INCARNADINE

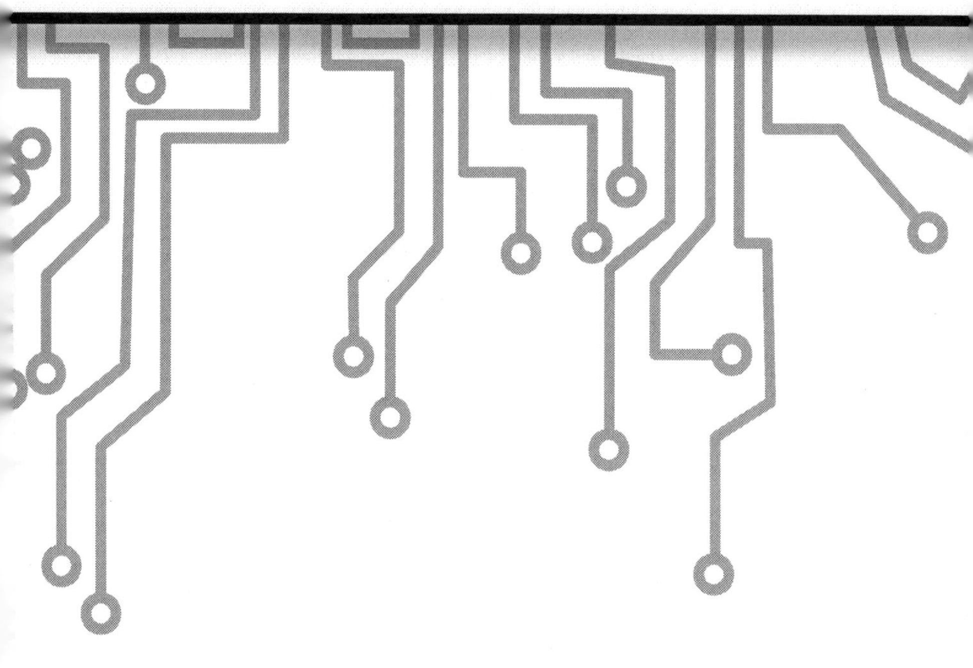

BOOKS BY TIM FRANKOVICH

Heart of Fire

Until All Curses Are Lifted
Until All Bonds Are Broken
Until All the Gods Return
Until All the Stars Fall *(coming soon)*

Dragontek Lore

Viridia
Incarnadine
Auric *(coming soon)*

INCARNADINE

DRAGONTEK LORE, BOOK 2

by Tim Frankovich

ISBN-13: 978-1-7379570-0-3

Published by Warpsteel Press, 2021

League City, Texas

Cover Design by Austin DeGroot

For that 13-year-old boy on his bicycle
on the way to the library

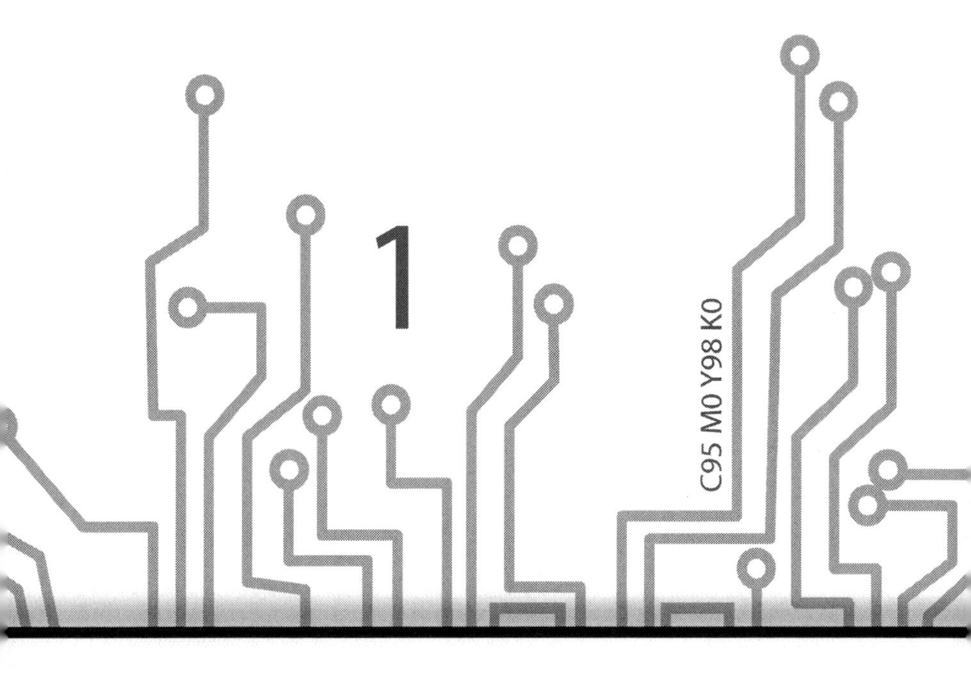

1

The dragons had gone to war. The thousand-year peace of the cities of The Circle had ended. And it was all my fault.

Okay, slight exaggeration. It wasn't my fault alone. I had help. And I guess the dragons hadn't been at peace for a thousand years, exactly. No one was really sure how long it had been, since our history lessons all came from the dragons. But it was a long, long time.

"Think it'll work this time?" Caedan asked. We stood on the tallest hill we could find, looking down at a battlefield.

A little over a month previous, my friends and I killed Caesious, the blue dragon, one of the six who ruled over The Circle. We arranged for the blame to fall on Viridia, the green dragon who ruled the city where most of us lived. Yes, it's an insane plan, but it somehow succeeded.

As a result, the other dragons turned on Viridia and the war began. Atramentous, the black dragon, came to Viridia's aid, as they had long been the closest of friends. Against them were the forces of the two red dragons, Incarnadine and Amaranth, along with the draconics and humans that had belonged to Caesious. The last of the dragons, Auric the gold, seemed to be staying neutral.

Except… the dragons weren't doing much of the actual fighting. Instead, they were sending their human subjects, led by their draconic servants, into battle. This was not what we wanted. Too many humans were dying.

We wanted the dragons dead.

"It's going to work," I said. "They won't see us coming."

"I'm more worried about their reaction time," Rick said.

Richard Onyx and Caedan Teal were my two closest friends. The three of us came from three different cities, but had somehow become united in this struggle. Rick adjusted the black leather gloves he used to hide his cybernetic hand. His black chromark made his face appear darker than it really was. Caedan's chromark was blue, which made for an odd contrast with his olive skin, though it perfectly matched his iridescent blue eyes. Those eyes, keener than mine, swept over the battle, evaluating everything. He gripped his baton tightly.

"It's going to work," I repeated. Maybe saying it enough times would make it true.

With the dragons staying mostly out of the fighting, our team was searching for a purpose. Bice, the former priest of the dragon religion and the oldest member of our team, had advocated staying quiet for a while. He was hoping one of the dragons would make some kind of mistake, leaving an opening for us to make a new plan.

I couldn't sit still, though. It had taken me weeks to recover from my battle with the draconic Troilus Green, the killing of the blue dragon, and the death of my friend and mentor, Loden.

Without a clear plan, and without Loden to help create one, I decided we needed more action. We couldn't get to any of the dragons right now, but their draconics, their most trusted servants, were leading the battles erupting across The Circle. We could target them.

"There it is," Caedan said, pointing.

"It's hanging back, directing the battle, like last time," Rick observed.

"Where?" I complained. "I don't see it."

Caedan turned my head for me and pointed again. Near the back of the red army, I finally spotted it: the draconic Zidanta Red, commander of Incarnadine's forces. It looked taller and perhaps slimmer than the green draconics we had encountered before. It directed a small army of red-clad soldiers charging across the open plain toward an army wearing green and black. Of course, calling them armies might be a stretch. Neither side included more than a hundred or so people. Weren't armies supposed to be thousands? I seemed to remember reading that in a history book somewhere.

"What kind of weapons do the red troops carry?" I asked.

"Mostly blades of some kind," Rick said. "I think I've seen a few crossbows. And one out of every ten carries a weapon that shoots flame three or four feet."

As he spoke, I caught a glimpse of a spurt of fire on the battlefield, just before the two armies met. Even from our distant vantage point, we heard the impact of them clashing into each other. The Viridian Guard, the green troops, carried shockspears. We were more than familiar with those.

"The green draconic leads up front," Caedan pointed out.

"Which is why we go for red." I pulled a pair of goggles over my eyes. "Let's do this."

"Don't know why we have to use the four-wheeler. Cyber boy can run almost as fast as it," Rick grumbled.

Caedan jumped up onto the four-wheeler, a small vehicle just big enough for the three of us. Invented by Loden, the four-wheeler ran on an engine similar to those used by the dragon's forces in their trucks. Caedan had spent the past two weeks practicing with it. "But then I wouldn't get to drive!" he said, grinning.

"And I'd get there already worn out," I added. "Come on, Rick." I gestured for him to board behind Caedan.

"I just don't trust this thing," he mumbled as he clambered on.

I mounted behind him. Before I could brace myself, Caedan revved the engine and took off. The four-wheeler flew down the hillside, gaining speed. Caedan guided it through the smoothest path… which wasn't all that smooth. We were jostled back and forth, side to side.

"Wait, go back," Rick said. "I think you missed a hole back there."

"You try driving!" Caedan shot back.

Ignoring their bickering, I gathered myself mentally. I could do this. I'd done it before. No difference. Really.

"Almost there," Caedan called. "We're starting to get noticed!"

I slipped to the side of the four wheeler and crouched on the step we used to mount it. Rick grasped the back of my shirt with his cybernetic hand, holding me in place. I hoped the shirt wouldn't tear; I liked this one.

"Now!" Caedan yelled.

Rick let go and I leaped. With a thought, I triggered the cybernetic implant in my brain to provide a "boost" to my legs. I leaped higher and further than any normal person could manage. Another boost strengthened my legs for the impact of my landing… right in front of the draconic as it turned to see me.

"Uh… hello." Even with that stupid line, I sounded more confident than I felt. This thing stood well over seven feet tall. Its glistening red scales shone in the afternoon sun, almost blinding me with the light reflection. It wore nothing more than a simple belt holding several devices and tools.

"The Viridians send an assassin? How unusually creative of them," it hissed.

I wore my Viridian Guard uniform for exactly that reason. Let the blame fall on Viridia, even if I didn't succeed. It would keep the conflict going.

"I am Zidanta Red, little one. You are doomed simply by wearing that outfit and coming into my presence!"

"Yeah, yeah. I'm doomed. Whatever." Out of the corner of my eye, I saw a pair of red-suited soldiers running to aid the draconic. The four-wheeler swept past them and both collapsed as Rick shocked them. The guys had my back.

Speaking of my back, I pulled my sword from it. Do you know how difficult it was to make sure I could draw a sword from a scabbard on my back? It took some weird modifications. But at least it looked cool when I drew it. Now I had a serious advantage over the lizard there, unless…

The draconic roared something I couldn't understand and lifted its palm toward me. Fewmets. I dove out of the way as a wave of power struck the spot I'd been standing. Magic. Ugh. Well, Bice tried to say it wasn't magic, just some power we didn't fully understand yet. Sounds like magic to me.

I boosted my legs again and charged the monster. I gripped the sword hilt in both hands, aiming for its side. At the last moment, it twisted. My blade scratched through some scales, but nothing more.

"You're fast," Zidanta Red observed. "Clearly some enhancements in play here." It swiped at me with its claws. I slipped out of the way a split-second away from being eviscerated.

"And you're ugly," I retorted. "Enhancements won't fix that." Actually, I didn't say that, but I thought of it a few seconds later. I think I managed a brief snort at best.

I tried again, this time giving my arm an extra boost as well, to speed my attack. I managed to get a solid stab into the draconic's upper thigh.

It snarled in rage and backhanded me. I tumbled across the grassy earth, holding on to my sword and somehow managing not to slice myself open in the process.

I looked up in time to see Zidanta Red spit at me. Except, as a red draconic, its spit wasn't just saliva. I threw myself to the side again as the flaming liquid struck the ground. A sizzling, smoking hole marked the spot. Ouch.

How often could it do that? This might be harder than I anticipated.

"Beryl!" someone shouted. Rick, I think. "Incoming! Incomindine!"

What? That made no sense.

An enormous burst of warm air almost knocked me over. A shadow blotted out the sun for a moment.

Oh. Incarnadine. That's what he said. The dragon was here.

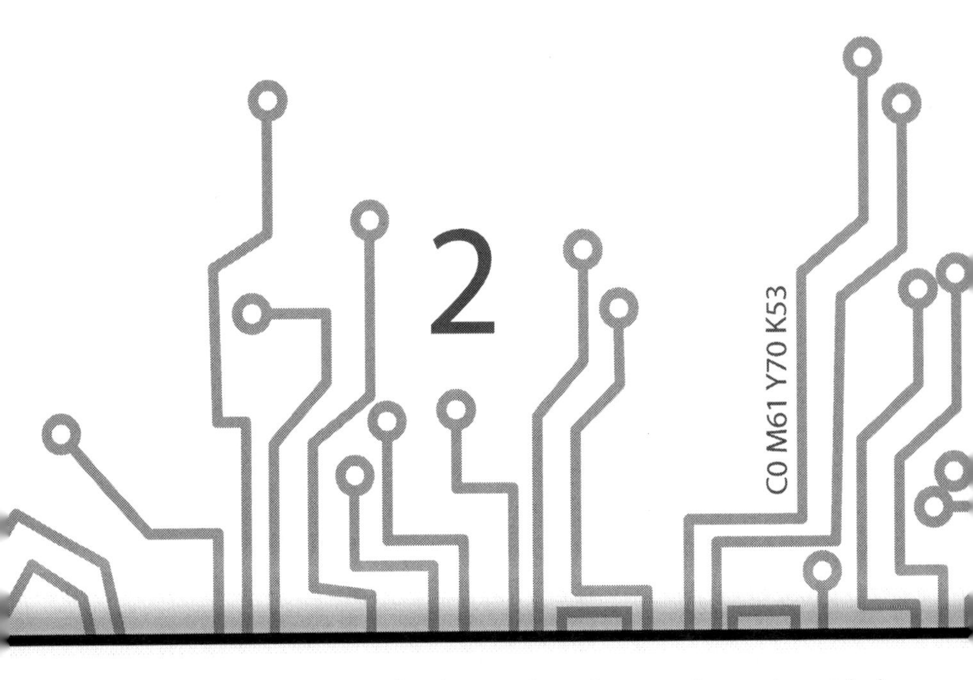

2

Incarnadine swept overhead again. Something was happening with the armies, but I couldn't take time to look. And where did my friends go?

"A god honors us with his presence," Zidanta Red announced. "Behold the epitome of true power and majesty!"

"Caedannnn!" I yelled, backing away, trying to keep an eye on the draconic and the circling dragon at the same time.

"Beryl! Over here!"

I boosted my legs, turned tail and ran for my life. Caedan slowed the four-wheeler just enough for me to leap aboard. Rick grabbed my shirt again, and Caedan accelerated.

"What is the bleaking dragon doing here?" Rick cried as he helped me get seated.

"The draconic couldn't have called him, could it?" I wanted to know.

Rick and I looked back. Incarnadine descended over the battlefield. He didn't seem to be looking toward us. Below, the two armies separated, running in opposite directions. I couldn't help but notice the bodies both sides left behind on the ground.

The dragon reared back its head and unleashed hell. A massive stream of fire exploded from his mouth and enveloped the fleeing green army. Another quick circle, and another burst of flame caught those few who escaped the first. In seconds, not a single soldier clad in green remained standing. Flames licked the edges of the now-blackened arena of death.

"Chromatic hells," Rick swore. I couldn't think of anything more appropriate to say. A dragon had entered the battle and shown his true power. In moments like this, I could understand why many people called them gods. The devastation gave me a sick feeling inside.

Incarnadine did not land with the destruction of the enemy, but turned and sped off toward the north. Heading home, I'd have to guess. At least it didn't come after us. That meant the draconic couldn't communicate with it... or more likely, it just didn't think we were worthy of pursuit.

We killed a dragon, but we made sure someone else got the blame. And so we could never claim credit for it. No one knew who we were. We couldn't call ourselves dragon slayers or anything like that. We had no reputation. No one feared us, even though we had killed a thousand-year-old god-like monster.

"So the dragons are joining the fight themselves now," Caedan stated the obvious.

"Maybe," Rick said. "Maybe this was a one-time thing. Maybe they're spying on each other and he knew Viridia and Atramentous wouldn't be around. I don't know."

"It's going to change everyone's tactics," I said. "Will any of them send troops out to fight when a dragon can destroy all of them at once?"

"The dragons don't care how many humans die. You know that."

"We don't even know what their objectives are," I countered. "They're not trying to actually capture each others' cities. So why send troops at all?"

"To control the rail lines? I don't know. We need to be smarter about this."

He had a point.

We rode mostly in silence for the duration of the trip. The four-wheeler had been designed for two riders, making our ride especially uncomfortable, complicated by how often all three of us kept scanning the sky. The skies belong to the dragons, as we were taught all our lives. I couldn't repress the sick feeling in my stomach every time I looked up, certain I would spot a growing red shape.

The concern over the skies led to the evolution of our current home. At first, we lived in a cave, including Loden's amazing workshop full of his inventions. But the cave did not provide a lot of room for the seven of us to do much more than sleep, or explore the workshop. The rest of our time, most of us would rather be out in the open air. All of us had grown up in the cities; outdoor living was a new and exciting experience. But too much time outside might get us spotted by one of the dragons.

Don, the most construction-minded of our team, came up with the solution. Every day, he worked on this new project: erecting a roof of sorts over a wide area outside the cave. With the help of Lovat, the orphan boy who excelled at scrounging, Don obtained a number of lengthy cables. He mounted a pair of them into the hill above the cave entrance and stretched them across open ground until he reached the next hill, at least a couple hundred feet. He added many more cables, stretched in various directions, criss-crossing each other to form a supportive web. Railroad ties, obtained from old and unused portions of the rail lines, were then used as pillars to help support the cables in the middle. After all that, he began the arduous process of covering the cables with whatever scrap wood or tree branches we could find, moving dirt on top of that, and even transplanting grass in patches. We hoped it would be camouflaged well from above. All of us did our part in the work, of course, but Don led the way. And all of us enjoyed the freedom of movement the new hideout gave us.

Kelly dubbed it the "Achromatic Asylum." I liked the "achromatic" part, meaning "freedom from color." But we all kept shortening it to just the Asylum. I guess because we all still believed we were crazy.

Bice came up with the idea of using one of our two four-wheelers to haul water from a nearby creek. Some empty barrels from Loden's workshop, once cleaned, provided ample storage for a few days' worth drinking and cooking water. Bathing still required a trip to the creek.

We brought large stores of imperishable food with us when we arrived, but they would not last forever. We had regular discussions about obtaining more, but no decisions had been made yet.

Caedan drove the four-wheeler under the Asylum roof and brought it to a stop. Kelly, the only one of our friends in sight, set down a glass of water on a table, one we had dragged out from Loden's workshop. As she approached, Rick and I jumped down from the four-wheeler. Kelly's eyes glanced at me for a moment before locking onto Rick.

I'm not going to lie. It still hurt. For a short, tumultuous, and glorious time, Kelly was my girlfriend. But I blew it. And now she and Rick were an item. Rick had offered to back off, but I didn't want to deny either of them any happiness they could find in this messed-up world. But yeah...

it still hurt.

"How'd it go?" Kelly asked.

Rick caught her up in a quick embrace before answering. "Not good." He set her back down. "Incarnadine showed up."

Kelly's eyes widened. "The dragon himself? Chroma! You three are lucky to be alive!"

I pulled my goggles off. "Lucky, tired, and dirty. Caedan likes driving us through the dustiest places he can find."

Caedan, still sitting on the four-wheeler with one knee pulled up, laughed. "Those parts are the most fun!"

Kelly looked over the three of us. "No question on the dirty part. You guys need to head down to the creek."

"I'll go right now if you come with," Rick suggested.

Kelly shoved him away. "Gods, you're incorrigible."

I still don't know what "incorrigible" means. If it describes Rick, does that mean I should try to be more incorrigible? Or was it a negative comment? I wasn't about to ask her what it meant, but who else could I ask? Bice?

At that precise moment, Bice emerged from the cave entrance. The ex-priest wiped his hands on a dirty cloth as he joined us, smiling as usual. "Did anyone see you?"

"I fought the draconic, but only scratched him before Big Red showed up," I said. "A few more minutes and the plan would have worked."

"You're lucky none of you were killed," Bice said.

"Here comes the 'I told you so,'" Rick complained, rolling his eyes.

"I did tell you," Bice said, tossing the cloth to Caedan. "You could have been killed, captured, led the enemy to our base, or any number of other possibilities. And even if you succeeded, what good would it do?"

"We would have killed another one of those lizards!" Heat rose into my face. "We've got to do something. We can't just hide here for the rest of our lives!"

"I agree. But if we work on getting better information, we can choose better targets. Something that may actually make a difference in this war."

Caedan looked up from cleaning his goggles. "You talk like you have a suggestion."

Bice's smile broadened for a moment. "Maybe I do. Once you're cleaned up, come see me in the workshop."

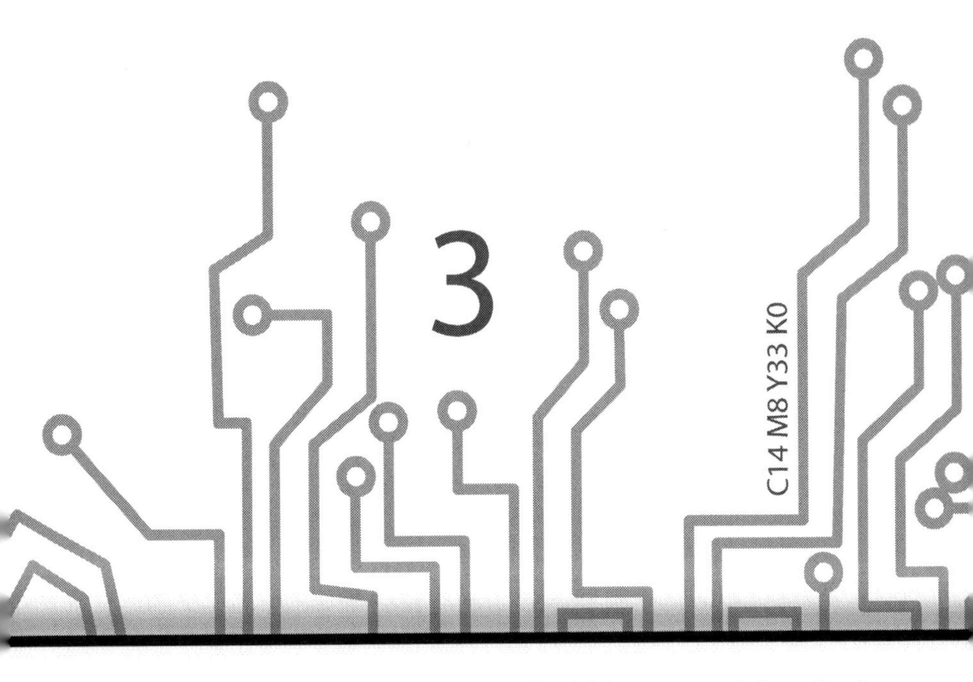

3

After a cold dip in the creek to wash off the sweat and dirt, the three of us found a change of clothes and made our way through the cave to Loden's workshop. Finding the hidden door had been a thrill, but if we shut it, we had to find it all over again. The process got annoying, so we left it open most of the time.

Bice waited for us in the workshop. I think he wanted to meet here because of the air conditioning, which was fine with me. The temperature seemed to always be perfect, even though we hadn't yet found the controls for it. I hadn't even figured out where the generator could be. The workshop provided a comfortable retreat during the hottest parts of the days, now that summer approached.

Kelly joined us and we gathered around a table cleared of most of its clutter. Loden's organization skills did not match his genius in other areas. Consequently, we had yet to even document everything in here. A number of curious inventions attracted me, but I was a little worried about turning them on without knowing what they could do.

"We need information," Bice started. "And we need it on a regular basis. We haven't heard from Stacy in weeks." Stacy, an actress and the final member of our team, remained in Viridia.

"We also need more recruits," Rick said. "We need people from all the cities if we're going to keep up this conspiracy."

"What do you suggest?" Caedan asked.

"I can't go anywhere," Bice said. "I'm too well known. None of you can travel to Viridia safely. Beryl and Kelly might get by for a little while, but if they're spotted, they'll be recognized. Rick and Caedan, obviously, have the wrong chromark."

"That leaves Don and Lovat," I said. "Where are they, anyway?"

Bice grinned. "On their way to Viridia."

"What?"

"I sent them soon after you left this morning. Don is unknown and Lovat… well, he's been keeping hidden in the city for most of his life. He'll find Stacy and hopefully set up a regular information exchange. Maybe once a week."

"So we'll send them back every week to pick up the news?" I asked.

"It's not ideal," Bice said. "But I can't think of any other method that would work, unless we can get someone on the trains to work with us."

"Even that might not be so great," Rick said. "Most of the trains aren't running right now because of the war."

"Did you ask Stacy to work on recruitment?" I wanted to know.

"That's part of her overall job, I think." Bice stretched and glanced at the door. "But she has to be careful. Ironically, she can't be spreading the news about our greatest victory."

"Because if the other dragons found out that we killed Caesious, then they wouldn't have any reason to be at war with each other." I groaned.

Rick wandered away from the table, then turned back. "I like what you've done, Bice, but I have one problem with it."

"What's that?"

"Who's in charge here? I thought we chose Beryl to be our leader. Shouldn't he be involved in decisions like this?"

Bice did not respond for a moment. Then he nodded. "You make a good point. I've been operating things on my own for so many years that I forgot we're a team. With a leader." He looked to me. "I apologize for acting without consulting you, Beryl. Do you have any problems with what I've done?"

I blinked repeatedly. "Uhhh, no. I think it's a good idea. I just wish… I wish we could move faster. Even with this plan, it may take weeks before we get information we can use. Or any new recruits."

Bice gestured around the room. "We need a new tech person most of all. I've tried to understand some of this stuff and gotten nowhere."

My eyes wandered around the room. As always, they were drawn to the one item I'd been itching to use since we found this place.

"What about the other cities?" Caedan asked. "Rick and I have the marks to visit Caesious and Atramentous. Maybe we could find out some things?"

"I can't go back there," Rick said. "They know me too well. And you…"

"You used to be one of their elite guards," Kelly said. "Do you really think you could move about without being recognized?"

As Caedan conceded, I stifled a smile. It wasn't just his face that would get him into trouble. Caedan was a fighter, not a spy. We needed him, but not for that kind of work.

"But I do have a long-range idea," Bice broke in. "Something for us to think about and possibly prepare for."

I turned my eyes back to him. "Let's hear it."

"Unless things change, I can see the dragons growing tired of this conflict before too long. So far, their fighting has been… well, it's a bit perfunctory, as if they don't really want to, but feel like they have to."

"A couple hundred crispy Viridian Guards might disagree with you there," Rick said. Kelly grimaced.

"I agree Incarnadine's actions today represent an escalation. But look." Bice spread a map of The Circle on the table and pointed at the center of it. "We're camped over here, near the Blasted Lands. But all of this other land, outside the cities, consists mostly of farms. Crops and herds. The dragons haven't attacked any of that yet. Why? Because they know in the long run, it would be detrimental. They're not planning a drawn-out war here."

"So… fight to show you're angry, but don't do anything that would threaten the future?" I thought I could see what he was saying.

"Essentially. And eventually, they're going to want to talk to each other."

"And that's when we hit them all at once!" Rick exclaimed.

Bice shook his head. "I still don't think the dragons themselves will get together. At least not at first. They're split too evenly, two against two, with Auric staying neutral. They don't want to risk the balance there. If Auric came in on one side or the other, it might change things. But he seems committed to staying out of it."

That confused me. When Caesious the dragon died, his last words had mentioned Auric. He was the most unknown of all the dragons. Even Stacy's acting troop didn't perform in his city.

"But the dragons will want to talk peace, one way or the other, eventually. And since they won't meet face-to-face, who will they send?"

"The draconics," Kelly answered.

"Right. Their most loyal servants. I can see a big gathering of draconics happening sometime in the not-too-distant future. And that's what we should prepare for."

"To kill them?" Rick asked.

"Or... to do something—I don't know what yet—that will inflame the war even more. Draw the dragons into it. Make them so angry they actually do fight each other. Because let's be honest: Loden's plan to kill a dragon was one in a million. I don't see it happening again."

"It takes a dragon to kill a dragon," Kelly said. "I mean, besides what we did."

"I don't know." I gestured at a shelf of strange devices. "There might be something else in here that would work. We just haven't found it yet."

"As much as I'd like to believe that, I just don't see it," Bice answered. "Loden worked long and hard to come up with that plan, and he never mentioned any back-up ideas."

"So, let's sum up." I gestured to Bice. "You're working to set up a way to get information. Beyond that, we need to be patient and wait for these eventual peace talks. And try to plan something for that occasion, something that will really anger the dragons."

"And make them fight," Rick added. "I'd rather we killed them ourselves, but them killing each other is almost as good."

"That about covers it." Bice nodded, arms folded across his chest.

"I think we can do more, though," I argued. "We might have other means of gathering information. We should work together on identifying everything in this room. Some of them might help us out. I mean, one of them has been staring at us this whole time. It's absurdly obvious."

"Which one?" Caedan asked, looking around.

"That one. I've been thinking about it since the beginning," I said. I pointed at the set of wings hanging from the ceiling. "I want to try that one out."

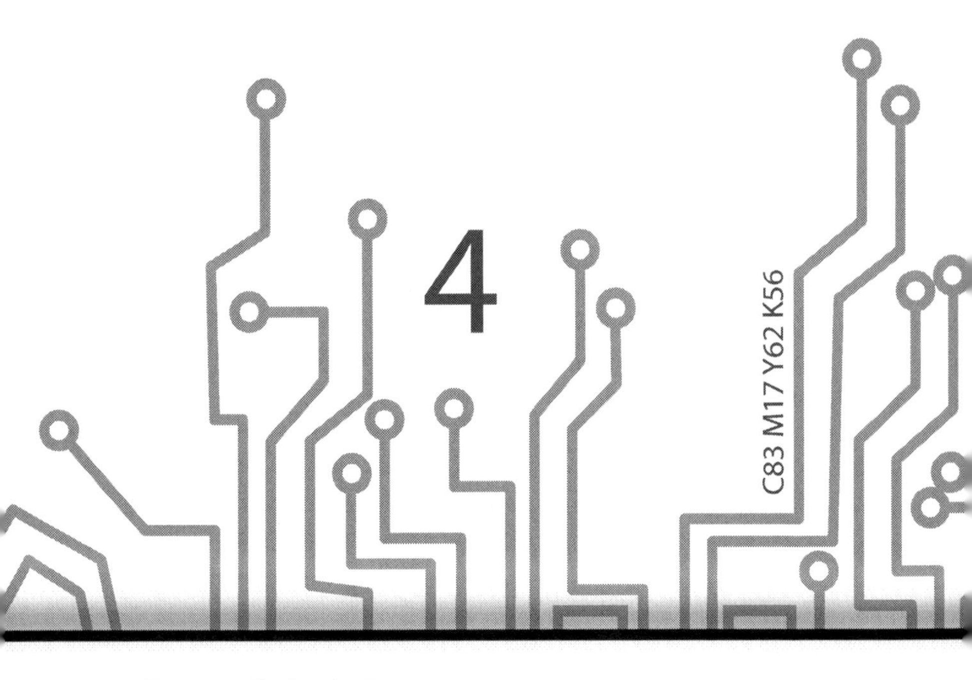

4

Bice actually laughed at me.

"I'm serious!" I insisted. "Think about what we could discover if we could get up in the air!"

"We know nothing about that device, nothing about how it works," he answered. "I agree it's full of potential, but… we don't know anything about it. I haven't found any documents related to it at all."

"We could at least try." I lowered my eyebrows and crossed my arms.

"I'll tell you what. I'll take it down and look it over. If I can figure anything out—anything at all—then I will show you what I find."

I snorted and looked around at the others. "We're done here." I left the workshop, exited through the cave and went to find some water. All the talking made me thirsty.

Rick followed me out. "You're not wrong, you know."

"Eh, I don't know. Bice has a point. It would be reckless to mess with something we don't understand."

"No. See, that's the whole problem! The dragons have kept us down so much, we think like that. And we shouldn't!" Rick paced around the water barrels. "Our technology should be so much higher than it is. And everyone who wants to should be able to learn about it. Loden had to do half of his research in secret to keep Viridia from finding out!"

"Ha!"

"What's so funny?"

"Just... you and me griping about technology. When I have a cyb implant in my head and you have a mechanical hand." I waved my fingers at him. "Which you still haven't told me about, by the way."

He sighed and took a seat on the table. "Is that still bothering you?"

"I've told you all of my past." I climbed onto the table beside him.

"You're right." He nodded. "It's only fair. It's just... I got burned in Atramentous, you know. Lost so many friends. I've been... reluctant to talk much about what happened there."

"So you got the hand there?"

He pulled off his glove and flexed his cybernetic fingers. Once again, I admired the beauty of the tech. No gears, exposed wires, rusty metal, or odd shapes. If it were covered in skin somehow, no one would know the difference.

"We had a tech guy there too. I called him Styg, because his real name was too long."

I sat up. Details. Rick didn't give out too many of those.

"He was a genius. Very different from your friend Loden. Younger. Crazy hair." Rick stared off into the distance. "He made me laugh. But like I said: genius."

"He built the hand?"

"No." Rick smiled. "But he was the one who... installed it. I lost my real hand in a fight with—oh, what was its name? One of the black draconics. Naram-Sin, I think."

I'd heard that name somewhere before, I think. But I couldn't remember where.

"Yeah, big bad draconic. Nasty. But as for the hand itself..." He lifted it up again and clenched it into a fist. "I stole it."

That didn't surprise me.

"Stygian Labs. One of the leading research sites in Atramentous. I used to tease Styg that it should belong to him because of the name. We snuck in one night, Raven and me." Rick paused. "They had some sick stuff in there, Beryl. Really sick. You think Viridia is bad? Atramentous is experimenting on people in ways Viridia hasn't even thought of yet."

Despite the warmth, I shivered. Every time I learned something new about the other dragons and their cities, it only cemented my desire to see them all dead and gone.

"Raven wanted to just blow the place up, and I agreed. We—"

"Blow it up?"

"Oh. Right." Rick's eyes darted around. "You don't know about explosives. It's like burning it down, only a lot faster and, uh, violent."

I narrowed my eyebrows. "That sounds like something we should have."

"I wish we did." Rick shrugged. "But if anyone in Viridia had that tech, I never saw it."

"Maybe we should run a mission to Atramentous then."

"Bice already pointed out the problem with that." Rick tapped his chromark. "I'm a fugitive and none of the rest of you would fit in."

I rubbed my own chromark. These identifiers, the markings the dragons had branded us with, caused a lot of difficulty. What would it take to change one? Or get rid of it?

"Anyway, we were setting things up to, uh, destroy the lab, when I saw it." Rick held his hand up vertically. "It was beautiful. Keep in mind, this was before I lost my real hand. I had no idea I would need this later. But I wanted it. Out of everything we saw in there, this was easily the most… advanced."

I nodded. I had seen cybernetic parts before, but none matched this one. Even Viridia's parts didn't appear this sophisticated.

"You really lucked out that you didn't lose your left hand."

"If you call having a big lizard bite your hand off lucky."

"You know what I meant."

"Yeah." He smiled. "It's awesome. Not as awesome as your extra brain, though."

I rolled my eyes. "It's not an extra brain."

"And how much have you been using it lately?"

"What?"

"How often have you even used your implant since we killed Caesious?" He wasn't smiling any more.

"Um, not much. I haven't needed to." The sudden change in Rick's demeanor bothered me. When did this switch from story time to inquisition?

"You should be. You should be testing it, finding out how far you can go, how much you can do." Rick pointed at me. "Chromatic hells, man! You possess something that the dragons have all been trying to develop for decades! Who knows what it's capable of?"

"I've been recovering. We've both been recovering!" I shot back. "You know this."

"Yeah, but you were sloppy out there today with the draconic. You could have taken him." I opened my mouth to protest, but he kept going. "Even before Incarnadine showed up. You haven't been using your implant, and it showed." He folded his arms across his chest. "You've lost your edge."

Heat rose up in my face. "I killed Troilus Green! No one's worked harder for this team than me! I pushed myself to the absolute limit on that train!"

"And then you quit. What have you done since?"

I scowled. But I had no answer. After the battle, the exhaustion, the grief… I wanted rest. My anger, my rage against the green dragon faded. I still wanted him dead. I wanted everyone free from their control. But my motivations were different. I felt different.

Rick unfolded his arms and shrugged. "You want to experiment with Loden's inventions. That's good. But why not start with his greatest invention?" He waved his arms. "Vehicles, talking boxes, whatever. How does that compare with what he did with you?"

"You've made your point," I answered.

"So?"

I looked around. "So?"

"Go for a run! Go see how far you can jump! Do handstands. I don't know." He paused. "Here's the other thing. If I didn't exercise my arm, this hand would eventually be worthless, because my upper arm has to be strong enough to use it. If you don't exercise, it doesn't how much you 'boost' your arms and legs. You have to have muscles in order to boost them. Am I right?"

In answer, I jumped off the table and started running. After a few steps, I triggered a boost into my legs. My pace picked up. I left the Asylum behind and ran over the hills. Up and down, faster and faster. Stacy taught me to trickle my boosts to sustain things, rather than channeling one huge burst of energy at once. I did that now, keeping the boosts flowing. My legs churned.

I crossed the creek, flying through the water so fast it barely registered. Up the next hill, and the next. Going downhill into an extended plain, I went all out, letting the boosts get stronger.

It felt good. It felt really good. Rick was right. I needed to practice.

Over another hill, a cliff forced me to turn left through a narrow valley, then up a steep incline. The top of this hill leveled out into a wide plateau. I approached the edge with blinding speed, judged the height of the drop-off... and leaped.

I soared out a couple of dozen yards at least before descending into the next plain. An extra boost into my legs allowed me to land without mishap, but I stumbled a few steps later. I cut off the boosts and came to a faltering stop. Only a yard or so from my feet, the green grass disappeared. I stared at dirt: ugly, corrupted dirt. I lifted my head and looked forward.

The Blasted Lands.

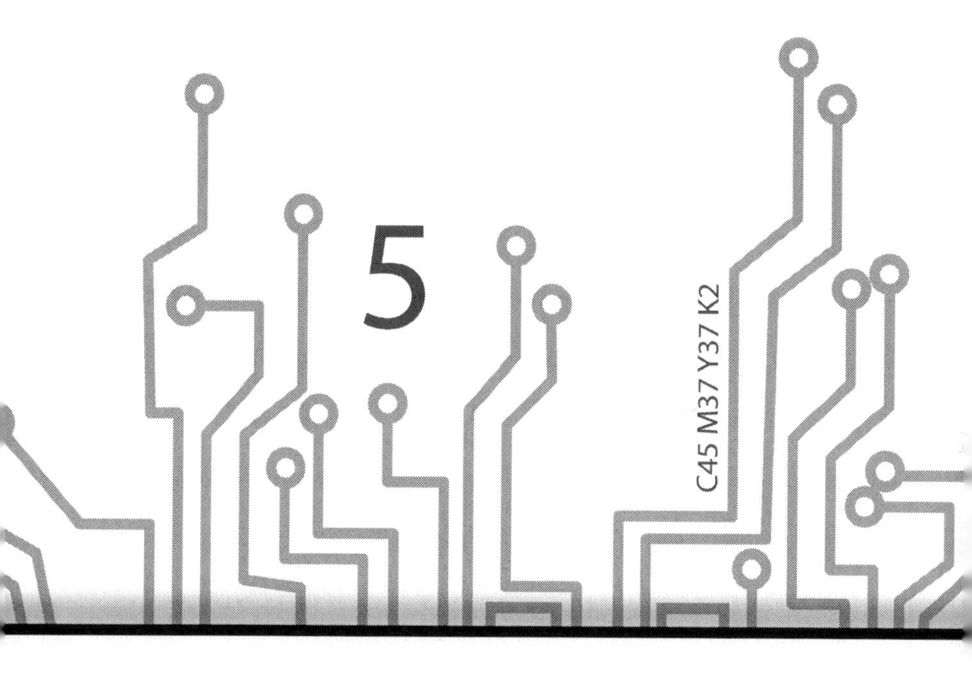

5

The dividing line between the green grass and the corrupted ground stretched as far as I could see in either direction. At first, the line appeared stark, a clean and abrupt division between the two. But as I looked closer, I could see "fingers" of corruption stretching out into the healthy land. Caedan said the Blasted Lands were growing. I guess he was right.

I looked out over the blight. Black and brown dirt stretched off into a haze. Did anything remain of the city which once stood within? Having seen a red dragon in action, I tried to imagine the devastation of that day. All six dragons—green, blue, two reds, black, gold—attacking and attacking until nothing and no one remained. The sky rained fire, venom, lightning, and more. What had that combination done to this area? How deep into the soil did the corruption sink?

Without thinking, I took a step forward. My foot crunched into the corrupted earth. I shifted my weight. The sound of my shoes in the dirt seemed wrong. I bent down and looked at its odd consistency. For a moment, I wished for Rick's cyb hand, or even his gloves. No way would I touch that with my bare fingers.

I straightened and looked around again. For some reason, I had assumed the air quality would change the second I stepped over the line. But now that I considered it, it made no sense. I had no doubt the air would not be pleasant if I went further in, but here at the fringes, it still tasted normal.

Even so, I shivered through my sweat. The wrongness of the place gnawed at my… gut? My spirit? I'm not sure.

One thing I did know: this would be the fate of my team and the Asylum if the dragons ever discovered what we had done and where we lived. They'd probably compete for the honor of taking us down.

The melancholy almost overwhelmed me. I took two steps backward into the grass and turned away.

That's when I realized the problem with running so far and so fast on my own: I didn't know how to get back. I almost panicked before I remembered the easy way to get home. I needed to keep going south or southwest until I ran into a railroad track. Then I could follow it to the Asylum's region. It would be longer than my run to get here, but no other options came to mind. I sighed and started running.

I kept my speed above average, but didn't push myself too hard on the way back. I wanted to arrive with my legs still working.

In the end, I got home, but my legs were so exhausted, it was all I could do to find my sleeping bag and collapse. Anything else would have to wait for the next day.

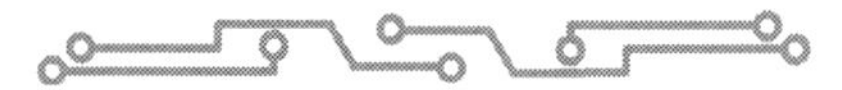

Don and Lovat returned the next morning. Bice called us all together in the workshop to hear their report.

As usual, Don said little, and what he did say contained almost no emotion. "We arrived in the city. Found a place to hide. Then I waited for Lovat to do his thing."

"If we do this again, we'll try to find something else for you to do," I suggested.

Don shrugged.

"Did you find Stacy?" Bice asked Lovat. I already knew the answer. Lovat wore a new set of clothes that actually fit. He didn't find those on his own.

"Yah." He nodded. "She talked a lot."

"What did she have to say?"

Lovat looked at me. "She wanna see you."

"Me?"

He cocked his head. "She wanna see all, but you most."

Rick nudged me. "You most." He arched his eyebrows suggestively.

I shoved him away. "Did she suggest a date and time, Lovat?"

The boy dug into a pocket on his new pants and pulled out a note. He looked it over and put it in a different pocket. Then he repeated the process with another note. Satisfied, he handed that one to me.

I opened the note and read aloud: "Tuesday, early evening. Backstage at The Citrine." I looked at Kelly. "That's the theater on the east side, isn't it?"

"Yeah, I've only been there a couple of times. It's a big place."

"How do I get backstage?"

"I show you," Lovat answered.

"Then I'm going too," Kelly announced.

"Uh…" I wanted to protest, to tell her it was too dangerous, or that it was a long trip. But a look at her determined face told me not to bother. "What day is it, anyway?"

"Today's Monday," Don said.

"So we'll have to leave early in the morning to make it in time."

"There's a chance someone will recognize you," Bice pointed out.

"I don't know anyone on the east side," I replied quickly. "Kelly, you know anyone over there?"

"No." She shook her head. "We hardly ever went to that side of town."

"I meant the Viridian Guard," Bice said. "You're both wanted criminals to them."

"We'll avoid them. Without Troilus Green, they don't scare me that much," I said.

"He's not the only draconic in Viridia, you know."

"Keep 'em safe," Lovat said. He patted his own chest.

Bice's smile broadened. "I have no doubt they're in good hands, Lovat."

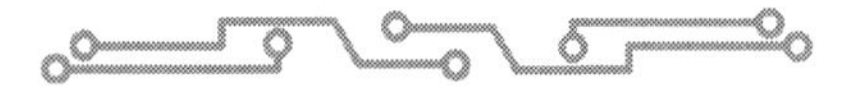

With the sun barely peeping over the nearest hill, the three of us set out. I wanted to use the four-wheelers to get halfway there, but Bice discouraged it. "Imagine a dragon does fly overhead. Will he be more likely to notice some people walking, or unauthorized vehicles zooming along?" I hated it when he was right.

I let Lovat take the lead, though I knew the way. He bounded on ahead of us, an endless ball of energy. Every so often, he paused, positioned himself like the start of a race, ran as hard as he could and then leaped into the air. He usually couldn't land on his feet, but always laughed at it. His constant delight with nature made me smile.

I glanced at Kelly. This was the first time the two of us had done anything together since she and Rick became a couple. Did she feel as awkward as I did?

"What do you think it'll be like?" she asked abruptly.

"Excuse me?"

"Viridia. What do you think it'll be like being there again? I'm not sure what to think."

"Me either." I hadn't given it much thought, to be honest. Viridia in my mind now was… just a place. Everyone I cared about was either dead or with me in the Asylum. The city meant little to me.

"It's going to be weird, no matter what. Walking around, seeing everyone else going about their regular business as if nothing has changed… when everything has changed!"

"We might see more changes than you think," I said. "Remember what Bice said about the trains and food. I don't know if it's far enough along to make a difference or not. Plus, just the fact that the city is at war."

"You might be right. It could be tense."

We walked in silence for a few minutes.

"What do you miss the most?" Kelly asked. "About life in the city?"

I thought for a moment. "My bicycle?"

"Seriously?" She shoved my shoulder. I missed her doing that. Such a fun, but slightly intimate moment.

"I don't know. Um, I miss my refrigerator. It had this annoying hum when you opened the door, but I miss being able to grab something to drink. Besides water."

She laughed. "That's better."

"What about you?"

"I miss showers. The creek is nice, but… I'm the only girl and it's… awkward. I never feel truly safe."

"None of us would spy on you."

She shot me a look. "I know you wouldn't. You're a good man, Beryl. Same with Bice. I still don't know Caedan or Don hardly at all. And Rick… well, he's Rick."

"He definitely is." I glanced ahead. "You didn't mention Lovat."

Kelly snorted. "Him I trust least of all."

Lovat looked back at us. "What?"

"Nothing," I said. "We're just being stupid."

"Why?"

"Um… I don't know. Kelly, why are we being stupid?"

"Beryl's being stupid," Kelly said. "It's what older boys do. I'm just talking."

"That's what girls do," I added.

She shoved me again.

Lovat eyed us both while taking a few steps backward. He rolled his eyes and spun around. Kelly and I looked at each other and both stifled a laugh.

If we hadn't distracted Lovat, maybe he would have been more alert. As it was, we came around the side of a hill next to the railroad tracks and stopped short.

A train stood still on the track. A dozen or more Viridian Guard swarmed about it.

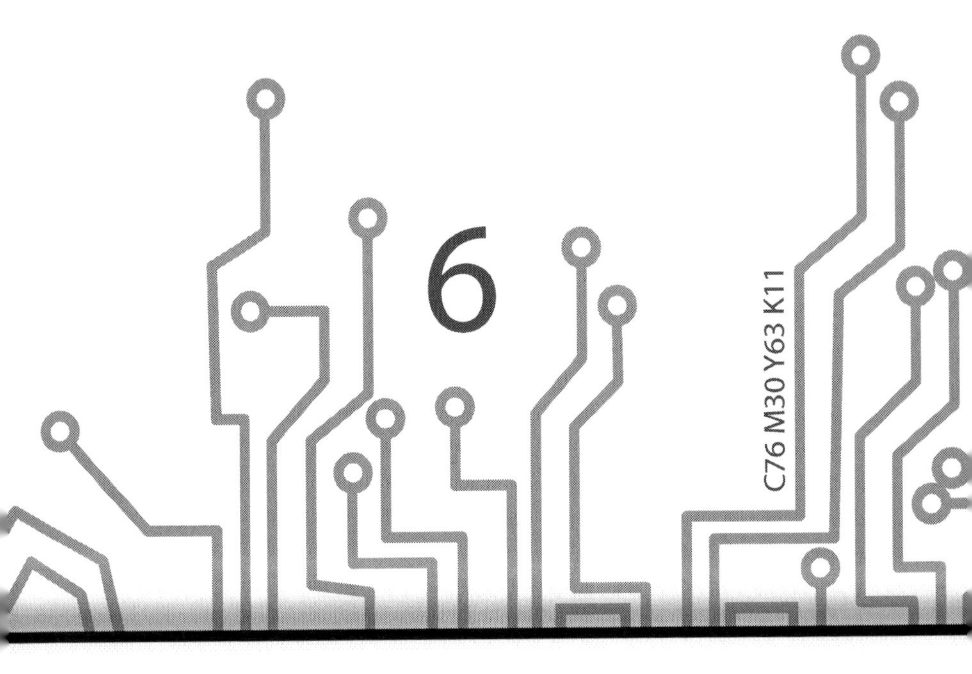

6

Fewmets. So many fewmets. No weapons. No other help. I couldn't run away without Kelly and Lovat, and I couldn't take on this many Guards without endangering them.

"You three! Stop there!" Four of the soldiers ran toward us.

Lovat darted behind Kelly. "Good idea," I whispered. "Hide behind your mom there."

"Sister," Kelly corrected.

"Sure. Go with that."

All four of the Viridian Guard slowed as they approached us and spread out. All of them carried shockspears, fully armored, helmets and everything. I spared a quick thought for the train. It looked like an engine with only a single passenger car of some kind. What could be inside necessitating all of these Guards? Why stop it out here?

The closest Guard pointed his shockspear at me. "Identify yourselves."

I held out my palms in as innocent a pose as I could imagine. "Hey, no problem. We're sorry to intrude. I'm Lauren Jade, and this is my, uh, wife, K-Kim."

The Guard to the left tried to get a closer look at Lovat, who buried his face behind Kelly. "This your kid?"

"Nephew," Kelly said. "He's visiting us at the farm."

"Yeah, his parents wanted him to see what life was like outside the city," I added.

"There aren't any farms near here," one of the Guards said. "You're a long way from where you should be." He glanced back at the train. I took a quick look too, but couldn't see anything significant. A bunch of green uniforms and… wait. One of them wasn't green.

"We took him camping," Kelly said, putting her arm back to pat Lovat awkwardly. "Wanted him to see what it was like way out here, where you can see the stars at night. We're on our way back to the farm now."

Blue. One of the uniforms was blue. That made no sense at all. Green and blue were at war. They couldn't be working together on anything.

The Guards exchanged looks. Did our story sound plausible enough? I resisted the urge to start babbling out more. Too many details would only catch me in a lie.

"All right." The nearest Guard lowered his shockspear and beckoned to me. "Come here." I glanced at Kelly and stepped up. "Hold still," he said, and reached up to my face. I flinched, but all he did was run a gloved thumb across my forehead.

"What was that?" I asked.

"Just checking your mark," he said. "We've had reports of infiltrators with fake chromarks." He gestured to Kelly and Lovat. "Check theirs."

Fewmets again. Just when it looked like it might work.

Kelly submitted to a Guard's testing of her mark. A brief flare of anger stirred in me watching one of them touch her. Lovat tried to keep his face buried in the back of Kelly's shirt.

"Come on, kid," the Guard said. "I won't hurt you."

"He's terrified of you." Kelly put her hand on the Guard's arm. "Can't you see that?"

"He's just a kid," I added. "Can't you let him be?"

The Guard next to Kelly hesitated, but the one beside me shook his head. "No exceptions."

I took one more glance toward the train. No one there seemed to be paying attention to us. Four against one at the moment. I could handle that.

I triggered my implant, sending boosts throughout my body. I needed speed and strength. "Lovat, run!" I yelled. Before the nearest Guard could even turn his head back toward me, I shot forward. I wrenched his shockspear from his hands and gave him a shove that sent him flying backward.

I barreled into the one next to Kelly next. No finesse, no fancy moves. I just lowered my shoulder and knocked him off his feet. Kelly turned to run after Lovat, already several yards away by now. I spun back to face the final two Guards.

"He's got cyb implants!" one of them shouted. He threw his shock-spear at me.

With my increased speed, I watched it coming and easily stepped out of its path. I could throw mine back at him, but the Viridian Guard's uniforms were insulated against their own weapons. Brute force seemed to be the only option, but one Guard still held his shockspear. I had to watch that.

Actually, I didn't have to fight them at all. I feinted lunging toward them and got them both to take a step back. Then I spun and ran, throwing an extra boost into my legs. Yells followed me, but a glance over my shoulder showed I didn't need to worry about the last spear. I escaped out of his accurate range in seconds.

I caught up to Kelly and swept her off her feet. Wish I could do that more metaphorically. Is that the right word? Anyway, I picked her up and kept running, much faster than she could. She didn't protest. As I passed Lovat, I said, "Be right back for you, buddy."

I carried Kelly up and over another hill, dropped her off, and went back for Lovat. I reached for him, but he spun around my grasp and jumped on my back. Sure, that works. I took off again and smiled at his laughter. "So hue!" he shouted.

When I reached the top of the hill, I looked back. My running had taken us at least a couple hundred yards from the enemy. One of the Guards had chased after me for a few dozen yards before realizing the futility. The two I had knocked down were back on their feet, staring after us. The fourth ran back to the train, no doubt telling them what had happened.

"Did you have to say I was your wife?" Kelly asked. She joined me in looking back.

"Easiest stories are the best," I answered. "It would have worked if not for the chromark thing."

"Sorry," Lovat said.

"Not your fault," I told him.

"We'd better get further away," Kelly said. "They can still see us right now."

"Yeah." But I hesitated. What was going on with that train?

"Are you coming?"

"Just a minute. I want to try something." I closed my eyes for a moment and concentrated. During the fight with the dragon, I did something with my eyes that let me see further. Or at least I thought I had. I triggered the implant, trying to instruct a small boost toward my eyes. I opened them and looked toward the train.

It was like looking through a telescope. My vision narrowed and zoomed in. I could see the train car, a dozen or more Viridian Guard, someone dressed in what might be a Cerulean Corps uniform—Caedan's old group—and a couple of other figures without uniforms. I couldn't make them out.

I tried to zoom in on the windows of the train car. I couldn't make out much, but what I saw looked like… medical equipment? And some other technology I didn't recognize. "The train car is some sort of lab," I said aloud.

"Who cares? They're coming this way!" Kelly interrupted me. Lovat pulled on my arm.

I released the boost and let my vision return to normal, but as my view pulled back from the train car, the back door opened. A green shape appeared.

"Draconic!" I exclaimed. "There's a draconic too!"

"Beryl, we've got to go!" Kelly insisted.

I turned and joined them in running down the hill. I took turns with carrying them again, this time for half a mile almost due east. Finding a secure spot on the edge of a grove, we stopped for a rest.

"Can we still meet Stacy?" Kelly wanted to know.

"I don't think it'll be a problem," I said. I stretched out on the ground, letting my body relax. Aching muscles reminded me of Rick's advice about exercise. "We've come further east now. We should be able to come down to the city without getting near those guys or the train station. Just give me some time to rest."

"You can't run us all the way to the city, can you?"

I looked up at her with my eyebrows raised. "I hope you're not serious. I'm worn out as it is."

She shrugged. "Just asking. I don't know what all you can do. What was that last bit where you were looking at them?"

“I can see further, if I concentrate on it. I could see the Viridian Guard, a draconic, the lab in the train car… and someone in a Cerulean Corps uniform.”

“What? That makes no sense!”

“I know! But he was there.”

Kelly paced around me. “A traitor, maybe? Bringing Caesious secrets to Viridia?”

“Maybe.” But it didn’t feel like that. Something about the train car and its contents gave me a sinking feeling in my gut. Like there was something much deeper going on than we imagined.

Maybe Stacy would know something about it.

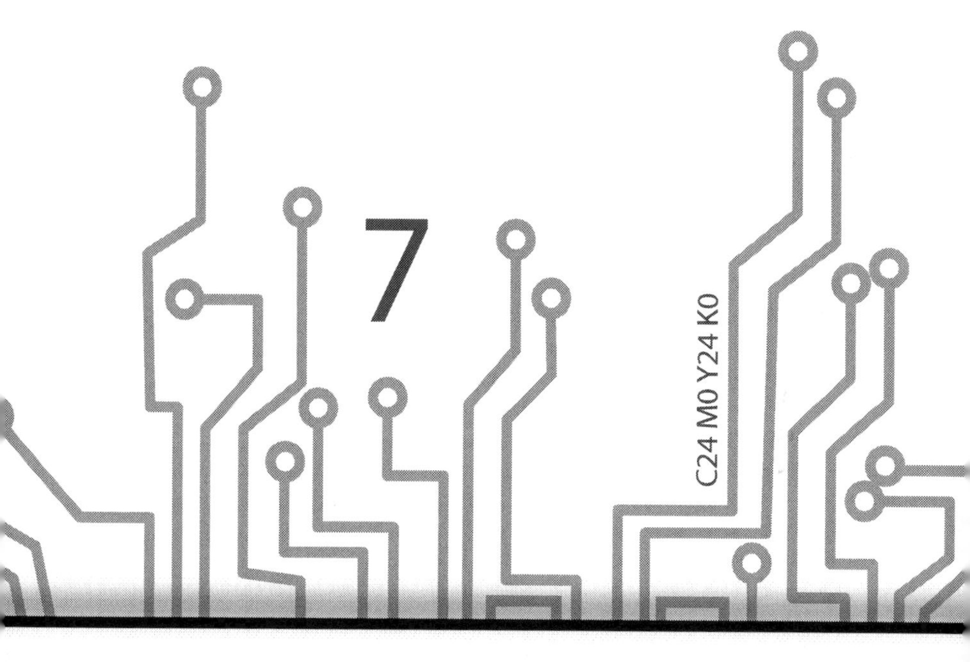

7

Walking the streets of Viridia again felt just as weird as Kelly suggested it would. Citizens of the city walked and rode their bicycles past us as they always did, faces down, little interaction with one another. In fact, everyone appeared more downcast and maybe even afraid. Who could blame them? In addition to the soul-crushing weight of the dragon's rule, they now had to worry about war and its side effects.

Within moments of entering the city, I felt an almost physical weight settle on my own shoulders. The still air contributed to the overall melancholy of the situation.

"This is… sad," Kelly whispered.

"Yeah. We haven't exactly set them free yet, have we?" I wondered what the streets of Caesious were like now. Did people feel freer there with the blue dragon dead? Or had the red dragon forces moved in fast enough to quash any delight?

"This way," Lovat told us, turning a corner. He kept his own head down with a hat (a beret!) hanging low to hide his lack of chromark.

The Citrine was one of the few all-wooden structures in Viridia. It stood apart from all of the concrete-and-brick structures around it. Though I had never thought much of the theater business, I suppose it was one of the few bright spots in this world. Kelly enjoyed it. Why had I never done so? Had I consciously avoided it in order to hold on to my rage and depression? And were there others out there like me, who might be prime for recruitment? We wouldn't find them at the theater.

I glanced at the position of the sun. "I guess it's early evening, or at least close. How do we get backstage?"

"Follow." Lovat beckoned and started down an alley to the left of the theater. At the end, we met a fence. Lovat shoved a trash can next to it and used it to clamber up and over.

I looked at Kelly. "Need a boost?"

"If he can do it, I can." With her mouth set like stone, Kelly pulled herself onto the trash can and then over the top of the fence.

I gave myself a little boost and jumped to the top of the fence, then over. I landed next to the other two and found myself in another alley which ran along the back of the building. I looked down a block where it opened into another street.

"Why didn't we come that way?" I asked.

Lovat shrugged. "My way faster." He pointed to a single door at the back of the theater.

Kelly glanced around and knocked. We waited for a minute or more. Nothing happened.

"Maybe no one's here." I looked at the sky again. The sun would reach the mountains any minute. Definitely evening.

Kelly knocked again. This time, the door swung open almost immediately. An unfamiliar young woman with curly blond hair and a perky nose looked out at us. She focused on me. "Do I know you?"

"We're looking for Stacy Moss," Kelly said.

"Oh, you're Stacy's gang. Hue. Come on in." She stepped back and beckoned.

I let Kelly and Lovat go ahead and then followed. As I passed the blonde, she reached out and squeezed my bicep. "Are you sure I don't know you?"

"Uh..."

"Olive, stop flirting with the boy. He's spoken for." Stacy's voice came from off to my left in a darkened hallway.

"Awww." Olive shut the door behind me, cutting off all the light.

"Not any more," I said.

"Oh, really?" A hand slid down my back. I had to admit: I wasn't used to this sort of attention, but... I didn't hate it, either. And a small part of me wanted to make Kelly jealous.

"Sounds like you might have as much news to share as I do," Stacy said. She turned on a flashlight right in my eyes. I blinked and she moved it around. "Sorry about this. The light in this hallway has been out for two days and Frank hasn't gotten around to replacing it."

We followed her flashlight through a hall crowded with stage paraphernalia. I saw masks, costumes, stands, furniture, and lots of other things I couldn't identify.

Stacy opened a door and led us into a well-lit hallway that led to a sharp right turn. She took the first left-hand door in the hall into a smaller room that held a clothing rack full of costumes, a small desk with a mirror, and a single chair. A changing room for the performers, I guessed.

The warmth of Olive's body right behind me drew my attention. I turned around and found her almost brushing up against me. She looked up into my face. "You *are* cute," she said, her voice accented a bit different than I expected. She drew out the "arr" sound. "Stacy already told you I'm Olive. What's your name?"

"Beryl," I answered without thinking.

"Beryl," she repeated. "Now that's a vibrant name."

"Olive, I'm sorry," Stacy said. "I invited them here for a private conversation. Show and tell will have to wait until later."

Olive pouted, but leaned even closer to me. "That means I show you something," she whispered, "and maybe you don't tell."

"I, uh…"

Olive patted me on the chest, flipped around with a bounce of her curls and disappeared down the hallway. I swallowed, disappointed to see her go. But I shut the door and turned to see Stacy.

She fell back into the lone chair and laughed. "Oh, Beryl. The look on your face. You're still the same innocent, aren't you?"

I scowled. I wasn't that innocent. Was I?

Stacy stood back up. She hadn't changed. Her deep green hair looked a little shorter, but didn't alter her sharp beauty, and contrasted well against her dark skin. Kelly smiled and stepped forward. The two girls fell into an embrace. Lovat wandered around the clothes rack, examining different items.

"So you two aren't a thing any more?" Stacy asked as she pulled back from Kelly. "That surprises me."

Kelly shrugged. "It's no big deal."

Stacy's eyebrows went up. "If you say so."

"There's not much to tell," I said. "What do you have for us?"

"Well, okay. Straight to business then. We'll get there. Lovat, how you doing, little guy?"

Lovat peeked around from behind the clothes rack. "Hue."

"Of course you are. Nothing fazes you, does it?" She looked Kelly over a little more critically. "You've lost some weight, dear. Outdoor food treating you okay?"

"I'm fine. It's the exercise." Kelly's smile never left her face. "What about you? Any new shows lately?"

"Business is down. Our travel is restricted, obviously." Stacy took her seat again. "We played a couple of shows in Atramentous, but then had to come straight back."

"How are people handling all this?" I asked.

"They're scared. Nothing like this has ever happened." She leaned back and crossed her long legs. "More and more young men have been yanked away from their jobs and placed into the Guard." She chuckled. "That's part of why Olive showed you so much attention. There haven't been as many boys hanging around her as she's used to."

Warmth rose into my face, and I turned away so the girls wouldn't see it.

"We saw the attitude on the streets," Kelly said. "Everyone seems frightened or worried."

"Why wouldn't they be?" Stacy asked. "Everything is changed. We're at war. Did you know Incarnadine killed several dozen of our men a couple days ago?"

"Yeah." I turned back. "I saw it happen."

Her eyebrows went up. "I guess I shouldn't be surprised." She paused a moment. "You people have altered everyone's lives, you know. In all the cities."

"But no one knows we did it." Kelly sat down on the floor and crossed her legs. "I sang to a dragon and no one will ever know!"

"Oh, they'll know. Someday. Things are changing, sweetheart." Stacy shook her head. "Everything is changing. And don't be so sure no one knows."

"Have you been trying to recruit other people?" I asked.

"Well, yes, that. I've been feeling some people out, but it's a slow process. I can't just say, 'hey, want to join up with the people who killed a dragon and started the war?'" She leaned forward. "But that's not what I meant. While in Atramentous, I got a message from someone and he mentioned you by name, Beryl."

"What? I don't know anyone in Atramentous."

"That's the crazy thing. He wasn't from there. He was from Caesious."

My mouth dropped. "And he was in Atramentous? But they're at war!"

She rolled her eyes. "Yes, I'm aware of that. He was disguised. Fake chromark and everything. And somehow, he knew to talk to me. I can tell you, it scared me."

"I'll bet," Kelly said.

"But he came, representing someone else. Someone who wants to join you, Beryl. Who knows your name and… I think he knows what you did."

"Who is this person?" I couldn't imagine anyone in Caesious knowing me, let alone our purpose.

Stacy made a slow wave through the air. "Prepare to have your mind blown." She put her hands together. "It's the high priest of Caesious."

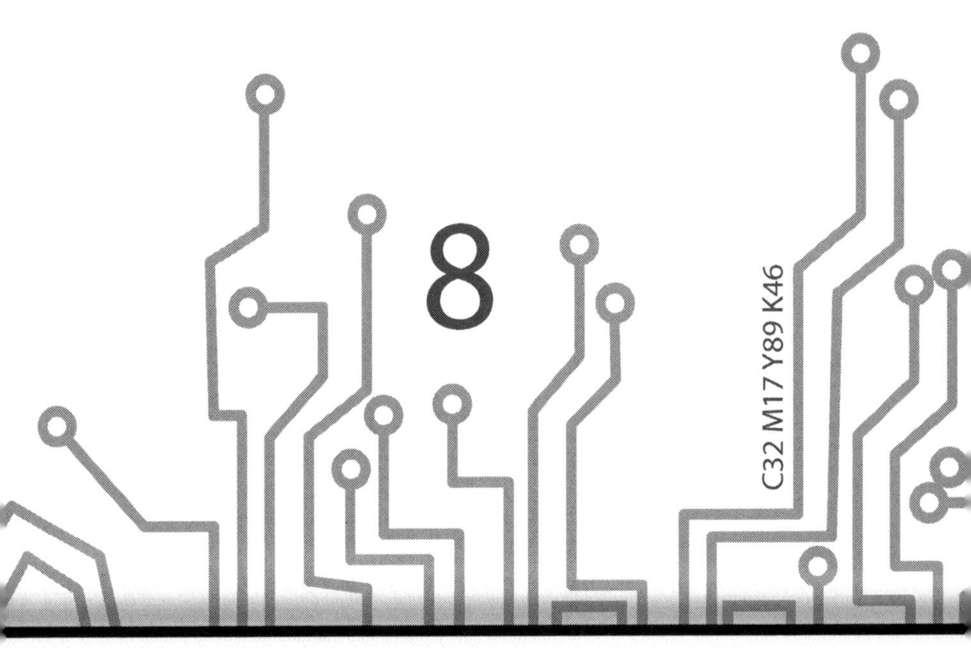

8

"I'm sorry. Who?" She couldn't have said what I thought she said.

"The high priest of Caesious. I believe you've met..."

That guy? "Maza-something-something? The guy with the sapphire on his head? Caedan's old boss?"

Stacy laughed. "I guess so."

"He wants to join us?"

"That's what the message says."

"This is a joke. Or a trap. It's got to be. No way that guy is rebelling."

"How does he know who you are?" Kelly asked.

"I, uh, may have told him my name." Not my brightest moment.

"Like you just did with Olive?"

Ouch. "But even with my name, how does he know everything else?" I protested. "It's not like we've been telling people what we're up to."

"Ohhh, he's the one you delivered the invitation to," Stacy realized. "And then you kidnapped his guard. I guess he's figured it out on his own."

"That's frightening," Kelly said. "If he's figured it out, and told anyone else... it could ruin everything."

"You mean like ending the war?" Stacy asked.

An awkward silence followed. "What did the message actually say?" I asked a few moments later.

"Oh, let me see... it went something like: 'tell Beryl I am coming to join his little band, and I would appreciate it if he didn't kill me like he did the green, at least until I can talk to him.'"

"He knows you killed Troilus Green?" Kelly exclaimed.

"Nobody outside our group knows that." I leaned against the wall. "This makes no sense."

"Then what do we do about it?"

I shrugged. "I guess we wait and see if he actually shows up."

Stacy laughed again. "Beryl, my friend, you are like a magnet for insanity. I don't know how else to explain how so many crazy things keep happening around you."

"Why can't I just be a magnet for beautiful women?" Except I didn't say that. I thought of it about ten seconds later. Oh well.

"We'll have to be prepared if it's a trap," Kelly mused. "Maybe Rick and I can hide nearby while you and Caedan meet with him."

"'Rick and I,'" Stacy echoed. "So that's how it is, huh?"

Kelly turned red. "How did you get that from what I said?" she demanded.

"I didn't. I got it from your face just now." Stacy laughed and leaned in. "Spill, girl. Tell me everything."

Kelly had the decency to glance at me. "Lovat and I will go out and let you two do your girl talk," I said. "But I do have one or two questions first."

"All right, we'll wait." Stacy pretended to groan. "What do you want to know?"

"So people… spies, whatever… are really making fake chromarks?"

"Sure. It's not complicated." She traced a finger around her own eye. "You just get someone to paint over your existing one with a different color. The trick is finding the right kind of makeup that won't wear off too quick."

"Has anyone…" I stopped, absently rubbed my own mark, then tried again: "Have you ever heard of someone having their chromark removed?"

Stacy cocked her head. "No, the marks are permanent. I don't think there is a way to remove one."

"Right." I beckoned to Lovat and we left the girls alone.

"Where to?" Lovat asked after we stepped into the hallway.

"I don't know. We shouldn't go outside." I looked around. "But I'm feeling cramped in here. Is there a larger room we can wait in?"

Lovat giggled and led the way down the hallway. I don't know what he thought was so funny. That is, until we turned a corner, went up a handful of stairs, and stepped out… onto the stage. Yeah. "Larger room." I'm an idiot.

I stared out in the semi-darkness at hundreds of empty seats. When Stacy and her friends performed their plays, those seats were full. What was that like? How did it affect a person to have so many people watching you? Admiring your accomplishments and laughing at your mistakes? I walked further out onto the stage, knowing this was something I'd never wanted.

And yet… isn't that what I was asking for in trying to lead this rebellion of ours? If we did recruit new people, wouldn't they all be watching me, like one of these performers? Waiting to see what I would do? All of a sudden, the idea of leadership didn't appeal to me.

"So. Actor or fan?" I jumped and turned to see Olive approaching from the other side of the stage. She didn't so much walk as she did… glide? Sashay? What did you call it when someone flirted through the way they walked? She wore a loose forest green shirt and tight pants that showed off her legs.

"Excuse me?"

She stopped a few feet away and cocked her head. "Are you an actor yourself, or just one of Stacy's fans?"

"Oh, I'm not an actor." I looked at all the empty seats again. "I was just thinking how I could never do this."

"Just a fan, then." She sat down on the edge of the stage, then patted the spot next to her and looked up at me.

I joined her, trying not to sit too close. "Does that disappoint you?"

"Depends." She leaned back, arching her back. "Are you a diehard Stacy Moss fan, or…?"

"Um, Kelly's the real fan." I tried not to stare at her, um, arching, and the way it pulled her shirt up. "I'm just a casual fan, I guess."

"Kelly. She the one Stacy thought you belonged to?"

"She, uh, she used to be my girlfriend. Yeah." I don't know why this kept coming up. Nor did I apparently know how to have a normal conversation with a girl. I kept stuttering and saying the wrong things.

A giggle echoed through the empty theater. I caught a glimpse of Lovat running through the chairs in the balcony. I was wondering where he'd gone.

"What about him?"

"Oh, he's Kelly's, uh, nephew. He's just hanging out with us for the day. I brought Kelly to see Stacy, and he tagged along."

"So no real connection to anyone, huh?"

"Well, we're friends. I mean… not related. Or in a relationship. If that's what you mean. I don't have anyone. Family, that is. Or a relationship." Great. Now I was babbling.

"Mm. Good to know." She lifted her arms above her head and stretched, lifting her shirt even higher.

"Are you an actor? Actress, I mean?"

She laughed, a high-pitched thing that echoed a little in the empty room. "Not like Stacy. I'm a bit player. I get parts with a couple of lines now and then. Nobody comes to the theater for me."

"Maybe they just don't know you well enough."

She looked up at me. Were her eyes really that green, or was she wearing contact lenses? "That may be the nicest thing anyone's ever said to me… Beryl."

"I'm… I, uh…" I didn't know what else to say. I wanted to spend more time with this girl, for obvious reasons, but I felt the weight of our mission more than ever. Stacy talked about the difficulties of trying to recruit other people. Maybe I should give it a try.

"Have you ever wanted life to be different than it is right now?"

"Who doesn't? I wish I were famous." She got to her feet and spread her arms out as if receiving acclaim from the audience. "Known throughout all six cities of the Circle!"

"Not just different for you, but for everyone," I clarified. "With more… freedom."

She crouched down and looked at me with one raised eyebrow. "What exactly did you want to be free to do?"

"No dragons."

She regarded me for a moment, then started to laugh. She lost her balance and sat down hard. "That can't happen!"

"Why not? One of them is already gone."

She spread her legs and leaned back on her arms. "Yeah? That still leaves five, by my count. You gonna take them down?" She giggled again. "You're cute and all, but you're not exactly some kind of super warrior."

I looked around for some kind of stage prop, anything I could use to demonstrate my strength. Finding nothing, I stood up and looked toward the balcony. I glanced at Olive, who sat watching me with both eyebrows raised now. I took a couple of steps back, nodded to her, then channeled a boost into my legs.

I ran to the edge of the stage and leaped. I flew across the darkened theater and landed in the back balcony. I'm sure it looked suitably impressive. I turned around, climbed onto the balcony railing and hopped back down, using an extra boost to control my landing. Then I trotted down the aisle to the stage again.

Olive, now on her hands and knees, stared at me with open mouth. "Who are you?" she whispered.

"I'm Beryl. I've killed one draconic and helped kill one dragon. And I'm not stopping until they're all dead."

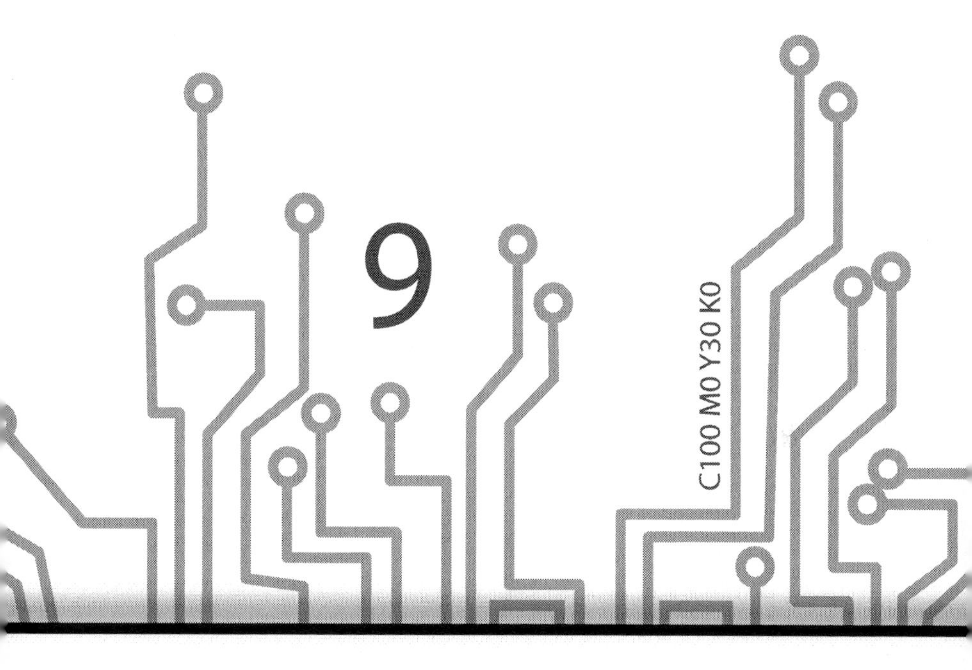

9

Olive continued to stare. I didn't mind. Maybe this is how performers felt. Olive's attractiveness and interest in me didn't hurt, either. I gave her my best smile, put my hands on the stage and leaned in closer.

"All right, Beryl, I'll talk to the director for you. Chroma. You didn't have to go that far." Stacy's voice startled me. Olive and I both turned and saw her entering the stage. Kelly and Lovat stood behind her in the shadows.

"What?"

"I'll admit that was pretty impressive," Stacy went on. "I forgot we left those wires up there from Legends of Greensleeves. How did you even know how to use them?"

I opened my mouth, but she kept talking. "You know what? Don't tell me. The surprise was worth it."

Olive looked toward the ceiling. "Oh, right… the wires…"

"But I—" I began.

"No, no. Don't ruin it," Stacy interrupted. "You wanted me to help you get a part. I'll help you get a part. I'll arrange a meeting with the director. But… Kelly says you need to get the kid home now."

Olive sat back. "That was an act? You've got potential, man! You really had me believing you for a minute there!"

Stacy didn't want Olive to know the truth for some reason. I felt both annoyed and curious. But I guess I could play along.

I climbed on to the stage and reached down to Olive. She put her hand in mine. I almost kissed it, but figured that might be over the top. Instead, I pulled her to her feet. "I'm sorry. I got caught up in my role," I told her.

"Don't apologize. That was fantastic." Her eyes sparkled.

"Apparently, I need to leave now." I glanced at the others. "I hope we meet again."

"If you make it big, take me with you," she whispered, moving a step closer to me.

"Nothing would please me more." I tilted my head closer.

To my delight, she let go of my hand, grabbed my head and kissed me. Her kiss might not have been as sweet as Kelly's, but it certainly had more… enthusiasm.

She broke off and pulled my head down to whisper in my ear. "Are you sure you have to leave right this minute? If we're going to perform together, shouldn't we—"

"All right, you two," Stacy interrupted, suddenly right beside us. "Break it up already."

I separated from Olive, though most of me didn't want to. I smiled at her one more time, then turned to follow the other two off the stage. I couldn't read Kelly's face at all. Was that good or bad?

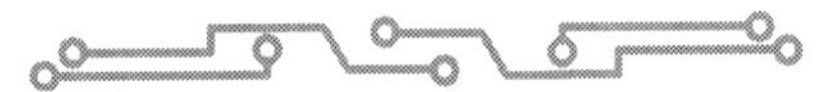

We slipped out of the city in the dark, circled around until we found the train tracks and followed them toward home. The night air whispered cool and pleasant against my face. Kelly, for some reason, didn't want to talk as we traveled.

"Are you mad at me?" I finally asked.

"Why would I be mad?"

"I don't know. That's why I'm asking."

"I'm not mad."

"Okay."

"Okay."

We kept walking. I had no idea what to think. She broke up with me because I kept secrets from her. But now she was with Rick, who kept all kinds of secrets of his own. I wondered if he'd told her all about his hand and the people in Atramentous.

After a few hours, Lovat led us to an unused storage barn and we found somewhat soft places to sleep. I kept waking up with a stick poking me. No matter which way I rolled, I couldn't get rid of it. The next morning, we walked the rest of the way and arrived, sore, tired, and a little annoyed. Well, Kelly and I were. Lovat seemed as blissful as ever.

Around noon, we gathered to let the others know of Stacy's news. Caedan, naturally, had the strongest reaction.

"I have a really hard time believing he'd want to join us," he said, shaking his head firmly.

"Tell us what you know about him," Bice suggested.

"Mazarine Chalybeous, High Priest of the Sapphire Robes, Guardian of the Cerulean Books of Lore, and Luminary of the Azure Hue?" Caedan chuckled. "I heard his full titles announced so many times, even I know them."

"That's curious." Bice rubbed the scruff on his chin. "In Viridia, none of the high priests had such elaborate titles. What do they mean?"

"I have no idea," Caedan admitted. "I always thought they were just to sound impressive."

"Maybe. Or maybe not. Sapphire robes is obvious."

"He had a sapphire on his head!" I offered.

"It's just a color," Caedan argued. "It doesn't mean anything."

"And the books?" Kelly asked.

Caedan shrugged. "I never saw any special books. I mean, priests look at books all the time, but they were pretty common looking."

"What was the last one?" I asked.

"Luminary of the Azure Hue," Caedan repeated. "Seriously, it's for show." He waved his fingers on both hands. "Oooh, the luminary! It's not like he actually glows or anything."

Luminary… luminous. Oh, I get it. I think.

"Let's move away from the titles. How… intelligent is he?" Bice asked.

"Oh, he's smart," Caedan said. "Streaking smart. No one could ever put anything over on him."

"So, based on what happened with Beryl, and then the dragon… could he have figured all that out on his own?" Kelly wanted to know.

"I guess. I don't know. I was his bodyguard for only five months. He's arrogant, thinks he's better than everyone else, even the draconics. And like I said, he's smart. Calculating."

"So." Bice leaned back. "Given that Beryl delivered the message that led to Caesious's death, I suppose it's possible that this priest thinks Beryl had something to do with it. That much is reasonable."

"But he mentioned killing the draconic!" I protested. "And how would he know to contact Stacy?"

"That's the most troubling part," Bice agreed. "As for the draconic, we did leave his body with the debris, so maybe he extrapolated that part. Or just guessed."

"Then why didn't he mention killing the dragon?" Rick spoke up for the first time. "Why only mention the draconic?"

"What was the message again?" Bice asked.

I repeated what Stacy had told me.

"That's vague enough that he might have been spreading it all over the place." Bice took a slow breath. "Maybe he didn't know about Stacy. Think about it: if he spread a message about killing the dragon, it would spark all kinds of questions and investigation. But 'killed the green'? That could mean a lot of things. The only thing not vague about the message is your name, Beryl."

"It's a common enough name," I pointed out.

"And that's all you told him, right?"

I nodded.

"Then he couldn't know which Beryl he was even looking for. So he spread the message as far as he could."

"Then we don't even need to worry about it?" Caedan wondered.

"I think we should keep an eye out," Bice said. "After all, he said he's coming to join us."

"How could he know where to come?" Rick asked.

"He couldn't," I said.

"Unless he just came to the spot where we killed the dragon. And waited for us to come to him," Don said.

Every time he spoke in one of our talks, it surprised me. "Why do you say that?"

"Because there's been a guy showing up there the last couple of days in the afternoon," he answered. "He hangs around for a few hours, and then leaves. I've been keeping an eye on him."

"Why didn't you tell us?" Rick exclaimed.

"Thank you, Don," Bice said in his usual calm voice. "The next time something like that happens, it might be best to share it with the rest of us."

Don shrugged.

"Think he'll be there today?" I asked.

"There's only one way to find out," Caedan said. He stood and picked up his own weapons. "Let's go see."

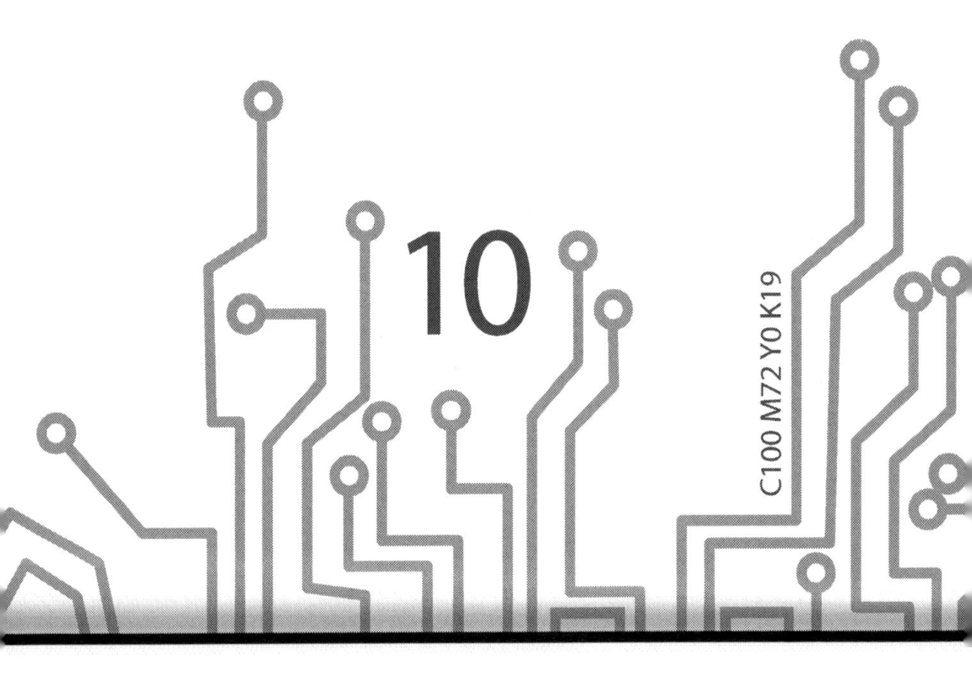

Everyone wanted to go, but Rick remained adamantly against it. "If it's a trap, we don't want all of us to fall into it!" I couldn't argue with that.

"If it is a priest, I shouldn't go," Bice said. "My reputation might be a detriment here."

In the end, only Rick, Caedan and I went. Kelly complained, but the decision was logical. If this was legitimate, then the priest would be expecting to see me and Caedan. If it was a trap, Rick would provide our backup. And the others would be safe.

Since the day we killed the blue dragon, I hadn't been back to the actual spot where it happened. I don't know what I expected to see, but little evidence remained of the momentous event. The dragon's body and all of the train debris had been taken away, of course. They'd even repaired the damaged rails. The ground remained torn apart in some places, but it felt insignificant considering what took place.

"Someday, we should build a monument or something here," I said. "At least some kind of marker with a plaque."

Caedan gave me a funny look. He and I hadn't discussed the death of Caesious, which felt wrong, now that I thought about it. The blue dragon had been his god, after all. He only joined our group because I forced him into it. After that, he threw himself into our work, especially while Rick and I had been sidelined from our injuries.

I looked at Caedan as we lay on top of a hill. I hadn't seen him wear his Cerulean Corps uniform in weeks. He put a pair of binoculars (from Loden's workshop) to his eyes. "I don't see anyone yet."

"How do you feel about all this now, Caedan?" I asked.

"What?"

"The death of the dragon. Our little rebellion. You didn't have to stay, but you did."

Caedan shrugged. "I told you I enjoyed action. This seems like the best place to find some, even though not much has happened lately."

"It's gotta be more than that. I mean, we killed the bleaking blue dragon! The god of your city! And you're okay with all this?"

Caedan lowered the binoculars and stared at me. "What do you want from me, Beryl? You dragged me into this, and it's been a fun ride. Why spoil it?"

"I'm not trying to." I tried to think of the right thing to say. "I'm just… I want you to know you're free to do whatever you think is right."

"So you don't want me here?" He looked through the binoculars again.

"No! Of course I do! You're awesome. I want you here. I'm…" I sighed. "I'm bad at this. Everyone wants me to be the leader, but I keep blowing things like simple conversations."

"Nah, you're good." Caedan made an adjustment to the binoculars. "I think I see our boy, though."

"Oh?" I took a look. Sure enough, I spotted a figure in a sky blue robe approaching the tracks. That couldn't be comfortable, walking around in this heat. "That's not the high priest, is it?"

"No. It's his assistant Peri. Minor priest. The one who usually recites the titles."

"Any sign of anything else? A trap?"

"I don't see anything."

I stood up. "Then let's go see what he has to say for himself."

We trotted down the hill. I spared a glance in the other direction, but couldn't see Rick's hiding place. I knew he could see us, though.

The priest looked up and stopped when he saw us approaching. He looked around as if he wanted to run. "Ho, Peri!" Caedan called. Recognizing his voice and uniform, the priest appeared to relax somewhat and watch us draw close. He didn't look very old, maybe in his late twenties at most. His head was shaved bald like all the priests I'd seen in Caesious, revealing a chromark that stretched across his scalp.

"Caedan Teal," he said. "I expected to see you here." He looked at me. "Are you Beryl?"

"I am. I hear your master has been trying to get in touch with me."

"Mazarine Chalybeous, High Priest of the Sapphire Robes, Guardian—"

"Right. That guy. What does he want?" I interrupted.

"He is coming." Peri gestured toward the west. "He awaits my return after finding you. Then he will approach."

"But what does he want once he approaches?"

"It is not my place to explain the Luminary's motives."

Caedan looked at me. I rolled my eyes. "Fine. Let him approach."

"Is he alone?" Caedan asked.

"Save for myself and one other servant of the Sapphire Robes," Peri answered. "The Luminary requests that you, Beryl, promise no harm will come to any of us."

"As long as you come in peace, I can say that." I narrowed my eyes.

"The Luminary means no injury toward any of you. I am told that you are a man of your word. I will report this to my master." Without another word, he turned and jogged away.

Once he moved out of sight, I waved at Rick's position. He trotted down to join us. I filled him in on the brief conversation. "Follow him," I suggested. "See if he's telling the truth, then come let us know."

Rick agreed and took off. Caedan offered to tell the others, who would be impatient for our news. He ran off, leaving me alone.

To occupy myself, I found a loose railroad tie. Rick said I needed to exercise and push my implant's abilities. Here was an opportunity. I grasped the wood and sent a strong boost to my arms. With effort, I managed to lift one side of the tie and flip it over. I considered trying to lift it over my head, but that much weight would put strain on all of my body. I didn't want to push things that far just yet. Instead, I flipped the railroad tie over and over across the open area.

Caedan returned and watched me for a while. I wondered what he thought, but didn't ask. When Rick returned, I gave the tie one final flip and watched it land in a satisfying cloud of dust. I wiped the sweat from my face and joined the two of them. "What did you see?"

"It looks like he's telling the truth," Rick reported. "The high priest is coming this way, riding on a little cart. The assistant that talked to you is walking alongside."

"And the third?"

"I didn't see a third person. He must be inside the cart."

"That's kind of suspicious."

Rick nodded. "It could still be a trap."

"Right. Let's face it the same way. Caedan and I are both armed, but if something happens…"

"I'll be ready."

Rick returned to his hiding place. Caedan and I went back to waiting. After another twenty minutes or so, the cart came into view. I tried to analyze things as it approached. I would have called it a covered wagon like those in the history books, but it looked smaller. The high priest sat at the front, holding the reins for the donkey pulling him along. Peri walked beside him.

"Two people could fit inside that thing." Caedan said what I was already thinking. "Maybe even three."

"Right." By instinct, he and I took several steps away from each other. If it was a trap, we wouldn't let both of us get taken out at once.

The cart came to a stop. With Peri's assistance, Mazarine What's-his-bous descended. As he came near, I shook my head. He still wore the elaborate robes and jewelry from the last time I had seen him. Who was he trying to impress?

To my everlasting shock, he removed the circlet with its sapphire from his head and knelt before me, holding it out. "Hail, Beryl Godslayer. I come to you in desperation, for you are my last hope for all the people who live within The Circle."

I blinked and looked at Caedan. How on earth did I react to that?

"Um… you can keep your sapphire. I don't need it. What in The Circle are you talking about?"

Mazarine rose to his feet and replaced the sapphire on his head. "Though you and, no doubt, those with you"—he glanced at Caedan—"have slain the great Caesious, it is that very act which drives me to you, for I know that you, out of all others within The Circle, will not betray what I have to say to the other dragons."

Okay, color me intrigued. If this was a trap, he knew how to bait it.

"Caedan, check the cart."

“Oh, there’s no need for that,” Mazarine protested, reaching toward Caedan.

“That only makes us want to know even more,” Caedan said, heading toward the back of the cart.

Mazarine spun back to face me. “You gave your word not to harm us.”

“And I won’t, as long as you come in peace, and aren’t trying to deceive me.”

“I mean no deception.” Yet he watched Caedan’s progress with wide eyes. His hands even trembled. Not good. I drew my sword.

Caedan grasped the cloth overhanging the back of the cart and pulled it aside. Immediately, he let it go and dove away. He rolled to his feet and pulled out his own weapons, yelling at the top of his lungs:

“Draconic!”

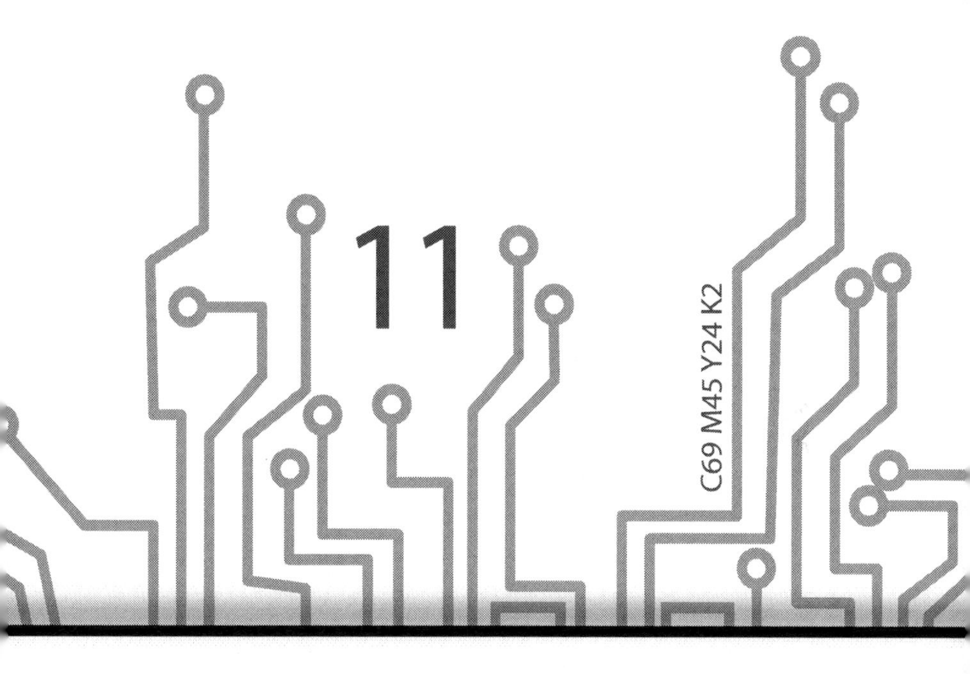

11

I shoved the high priest out of my way and charged the cart. Out of the corner of my eye, I saw Rick coming down the hill, drawing his own sword. Caedan knelt a few feet from the cart, his projectile weapon aimed at it.

The cart hadn't moved. I expected a monster to leap out, claws and teeth raking the air, searching for its prey. But nothing happened. I came to a stop and looked at Caedan.

"It's in there, I tell you!" He held his weapon steady, eyes never leaving the back of the cart.

"Please!" Mazarine called. "He is old and infirm. He will do you no injury!" I glanced at him. Peri had helped the high priest back to his feet from where I shoved him. They both looked… concerned?

I approached the cart with sword leveled. I triggered a short boost throughout my body, preparing for anything. Still nothing happened. I looked to Caedan again, then to Rick, who stopped a couple dozen yards away, watching me.

I reached forward with my sword and pushed at the covering cloth. It fell back into place without a sound.

"If you wish to see me, you will have to open it," said a deep voice from inside. "I will not harm you. In fact, I do not believe I am capable of causing you harm, if you are who I think you are."

I glanced at the others again, then climbed onto the back of the cart. I shoved the cloth aside and held my sword at ready.

Inside the cart sat a blue draconic all right. But I felt inclined to believe Mazarine's words. The draconic's scales, while still blue, looked faded and dull. A few were missing. Its claws, though longer than usual, looked chipped and damaged. One of its eyes appeared glazed over, whitened. A wave of heat, along with the familiar sickly-sweet smell, washed over me.

"Greetings, Beryl, slayer of my father Caesious," it said. "I am pleased to meet you, though I know you will not believe my intentions at first. My name is Protogonus Blue, and I am at your service."

There are times in my life where I have been dumbfounded, speechless even. When Kelly and I shared our first kiss, for example. But nothing compared to this moment. I had no idea what to say, how to react, how to even move…

"Beryl?" Caedan called. "Are you all right?"

I blinked, teetered unsteadily, then dropped back down to the ground.

"What is it?" Rick asked.

"It's… a draconic. It doesn't look well." I turned toward the high priest. "I think he's telling the truth."

Mazarine folded his arms across his chest. "Of course I'm telling the truth. Do you think I would come all the way out here to the middle of nowhere to lie to you?"

"We didn't know what to think," I said. "You have to admit: you're the absolute last person I would expect to be coming out to find us."

"Which should further solidify your trust in me! Protogonus Blue and I need to speak with you. Our world, our very existence is in grave danger!"

I studied him for a moment. He seemed sincere, but his words made no sense. Had he lost his mind? The death of his god could have driven him insane, I suppose.

"Beryl?" Rick came closer.

I beckoned him and Caedan. "Let's talk, guys."

The three of us retreated some distance away, but kept our eyes on the visitors.

"What do you think?" I asked, sheathing my sword.

"I don't know," Caedan said. "It doesn't seem like a trap. It looks like he actually wants our help. And it's absolutely crazy to even hear those words come out of my mouth."

"I don't trust them," Rick said. "I say we kill the draconic and then get answers from the priests."

My eyebrows almost went up. I knew Rick to be more suspicious by nature, but his reaction seemed a bit extreme. "I'm, uh, not ready to go that far just yet," I said. "But keep your sword ready."

"Why not just ask them to explain?" Caedan suggested. "We don't have to take them back to the Asylum for that."

"We shouldn't take them back, no matter what they say!" Rick insisted. "They could bring the wrath of all the other dragons down on us!"

"Then why haven't they done that already?" Caedan asked. "If they knew the truth, and told the red dragons, it wouldn't have taken them too long to search us out. We'd be dead already."

"What do you know of this draconic?" I asked him.

Caedan shrugged. "I've heard of him. He spent a lot of time with the priests. Other than that, nothing."

"Then let's see what they have to say for themselves. If it makes sense, then we discuss taking them to the Asylum or not." I had to admit I was seriously curious now.

We returned to the priests. Peri had pulled aside the cart's flap so we could all see the draconic sitting inside now. It hadn't moved.

"All right, we'll hear you out," I announced. "Why have you come looking for us?"

"Here?" Mazarine asked, gesturing with both hands. "Don't you have somewhere more comfortable we could talk?"

"It'll get a lot more uncomfortable if we don't like what you have to say," Rick said.

Mazarine examined him. "There's something familiar about you," he muttered.

"Why have you come?" I repeated.

Mazarine sighed. He straightened his circlet and stood a little taller. "As the most senior and honored priest of the great Caesious, one of my titles was Guardian of the Cerulean Books of Lore." He paused. "This is not just fancy words for the sake of my ego. The Cerulean Books of Lore exist."

"Yes, and…?"

"They really exist," he repeated, as if it would mean something to me.

"All right. You have some books about your religion. What does that have to do with me?"

"You… don't know?" He looked from one to the other of us. "How do you not know?"

"Much has been forgotten," the draconic rumbled. "The cities have grown distant from one another. This is not surprising."

"The Books contain the history of The Circle," Mazarine declared. "Its true history, not the propaganda you all received in your Learning Years."

That sounded interesting. "You mean how we got here?"

"And the true story of the dragons themselves," Protogonus Blue said. "And thus, no one is allowed to read them, save for Caesious's most trusted and valuable researchers, should they need guidance in their efforts to help the dragons. The high priest was responsible for guarding them, though he was not allowed to read them himself."

"And now they're gone!" Mazarine interjected. "Incarnadine sent his troops to steal them the moment we received word of the death of Caesious!"

"You're lucky you left when you did," Peri said to Caedan. "The Luminary's other guards were slaughtered during the theft."

I glanced at Caedan, but couldn't tell anything from his face. I wondered how well he knew the other guards.

"This is all fascinating, but what does it have to do with us?" Rick asked.

"You are the only ones who might be able to recover the books," Mazarine said.

"You have demonstrated remarkable capability with your recent actions," the draconic added. "And it appears you are unaffiliated with any of the other cities or dragons."

"What do you have to do with all of this?" Rick demanded. "I get the priests, but you?"

"You must try to understand," Protogonus Blue said. "I am a child of Caesious. All my life, I have been inculcated to recognize him as my father and god. When you killed him, my whole world fell apart. How could my god die? I went to the high priest, long my confidant, and he told me of the books. I seek them now, because… I must know the truth. Who am I? What am I? I want to know before I die."

As much as I hated the dragons and by extension, the draconics, his words affected me. It reminded me of what Bice would say about the dragons and the nature of gods. He needed to talk to them about these kind of things.

"So you want us to invade the city of Incarnadine and get them back for you?" I scratched an itch on the back of my head. "Why would we want to do that?"

"Because you managed to convince everyone that Viridia killed Caesious," the draconic said. "You have higher aims. One dragon is not enough for you, is it?"

I stared at him, but didn't answer.

"If we recover the Books of Lore, you may find what you are seeking as well: the means by which to rid us of all the dragons!"

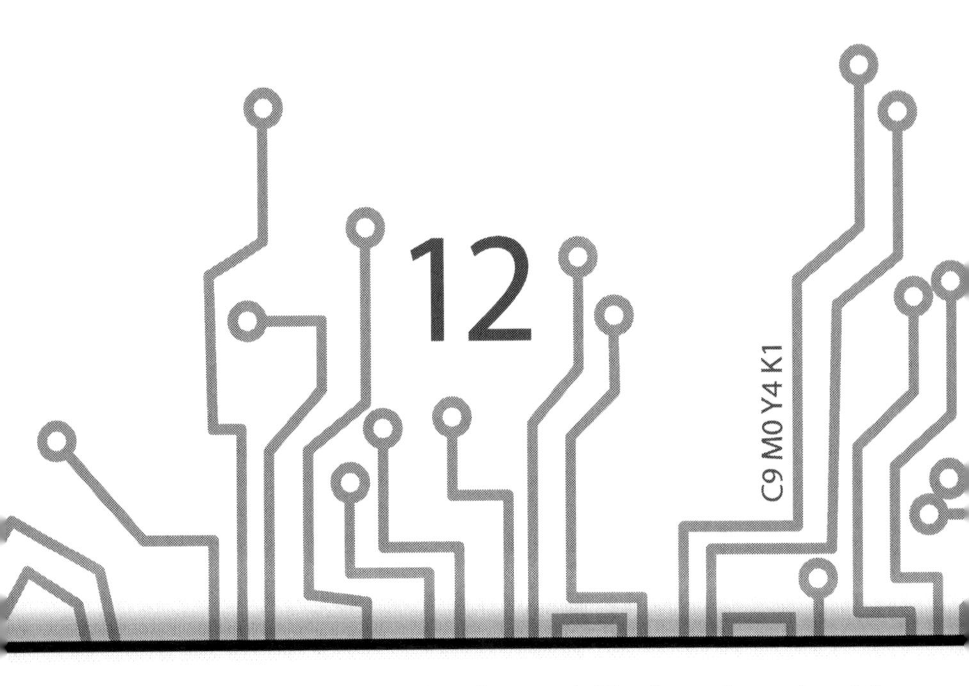

12

"We still can't trust them!" Rick insisted. The three of us gathered for another discussion.

"The draconic at least seems… sincere," I said.

"All right, let's say it is." Rick glanced back toward the cart. "Let's assume that it's defying everything it's every believed and everything that defines its very existence. Sure, let's assume that. Why not? What about the priests?"

"What about them?" Caedan asked.

"The high priest is only interested in getting these books back. He's not on our side. And we know nothing about the other one."

I couldn't argue with him. My own brain kept arguing with me: out of all these suspicious people, I believed the draconic? The draconic! What was wrong with me?

"So what are they going to do?" Caedan put in. "Betray us? To who? They've abandoned their own city. They can't go to green or black because of the war. And they're wanting us to steal something from the reds."

"Gold," I said automatically.

"You think something like this will suddenly bring the gold dragon in?"

"I don't know. It was the only color you didn't mention."

"The draconic isn't going anywhere without help," Caedan said. "And

I can't see the priests getting far on their own, anyway. I don't think it'll be hard to keep an eye them."

"So you want to bring them back to the Asylum?"

"Sure."

"No way," Rick argued. "We can't let them see our capabilities."

"We wouldn't allow them in the workshop," Caedan said. "I'm not saying make them part of our team."

"They can't come in the cave at all," I said. "I don't want them even close to Loden's stuff."

"In the face."

"What?"

"I'm good with that."

"I'm not." Rick folded his arms.

"Look, you keep wanting me to be the leader here," I complained. "Then let me make decisions, even if they're bad ones."

"This is a bad one."

"Fine. We'll see what happens. At the very least, Bice will be thrilled that he gets to talk religion with someone that'll actually listen."

Rick snorted.

"And," I added, "it gives us something to do. A mission. Don't tell me you don't want to steal something out from under the red dragon's nose."

"Sounds like fun to me," Caedan said, grinning.

After explaining a bit to our visitors, Caedan led the way to the Asylum. The priests and the draconic were suitably impressed with our efforts on overhead disguise, and even more impressed when they saw the four-wheelers. Peri ran straight to one of them and walked around it, examining everything.

"You like that?" I asked him.

"In Caesious, all priests are required to learn another profession during their early training. I chose mechanical engineering."

Maybe this guy wouldn't be completely useless. "You know how these work, then?"

He nodded. "I'm not an expert, and I don't know anything advanced, but engines? I know those."

Mazarine brought the cart under cover and called Peri back to take care of the donkey. Rick stood near, fingering his sword hilt and watching their every move.

Bice and the others emerged from the cave. I waved and went to meet them.

"So… we have some guests." I quickly explained who and why. While we spoke, Lovat abandoned us and went to look at the donkey.

"Not what I expected," Kelly said. "Can we trust them?"

"Caedan thinks so, Rick doesn't, and I'm in the middle," I answered. "At the very least, we need to keep a close eye on them."

"Let's see how they react to me," Bice said, rubbing his hands together.

"I'm sure that'll be fun. And then can you and Don help find a place out here for them to get settled? They're definitely not allowed in the cave."

Bice agreed. I started to follow him, when Kelly grabbed my arm and pulled me aside.

"You're doing it again," she said.

"Doing what?"

"Making decisions for everyone. Like when you brought Caedan."

"That worked out pretty well, I thought."

"And maybe this will too." She sighed. "Beryl, we just want to be in on the discussions."

"Caedan and Rick—"

"Not just the three of you! You should consult with all of us." She glanced at the priests, now reacting in shock to Bice. I wished I were listening to that conversation instead. "Look, I'll be honest. I'm the only girl here, and… bringing in more men I don't know makes me feel… less safe."

"I would never let anyone hurt you!" I felt a surge of anger at the very thought.

"I know that's your intention, and I love you for it. It's part of what makes you… you."

If she loved me, why were we apart?

"But you and Rick can't watch over me every moment of the day and night, you know. And you shouldn't have to."

Ah. Rick. Of course.

"Do you understand what I'm saying?" She looked at me with pleading eyes.

"I hear you," I said. "I'll try to do better. In fact, I want you to be a part of this books thing. You'll probably have saner ideas than us guys."

"Yeah, you'll just want to charge in waving your swords or something."

I grunted. "We men. We break things. Ugh."

She shoved me. Did I mention I love that?

"Let's go see the others." I led her to join the rest of the group.

"All right," I called. "Everyone acquainted now? Kelly, this is Mazarine Something-or-other, the high priest of Caesious, and his assistant Peri. That over there is Protogonus Blue. You three, this is Kelly."

"Mazarine Chalybeous," the priest corrected me.

After some more interaction, Bice and Don, joined by Caedan, worked to set up suitable living quarters for the newcomers before it got too dark. Mazarine seemed on the verge of outrage after being told he would be sleeping outside, but after a look around at the rest of our base, he accepted it. We didn't tell him about the cave just yet.

Rick, Kelly and I retreated to Loden's workshop. "All right," I said. "Let's assume for the moment that we want to go after these books. How in The Circle would we do that?"

"First we'd need to find out where they are," Kelly pointed out.

I took a seat and looked up at the winged device. "Viridia has the Emerald Ascendancy. Caesious had a tower. Rick, what's the red… Incarnadine's place look like?"

"It's not as huge as Viridia's, but the architecture is pretty amazing." Rick tried to illustrate with his hands. "It's a circular structure at its base, but it rises up in the shape of—surprise!—fire. Incarnadine flies up from the middle of it. They just call it The Flame."

"What about the other red dragon?" Kelly wanted to know.

"Amaranth has the same place, almost a mirror image."

"What's it called?"

Rick frowned. "I… don't remember."

"So… let's assume these books, since they're so valuable will be taken to this Flame place," I suggested. "How do we get information from inside it? We don't know anyone in Incarnadine."

"No… but Stacy does," Kelly said. "She knows people in every city."

"But she can't go there right now," I said. "Greens aren't welcome."

"She could give us their names," Rick said. "And we could find them ourselves. No one's stopping us from traveling."

"Yeah, but we'll get noticed once we're there."

"Maybe not." Kelly paced the room. "We already know that some people are wearing fake chromarks. We should look into that."

"Sounds like something else to talk with Stacy about. Maybe some kind of stage makeup?" I knew nothing about such things, but figured Kelly might.

"Maybe. I'll need to go see her again."

"We were just there." Was that only yesterday?

"Do you want to wait until our next regular meeting in a week?"

I hesitated.

"Your priest out there seemed pretty upset. If we sit around and do nothing for a week, he might regret coming to us," Rick observed.

"You're right. We'll have to go back."

"We?"

"I'm not sending you alone. And we're still the least likely to be noticed." And, I'll admit it, the thought of seeing Olive again popped into my head. "But… it can wait until morning, at least. Then we'll tell Mazzy out there that we're going to talk to our contacts."

"Oh good," Rick said. "You're smart enough to keep Stacy a secret, at least."

"Seriously, Onyx. I'm doing the best I can here."

He lifted his palms. "No, you're right. I'm sorry. Just… having a draconic around puts me on edge."

"I'm not all that comfortable with it myself, but you saw it."

Rick stood up. "Yeah, I saw it. And so did you. Now let me ask you this: are you an expert on draconic aging? How do we even know what an 'old' draconic looks like?"

I had no answer to that.

"We don't know," Rick concluded. "And that means we've let one of our worst enemies into our camp."

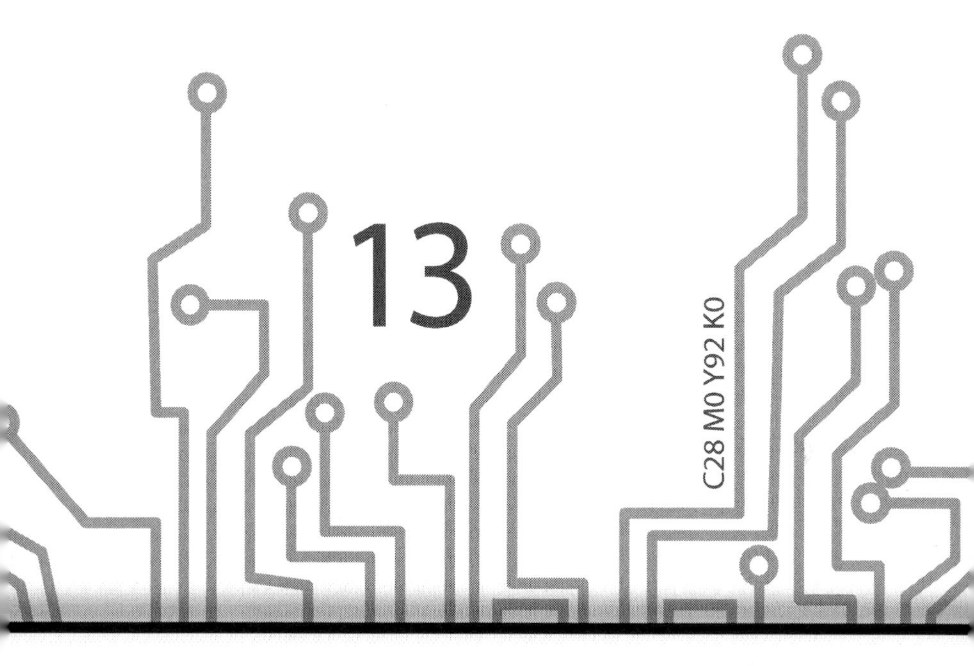

13

At least this time, Lovat led us to the theater through the alley without having to climb fences. The walk back to Viridia had been long and boring. Kelly apparently wasn't interested in talking… again. Since Lovat often traveled with Don, I guess he was used to it. I wasn't. I guess I don't do well with silence.

No one answered our knocks at the Citrine. I tried the door and found it open. "Lovat, go see if you can find Stacy." The boy slipped past me, wove his way through the back hallway and disappeared from view. I stepped back to wait with Kelly.

"Disappointed Olive didn't answer the door?" she asked.

I blinked and looked back at her. Now she wanted to talk? "Maybe. Why?"

"She's not worth it, Beryl."

"Excuse me?" I mean, seriously. "Why do you care?"

"Because in spite of everything else, we're still… friends. And as your friend, I need to tell you this." Every time she used the word "friend," it was like a knife in my gut.

Kelly grasped her hands together and put them near her mouth. "I just… you're still a great guy, Beryl. You deserve someone… someone amazing. Olive doesn't deserve you." She paused and added much quieter, "And neither do I."

Wait… neither did she? Did we break up because she didn't think she was good enough for me? I couldn't fathom that. I mean, I'm nobody special.

"Maybe…" I started to say, then stopped. No matter what I said, it would be wrong here.

"I'm serious," Kelly said. "You deserve better than her."

"What if I don't want to wait for better?" I asked. "We're in a revolution against almost omnipotent dragons, Kelly. I may not have time to wait for the perfect woman." I wanted to add: "Besides, I already found her, but she's with my best friend now."

The door burst open and Lovat popped out, followed by Stacy. She wore a skin-tight bright green jumpsuit and looked fit to burst, both out of the jumpsuit and out of her mind.

"Are you two insane? What are you doing back again so soon? Are you trying to get me in trouble?"

"We need some quick information, and then we'll get out of your… hair," I said. Since when had Stacy's hair spiked up in every direction?

"You, you—" She leveled her finger at me.

"We need some contacts in Incarnadine," Kelly interrupted. "It's important, or we wouldn't be here. Obviously."

"I'm not just giving away my information network!" Stacy whirled on her. "You should know better than that."

"You can't even connect with them. We can. Don't you want to know how they're doing?"

Stacy crossed her arms. I swear that jumpsuit was about to explode.

Kelly looked around to be sure no one could hear us. "Listen, we've been visited by the high priest of Caesious. He's got a job for us in Incarnadine. But we can't just waltz in there without knowing anyone."

"You're doing jobs for the blue priests now? I expect this from him, Kelly"—she pointed at me—"but you're usually a bit smarter. Is this Rick's influence?"

"We're after some books that might reveal the dragons' weaknesses," I said. "Since killing them is our whole purpose, I think we should try it."

"You'll never be able to pass for Incarnadine natives," Stacy said, but at least she didn't seem so angry any more.

"We know. Do you have any, um, makeup or something to disguise our chromarks?"

She studied us for a few moments, then sighed. "Anything else I can get you? Ticket to tonight's premier, maybe?"

"Oh, there was one thing." I had a sudden thought. "Have you heard anything about a train a few days ago?"

"The trains aren't running."

"One of them was… it was doing something, anyway. We saw it on our last trip here. Lots of Viridian Guard. And at least one member of the Cerulean Corps." I wanted to kick myself for not mentioning it last time. But I guess I got a little distracted.

"That doesn't make sense."

"We know."

She nodded. "I'll ask around." She glanced from one to the other of us, then nodded. "Wait here."

A few minutes later, she returned with a bottle she handed to Kelly. "We use this during plays in the red cities. Strongest stuff we have."

Kelly unscrewed the lid and looked inside. "Works with a normal makeup brush?"

"Sure. The ones I gave you last time you were here should work."

Huh. They were exchanging makeup brushes? What else was changing hands? Actually… I didn't want to know the answer to that question.

Stacy turned to me and offered a slip of paper. "Here are the names of my two best friends in Incarnadine." She swallowed hard. "I'm trusting you, Beryl. Don't put them in danger, if you can help it. Please."

"I'll do my best."

"I'm not sure that's comforting. Anything else? I need to get back to the rehearsal."

I looked at Kelly, and she shook her head. "Guess not," I said. "Say hi to Olive for me."

Stacy rolled her eyes and turned back to the door. "You're incorrigible!"

Like Rick? Wait, was that a good thing or not?

We trudged through another day-long hike back to the Asylum, broken up by another night in the barn. If Lovat hadn't been with us, and if Kelly and I were still together, it would have been… Never mind. I needed to stop thinking about things like that.

Caedan shortened our trip a little by showing up on a four-wheeler a few miles out. He gave Kelly and Lovat a ride and I ran the rest of the way. The exercise helped clear my head, though I still wanted a nap when we got there.

Bice met me as I came under our shelter. "We got the contacts in Incarnadine," I announced.

He nodded. "Good to hear." He glanced at the others getting off the four-wheeler. "There's someone waiting to talk to you in private. It's a conversation you shouldn't avoid."

I suspected what he was going to say. "I'm tired, Bice. Two trips in a row to Viridia is a lot of walking."

"I know. But he just wants to talk."

"Who does?"

"Protogonus Blue."

It did not escape my notice that Bice referred to the draconic as "he." As far as I knew, the draconics had no gender, and giving one a personal pronoun felt… completely wrong.

"Do I have to?" Even as I said it, I knew it sounded like whining. "Never mind. Where is it?"

Bice pointed. "We've set up a space for him over there."

I walked around the water barrels and found an odd construction. It looked like they had taken the cart apart and used its lumber and cloth to erect three walls with an opening on one side. I approached the opening and looked inside. The draconic sat cross-legged on the ground, hands resting on its knees.

"Ah, you have returned," it uttered. As always, it felt strange to hear words coming from the reptilian snout. It didn't move anything like our mouths.

"You wanted to see me?" I stood on the edge of the structure. The crude walls blocked all of the breezes that swept through the Asylum. Did draconics prefer heat, or just this one?

The creature's eyes blinked like a lizard as it watched me. "I have desired to see you for weeks. Our brief meeting before was not sufficient for my curiosity, I am afraid."

I spread my arms. "Well, here I am. Get a good look."

"You are a conundrum, Beryl. A mere human, barely on the cusp of what you consider adulthood. Yet you have accomplished a task far beyond any in your history."

"I didn't do it alone. I had a lot of help," I pointed out. "And Rick did the final bit."

"Ah, yes. The Wanderer. He is a mystery in himself."

There was that name again. Troilus Green called Rick the Wanderer. I knew he had visited most, if not all, of the cities, but the way the draconic said it... they seemed to be implying something more.

"But you are the impetus, the primary trigger for all that has happened," it went on. "It all revolves around you."

"I'm not anyone important," I said. "I just want... freedom for my people." I sat down on the ground to face him. Everyone seemed determined to tell me I was important and great. If this kept up, I might start believing it.

"A laudable goal, though one I would have thought preposterous mere weeks ago." The draconic lifted a clawed hand and flipped it in the air in an odd gesture. "Yet now it seems entirely possible. However, you still have far to go. Tell me, how did you feel when you saw him lying there?"

"How did I feel?" I paused. "Satisfied, I guess."

"No anger? No joy?"

"Maybe. I guess. I'd probably feel more at the death of the green dragon."

"Oh. Oh, you misunderstand me. I do not speak of the death of Caesious. I am not entirely able to deal with that yet. I speak of my cousin, the green one."

"Troilus Green?" I blinked. "I, uh, definitely felt pleasure at its death after what it did to me. I'm happy I'll never see it again."

"Ah, again a misunderstanding. There is so much you do not yet know."

"What do you mean?"

"Troilus Green will return."

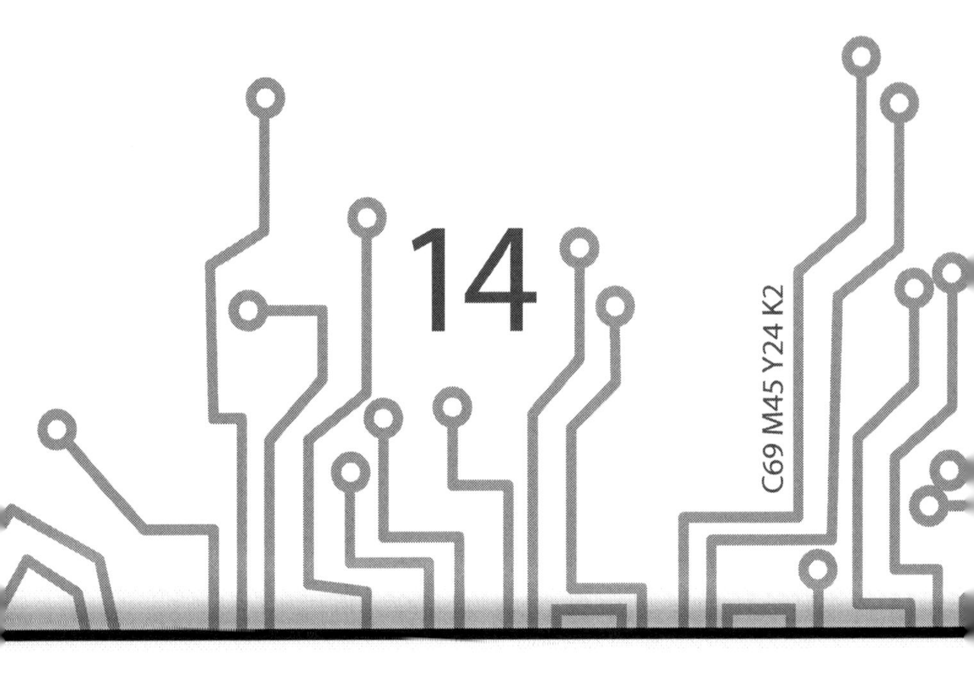

14

I jumped to my feet. "What? What do you mean it'll return?"

The draconic held up a palm to calm me. "Perhaps not for quite some time, but eventually, that one will come back."

"How? I killed it!" My hand went to my sword hilt. The memory of driving my sword down through Troilus Green's maw made regular appearances in my dreams at night.

"We draconics are the children of the dragons," Protogonus Blue explained. "There is a… limit to the number that may exist at any one time. We live perhaps twice your lifespan, but when one of us dies, we are… reborn later."

I tried to understand. "So… Troilus Green will be… reborn? Grow all over again? Will it have the memories of its past life?"

"Some of them." The draconic sighed. "Some memories are lost as our spirit waits for the birth of a new body. And then when it finds one, it must grow again, as you said, learning what a child must learn to survive. In time, it regains most of what it knew before… though not all."

I relaxed. "So even if Troilus Green had a new body born today, it would be years before it could recall how it died and tell others about it?"

"Ah, I see your concern. No, you need have no worries there. But years from now, my green cousin may come looking for you."

That was a pleasant thought. "Then," I said, sitting down once again, "you have memories from previous lives, er, bodies?"

It nodded. "This is my third incarnation, and my last, since the death of my sire. I have, as I said, lost some memories, but I recall a great deal."

I did some calculations. That would mean this thing's memories stretched back almost six hundred years or more! "You could tell us a lot about the past."

"I could, and I would be happy to. Though the books you seek will tell you of the time you wish to know about. I'm afraid my own memories do not cover such monumental times."

"But… three hundred years ago. The black city rebellion and death of its dragon. You were alive for that?"

"Oh." The draconic looked down and to the side. Was it nervous? "Yes, I recall some of that time."

"How did they do it?" I asked. "How did they kill the dragon?"

"I'm afraid I do not know that particular detail. Only that it happened, and how the other dragons reacted."

"The Blasted Lands."

It nodded. "A horrific reprisal, but one, you must admit, that has kept the human population in fear and servitude ever since. Until you, of course."

I wanted more information than that, but didn't know what else to ask. He told me nothing more than the history books.

"Why did you ask how I felt?"

"What?"

"You asked how I felt when I killed Troilus Green. Why?"

"Because it is a rarity. Not as rare as killing a dragon, obviously, but not something that happens very often. And, as you yourself said, you did that on your own. Killing Caesious was a team effort. I am, admittedly, most intrigued in knowing how one such as you"—it gestured at me—"was able to accomplish this. You do not appear to be a mighty warrior. Perhaps you caught the green one by surprise?"

I didn't answer. I had no desire to share the secrets of my implant with this creature.

"Ah, well. My curiosity shall sustain me, I suppose, helping me live on until I can learn the answers I seek."

"Good luck with that." I wasn't sure if I were being snarky or serious.

"Are there any other answers I can provide you?"

"What's beyond The Circle?" The question popped into my head.

The draconic's eyes widened. "Why do you ask this?"

"Troilus Green bragged about seeing what was beyond The Circle. I want to know."

"I... have never seen beyond The Circle myself. If he told you this, then I am surprised. I do not think he would lie, but I can see no reason for him to have been there."

"And you don't know the answer?" I got back to my feet.

"There is nothing beyond The Circle." Protogonus Blue spread its arms. "The dragons brought us here because the land is good. Outside, there is nothing."

"So basically you have no answers for me at all." I threw up my hands. "You've gone on about draconics being reborn, but other than that, everything you've said is the same garbage they fed me in history class."

"Perhaps because it is the truth."

"I don't buy that." I stalked away toward the cave. Mazarine had better be right about those books. The truth had to be somewhere.

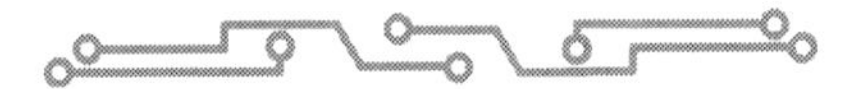

After some discussion with the main team, we agreed Kelly, Rick, and I would travel to Incarnadine and meet with Stacy's contacts. We would try to ascertain the location of the Books of Lore and what it would take to steal them. Caedan wanted to come, but too many of us at once might be intimidating to Stacy's friends. Once we knew what we were up against, we would bring in whoever we needed.

Caedan's job, for now, was driving one of the four-wheelers. I rode behind him while Rick and Kelly took the other one. Peri had helped Caedan understand more about the vehicles, including their fuel capacity. We brought along an extra can of gasoline from the cave (Loden had quite a stockpile), just in case.

We rode for miles and miles across hills and plains, past abandoned farms. The farmers and workers of these distant places had no doubt been evacuated back to their home cities. We had to cover our faces as we passed a smoking field. It must have once been full of some type of grain. Either Incarnadine had been here, or some soldiers had set it ablaze to keep it from enemy cities.

At a pause for lunch, Rick had a suggestion: "We should see what's happening at the Hub."

"Will it be safe?" Kelly asked.

The Hub lay at the very center of the Circle. Rail lines from all six cities led to and from it. Controlling it could be crucial in this ongoing war between the dragons.

"How about Caedan and I check that out?" I offered. "No need for all of us to go."

Rick frowned but agreed.

Once we drew close enough, Rick and Kelly stopped and waited with the four-wheelers while Caedan and I took off on foot. We moved at a brisk jog, but keeping our eyes and ears peeled for any sign of danger.

I had never been to the Hub directly, but the train Caedan and I rode from Caesious to Viridia had passed through it. I remembered little about that part of the trip. Caedan, fortunately, knew more about the landscape than I did.

"If I remember right, there's a fold in the earth up here," he explained. "It forms into a narrow valley that should take us right up within a few yards of the Hub itself."

We crossed over another set of tracks, probably the ones heading toward Atramentous. Only a few minutes later, we found the fold Caedan described. We climbed down and followed the tiny valley. A number of brambles made it a difficult passage, but not impossible. I had to use my sword a couple of times to carve us a way forward.

As we drew near the end, we moved as silently as we could. Caedan took out his binoculars and lifted his head just above the main ground's surface. He looked for a few minutes, then stepped back and handed the binoculars to me. "Not what I was expecting," he said.

Curious, I took his place and looked. I could have zoomed my eyes myself, but the binoculars didn't require extra thought. The Hub, a massive but low-set building, loomed very close to our hiding spot. I guessed it to be circular in shape, with large openings for each of the rail lines that extruded from its depths. The architecture looked to be a blend of concrete, brick, and wood: all very practical.

Captivated by the building itself, it took me a moment to notice the figures moving in and out of one of the entrances. I adjusted the binoculars and looked closer.

Soldiers moved here and there, carrying large crates, directed by their leaders. A few carried tall, bladed weapons of some kind while others had thin swords strapped to their backs. All wore glistening, layered armor of some sort.

I lowered the binoculars and tried to wrap my brain around it. Soldiers of Auric, the gold dragon.

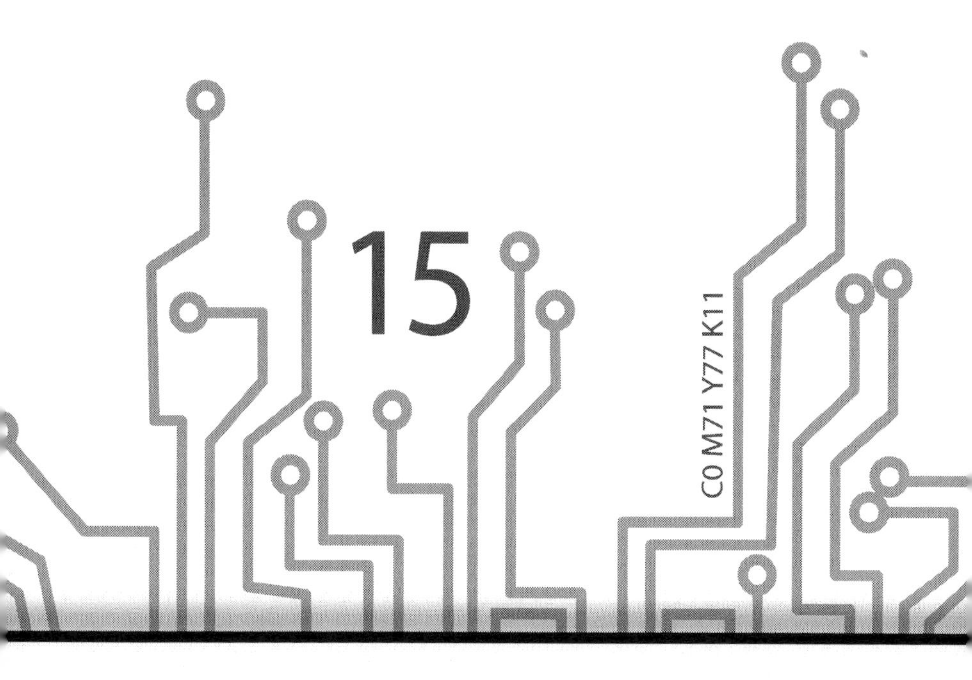

15

The mystery of the gold soldiers at the Hub nagged at me as we drew near Incarnadine, but it would have to wait for another time. The current mission came first.

If anyone walks around a city staring wide-eyed at everything, it attracts attention. Normal city residents don't behave that way. They spend their whole life in the city; nothing about it was worth staring at. Consequently, keeping our eyes down when we walked through Incarnadine was both vital to blending in and difficult to do. We had never seen it before.

The paint on my face only added to the struggle. At the spot we left Caedan, Kelly painstakingly gave all three of us red chromarks. While they looked perfect in the mirror, I couldn't help the constant knowledge of the paint being there. I felt paranoid, certain at any moment, someone would point at me and tell everyone my mark was fake.

Caedan waited with the four-wheelers, though he kept complaining about the cold. He agreed to camp out for three days, at least. We could communicate with him via Loden's talkers, or at least we hoped. None of us fully understood the technology yet.

As we approached the edges of Incarnadine, I tried to get all of my staring in. The architecture was something altogether different from Viridia or Caesious. Each city had its own personality. I wondered how much of that came about as a reflection of the dragon who ruled it. Unlike Viridia, this city had no definable starting point. Tiny homes and small buildings dotted the outskirts without rhyme or reason, gradually leading into the more organized city proper. Once there, we saw larger buildings, mostly apartments and shops, all reflecting the same stylistic choices. Most of them were made of stone, featuring two different colors, usually contrasting and almost always including some red. Every building also sported geometric patterns of some sort carved into the stone.

Toward the center of the city, the buildings looked more like those of Caesious: lots of glass and metal. A large cluster of very tall buildings stood off to the right of the true center of the city: the Flame.

Rick had undersold the structure. Maybe it didn't have the total square footage of the Emerald Ascendancy, but it towered high into the air. Made entirely of some kind of red stone, it stabbed upward with a dozen or so peaks of differing heights. Rather than shooting straight up, it bulged outward from its base, furthering the impression of active fire.

Far to the right of the city center, I caught a glimpse of more tall buildings. I wasn't sure, but it might actually be part of Amaranth, the other red city.

All of this, I had to take in with quick glances, keeping my face down most of the time to avoid eye contact. After a lifetime walking the streets of Viridia, that part felt completely normal.

Kelly checked the address and directions on Stacy's note and led the way. I couldn't fault her for a couple of wrong turns, considering the strangeness of this place to all of us. About halfway between the outskirts and the Flame itself, we found the apartment building we sought.

It was an odd structure, composed like many of reddish and tan stone. The first floor consisted of a number of shops, lined with windows and arches. Apartments filled the next three floors, though some of them protruded out from the main structure. Some even extended higher than the four floors, sporting their own fancy (red) roofs.

"It's awfully cold here for this time of year," Kelly noted, rubbing her arms.

I agreed. Ever since we entered the city, the temperature had been dropping. Now that evening approached, I wondered how cold it would get in the dark.

Kelly found an entrance leading to an elevator. We ascended to the third floor and found the door labeled 326, referenced on Stacy's note.

With a nervous glance at Rick, Kelly knocked.

"Coming!" a voice called from inside. A moment later, the door swung open to reveal a young man in his early twenties with dark skin and curly black hair piled atop his head. His eyes swept over us. "Can I help you?"

"Are you Marcus Vermeil?" Kelly asked. "Stacy Moss sent us."

His eyes widened only a tiny bit. "Oh, yeah? Well, come on in!" He stood to one side and beckoned. With a last look in either direction of the hallway, I followed the other two into the apartment. Marcus also took a quick look, then shut the door and joined us.

The interior of the apartment reminded me of Kelly's parents' home. The furniture was nice without being extravagant. A separate kitchen stood to one side with a bar separating it from the living area. A hall opened to the right, no doubt leading to the bedroom and bath.

"Stacy's friends, huh?" Marcus gestured to the living area. "Make yourselves at home. My wife works at the Flame, so we don't eat until she gets home. It can be late sometimes. But you're welcome to hang out for now."

I could sense nervousness in his voice. He didn't want to say anything to give himself away in case we weren't who we said we were. Then again, we didn't know whether he was truly who he said he was. Stacy hadn't told us how much this guy knew. We really needed a better system for identifying allies.

"Thanks." Kelly took a seat on his couch. "I'm Kelly. This is Rick and Beryl. How long has it been since you saw Stacy?"

"Before the war, of course," he said. "During her last tour. She was doing Scarlet Jade, I think."

"I love that one!" Kelly exclaimed. "It's not my favorite one of the Jade stories, but it's probably a close second."

"I got to play Jade's boyfriend Agate." The way Marcus said it made me wonder if he were testing Kelly somehow.

Rick had enough. He had started to sit down next to Kelly, but got back to his feet. "I'm going to be straight with you, Marcus." He leveled his gaze at our host. "We're the ones who killed Caesious. We're here for the next step of our plan, and we want your help."

Marcus took the news without reaction. He walked to the window and made sure it was shut before turning back to look at us. "Give me your names again."

"I'm Beryl. This is Kelly. We're from Viridia. This is Richard Onyx from Atramentous. We're all in this together. Against the dragons." I held both palms out. "And Rick is right. We need your help."

Marcus stepped up to me and lifted his hand toward my face. "Do you mind?" I shook my head, though I didn't know what he meant. He placed his thumb above my eye and rubbed at the chromark. He pulled his hand away with some of the red makeup on his thumb.

"You seem to be telling the truth." He relaxed and dropped into an easy chair. "That's a relief. I was sure this was some kind of sting operation from the Crimson Elite." He closed his eyes for a moment.

"I can understand," I said. "We've all got to be careful." I shot a quick look at Rick. It worked out, but what if Marcus hadn't been right? Blurting out the truth like that might have gotten us all killed.

Marcus opened his eyes and leaned forward. "You killed Caesious and started all this? I have so many questions!"

"I'm sure you do," Rick said. "We have some too."

"Right, right. You need our help. Should we wait for Cerise?"

"It's not a rush," I assured him. "We need information, and then we'll make some plans. Have you ever heard of the Cerulean Books of Lore?"

"No. Should I have?"

"Not necessarily. They were stolen from the city of Caesious by red soldiers. We want to find them."

"Some blue books? Why?"

"They hold the true history of the dragons," Rick said. "And maybe their weaknesses."

Marcus rubbed at his light mustache. "If they're here, they've been taken to the Flame. It's the most secure place in the city. Unless they've taken them to Amaranth instead."

I hadn't thought of that. Two red cities, two red dragons, two red armies… it made things complicated.

"I wouldn't think so, though," Marcus went on. "Incarnadine has always seemed like the dominant one of the two dragons. He takes the lead in almost everything."

I wanted to ask what that was like. How did the relationship between the two dragons play out in the two cities? What did it mean for the common people? If we stuck around long, maybe I could find out.

"You said your wife works at the Flame," Rick said. "Can she find out? And more importantly, can she get us inside?"

Marcus shook his head. "I don't see how that's possible. The Flame is just too well guarded. You wouldn't stand a chance."

"We killed a dragon," I answered. "Don't tell us what's not possible."

Marcus's expression didn't change. "This might be harder."

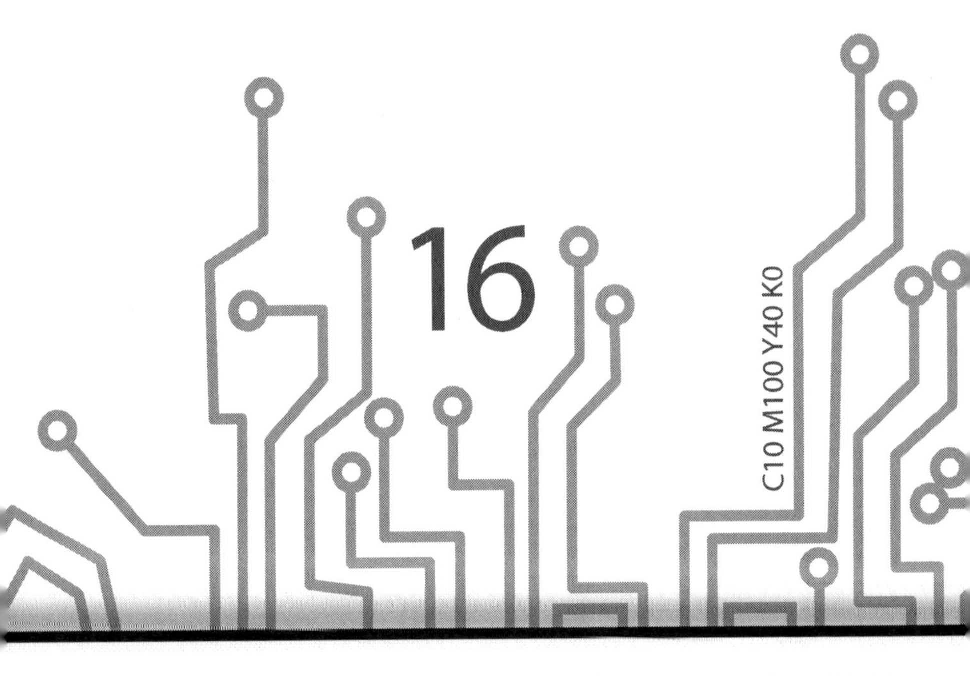

16

"We made it into the secure area of the Emerald Ascendancy," Rick said. "All we needed was an inside guy. And it sounds like we've already got that here."

"Cerise doesn't… you know, I'll let her explain it to you. I'll start supper." Marcus went to the kitchen and left us alone to wait. So much for all of his questions.

"So what is the overall plan, then?" Kelly asked.

"First we need to be sure the books are here," I said. "We may have to get inside the Flame just to figure that out. And then we can make plans for stealing them."

"It's not going to happen overnight," Rick added. "We may be here a while."

I glanced at the kitchen. "I hope our hosts are all right with that."

While we waited, I took one of the talkers out of my pack and contacted Caedan. The signal was weak, but we could hear each other well enough. I updated him and promised to call back when I had more information.

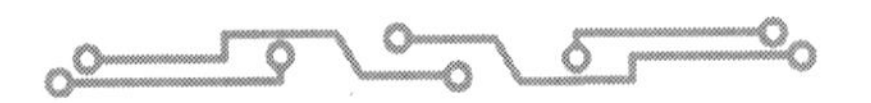

Cerise arrived home about half an hour later. She entered the apartment in a rush, then stopped upon seeing us in her living room. "Cerise, honey! These are friends of Stacy's!" Marcus called. He emerged from the kitchen, wiping his hands on a dishtowel.

Cerise, a tall woman with pale skin, unwrapped a scarf from her neck. How cold did it get here, anyway? She shook out her hair, blond with a thick red stripe down the middle. I honestly couldn't tell which color was natural and which was dye.

"More performers, Marc?" She smiled at us. "I hope he hasn't abandoned you for long."

"It's quite all right," Kelly said, standing. "We know we're intruding here."

"Cerise, it's them," Marcus said quietly. "The ones who killed Caesious."

"Oh… Oh!" Her already wide eyes grew wider. "Those kind of friends…"

After introductions, Marcus announced that supper was ready. All five of us crowded around their glass-top table intended for three or four. The meal was simple, pan-fried chicken with brown rice, but spicier than I was accustomed to, especially after a few weeks of eating at the Asylum. We put off further business talk to enjoy the food and company. At the end of the meal, Marcus produced a half-frozen sweet drink, and we returned to the living room, savoring the cold flavor.

Kelly explained our mission again, leaving out details such as where we got the information about the books. As much as we were delighted to meet new allies, it couldn't hurt to keep some information private for now.

"I haven't heard anything about these books," Cerise said when Kelly finished, "but I'm only a receptionist. I don't know a lot about what's going on in the rest of the Flame."

"Is any part of the Flame public?" Rick asked.

"Yes, the first two floors. That's where I work. My desk is literally the first thing most people see on entering." She took a sip from her drink. "There's not much of interest there. Some labs that appear to be working on medical advances, et cetera. It's all for show, to make people think the dragon has their best interests at heart."

"That sounds familiar," I muttered.

"Maybe we should visit it," Kelly said. "Isn't that how you two did with the Emerald Ascendancy?"

"It can be a start," I said cautiously. "But we have to take it slow. We knew much more going in there."

"Come tomorrow morning," Cerise suggested. "Then you can get an idea of what you're up against." She glanced at me. "But you might want to touch up your makeup first."

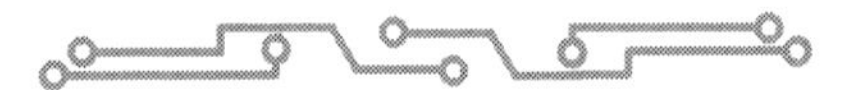

The next morning, we waited an hour after Cerise left for work before setting out ourselves. As we approached the Flame, we abandoned pretense and stared. Surely even the residents of this city could be impressed with this structure. I paid special attention to the "peaks" of fire, the blazes. From differing angles, I thought I could make out more details. It looked like the peaks themselves were only walls of stone around balconies or platforms of some kind extruding from the central building. If we could get to one of those, it might provide another entrance, but the lowest one looked to be about ten floors up.

"Do you think those walls are climbable?" I asked Rick.

He pointed toward the peaks, feigning excitement. "Not without some kind of climbing gear, I would think. Even you would need help getting up that surface, cyber boy."

"That's enough, you two," Kelly warned. "Let's go inside."

We climbed a wide set of stairs to the Flame's main entrance: glass doors turning on hidden hinges. I'll admit I spent more time trying to figure that out than I did examining the two guards standing just inside.

Cerise hadn't been kidding. We spotted her almost immediately. She and several other receptionists sat within a huge octagon desk in the center of the enormous open lobby.

Our eyes went up almost at once, drawn by the flickering red lights above. We could see four floors upward before a ceiling appeared. Balconies from those floors overlooked our current position. Beneath each one of those shone a different form of red spotlight, shining out into the open, reflecting off twisting pieces of mirrored steel to create the blazing effect.

"Could you jump that high?" Rick whispered.

"I could get to the second floor and then make another jump to one of those other balconies." I considered the difficulty. It wouldn't be too hard.

I looked around at the guards, the desk, and some other people coming and going. "It would require a good distraction to keep eyes off me."

Rick nodded.

Kelly led the way toward the desk. On either side of it, a wide, curving staircase ascended to the second floor. On the wall a couple dozen yards behind the desk, I saw a bank of elevators. Two more guards stood there. I watched a woman approach and show them a badge hanging from her neck on a lanyard. A guard examined it, nodded, and pushed a button on the wall to open the elevator for her. Getting past those two would not be easy.

Kelly ignored Cerise and approached one of the other receptionists. "Hi! We're here for a tour, I guess?" She giggled. "All three of us have never been, can you believe it?"

"I didn't say that!" Rick interrupted. "I've been here. It was just..." He gestured. "Um, before some of the newer construction."

The receptionist, a middle-aged woman, raised an eyebrow at him. "You must be older than you look, son. Unless you were a baby at the time."

"I was very precocious."

She chuckled. "I guess so." She opened a drawer and removed three lanyards. We took them and hung them around our necks, noting the enormous "VISITOR" tags.

"There are no live tours any more," the receptionist explained. She handed Kelly a small electronic device with several buttons in a row across one side. "When you see a number on a door or above a window, enter it here and you'll hear a recording explaining what you're seeing."

"How clever," Kelly gushed.

"Start with either set of stairs. Enjoy your visit. May the sacred flame of Incarnadine's blessing be with you."

"Oh, and, uh, with you." Kelly pretended to be distracted with the device to cover her stumbling over the blessing thing. I made a note to ask Marcus and Cerise about things like that. How prevalent was the dragon religion here? Did everyone talk like that?

We climbed the stairs on the right, examining everything we could see. Rick pointed out a couple of small windows on the curved wall to either side of the elevators. There might be other eyes watching in addition to the two guards.

Halfway up the stairs, we found a landing and a large number three inscribed in red on the railing. "She said doors and windows, not railings," Kelly grumbled, but she entered the number anyway.

"Welcome to the Flame, home of the immortal Incarnadine, the living and sacred incarnation of fire itself," a clear voice spoke from the device. "This lobby and the tour you're about to begin, were constructed around twenty years ago as a way of showing Incarnadine's beloved people the lengths to which he is willing to go to ensure their continued prosperity."

"I think I'm going to throw up," Rick complained.

"What happened to numbers one and two?" I wondered.

"It's probably the other stairs," Kelly said. "Or maybe we missed something down in the lobby."

I lifted my foot onto the next step when a voice came from behind: "You three. Stop there."

We turned and saw a pair of Crimson Elite ascending the stairs behind us, followed by the unmistakable form of a red draconic.

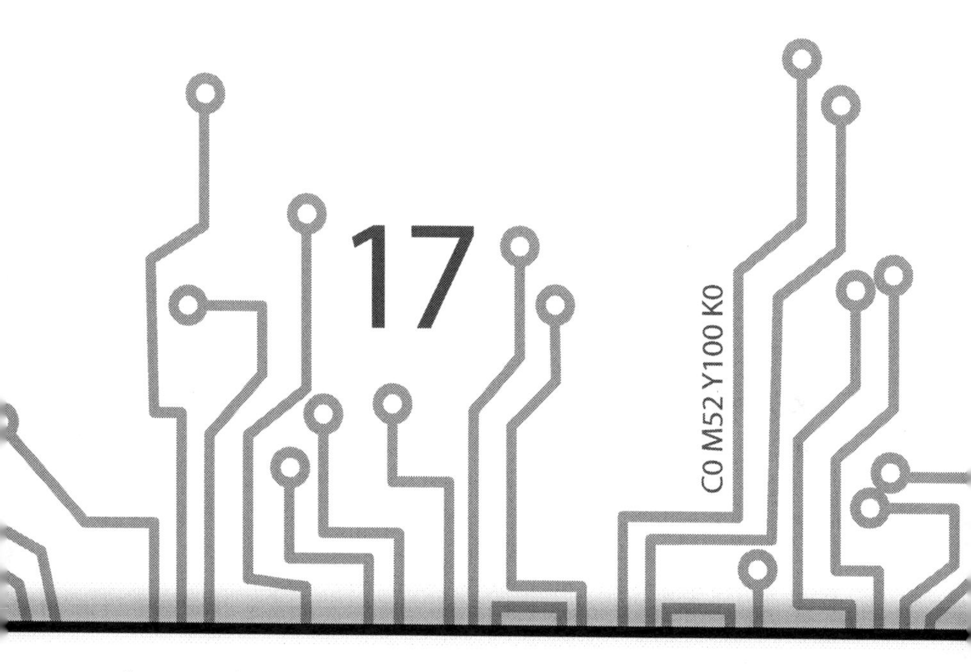

"Move aside there!" one of the guards called. Trying not to display too much relief, I joined Rick and Kelly in moving against the railing to make room for our betters.

My eyes darted to the draconic's left thigh. Sure enough, I saw a recent scar. It was Zidanta Red, the draconic we tried to kill on the battlefield. I dropped my face and tried to appear nondescript.

It passed me by without a glance, but stopped a step later. It turned and reached out its hand toward Kelly. It reached past her face and ran its fingers through her hair. I clenched my fist and prepared to trigger my implant. I might not win a fight with everyone here, but I could keep them occupied while Rick got Kelly out.

"Your hair," Zidanta Red rumbled. "So unusual to see a female without at least some red."

"I, I'm from the outskirts, my lord," Kelly stammered. "Hair dye is not cheap."

The draconic kept its hand next to her face. "The outskirts. Perhaps that explains your accent as well."

Accent? We didn't have accents, did we? I hadn't noticed any real difference in our voices from anyone in Incarnadine. Was this a trick? An attempt to make Kelly give something away?

"Sir?" One of the guards looked up at the draconic. "They're waiting for you."

"Yes, yes. Of course." The draconic turned away from Kelly and ascended the stairs with its escorts.

Cerise hurried up the stairs behind us. "Are you all right?"

Kelly gave Rick a quick hug, then straightened herself. "I will be. It's not the first draconic I've been that close to." For that matter, she sang to a dragon. It still doesn't stop the fear. I had been scared for her.

"We're good," Rick said. Cerise nodded and headed back to her post. I'm sure she would regale her co-workers about the first-time visitors scared to death by a draconic.

I moved on up the stairs to the second floor, followed by the other two. Kelly found another number and started listening to the tourist spiel, talking about the red spotlights, I think. I ignored it and looked around. The balcony here overlooked the lobby, both with a central circular platform, and extended walkways toward either side of the building, where they eventually curved to follow the outer wall. Two hallways curved around the central column that held the elevators from below. I walked around the column and found what I expected: another elevator door, separate from the ones below. Zidanta Red and his guards must have entered there.

The wall beside the elevator door held only one button, key-activated. If we could get one of those keys, we could bypass the lower elevators and come here. I wondered where each set of elevators led.

"We could do it right now, you know." Rick stepped up beside me.

"What do you mean?"

He flexed his cybernetic hand, hidden by his usual glove. "Between the two of us, we could get this door open. With your abilities, you could climb the shaft as high as you wanted."

He was right. I looked around. "I don't even see any cameras or windows here."

Climbing up an elevator shaft. I don't know if I would have even thought of the possibility. Just another way that Rick's mind worked different from mine.

"No time like the present." Rick pulled his glove off and approached the elevator doors.

Kelly came around the corner. "What are you doing?"

Rick forced his fingers between the doors, prying them ajar just enough for me to get my hands in. "Beryl's going to climb the elevator."

I triggered a boost to my arms and pulled. The weight of the doors surprised me. I gave myself another boost and managed to pull them far enough to look inside. The shaft rose higher than I could see. For that matter, I couldn't see the elevator itself. How high had it gone?

"Are you two insane?" Kelly hissed. "I thought we were here just to look around!"

"We are," Rick protested. "And now we've got a chance to look around in more secret places."

"It's just like the Emerald Ascendancy," I argued.

"And that almost got you killed! You were incredibly lucky, Beryl. Are you really willing to base everything on that luck again?"

I hesitated and looked at Rick. Things were different now. I had more friends that I cared about. But the two I cared about most were right here. And they... they'd be okay if I didn't come back. I nodded. "At the very least, this will let us know if this is a viable way of infiltrating the Flame." I grinned at Kelly. "Enjoy the rest of the tour. If I'm not back by the end of it..."

"We'll wait for you."

"Don't wait too long."

I leaned into the shaft and grabbed hold of the frame surrounding the doors. I looked up. With careful boosts, I should be able to jump to each floor one at a time. Every floor had a tiny bit of a platform. I could either land on one or grab hold of the next one. The problem would be maintaining my balance. The higher I climbed, the further the fall.

Massive cables hung down the middle of the shaft, but I didn't like the idea of trying to hold on to those. Shredding my palms did not sound like fun.

I took a deep breath, triggered a boost, and made my first jump. I caught hold of the next floor's platform, boosted my arms, and vaulted up onto it, catching hold of the side for stability.

Below, I heard a soft thunk as Rick let the doors slide back into place. A few scratches from his cybernetic hand would be the only evidence we had been there.

With that, I lost most of my light. Almost no illumination escaped around the elevator doors. Every three floors, a pair of emergency lights gleamed with a dull light which didn't show very much. I waited at my perch until my eyes adjusted, then leaped to the next floor.

It suddenly occurred to me that I didn't know how to open the doors from inside. I searched around the doorway mechanisms until I found a roller that would be triggered by the elevator car itself. I pushed on the roller. To my relief, it pulled a lock from within the doors and I was able to slide them open. Since this was only the fourth floor, I let the doors shut again with only a brief glance. I saw nothing but a hallway.

How high should I go? The only real limit would be the elevator car, wherever it was. If it started descending, obviously I would need to get out. But until then, going up seemed like the best course of action. Logically, the greater secrets would be higher up, wouldn't they?

Jump. Grab. Pull. Balance. I repeated the process several more times. Out of all the possibilities of investigation today, I had to admit this one had never occurred to me. Chance opportunities. My life seemed full of them the past few months. Maybe Kelly was right. I relied on luck way too much.

Jump. Grab. Pull. Balance. Or maybe I just took advantage of what I found. Maybe I made my own luck. Bice would probably see some mysterious spiritual force behind all of it.

Jump. Grab. Pull. Balance. Thinking of Bice made me think about the "magic" he and Troilus Green used. Zidanta Red used it once in our first meeting. How many others inside this place might be able to do that?

I shivered. The elevator shaft did not seem to be heated. Who would have thought I would get cold inside a place called "the Flame"? And why was it so cold, anyway? The red dragon breathed fire. You'd think everything would be hot.

Jump. Grab. Pull. Balance. How many floors had I climbed now? At least ten, I think. I looked up again. The elevator car waited six floors above me. Better not to get too close to it in case it started moving. One more floor, and I'd stop.

Jump. Grab. Whoa. My arms felt like noodles. I had been feeding them a lot of boosts to get this far. That usually wore my muscles out at a rapid pace. Just needed to lift myself up one more time.

I triggered the boost to my arms and pulled. At the exact same moment, I heard a loud thunk above me, and the sound of an electrical engine humming. As I scrambled into place on the next floor, I glanced up. The elevator car descended toward me at a much faster rate than anticipated.

I shoved the roller to unlock the doors and fumbled for the door itself.

My fingers slipped. The car came closer. I snagged the edge and pulled, boosting my arms one more time. The door slid open and I tumbled through. Behind me, the elevator car passed by. A few more seconds, and I would have been crushed.

I pushed myself up onto my hands and knees and looked around. I had made it high within the Flame, but had no idea where I was, or where to go from here.

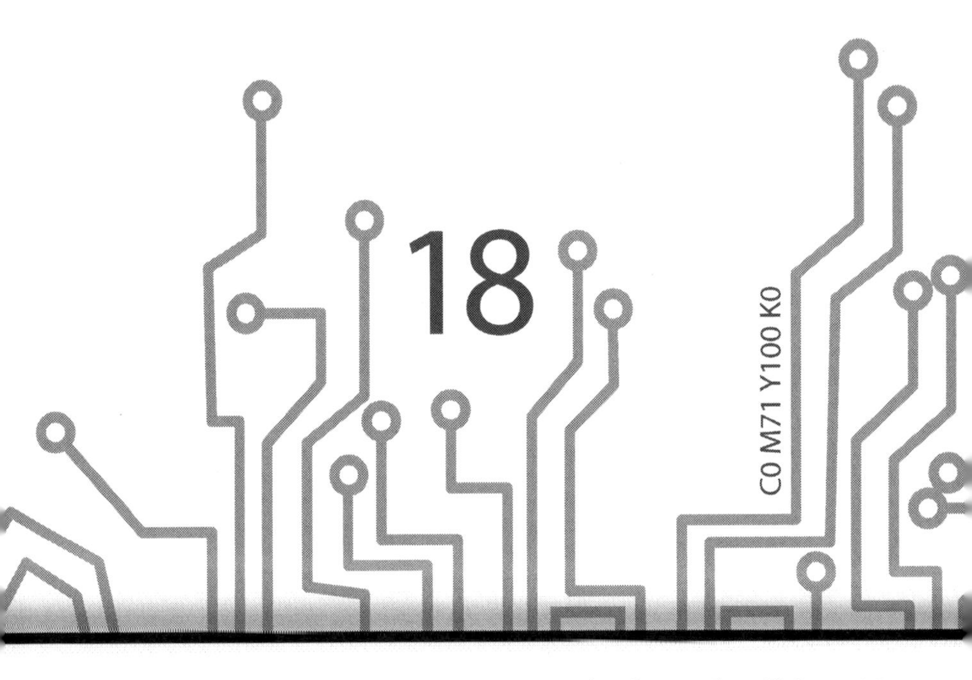

18

My arms almost gave way. I sat up to take the weight off them. My hands shook. Guess Rick was right about needing more exercise. If I were in better shape, maybe this wouldn't be that much of a problem.

Voices came from my left: someone coming down the hall. I scrambled to my feet and looked around. The wall opposite the elevator formed a slight curve bordering the wide hallway that stretched both to the left and right. It looked like solid red stone. "The dragon flies out of the middle of the Flame," Rick had said. The dragon's nest or at least the shaft leading to it must be on the other side of that wall.

But that didn't help me with the voices coming down the hall. I turned and jogged toward the right. The hall followed the inner stone wall. I passed a couple of doors on my right, but didn't try them. The voices were too close.

At the very end of the hall, a door stood partly open. As I drew near, I noticed sunlight coming through. I glanced back, then darted through the door.

The sun blinded me for a moment. I stood in the open air on a large round platform, surrounded by high stone walls that curved up to form a peak. It must have been one of the blaze platforms we saw from below. The sun shone into the platform from either side. Benches lined the walls. I could see no purpose for the platform other than decoration.

The voices continued to follow me. Were they coming out here? Maybe the building's workers used this for lunch or breaks on pleasant days.

Next to the main building wall, a narrow set of stairs led up the side, following the curve of the wall. With no place to hide, I climbed up the first few steps. Then I stopped. The stairs, made of the same stone as the wall, had no railing. They would be invisible from below. But that didn't matter much to me. Right now, I fought against a wave of dizziness. I must have been close to two hundred feet from the ground. I didn't think I was afraid of heights, but the narrow stairs and lack of railing would have daunted anyone.

I didn't have time to be dizzy. I pushed on up the stairs as fast as I dared. Thankfully, it did not take very long to reach another of the fiery platforms. This one was empty, so I took a moment to catch my breath. The strain of climbing the elevator shaft combined with the tension of near-discovery and the dangerous stairs made me want to take a long nap. I stretched out on one of the benches and allowed myself to relax.

Only for a moment. The longer I stayed in one place, the greater the risk of discovery. Plus, Rick and Kelly were waiting on me. I needed to make this whole endeavor worthwhile, which meant I needed to find something significant.

I listened at the door and heard nothing. I pushed it open and stepped into yet another hallway. Why so many hallways? I mean, I know it's the way to connect rooms, but this was getting ridiculous.

After a few feet, I realized this hallway was different. Many of the rooms on either side had wide glass windows. I could see anything inside the rooms... but they could see me. My only option was to act like I belonged.

I flipped my Visitor pass around so the title didn't show, and walked with a casual but firm stride down the center of the hall. I glanced to and fro, trying to appear indifferent, but still needing to see whatever I could.

The first two rooms reminded me of similar labs back in the Emerald Ascendancy. White-coated scientists worked at odd devices on wide tables. I couldn't make out what they were doing, but it appeared to involve chemicals of some kind. The third room caught my attention a little more. Engineers worked on what looked like an enormous cybernetic hand. No, not a hand. Claws. A replacement for the dragon?

The fourth room made me stop in my tracks and stare, despite the danger. On one table lay a red draconic, unmoving. On a second table lay a man, also unmoving. Except his chest had been cut open, and a masked doctor was removing something from inside his chest. I swallowed to keep from gagging.

Together with two assistants, the doctor took the heart or whatever it was to the draconic. The assistants worked to open the draconic's chest. With skilled moves, the doctor placed the object inside, and began to work on it.

I turned away, sickened. They were harvesting human organs to help the draconics. It was the only conclusion I could draw. In my turning, I noticed a window inside the operating room, opening to the next room. Zidanta Red and five or six humans stood watching the procedure intently. I froze. Had anyone seen me? No one rushed to the door. No one yelled and pointed. They were too caught up in watching. Even so, I moved with slow, smooth steps as I passed them by.

I came to a fork in the hall. Ahead, I could see the elevator. To the left, the hall curved around the central region again. I turned that way. If Zidanta Red and his guards came back out, they would head to the elevator. No need to put myself directly in their path.

None of the rooms along this hall were windowed. I didn't see any signs on the doors. I listened at a couple and tried to open them. Both locked. The hall ended in a stair that led to the next floor. I glanced back, considering. A lot of time was passing, or at least it seemed like it. Rick and Kelly would be concerned. I could run back now to the elevator shaft, but that still left a significant danger of discovery. On the other hand, I could get to the elevator from the next floor as well. I trotted up the stairs.

The hall looked the same. I ignored the doors and made straight for the elevator. When I got there, I stopped and stared. Kelly complained that I relied too much on luck. If this wasn't luck, I didn't know what it could be. Next to the elevator, a directory was posted on the wall, with labels for every floor.

Somehow, I had ended up on level nineteen. It didn't add up in my head, but that didn't matter. This level, along with the one below it were labeled "Practical Applications." Most of the floors below were labeled "Research" of one kind or another: cybernetic, medical, chemical… Wait. What was "Resomancy"? I'd never seen the word before. It took up floors 11-13. Strange.

My eyes rose to the floors above. Only four levels remained. Two labels read only "Restricted." The top level read "Observatory." But the one just below it, level 22, read "Library." I wanted to find books? A library seemed the most logical choice. To get there from here, I'd have to pass through two restricted levels, whatever that meant. At the very least, it meant climbing up three more flights of stairs.

I clenched my fists. I might not have another opportunity. Getting to that library right now might solve all our problems. But I had used so much time getting this far. I wavered.

Then I almost slapped myself. Rick wasn't here. Without his cybernetic hand, I couldn't get the door open to climb down the shaft. The elevator here had a normal set of buttons. No key required. Did I dare actually ride it?

"Do you know one of the advantages of eye placement on the reptilian snout is a very wide range of vision?"

I knew that voice. I turned to see Zidanta Red standing not far down the hall, along with a pair of his guards. I took a quick glance behind me and saw two more guards approaching, short swords drawn.

"When you observed the operation taking place below us, I saw you, of course," it went on. "While you were watching us, I was watching you. I warned everyone else not to look."

I backed against the wall.

"Now. Who are you and what are you doing here?"

Maybe Kelly was right.

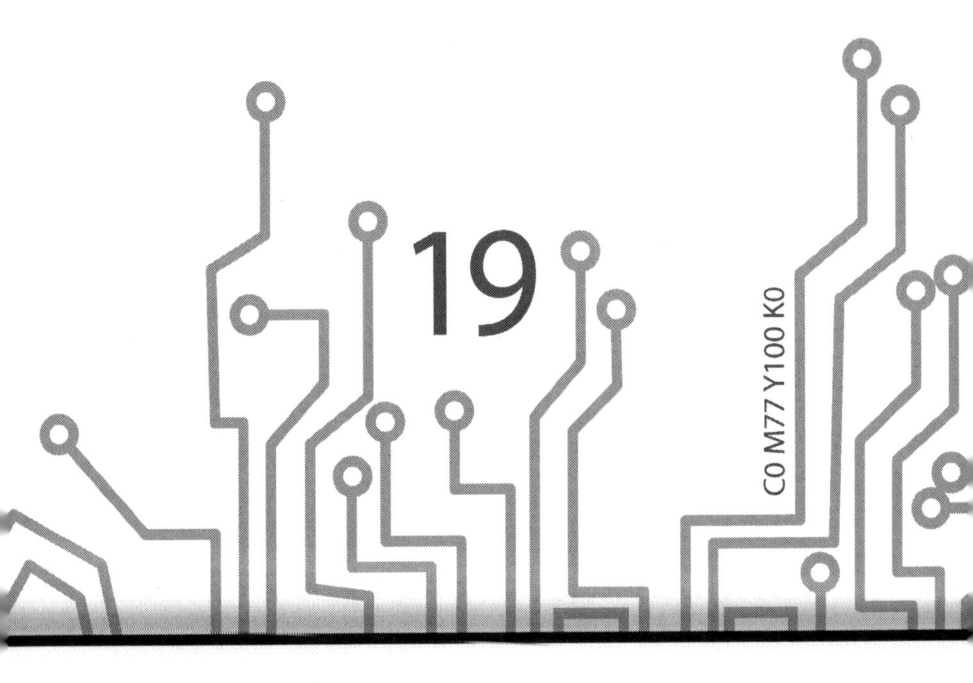

19

Trapped. Do I fight or run?

"Your life hangs by a thread," Zidanta Red said. "Tell me why you're here and maybe you'll live a little longer."

"I got lost. Sorry." I held up my Visitor tag. "Took a wrong turn."

"I know you, don't I?" The draconic sniffed. "Yes… fascinating. We have met before."

"Downstairs," I said.

"No, not that… the battlefield. You attacked me by yourself." It turned to the guards. "This man is a Viridian spy. Be careful. He's very—"

I think it was about to say "fast." But at that moment, I chose to run. The weakest link was to my left, through the two guards, rather than trying to get past the draconic itself. It led away from the stairs, but my options were limited. I boosted my legs and charged.

One of the Crimson Elite had the presence of mind to at least swing his sword at me. I dodged around it and gave him a boost-enhanced shove as I passed. He flew into his companion and both of them smacked against the wall.

I raced down the hall. A roar of anger followed me. If this level were like the others, this hall wouldn't go very far before… there. It ended in a door to the outside. Not my best option, but right now… the only one.

I shut the door behind me and looked out at another of the blaze platforms. At least the side stair from this one led down. Again, the only option. I started down the stairs, resisting the urge to look down, swallowing back my nervousness.

And then two more Crimson Elite appeared at the platform below me. If this was luck, Kelly, it wasn't any good.

I looked back up. A shout told me the guards I left behind were entering the platform. They'd start down the stairs toward me at any moment. I gritted my teeth, summoned my courage, and looked down.

Even the act of looking made me waver, almost losing my balance.

I could see another of the platforms below and to my left. I could leap in that direction and make it. That much I knew. I didn't know whether I could survive the fall, even with my implant's help.

"Nowhere to go, Greenie!" The guard's voice came from above. I glanced up and saw him take a step down toward me. He clearly did not want to come after me on the narrow stairs. The same appeared true of the guards below. One advanced a couple of steps up, but came no further.

A cold breeze made the hair on my arms stand up. I shivered. Would giving up be so bad? If they thought I was a spy for Viridia, maybe I could feed them false information, keep myself alive. It might work. And then the image of the doctor removing a man's heart filled my head. For me, it would be worse. They would take the implant from my brain so they could study it. My body would help the dragons live even longer.

Better to die. I crouched and took a deep breath.

"If you jump from here, you won't be anything more than a wet spot on the pavement!"

I looked to the guard above and smiled at him. I looked to the guard below and saluted. May as well go out in style.

And then I jumped.

For a moment, I thought I would throw up. Then the feeling vanished. The air rushed about me, tearing at my clothes. My fear melted away, replaced by absolute euphoria. I knew I wasn't flying, but the sensation had to be similar. I laughed out loud.

The blaze platform came rushing toward me faster than I expected. I channeled every bit of boost energy I could into my legs, triggering the implant over and over. I threw a couple of boosts into my arms as well. I would need to roll when I struck. I bent my knees and waited. The stone looked ready to welcome me to my death. Even as the thought passed through my mind, I couldn't grasp at the fear.

My feet hit the platform with an impact that jarred every bone in my body. I rolled to the right, tucking myself as tight as possible. Something snapped in my shoulder when it hit. I screamed. I flipped over and rolled. I tried to slam my left arm against the ground to slow my progress, but it didn't do much. I kept rolling until I hit the outer wall.

My vision blurred. I think I kept myself from blacking out by willpower alone. I tried to get up and fell again. I couldn't control my right arm. Pain radiated from my knees, my hips, my back, and my shoulder most of all.

I triggered more boosts and used the energy to get to my feet. I still had a long way to go.

I staggered to the door and entered this level's hall. Stumbling with every step, I made my way to the elevator. The sign identified this as level twelve. My brain tried to do the math on the fall, but the numbers slipped away. I pushed the down button.

With my shoulder injured, I couldn't climb the shaft, even if I could get into it. I could try running down the stairs, but I'm sure they would catch up to me. The elevator was an enormous risk, but it might be my only way out. I backed to the opposite wall, ready to run if the elevator were occupied.

A ding sounded. The doors opened. Empty.

I faltered into the elevator and punched the button for level two. A dim corner of my brain noted there were multiple buttons below that. The doors slid closed. The car shook and started down.

I leaned against the wall, then slid to the floor. I kept my eyes up, watching the numbers decrease as I descended. Eleven. Ten. Nine. Darkness pulled at the edges of my vision. Maybe it wouldn't hurt to close my eyes until I got there. I jerked my head. Level three already? How?

The elevator came to a stop. I had to trigger more boosts just to stand up. The door opened and I stumbled out. No one in sight. No guards: good. No Rick or Kelly: not so good.

I circled around to the stairs and looked down. Two guards still stood at the front door. They hadn't noticed me yet, but that would change. I'm sure my appearance would draw attention now. I would have to charge them and hope my momentum could carry me through.

But first I had to get down the stairs. Every step transmitted pain up through my knees and hips. I held my mouth shut, suppressing the desire to yell from the agony.

Halfway down, one of the guards noticed me. He nudged his partner and pointed. They stepped away from the door, coming toward me. I needed to charge, but I didn't trust myself until I got to the floor. I tried to speed up my descent.

The guards stopped a few feet from the door and waited. Maybe they had orders not to abandon it. Maybe they figured I couldn't go anywhere else. Whatever. It was all I needed. My foot stepped off the last stair and I inhaled through my nose. Time to go.

At that moment, the front door opened and Rick appeared. "Pardon me, guys, can either of you tell me the way to a restaurant called Ruby's?"

The guards instinctively turned. I gave my boosts everything I could and ran. I charged across the open space and slammed my left shoulder into one of the guards. He flew back against the glass. I ran into Rick, who pretended to be surprised, yelling his head off. We both tumbled down the stairs outside the Flame.

"Go!" he hissed when we came to a stop. "I'll get in their way again."

I got to my feet and tried to run. I fell again three steps later, scraping everything against the concrete.

"Gods, you're in worse shape than I thought." Rick grabbed my left arm (fortunately), and pulled me up. Together, we hurried down the sidewalk at a stumbling speed.

"Where's Lovat when you need him?" I muttered. I didn't see any way we could escape through the streets of an unknown city. We didn't even know where we were going. The Crimson Elite would be on us in seconds.

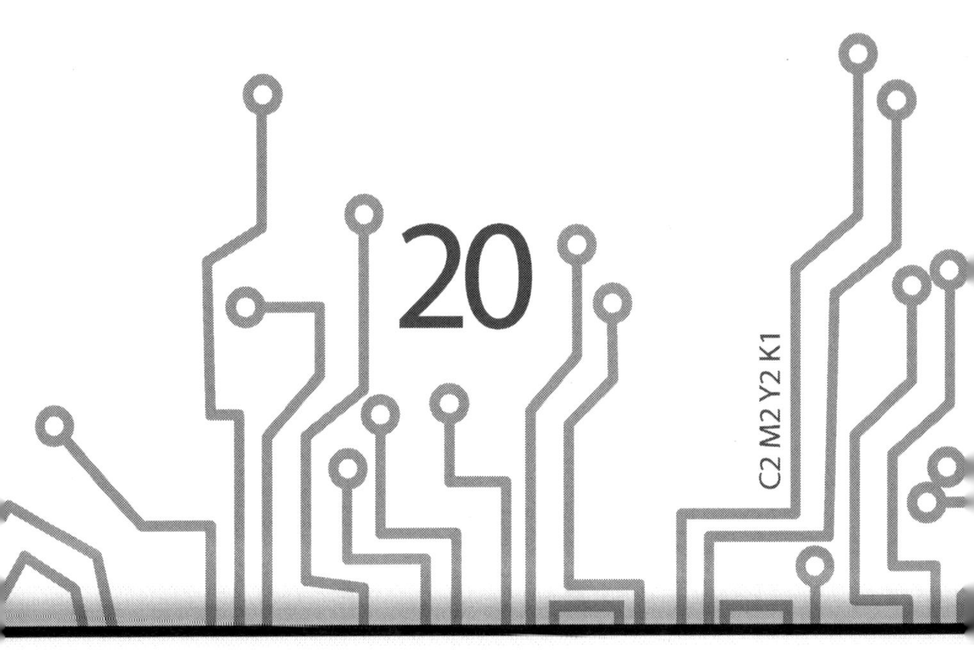

20

"This way!" Rick pulled me around a corner.

"Do you have a plan?" I gasped. I couldn't see any way out of this.

"It's more fun when it's a surprise." He looked up and smiled.

I turned to see the cause of his smile. A truck pulled up beside us, a beat-up delivery truck that had certainly seen better days. Even so, I never saw trucks in Viridia not being used by the dragon's servants.

The front door of the truck flew open to reveal Marcus behind the wheel. "Get in!"

Trying to push aside my incredulity, I pulled myself into the truck's cab and scooted to the middle of the seat, next to Marcus. Rick jumped up beside me as the truck started moving. He slammed the door shut, but bumped hard against my right shoulder. I'll admit I screamed a little.

"What's wrong?" Marcus demanded, eyes focused on the road.

"S-shoulder," I managed.

Rick moved closer to the door. "Sorry, man. We'll look at it when we get back."

The uneven cadence of the truck's engine was somehow worse than riding the four-wheelers across the countryside. I almost felt like I would bounce off the seat.

"What about Kelly?" I asked.

"She's already back at the apartment," Rick said. "This was her idea, from the moment you left us. She broke off the tour and went to find Marcus in case… well, in the probable outcome that you would need help. I stuck around to finish the tour myself and wait to see what happened. You certainly didn't disappoint us."

I tried to hold my right arm with my left. Everything hurt, but… I knew I could survive this. I'd been through worse. My shoulder worried me, though. Everything about it felt wrong.

"What did he do, exactly?" Marcus asked.

"Climbed up the elevator shaft in the Flame," Rick said. "I'm guessing he saw all kinds of stuff you're not supposed to see."

I nodded, but the jarring hurt. I didn't want to talk. One question did demand an answer, though: "How do you have a truck?"

"It belongs to the theater," Marcus explained. "I use it to transport props and costumes between theaters in the twin cities. It's a piece of junk, but it runs."

"Thanks," I whispered.

"Was it worth it?" Rick asked. "Did you find out anything important?"

"I think so." I closed my eyes and gritted my teeth. "Tell you later."

"You keep surviving things you have no business surviving!" Kelly ranted at me as I collapsed on Marcus and Cerise's couch. I didn't argue with her.

Marcus hung up his jacket in the entry and joined us. "I think he dislocated his shoulder," he said. "Unless it's something worse."

"What could be worse?" I groaned.

He shrugged. "Shattered bones, I guess? I dunno. I think you'd be in a lot more pain if that were true."

"So we need to pop it back in place, right?" Rick asked.

"Don't look at me. I'm an actor!" Marcus paused. "And apparently escape driver."

Kelly rolled her eyes. "Yes, it has to be put back in place. We can do it here." She looked down at me. "But it's going to hurt. A lot."

"Do it."

"All right. To get the bone back into the shoulder, we have to pull it further out and pop it back in." She moved around behind the couch. "Beryl, give me your good hand."

I reached up and she took it. I tried not to let the memories of our hands together affect me. She shifted to hold it more firmly. "Whatever you do, do not let go of me." I nodded. She looked at the other two. "All right, guys. Take his arm. When I give the word, pull."

Marcus and Rick looked at each other with wide eyes, then positioned themselves. They each took hold of my arm. The movement from that little motion sent waves of pain cascading through my body. Kelly braced herself against the couch, and took hold of my good hand with her other hand as well.

"Pull!"

I didn't feel the movement, only excruciating pain. I screamed.

"Harder!" Kelly urged.

Marcus and Rick obeyed and I screamed again. Rick let go with one hand and gave the upper part of my arm a quick pop. Bone scraped on bone, I think, and I almost lost consciousness.

When my vision cleared, all three had released me. Kelly moved around to the other side. "Can you move it?"

I wanted to ask if she were serious, but I closed my eyes and tried. My arm obeyed my command to move, but it still hurt. Nowhere near as bad as a moment ago, but still pretty bad. "Hurts," I managed between gasps.

"We did it." Kelly wiped her forehead. "I honestly didn't know whether we could do it on our own."

"Have you seen that done before?" Marcus asked.

"No, but I've read about it." Kelly grinned. She did all of that to me based on a book? Ow.

She looked back at me. "Let's make him a sling. Marcus, if you have any pain meds—"

Heavy knocks at the front door interrupted her. She and the others exchanged fearful looks.

"The neighbors," Marcus said. "They heard the screams. I'll deal with it." He went to the door, while Kelly and Rick moved out of sight.

I couldn't move, so I waited and tried to listen. I could hear raised voices, definitely asking about screams. Marcus said something about a rat, I think. He laughed and kept talking. After a few more exchanges, the neighbor left and he shut the door.

"Good performance," Rick noted.

Marcus shrugged. "I am an actor." He went to the bedroom and returned with an old shirt he tossed to Kelly. While she tore it into a sling for me, Marcus brought a glass of water and some pills. I took them gratefully.

"You couldn't give me these before that trick?"

"Sorry." Kelly looked down. "I wasn't thinking about that part."

I chuckled, then winced. "It's okay. You did great."

The front door flew open and Cerise charged in. Seeing all of us, she slowed and relaxed. Marcus hurried to her side. "What are you doing home so soon, babe?"

"After the mess this guy caused"—she pointed at me—"they shut down the whole Flame. After questioning us, they sent us home."

"Did they connect you with us?" Kelly asked.

"They asked about talking with you on the stairs," Cerise said. "But I don't think it mattered much. They don't think anyone of my low status could have helped with anything that happened. I mean, I wasn't even the one who started you on the tour."

"Good to hear." Marcus embraced her. Everyone found a seat and we all relaxed as the others told Cerise what they had experienced. Then all eyes turned to me.

"So…" Rick said.

"What?"

"What did you find?"

I still hurt, especially my joints and shoulder, but after drinking some more water, I found I could talk all right. I described what took place on the upper floors. My description of the directory inspired a lot of interest.

"Resomancy?" Rick repeated. "You're sure that's what it said?" I nodded. He wrinkled his forehead. "I've never heard that word." His frown deepened.

"But the library!" Kelly exclaimed. "That has to be where they took the Books of Lore!"

"That's my guess," I agreed. "Second to the top floor."

"Did you go see it?"

"Not exactly…" So I told them about the draconic and my escape. When I described my jump, Kelly put her face in her hands.

"Did I say you had no business surviving? I did say that, right? You should not have survived that!"

I started to shrug, but gritted my teeth in pain instead. Guess I needed to avoid that particular motion for a while. "It wasn't that far."

"You jumped from the nineteenth floor," Cerise said.

"Well, between the eighteenth and nineteenth."

"What floor did you land on?"

"Um... twelve, I think."

She shook her head. "At the very least, you fell over seventy feet, Beryl. There's no way you should have lived through that."

"I did mention the cybernetic implant, right?"

"Even so." She pushed her hair back. "Does it strengthen your bones? Your joints? Prevent your brain from getting shaken up? You should have shattered both legs, at the very least, not to mention having one serious concussion. But you only dislocated your shoulder?"

She looked me over. "It really strains believability, Beryl."

"Like when you survived the dragon poison," Kelly added. "Bice said you shouldn't have lived through that."

"But he healed me."

"No, he didn't. He did what he could, but he said you should have died before you ever got back to us."

I didn't like the way this conversation was going. Couldn't they just be happy for me?

Cerise continued to stare at me. She shook her head again. "What *are* you?"

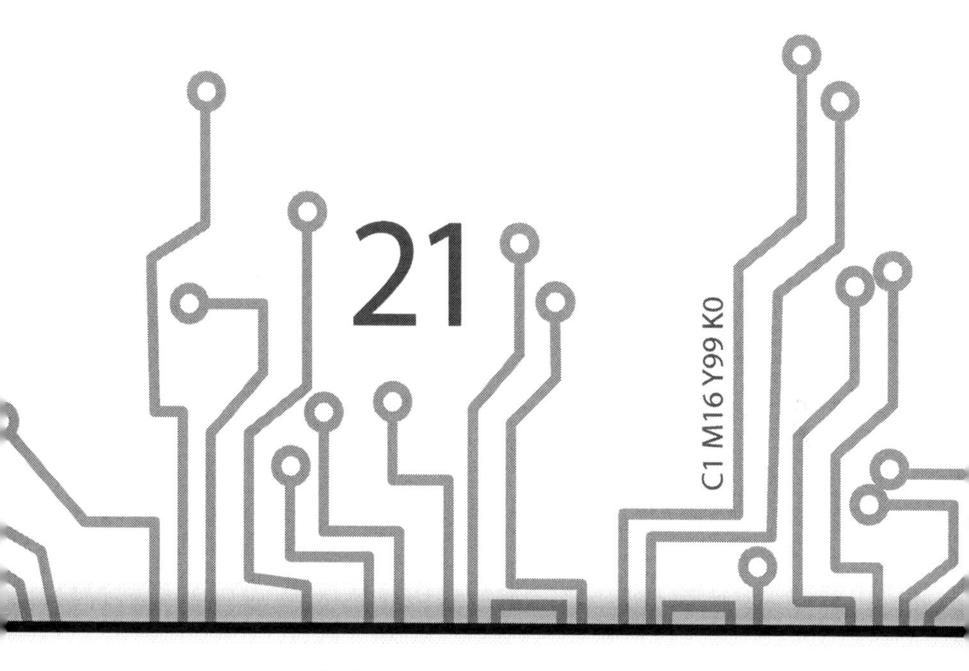

21

For a moment, nobody said anything.

"Look," Rick broke the silence. "Beryl is special. We know that. What Loden did to save his life… it's never been done before. We still have no idea how much he's capable of. He doesn't even know himself, am I right?"

"No." I managed to sit up without too much pain. "I keep discovering new things."

"Like what?" Cerise asked.

"If I aim the boost at my eyes, I can… see further. Like binoculars."

Again with the stares. It wasn't that crazy. Was it?

"That's… amazing," Kelly said.

"Does it work in reverse?" Rick asked. "Can you look at tiny things? Like a microscope?"

"I've never tried." Now that sounded crazy. "Listen, I can't deny that I don't know everything that's going on with, with my implant. But everything I do, everything I am is all about ending the dragons. Can we get back to that?"

Rick blinked and shook his head. "Right, right. So… the library. Second to the top floor. How do we get in there?"

"You won't be able to get anywhere for a while," Cerise said. "They've locked the building down. It will probably stay closed to the public for a week or even more."

"That gives us time to come up with a real plan," Kelly said. "You know, instead of just charging in, like some people..."

"Those people are idiots." I smiled and tried to shift to a more comfortable position.

Marcus got to his feet. "I'll start on supper."

As he left, Rick repeated his earlier question: "So how do we get into that library?"

"We probably can't get away with the same thing twice," Kelly said.

"Are you kidding?" Cerise asked. "Beryl's face will be on wanted posters across town by tomorrow. He can't go anywhere." She pointed at Rick. "And I'll bet your face was noticed too."

"Then we need disguises, or... we don't go in through the front entrance," I said.

"Both are problematic."

"Do we know of any other entrances?" Kelly asked.

Cerise shrugged. "I wouldn't be surprised. There must be a back door for large deliveries. But I've never seen it."

"There would probably be an entrance from within the dragon's lair," I said, mostly to myself.

"You're not doing that again!" Kelly exclaimed.

"I wasn't planning on it! Just... listing options."

"That isn't one."

We spent the next half hour discussing any ideas that popped into our heads. We didn't get very far. Yet as the conversation continued, another idea kept pushing its way back into my brain. I didn't bring it up because I knew what the reaction might be. Except for Rick; I think he'd love it. And Caedan. That solidified my thinking.

At supper, Marcus brought up the topic he must have been thinking about throughout our conversation. "I don't want to complain, because we're all kind of in this together," he began. "But I have to wonder—"

"How long we'll be staying in your place?" I interrupted.

He nodded.

"I'm leaving tonight," I said.

"You're what?" Rick and Kelly both exclaimed.

"I'm going to bring too much heat down on all of you. I'll sneak out and meet up with Caedan. He'll take me back to the, uh, base, and I'll recover there."

"Are you sure, Beryl?" Kelly asked.

I nodded. "Yeah, I think it's for the best. Besides, Bice might have some ideas. Or Don. And I can get the latest news from Stacy. Once I'm doing better and have some information to share, I'll come back."

"And we can keep looking for information here," Rick said. He looked at Marcus. "Is that okay with you?"

"I think so," Cerise said. "But to be honest, we can't afford to keep permanent house guests."

"It won't be permanent," Kelly assured her. She looked at me. "A week. Two at the most, I would think."

"Yeah, and I'll see if I can get hold of some money for you," I added. "Maybe Stacy can help out with that. Or, you never know. I might stumble over a bucket of gold that Loden left behind."

"Who's Loden?" Marcus asked.

I winced.

"Loden was… the man who made all that we do possible," Kelly answered. "He died when we killed the dragon."

"We really need to hear the whole story," Cerise said. "We've only gotten bits and pieces of it."

I exchanged glances with Rick. Was it wise to tell them everything? They had been trustworthy so far, but if things kept getting scarier…

"I'll tell it," Kelly offered.

I leaned in to her and whispered, "Just don't tell them anything about the Asylum. Not yet, anyway."

She gave me a skeptical look, but nodded. Then she launched into her own version of what happened the day we killed the blue dragon. As she went on, I drifted back into my own thoughts, considering my own ideas for getting back into the Flame. The feeling of euphoria while falling kept coming back into my head for some reason. It would be nice to repeat that… without the rough landing, of course.

I looked up as Kelly got to the part about her song. Rick put his arm around the back of her chair as she spoke. Yeah… being around the two of them was great sometimes, not so great in moments like this. Another good reason for leaving by myself.

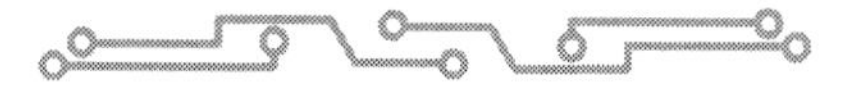

Before I set out that night, I made sure I knew multiple ways to get out of the city. The Crimson Elite might be wandering the streets, making me change direction.

"Are you sure you're up to this?" Kelly asked, looking me over.

I didn't want to tell her the truth. I still hurt all over. But we already covered all the reasons I should leave. "I'll be fine."

Rick stepped up. "I'll go with you down to the street," he offered.

I said goodbye to the Vermeils, and we left their apartment. Once in the elevator, Rick turned to me. "You've got an idea already, don't you?" he asked. "I can tell."

"What makes you say that?"

"Come on, Beryl. Back up there, you had the same look you had when we first thought of blaming a dragon's death on another dragon. I know you, man."

I sighed. "Loden's flying machine," I said quietly.

"Huh." Rick looked away and bit his lip. "Yeah, yeah. That could work. As long as the dragon doesn't show up."

"Right. And if anyone else saw me, the news would get to him. But it's something to think about."

"You going to try to get it working back at the Asylum, then?"

"Yep." I grinned.

"Now I wish I were going with you." He chuckled as the elevator doors opened to the ground floor. "Good luck, my friend."

"Same to you." I handed him Loden's talker. "I'll contact you when we come back." I stepped out and paused. "Keep Kelly safe," I added.

"You know it."

I slipped out into the darkness and made my way to the edge of the city. I stayed out of street lights as much as possible. Twice I saw Crimson Elite patrolling. I slipped into alleys and sought out new routes. I had learned a lot from Lovat. I wondered how he would handle this city. Considering how much he now loved our outdoor living, he probably wouldn't think much of it.

Getting to Marcus and Cerise's apartment in the first place had taken us about an hour of walking. Getting back out took me almost twice as long, with my route changes and stops to hide every so often. Finally, I left Incarnadine behind and hiked into the hills. It took another twenty minutes to find Caedan's hiding place.

"That you, Beryl?" Caedan's voice asked from the darkness.

"No. I'm the red dragon taking human form," I answered. "Of course it's me."

He turned on a lantern. "I had to check," he said. "About time you got here. I've been bored out of my head."

Leaving our self-proclaimed action junkie with nothing to occupy himself might not have been the best idea, I reflected. "Sorry about that. But if we come up with a good plan to get into the Flame, you'll be a part of it."

He grunted. "We going back to the Asylum?"

"Yeah, as soon as possible."

"Good. It's freezing out here at night." He looked at my sling. "So what happened to you?"

"I'll tell you on the ride."

I made sure Caedan had concealed one of the four-wheelers well enough. Then we climbed on the other one and set out. Our headlights would be visible for miles, but… no one was out here to see them.

Except those soldiers at the Hub. We should stay away from there, even if my curiosity about their actions kept pushing back into my mind. I couldn't help but think it might be more important than anything else going on between the cities.

"Spill it!" Caedan demanded. "What did I miss out on?"

I took a deep breath and began. The miles rolled by in the silent darkness, broken only by our headlights and the sound of my voice.

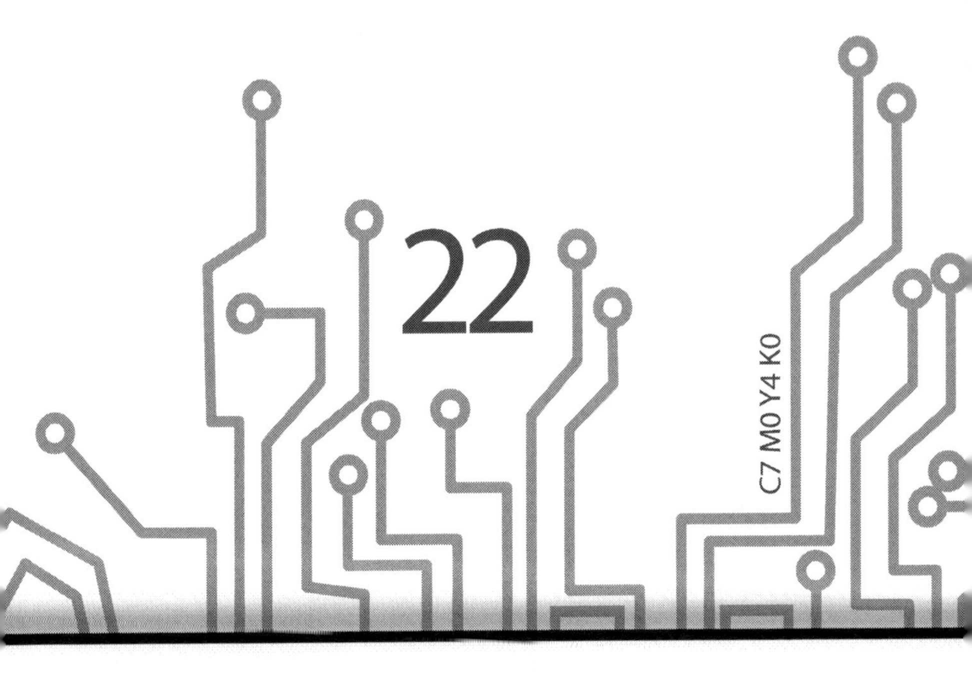

We only traveled a couple of hours by dark. Even though it took me a while to admit it, I needed more rest after the insanity of this day. A few hours on the couch in the afternoon were not enough. Caedan found a good spot, and we rolled out the sleeping bags.

I thought I would fall off immediately, but my mind kept replaying the scene in the Flame: the human heart being cut out and placed in a draconic. I had no doubt the man involved had not volunteered for that operation. This was all we were to the dragons, valuable only in what we could give them. My motivation hardened. We would take them down. Whatever it took.

In the morning, I crawled out of the sleeping bag into cool air. Cool, not cold. "Much better," Caedan muttered. "Not so cold any more."

Something about that bothered me. I looked back in the direction we had come, toward the red city. I pointed. "Caedan, what direction is this?"

He glanced at the rising sun. "That's northeast."

"And which way is Caesious?"

He pointed now. "East."

"You grew up in Caesious, but think Incarnadine is so much colder. Is there that much difference between the two?"

"It feels like it to me!"

Huh. It didn't seem right that the climate would be so different between two cities so near each other. Yet another strange thing about this world we lived in.

We munched a snack, drank some water, and got back on the four-wheeler. Caedan suggested swinging by the Hub again, but I turned him down this time. I was curious, but needed time to heal. My shoulder felt better, but I kept it in the sling. I could afford to give it time. We weren't under a huge deadline right now.

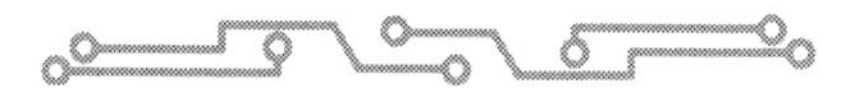

As we approached the Asylum, I saw the form of the blue draconic moving about. My first thought: we took all our warriors away and left a live draconic with the others. Before Caedan could bring the four-wheeler to a complete stop, I jumped off and looked about. To my relief, Lovat came running to greet me.

"Hey, buddy." I tousled his hair. It was getting pretty long out here. "Where's Bice?"

"Over there." He pointed toward the quarters for the priests, then jumped on the four-wheeler with Caedan.

I ignored the draconic and hurried over to the priests's lodgings: a couple of tarps hanging off our roof. Peri emerged and jerked when he saw me. "You're back!" He had abandoned the priestly robes and was dressed in more casual garb. The pants were too large for him, tied with a rope belt. The shirt, at least, seemed to fit. Most amusing to me, his hair had started to grow back, creating a light fuzz all over his skull.

"So I am." I eyed him, recalling his interest in motors. That might prove beneficial.

Peri pulled aside the tarp and let me enter. Inside, I found Bice and Mazarine seated at a rough-hewn new table (courtesy of Don, I assumed). Mazarine still wore his priestly robes, and had apparently persuaded someone to keep shaving his head. Or was he permanently bald? At least he wasn't wearing the sapphire thing any more.

Bice got to his feet with a smile. "Beryl! Back already. What happened to you?"

"Did you find the Cerulean Books of Lore?" Mazarine demanded.

"One thing at a time," I said. "Any word from Stacy?"

"No. Don and Lovat don't go back to check in with her until tomorrow." Bice came around the table and examined the sling on my arm as if he wanted to re-arrange it.

Tomorrow? Had it been a week? I didn't even know what day it was now.

"I dislocated my shoulder," I told him. "The others got it back in place. I'll be fine."

"What about the Books?" Mazarine's impatience radiated from his bald head.

"I know where they are," I said. "We're going to work on a plan to get them. Bice? The workshop?"

He nodded and followed me toward the cave. Despite my attempts to ignore it, Protogonus Blue moved to intercept us. "Welcome back, Beryl Godslayer. Have you slain any more of my kin?"

"Not for lack of trying." I looked up at its face. "What's it to you, anyway? I thought you had abandoned the dragon gods."

"I still retain interest in the happenings of this world. The fate of those to whom I am related is, naturally, a significant part of that."

"You do know I plan to kill all of them, right?"

The draconic's large snout went down in a slow nod.

"Good. Just so we're clear." I stalked past him into the cave, followed by Bice.

"Is it necessary to antagonize him? His curiosity is natural."

I stopped. "*It* is a thing, Bice. It's not a person like you or me."

"Isn't that how the dragons see us?"

I glared at him. He could still infuriate me with a handful of words. Sometimes because he was right. But this time… No. I was nothing like the dragons. I wasn't planning on cutting out the draconic's heart and giving it to someone else.

"Come on." I resumed walking and made my way into Loden's workshop. I found a chair and sat down. I took the sling off and rotated my arm a couple of times. It still hurt, but nowhere near as much as before. I rested the arm on the table.

"Are you going to tell me how that happened?" Bice asked, nodding at it.

"Maybe." It was petty, but I was annoyed. "Bice, have you found anything else in here about my implant? Notes from Loden?"

"No. You know his notes here are a mess." Bice gestured at the shelves packed with objects and papers. "I've run across a few things about cybernetics in general, but not yours. Why do you ask?"

"I scared the others with my abilities." I looked down, feeling the annoyance fade. "Bice, I… scared myself."

"Tell me."

I related the events of the past few days to him, beginning with what Caedan and I saw at the Hub. Bice found that particularly interesting. "We should run that by our blue friends and see what they think," he suggested.

"You think they know more about the gold city than we do?"

He shrugged. "I won't know until I ask them."

"No one seems to know much," I grumbled. I went back to my story, describing the city of Incarnadine, meeting Marcus and Cerise, and finally the Flame. Bice shook his head when I told of climbing the elevator shaft, but he didn't say anything. He was suitably horrified at the heart transplant story.

"You're sure it was a heart?"

"I'm not an expert on what a heart looks like," I said, a little annoyed again. "It was a red thing from inside the man's chest."

Bice chuckled, but lost the smile. "That actually includes several different possibilities. Regardless of which one you saw, it's still horrible."

Then I got to the part about being discovered and chased. "I dislocated my shoulder when I landed," I said. "But… everyone says it should have been much worse. I know it should have been worse. I fell over seventy feet, Bice. How am I still walking?"

Bice studied me for a moment. "I don't have the answers you need," he said at last. "Only Loden did."

"You were there during my recovery," I argued. "He didn't tell you anything?"

"He told me you required a cybernetic implant to save your life and let you walk again. That's all I know, Beryl."

My shoulders slumped and I looked around the workshop again. "Then we have to find his notes." I looked back at Bice, knowing that I sounded somewhat pathetic. "They all looked at me strange, Bice. I don't think… I don't think they believe I'm human."

"Of course you're human! What else would you be?" Bice leaned over the table. "Loden was a genius, Beryl. He saved your life, and gave you some pretty impressive abilities. Why do you need to know any more than that?"

"I don't know." But I did know.

Rick, Kelly, Bice, Lovat... even Don and Stacy... they were my family now. With my parents and Loden gone, they were all I had. It was why I told Rick I didn't mind if he pursued Kelly. I didn't want to do anything to risk losing them. Any of them. I had lost too much already.

And everything I had lost, everyone who had died, was the fault of the green dragon. Whatever we did now, whatever our goals... the green dragon still dominated my thoughts. I would not be satisfied until he was dead.

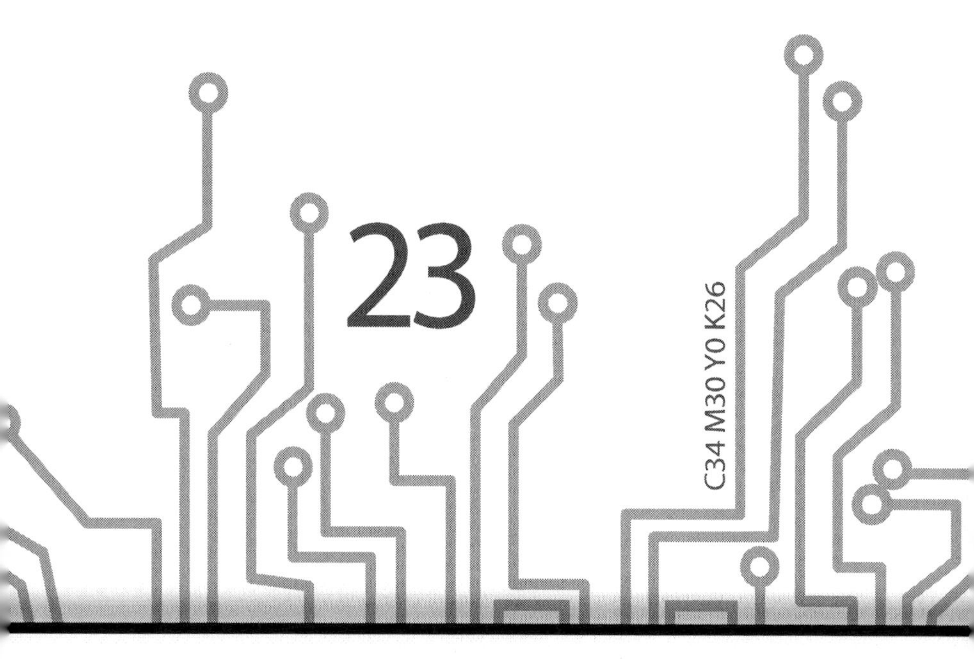

I avoided everyone else for the rest of the day. I stayed in the cave and rested. Kelly would have been proud of me for that, at least. Bice checked on me a couple of times, but I didn't want to talk any more. My thoughts trended dark. I wanted to entertain those thoughts, but didn't want to share them with anyone else. No good giving them more reason to worry about me.

I slept well through the night. The next morning, my shoulder still ached, but most of the other joint pain had faded to the point of not bothering me. I came out to relieve myself and find something to eat.

"Don and Lovat are about to leave for Viridia," Bice reported, finding me by the water barrels. "I've told Don what I could. Did you want him to ask Stacy anything else?"

I nodded. "Yeah, I'll talk to him."

Don stood just outside the Asylum, watching the sun rise. He greeted me with a grunt. I didn't expect anything more from him.

"Bice told you what we learned in Incarnadine?"

"Yep."

"Tell Stacy everything. See what she's heard. Maybe she'll have an idea for us."

Don nodded. For a few moments, neither of us said anything else. Lovat ran up, hugged us both, then bounded up the next hill. Don looked at me, as if waiting for permission to join him.

"Don… do you think I'm… strange? Because of the cyb implant?"

His well-worn face regarded me for a moment, then looked back toward Lovat. "Watch him," he said.

"What?"

He pointed at Lovat. "Just watch."

Lovat positioned himself, as I'd seen him do many times recently. He took off running, then leaped as far as he could.

"Do you know why he does that?" Don asked.

"I just thought he was having fun."

"He wants to be like you."

Running and jumping. Lovat was imitating what he had seen me do with my implant.

"And that's just fine."

With those words, Don started walking. He waved at Lovat and they joined together and moved over the hill.

A man of few words… but when he spoke, I listened. Or at least I should listen. Listening hadn't always been my strongest skill.

After getting some dry breakfast, I found Caedan and asked him to join me in the workshop. Once there, I pointed to the wings. "It's time. We need to figure those out."

His face brightened. "I've been wanting to get back into the air since that day." I knew which one he meant. On the day we killed the blue dragon, Caedan flew. Well, sort of. He shot into the air and floated down with a big balloon thing of Loden's. We discovered three more of those devices leaning against the wall.

"First we have to get it down." Caedan dragged a table beneath the wings. "It'll take both of us." He looked at my sling. "Are you up to this?"

"I'll be fine." I climbed onto the table. While I waited for Caedan to join me, I looked over a set of high shelves on the wall beside me. I didn't remember seeing these items before. Either I hadn't gotten up to this shelf, or Bice had moved things around.

Three cybernetic hands rested on the shelf, in varying stages of completion. One of them looked almost as elegant as Rick's. I knew Loden worked with cybernetics, obviously, but I hadn't seen this kind of evidence.

I looked for any papers or notebooks that might document some of it, maybe even my own.

I found one small case. Curious, I took it down.

"What's that?" Caedan asked.

"I don't know." I flipped the latch and opened the case.

And almost dropped it. Six eyes stared back at me, sheltered in foam.

"Creepy." Caedan reached over and took one of the eyes out. He flipped it over to reveal a metal socket of some kind. "I didn't know they made cybernetic eyes. They look completely real."

"I've heard of it," I said. "It seems like one of the dragons has one, but I can't remember which. Still…" I shivered. "It's pretty weird. Put it back."

Caedan replaced the eye, and I closed the case. I put it back on the shelf where we found it. Something to consider later, though I couldn't imagine what use they might be.

For now, the flying machine mattered more. Caedan reached up and unclasped a latch on one of the belts holding the machine to the ceiling. He let it slip loose, but kept a good hold on it. "It's not very heavy," he reported.

I examined the other belt. It wouldn't be hard to unbuckle it, but I knew my shoulder would give me some difficulty. I should have asked Don to do this before he left.

"I could get Peri to help," Caedan suggested.

"No, he shouldn't be in the workshop." I grasped the wing with my good arm, then used my injured one to unclasp the latch. I experienced only a little pain from the movement.

The wings came loose. To my surprise and relief, I could hold up my end with only one arm. Caedan was right about the weight. We lowered it to the table, then climbed down.

"Better be careful going through the cave. Don't want to break it before we get to try it." Caedan lifted his end and I took mine. He led the way. The cave twisted and turned a couple of times before emerging. On one of the turns, we had to tilt the machine at a angle to get it around the curve without scraping it on the rock. But with careful movements, we got it out into the open. We set it down on the ground and took time to look it over.

The whole thing looked about seven feet wide. Or it did until Caedan said, "Look at this," and pulled one of the wingtips. It extended out another foot and snapped into place. He did the same on the other side. In the sunlight, I could now see the true color of the device. I thought it was white, but now…

"It's light blue," said a voice beside me. I turned to see Peri staring at the wings.

"Camouflage," Caedan declared. "If you're in the sky, the light color will make it harder to see."

I pointed to the twin engines, one to either side of where the pilot would be. "These look like they spit out fire. That wouldn't provide much camouflage."

"Maybe." Caedan got down and crawled underneath the wings to simulate a pilot's position. "Look at the two extensions down low. I think they're for protecting your legs from the blast." He fingered the handlebar that extended in the front. "I think these are the controls here."

"Don't push any buttons," I warned. I examined the rest of the device. It didn't take long to discover two more parts that folded up from the back and snapped into place. I stepped back to examine the effect.

"Stabilizers," Peri said. "You would need them to help with control." He moved to the other side. "And here. These flaps move up and down. That must also help."

"So you think this will fly?" I asked.

He nodded. "I don't see why not. But… I'd be terrified to do it myself. The skies belong to the dragons."

"Not any more," Caedan replied, crawling back out. "We're going to take them away."

"Laudable, but…"

"What are you thinking?" I asked.

Peri gestured at the device. "This looks impressive, and it may work, but it's very small. Have you seen the size of the dragons?" He paused. "Of course you have. That was a stupid thing for me to say."

"No, you're right." I nodded. "I'm definitely not thinking of using this to fight a dragon. I'm not that crazy."

"No weapons, anyway," Caedan said. "Or at least, I haven't found any yet." He grasped the machine and pulled it upright, balancing it vertically.

I examined the pilot's position. As Caedan observed, the controls were mounted on a handlebar at the top. A set of straps and belts would wrap around the pilot's chest and waist, keeping him firmly attached. It would not be easy to strap and unstrap myself without anyone to help. The pilot's legs would hang free, but were shielded by the extensions.

"What do you make of the engines?" I asked Peri.

He walked around and crouched to examine them. "Obviously, they run on some kind of fuel. Where did this come from? Do you have more of the fuel?"

Caedan and I exchanged glances. We would have to search the workshop for fuel. "It's not the same fuel as the four-wheelers?" I asked.

"No, I wouldn't think so. Your four-wheelers are internal combustion engines, similar to those used on trucks in the cities. It moves the wheels, which propels you forward. This is something different. You can't exactly turn wheels in the sky. As you said, it looks like some kind of propulsion." Peri pointed at the two huge nozzle-like parts at the bottom. "You said these looked like they spit fire. That's probably accurate, as far as it goes. It would need something like that to launch it into the air and then keep it moving."

I understood most of that. I think.

"I do notice, of course," Peri went on, "that you didn't answer my other question. You don't want to tell me where this came from."

"No offense, Peri," I said. "But, to be honest, we don't know if we can trust you with everything yet."

He nodded. "You're wise to be cautious, of course. But I want you to know this: after seeing what you're doing here, and all the conversations I've had with your friend Bice, I see no reason to ever leave, regardless of what happens with the Books of Lore. I'm here to help, in whatever way you will allow me. In time, maybe, I will earn your trust."

It was an impressive speech. If I believed it, which I wanted to do, I'd tell him everything. But not yet. I gave him a short nod of acknowledgement instead.

"So..." Caedan said. "Who gets to try it first?"

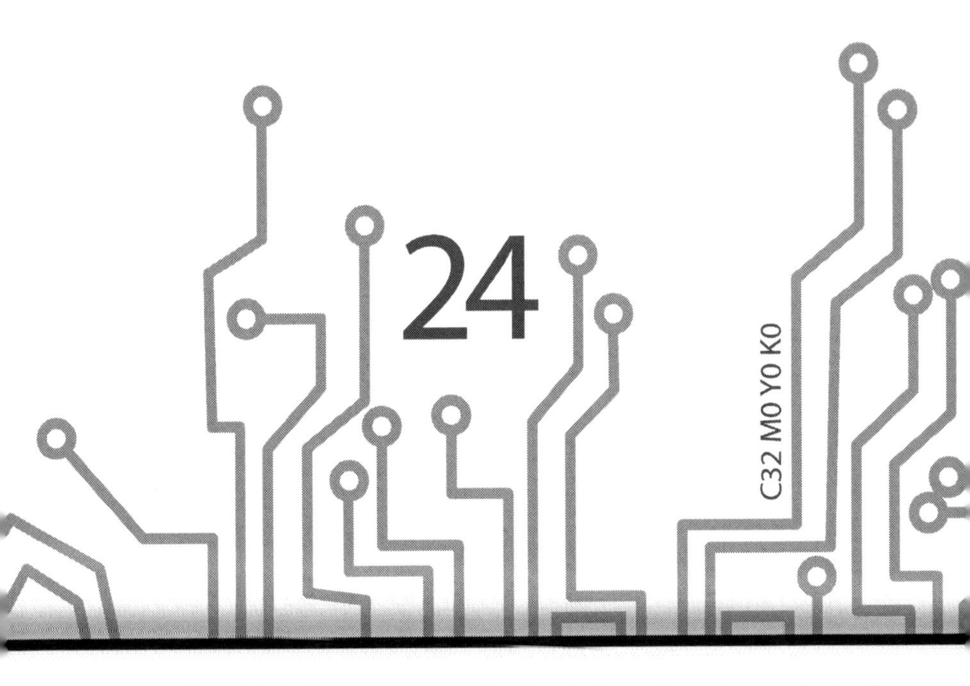

Caedan didn't like my answer, but he had to admit the truth. In the likelihood of an accident, I had a higher chance of survival than he did, even with my hurt shoulder.

We carried the wings to the top of the next hill. We checked the fuel and the tank seemed to be at capacity. Peri warned us to keep the flights short, since we had no idea how much fuel it would consume.

I moved to the pilot's side. "We need a name for this thing."

"Given that you call your other vehicles 'four-wheelers,' perhaps you should just call this 'wings,'" Peri said drily.

"Works for me." Caedan grinned.

"We'll think of something," I said. "Help me strap in here."

"Shouldn't you figure out the controls first?" Peri asked.

"I'll understand them better from the proper position." I got in place and Caedan helped me with the straps. They looped across my chest and even between my legs. "This isn't very comfortable." And it made me somewhat nervous…

"Maybe it'll feel better when you're in the air."

"All right, Peri. Help me figure this out." I examined the handlebars that came down beside my head and connected in front of me.

"Well… this switch here must turn on the engines. It's the only thing that resembles an activation." He pointed at a grip on the right. "And this appears to be the throttle. Turning it should give more fuel to the engines, increasing your speed."

"Just like on the four-wheelers," Caedan put in, watching closely.

"How do I steer?"

Peri frowned, looking it over. "Do these handles moves?"

I grasped them and pulled. "A little bit. Very strong resistance, though."

"Then that would turn the entire thing in the air. That is, it would move one wing down and the other up, allowing you to turn. I can't imagine it does that very fast, though. The real question is how you control your own angle."

"What?"

He gestured. "Well, I mean you're going to take off with your head up. But the way this is designed to fly, it looks like you need to be moving with your head down, your body horizontal, that is. How do you make that transition?"

I grasped the handle with my left hand. "This one moves too. Is that it?"

He walked around behind me. "Do it again."

I obliged. "Yes, that's moving the rudders back here. I think that's it."

"Go for it!" Caedan said. "Let's take the sky!"

"This is practice. I'm not taking the sky just yet."

I flipped the switch. A low rumble combined with a vibration shook me. Caedan and Peri both backed away a few feet.

"Give it some throttle!" Peri called. "Just a little!"

I swallowed and turned the throttle. The engines responded by growing louder. All of the grass went flat in a ten-foot radius around me. The others stepped further back. Was I giving it enough throttle? Caedan whooped. And then I realized I couldn't feel the ground any more.

I waved my feet in the air, like a toddler being held up by his father.

"Try the left hand!" Peri suggested.

I turned the other handle. The machine rotated forward, and I found myself looking at the ground about a yard beneath my face. At the same time, I began moving. I turned the left handle back just a little, to aim myself up instead of straight horizontal. Then I turned the throttle again.

I rose into the air in a smooth motion. I could feel the vibration at my back and a little wind in my face, but little else. I tried to turn the handles up and to the right. They moved, but only with an effort. A brief spasm of pain hit my shoulder. The machine tilted down and to the left. That wasn't what I meant to do. I let off on the throttle to slow down, but instead started to fall. The ground was now about twelve feet down. I added more throttle and stabilized.

Caedan and Peri ran below me, shouting and waving. Though I had leveled off, they grew further away, thanks to the hilltop we started on.

I rotated the machine to get my feet aimed down again, then let off the throttle bit by bit. I descended much more smoothly than I expected. As my feet touched the ground, I released the throttle and flipped the off switch. The engines died. I stumbled a little, but managed to stay upright.

Caedan and Peri appeared beside me, laughing. "You did it! You flew!" Caedan was beside himself. "My turn!"

I laughed too. The sensation had not been what I expected, but the reality of it kept a grin on my face. I began to undo the straps with reluctance. I wanted to do it again.

As we strapped Caedan in, Peri asked, "How did it feel?"

"I don't know how to explain it. Like riding the four-wheeler, but without the bumps? And… I don't know."

"I'll see if I can describe it better after I show him how it's done," Caedan promised.

"Caedan…" I rolled my eyes. "I know how you are. Don't get carried away here. Short flight."

He grinned, lifting his eyebrows up and down. "Step back. Here goes." He flipped the switch.

With a yell, Caedan shot twenty feet straight up in the air. He rotated the machine and kept going up at an angle. Then he kept rotating until he did a complete flip. Peri and I both laughed and ran along the ground below him. He roared over us, turned left, then right, accelerated up another short distance, and repeated most of the process again.

Peri and I stopped trying to chase him and waited. "He'll be back," I said. "Hopefully before he runs out of fuel."

"It is an amazing device," Peri said. "Is it going to help you get the Books of Lore?"

"I think so. I'm thinking of using it to get into the Flame from above."

Caedan circled back toward us and began to descend.

Peri ran a hand through the fuzz on his head. "I do not think you would be able to carry the books while flying this thing," he pointed out.

"They are... not light."

I frowned. "Even if they were in a bag or something?"

"I just don't see how it would be possible. The bag would need to be very large, and then how would you hold it?" Peri gave me an amused look. "Do you even know how many books there are, or what they look like?"

"Um..."

Peri laughed. "The high priest never included those details, did he? His arrogance knows no bounds."

His arrogance and my ignorance. I'll admit: I never even thought to ask these questions. How would I even know I had found the stupid books in the Flame? "Do you know?"

"There are seven books with dark blue covers," Peri explained. "Each is... about this big." He tried to show me with his hands. I didn't know books got that big. The plan I had begun to form fizzled in my head.

"I guess we'll have to do some more thinking."

Caedan zoomed in for a landing not far from us. He came in a little too fast, stumbled several steps, then fell on his face, the device atop him.

Peri and I ran to him, but he got back up, laughing, his face covered in dirt. "That was so streak!"

We helped him get loose, then I took the wings one more time. Now that I understood how they worked, I wanted to test more of the possibilities.

Like Caedan, I shot straight up into the air, except I went further. I kept going up, but started to turn the left handle gradually. This took me higher, but I eventually leveled off. I couldn't tell the elevation, but it was much higher than Caedan had taken it. He and Peri looked very small below me.

I stared out over the landscape, amazed at how far I could see. Rolling hills, clumps of trees, railroad tracks, farm lands... I climbed even higher. A haze lay off to my left, marking the Blasted Lands. And beyond that, the mountains. As high as I might be right now, they towered far higher. Part of me wanted to take the wings as high as I could, to see if I might even be able to cross the mountains one day. But my rational side reminded me I had no clue about how high or long this thing could fly. Also, the wind in my face was becoming a problem. Next time, I should wear goggles.

I turned to the left, drawn once again toward the Blasted Lands. I descended a few feet out of caution, but kept going. I'd head back in another minute, but curiosity pushed me on. And I needed to try something else.

I pushed a boost to my eyes and concentrated. It got easier every time I did this. My vision narrowed and zoomed forward, exactly like binoculars. Maybe better. Once again, the haze of the Blasted Lands made it difficult to see much of anything. But I thought I caught glimpses of some broken walls deep within, where the city once stood.

I lifted my eyes, intending to release the zoom vision and return to the others. My gaze swept up to the mountains overlooking the ruination, and my brain refused to accept the sight.

Whether I meant to or not, my vision snapped back to normal. Knowing I had been in the air too long, I immediately turned back toward the Asylum. But I argued with myself about what I had seen. It couldn't be possible, but what else could that have been?

Built into the side of the mountain, overlooking the Blasted Lands. A tower.

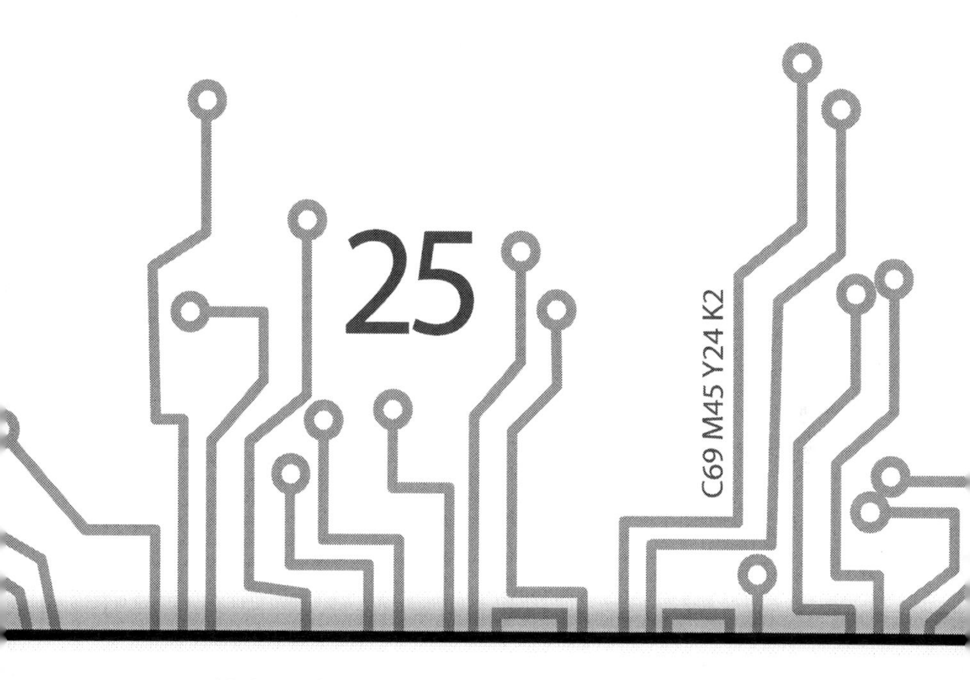

25

Bice scolded me for not taking it easy with my shoulder. He might have had a point. It definitely hurt more after the flights. I promised to spend the rest of the day relaxing. He also griped at me for not letting him watch the flights. I promised to let him know next time. I made a lot of promises.

I needed time to think, anyway. My brain bounced around so many topics: the flying itself, trying to think of plans to steal the Books, and most of all: what was up with that tower?

I seriously considered sending Caedan to investigate. Unfortunately, he would have to get to the mountains, climb them to the level of the tower, then move across the mountains to get there, all to avoid the Blasted Lands. It would be a long, complicated trip, and there was no guarantee he could pull it off.

Who would know anything more about it? Only one possibility came to mind. I dreaded it, but the desire for answers drove me.

I found Protogonus Blue in its shelter. Though I knew it got up and moved about from time to time, it spent most of the day in this spot, either alone or talking with Mazarine or Bice. It looked up as I entered. "Ah, Beryl Godslayer. How may I assist you?"

"You can start by not calling me that." I'm not sure why, but hearing that title from this creature annoyed me. "I have more questions for you."

"I will answer to the best of my ability."

"The Blasted Lands. Why would anyone want to watch over them?"

The draconic tilted its head in what I took for confusion. "I'm not sure I understand the question. Watch over them? Do you mean guard them?"

"No. I mean… well, maybe. Why would anyone want to watch them at all?"

"I cannot think of a reason that would make sense. There is nothing of value to be found there. No life. No anything."

I would have paced, but the entrance to the draconic's shelter was too narrow. I wanted to ask more, but didn't know how. I think part of me would always hate this creature. If the draconics truly were children of the dragons as they claimed, they deserved my hatred and anger just as much as their "fathers." Regardless of their origins, they helped enforce the dragons' will on everyone throughout the history of the six cities. By its own admission, this one had lived multiple lives, hundreds of years of oppression!

"May I ask why you are asking this?"

I looked around, then sighed. I sat down facing it. The smell bothered me, as always. "I believe I saw a tower on the mountains, overlooking the Blasted Lands."

It regarded me for a long moment with those reptilian eyes. "I will not ask how you were able to see such a thing, though naturally I wonder. Instead, let us consider the possibilities. An exercise in logic, if you will."

"So you don't know who built it." This was a waste of time.

"No, I do not. But as I said, there are limited logical possibilities. It will not take long to run through them." It held up a clawed finger. "First, perhaps this tower was built long ago, by the residents of the city, and was not destroyed at the same time. Maybe some residents even escaped there during the devastation."

"But wouldn't the dragons notice and destroy it too?"

The draconic nodded. "One would think. So that possibility is very unlikely. The second possibility is that after the destruction, one of the other dragons had it built to observe the devastation, to see if the land recovered. The most likely choices would be Viridia or Auric, as the nearest cities."

"It's not Viridia." I shook my head. "The architecture was nothing like Viridia." And while I didn't know what the city of Auric looked like, that didn't feel right, either. At the very least, the tower contained no strong colors of any kind.

"As you say. Again, I do not think that possibility very likely either. But the third possibility is least likely of all. That this tower was built by someone else."

"Who?"

"I do not know. Someone not of The Circle. From beyond it, as you asked about the other day."

"You said there wasn't anything beyond The Circle."

"I did not believe there was. But someone must have built it. If neither of the other possibilities are true, then it becomes more likely. Not much more, in my mind, but it is... imaginable, at the least."

It hesitated and looked off past my head. I glanced behind me and saw nothing. "What is it?"

"I can think of one final possibility, though you will scorn it."

"Try me."

"As a child, did you and your friends ever entertain... ghost stories? Tales of unliving beings returned from the grave?"

"I didn't have many friends, but... yeah, I know what you mean. My father told me a few of those." I entertained brief memories of spooky stories told by flashlight under a blanket tent.

"We draconics have our own such stories, tales told to frighten, to warn, and in some cases, merely to entertain. They are shared in our gatherings, on the rare occasions we have them. Often, the oldest of the draconics will recite a favorite story. One such tale involves the Blasted Lands."

"A ghost draconic?"

"Not exactly. The story tells of the humans uprising, killing the dragon and all of his draconics and guards. But one draconic survived somehow. He fled the attacks and escaped to a cave in the mountain. There he hid while the city was destroyed, fearing to reveal himself to the other dragons, for surely they would slay him for failing his god. He emerged when they were gone and stood amidst the destruction, not knowing what to do with himself. For decades, he wandered the Blasted Lands. The poisoned environment warped his mind and drove him insane. The story often ends with the mad draconic emerging and haunting the city of the storyteller." Protogonus Blue chuckled. "The ways we amuse ourselves. Still, many stories have a grain of truth to them."

I wrinkled my brow. "So you're suggesting that one of the black dragon's draconics survived everything, then built itself a tower overlooking its former home?"

"I do not suggest it. I think the whole idea quite ridiculous. But I promised to answer your questions, and in this case, I wanted to give you every possibility."

"Thanks, I think."

"Even if one of the children of Onyx survived the devastation, he could not still be alive after all this time. It has been over three hundred years since the city fell. We draconics live long lives, but not that long."

"Yeah, I didn't think so." And then it struck me. "The city's name was Onyx?"

"Onyx was the seventh dragon, yes. How do you not know this?"

Truth was, I never cared about the dragons' names. I remembered them based on their colors. The names were for the cities. I'm certain I must have heard the name Onyx in history classes, but didn't care to remember it. "Rick's name is Onyx," I said aloud.

"The wanderer from Atramentous? Yes, that would make sense. The black dragons were close, much as the red ones are now. And there are only so many different words to refer to any given color."

I shook off the weird feeling it gave me. I considered mentioning this little detail to Rick the next time I saw him. But if I did, he would laugh at me for not recognizing it when we first met. I had no desire to look like an idiot.

"Your own name, for example," the draconic went on. "I'm sure your parents gave it to you because a beryl is known as a green gemstone."

"But it can be other colors too," I said. "Mazarine told me that once."

"Yes. It can also be blue or red, or even gold." It chuckled again. "Not black, though. Very few black gems." It stared at me for so long, I grew uncomfortable. "Perhaps that's why..." it murmured.

"Why what?"

"A man whose name can be many colors, to lead the people of many colors." It nodded. "Your parents chose your name beyond their own wisdom."

"You think my name is what? Some kind of prophecy, then?" I got to my feet.

The draconic ducked its head. "We are a superstitious people. I told you one of our ghost stories. Prophecies, omens, portents: these are common parts of our beliefs."

"Maybe there's a way to use that."

"Excuse me?"

I sat back down. "Tell me more about these superstitions."

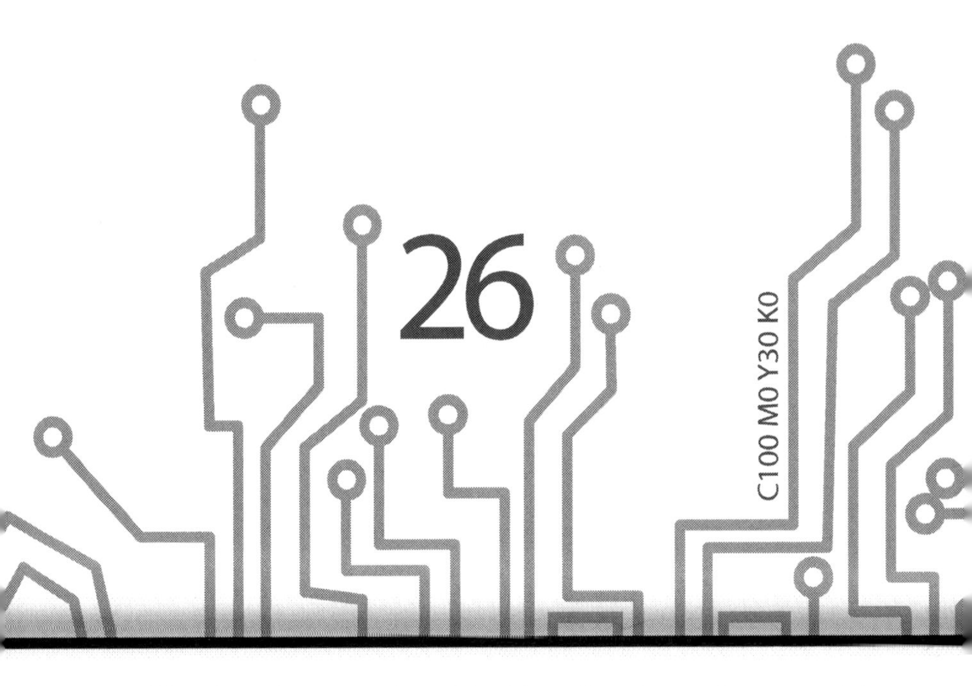

When Bice found me there, I had been listening to Protogonus Blue talk about draconic beliefs for at least an hour. It fascinated me how these creatures could be so advanced technologically, yet believe so many strange and weird things about the world. They feared the supernatural. And yet they wielded it… depending on what you believed about the power Troilus Green and Bice used.

"Ah, the Heretic," the draconic greeted Bice. "We have been having a most engaging conversation."

I got to my feet. "Bice, I think you would find some of this very interesting. Um, right now, I need to go think about how to use this information."

I found some lunch and headed to the workshop to be alone. Caedan and Peri were working on the four-wheeler for some reason. I didn't know where Mazarine might be, and didn't much care. I liked him even less than the draconic, especially after this conversation.

That thought stopped me in my tracks. Was I beginning to trust Protogonus Blue? It seemed to be completely open in our conversations, even if I didn't always get what I wanted from it. Could it really be a… decent… draconic?

Back in the workshop, I sat and thought for a while. I had so much information, but none of it worked together as well as I'd like. When Don returned tomorrow, he might have still more information from Stacy. That could complicate things even further.

"I can't do this alone," I said aloud.

It only took a few minutes to find Bice and Caedan and persuade them to join me. Peri looked disappointed as we left him, but I couldn't quite trust him yet. Maybe in time.

Once together, I laid out the situation. "We have all this information, but I'm no closer to coming up with a plan to get the Books. I need more minds thinking about it."

"All right. Let's brainstorm," Bice said, taking a seat. "What are your initial thoughts?"

"Well… even before I got back here, I was thinking about using the flying device to enter the Flame at one of the upper floors."

"Wouldn't people see you coming?"

"Right. So we'd need some kind of distraction below, to keep everyone focused at ground level. I did think of that." I scratched the back of my head. "But Peri told me the Books of Lore are too big for me to carry with the wings. So I can get in to get them, but can't get them out."

"That's a tough one," Caedan agreed.

"Then we have all this other information," I went on. "The war. Whatever is happening at the Hub. Everything I saw in the Flame. This stuff about draconic superstitions. There has to be something in all of this that we can use to our advantage."

"You're right," Bice said. "We should be able to use this. But." He held up a finger. "Great plans don't come together in a day. Do you know how long Loden worked on the idea of using a train to kill a dragon? It took him years."

"We don't have years."

"Maybe not. But there's not an urgent rush, either. You can rest, heal, and think. Caedan and I will also think about it. I may run pieces of information—not all of it, mind you!—past Mazarine or Protogonus. Don will be back tomorrow with Stacy's latest report. Let's take our time on this and do it right."

I knew he was right, but didn't want to admit it. "Rick and Kelly are waiting on us," I pointed out.

"They can wait a little longer."

"And they're getting to sleep indoors," Caedan added.

Yes, they were. And I couldn't admit that it bothered me. Not the indoors part. But they were together. Sleeping.

"We can trust these new friends to keep them safe, can't we?" Bice asked.

"Marcus and Cerise? Sure, they seem like good people."

"Then don't worry about it. Focus on what you can do. Let yourself heal, so you can be of use to them."

Wise words, but they didn't make it any easier.

"Also, keep in mind that not everything you learn has to fit in to the plan. If something works well, then use it. If you can't find a way, don't force it. Sometimes, simpler plans are better."

"But I get scolded if I run off on my own simple plans. Some people think I take too many risks."

"Plans can be simple without being reckless." Bice got to his feet.

"I'll have to take your word for it."

Waiting for Don to return was interminable. I rested my arm and shoulder, but tried to find other things to do to keep myself busy. I took a long walk to the edge of the Blasted Lands again, and looked out over the desolation. I half expected to see an ancient draconic come walking out of the haze. I laughed at myself. What a bizarre story. But I couldn't get the image of the tower out of my head. It had nothing to do with our current predicament, and as Bice pointed out, probably wouldn't factor into our current plans, but it bothered my imagination.

To clear my head, I dug out the wooden practice swords and found Caedan. He didn't require any persuasion to spar, but he had one condition: "No cyb tricks."

"Sure. Unless you give me permission."

He grinned. "Then I'm not giving it."

We chose an open area just outside the Asylum, out in the noonday sunlight. Peri followed us to watch.

"Go easy on me," I said. "I only have one arm."

"Okay, I won't use my left arm, either." Caedan flipped his practice sword to shield his forearm, his usual style. He dropped back to his defensive stance and beckoned.

I stepped into my usual opening stance, the one Stacy taught me, with sword leveled toward my opponent. I circled to my right, Caedan's left, watching his eyes. Stacy assured me that's what you should do. Unfortunately, it didn't help much. In under a minute, Caedan disarmed me and gave me a good whack across my back with his practice sword.

We lined up again. This time, I managed to go maybe a few seconds longer, but ended up getting a smack on the side of my head as a reward. Peri laughed. I couldn't blame him.

"Okay, okay." I tried to catch my breath. Caedan waited. "Since there's no way I can beat you like this, do you mind if I try boosting just my arm? No legs. Everyone keeps telling me to experiment with my abilities, so…"

Caedan's eyes narrowed, but he nodded.

I started the duel with slow boosts into my right arm, giving it more strength and speed. This helped, as I was able to get my sword in position more often to deflect some of Caedan's blows. I couldn't move the rest of me fast enough, though. He managed to get a couple of strikes against my legs, and one short tap against my left arm that hurt a lot more than it should have. Stupid shoulder.

Caedan soon realized my weakness and began moving faster himself. He aimed for strikes that would force me to dodge instead of parry. It worked. A series of blows made me stumble. Caedan dodged to the side, caught my foot with his sword and sent me into the dirt.

I spat and wiped my face off.

"Can you teach me how to do this?" Peri called.

"Sure. I'll be glad to," Caedan said. "Once I'm done teaching this greenie."

"One more," I growled.

This time, I augmented the slow boosts with stronger ones when the time seemed right. As I parried one of Caedan's side strikes, I gave my arm an extra boost. The impact of the swords staggered Caedan. I took advantage and stabbed forward, poking him in the stomach.

"Good one. Keep going." He moved back into his defensive posture and circled me. I feinted a couple of times, but waited on him to make the next big move.

As it always did, Caedan's patience ran out. He launched into a series of rapid attacks, intending to wear me down. I boosted my arm, and… I may have sent a little boost toward my eyes. I followed every one of his attacks and parried them all. With the last one, I threw him off balance enough to allow me a follow-up strike on his back.

"Yes!" I'm not ashamed to admit I yelled.

Caedan laughed and wiped sweat from his brow. "You're barely passable without the cyb stuff, but with it..." He shook his head. "Keep practicing and you'll be streak."

I grinned and looked at Peri. To my surprise, Lovat crouched on the ground beside him. "Lovat! You're back! Is Don here?"

"Yah."

"Where is he?" I looked around. "Does he have news from Stacy?"

Lovat pointed into the Asylum. "Oh yah. Big news."

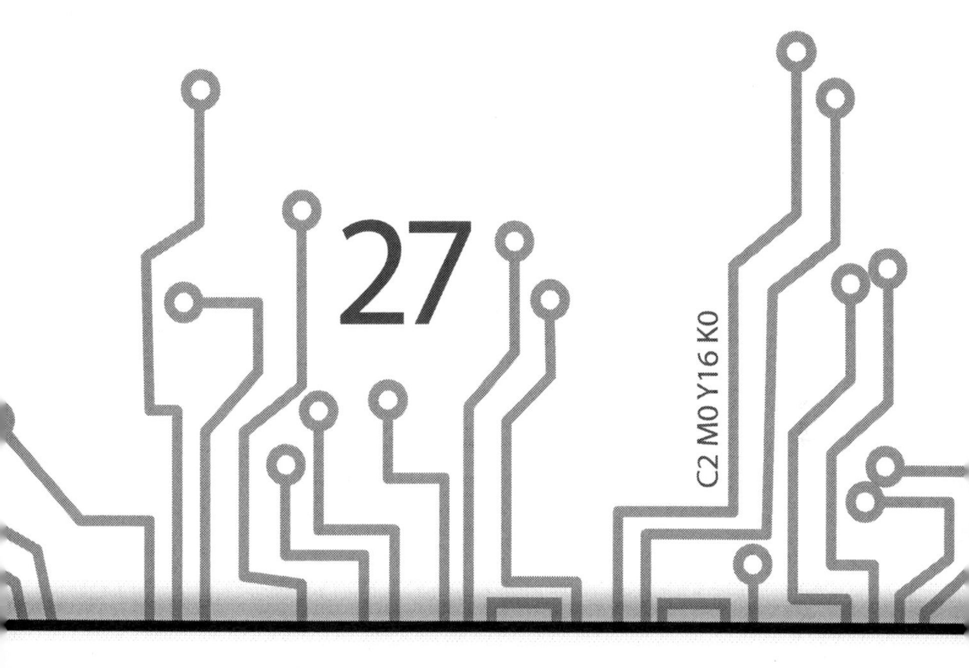

27

"You are a prophet," Don said to Bice. "How did you know?"

We gathered in the workshop to hear Stacy's news: Bice, Don, Caedan, myself, and Lovat. I did always feel just a little nervous whenever Lovat was in the workshop. Some of the stuff in here could be dangerous, and curiosity has always been one of his defining traits.

"How did I know what?" Bice handed Don a glass of water and smiled.

"The draconics are going to have a peace conference." He gave Bice a folded piece of paper.

Bice took the note, glanced at me, and opened it. "So it appears. Stacy says the draconics have agreed in principle to a gathering, one from each city, in Caesious. Makes sense. The city without a dragon."

"When?" I asked.

"It hasn't been decided."

"It's what you said would happen," Don said. "How did you know?"

Bice shook his head. "It's not prophecy, Don. I just tried to think about what I would do if I were running one of the cities right now. That's all. I made a good guess."

"I wonder if a draconic would be impressed by your logic, or superstitious about your prediction," I said. "Maybe both."

"Maybe this is where we could use those beliefs against them," Bice mused. "Guide them with some kind of omens or portents."

"Guide them to what?" Caedan asked.

"To hold this gathering on a day of our choosing," Bice answered. "Whatever that might be."

"And that's the day we steal the books!" I jumped up. "All of the attention will be focused on Caesious and this gathering. Maybe Incarnadine sends the top draconic, even. Less trouble for us at the Flame!"

"That sounds like the beginnings of a plan." Bice nodded in approval.

"Did Stacy have anything else to say?"

Bice looked over the rest of the note. "Let's see… nothing specific, really… vague rumors about troop movements… black and green draconics have been seen meeting… nothing surprising about that…"

"Nothing about the Hub?" Caedan asked.

"Or the books?" I added.

Don shook his head, and Bice confirmed it. "That's all."

"Weird. Do you think anyone even knows about the Hub?" Caedan leaned back in his chair. "Seems like that would be a big deal, for both sides of the war."

That triggered a thought, just the beginning of a plan.

"Oh." Lovat's head popped up from under the table and looked at me. "Olive says hi."

"Who's Olive?" Caedan looked at me.

"Another friend of Stacy's." I smiled at the memory.

"So…" Bice put the note down. "We have more information to work with. Beryl, how do you want to proceed?"

I couldn't believe the next words that came out of my mouth. "Let's go talk with Protogonus Blue."

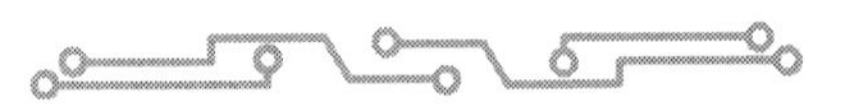

We found Mazarine and Peri with the draconic. I was reluctant to discuss anything with all three of them, but Bice launched right in: "Protogonus Blue, we have information that the draconics will be having a peace summit soon. How do you think they would go about choosing the day for such a gathering?"

"A peace summit?" Mazarine exclaimed. "What does that have to do with the Cerulean Books of Lore?"

"Everything," I told him. "If it's big enough and important enough, it will draw attention away from Incarnadine, so we can get the books."

He harrumphed but said nothing more.

Protogonus Blue pointed up. "They will start by consulting the stars."

"The stars?" Caedan wrinkled his brow.

"Yeah, it's a superstition thing," I told him. "They think events can be shaped by which stars are in the sky at a particular time of year."

"Or the phase of the moon," the draconic added. "All of it works together. The movements of the heavenly lights shape the movements of those here below."

"How?"

"Astromancy is not an area I have spent much time investigating myself." The draconic gave its version of a shrug. "There are draconics who spend many years on the topic."

That name triggered a thought in my head. "What's resomancy?" I asked.

Protogonus Blue turned to look at me. "I am unfamiliar with that branch of science. Why do you ask?"

"They have several floors dedicated to it on the Flame. You sure you never heard of it?"

"I know nothing of that name. Perhaps it is called by something different in other cities." The draconic paused. "The name is not helpful. 'Reso' could be resonance, I suppose. Something related to sound?"

I looked at Bice. He knew what I was thinking about, but wasn't going to say it out loud if I didn't. "Could it be..." I began. I stopped myself, and looked around the group.

"Could it be what?" Mazarine asked.

"Never mind. Bice, would you work with the draconic here, and try to figure out when the peace gathering might happen, and if we can manipulate that." They both nodded. "Caedan, with me. I've got another idea."

We separated from the others and walked to the edge of the Asylum. "The Hub thing is really bothering you, isn't it?" I asked.

"It doesn't make sense. Why would Auric step in like that? And what were they hauling around?"

"I agree. More importantly, there may be something there we can use to disrupt the peace summit. Or maybe even help us get the books. If it's important to them, it might be important to us."

Caedan looked toward the four-wheeler. "So you want to run another scout mission?"

"I don't know. We couldn't see much last time."

"Maybe if we… flew… over it?"

Tempting. "I think I'd rather keep the wings a secret until we have to."

Caedan spread his hands out. "Then what else is there?"

"I think we should walk in and ask them what's going on."

He studied me for a moment with that steely gaze of his. "I can't tell if you're joking. You haven't always been that good at it, but it's hard to imagine you're being serious here."

"I am serious." I glanced around to make sure no one could hear us. "Look, you said this should concern both sides of the war. And it should!" I pointed at my chromark. "I'm green. You're blue. We represent both sides. You put on your Cerulean Corps uniform. I'll put on my Viridian Guard uniform. Then we walk in together, saying we represent both sides and want to know what's going on."

"I could do that." He raised an eyebrow at me. "But I don't know if you could. I told you when we met: you don't look like a soldier, even with the uniform."

"Maybe," I conceded. "But they're drafting lots of new people into the Guard now. Maybe I'm just a rookie."

Caedan chuckled. "You always have the craziest ideas."

"But do they work?"

"More often than they should. So just to sum up: we're going to dress up, walk into an enemy camp, and ask them to explain themselves."

"Pretty much."

"Let's do it."

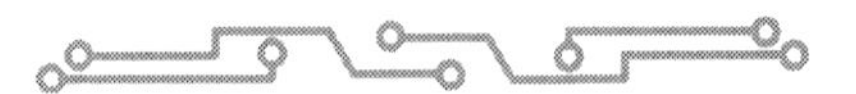

I told Bice we were going to scout the Hub again, and would be back in around a day. He warned me to take it easy with my shoulder, of course. We gathered the supplies we needed and set out.

We got within a mile from the Hub by twilight, so we stopped for the night. We could implement the plan in the morning. Though I had gotten used to sleeping outside, I tossed and turned all night. So many ideas and concepts kept running through my head. I tried not to think about the tower any more, and focus my thoughts on the Flame. But I was no closer to a plan than ever before.

In the morning, we dressed in the uniforms, and armed ourselves.

"They'll probably take our weapons away," Caedan pointed out. "Maybe we shouldn't bring them."

"We're soldiers," I said. "Why would we walk into an enemy camp without them?"

"Because we have peaceful intentions. I don't want to lose my weapons."

It was a fair point, so I agreed, but the thought of walking into the enemy camp without weapons bothered me.

"It shouldn't," Caedan said. "You are a weapon."

I rolled my eyes and we started walking. Caedan stopped and ran back to our supplies. "One more thing!" he called.

He came back carrying a white shirt. "What's that for?"

"When you want to talk to an enemy, not fight, you wave a white flag," he explained, waving the shirt in the air.

"Why?"

"I don't know. It's just what you do."

I hoped the golden soldiers knew that particular tradition. We set out walking. The closer we got to the Hub, the more nervous I became. The more I thought about it, the more I second-guessed myself. We could be walking into a deathtrap here. I knew that, which is why I hadn't told anyone but Caedan. Bice, Don, any of them would have tried to talk me out of it. And they probably would have been right. We should turn back.

Caedan pointed. "There they are. I think they've seen us."

Too late now.

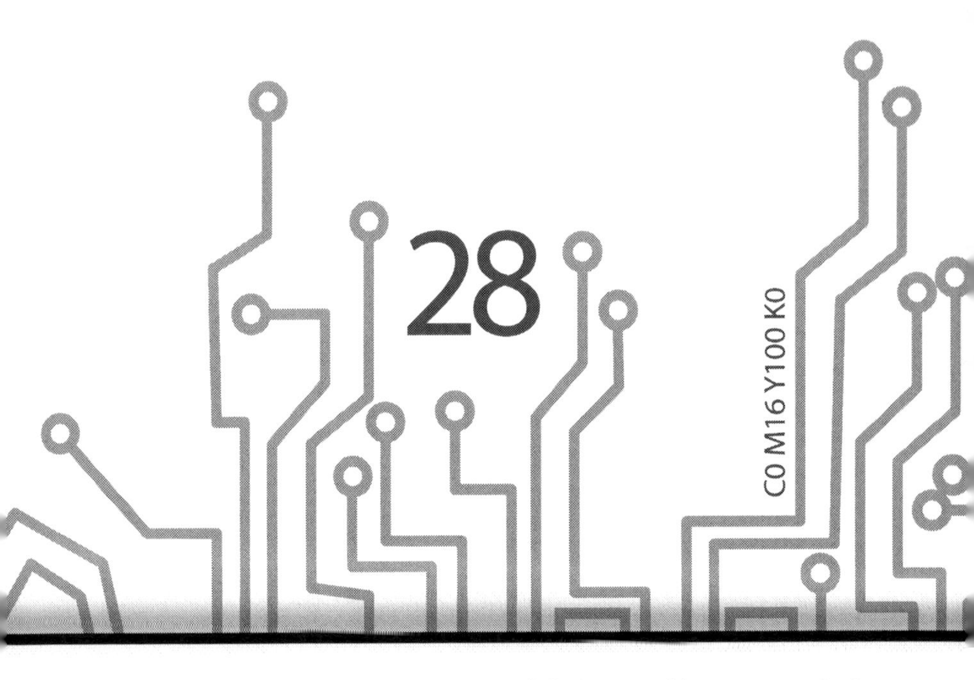

28

Caedan waved the white shirt. A full dozen soldiers approached us, and I could see more moving about the massive Hub building. All of them carried weapons: half with some type of bladed device on a six-foot staff, and the other half with thin swords, much longer than the one I usually carried. And we were walking into the middle of this. Stupid, stupid, stupid.

As we all drew closer, I examined their outfits. Most wore helmets that left their face open, but covered all of the rest of their head, extending down even to protect the back and sides of their necks. All wore armor: layered chest plates with shoulder guards and vambraces on their lower arms, and a kind of short skirt of long armor plates hanging from their belt to mid-thigh. All of it, from helmet to their tall boots, glistened in the morning light, shining like gold. At first, I thought it must be some kind of polished metal, but the closer we got, I became convinced it was some other type of material. It almost looked like plastic, but I knew it had to be something stronger.

The soldiers moved to encircle us, leveling their weapons. Caedan continued to wave the shirt, and I lifted my hands to show they were empty.

One soldier without a helmet stepped forward to face us. A crimson cape hung from his shoulders, a bright spot of color amidst all the gold. He eyed us with dark brown eyes framed by a dark tan face. His black hair hung straight and smooth past his shoulders, while his narrow beard reached only to the length of his neck.

"What are you doing here?" he demanded in a firm voice.

"We came to ask you the same question," I said, keeping my hands up. "As you can tell, we represent both Viridia and Caesious. Your actions here are concerning enough for our leaders to send us together to investigate." As I spoke, the other soldiers completed their circle around us. We stood surrounded by blades.

The officer, or whatever he was, looked to Caedan.

"Would I be standing here with someone in that color"—Caedan pointed at me—"under any other circumstances?" He took a step closer. "If it were up to me, I'd put a dagger in his neck," he said in a lower voice, as if I couldn't hear him. "Idiot's not even a real soldier. The greens are getting desperate."

The officer's eyes darted between us. "Neither of you are real soldiers, nor are any outside of Auric," he declared.

"We're outside Auric right now," Caedan said. "What does that make you?"

I closed my eyes, certain we were dead. Why hadn't I told Caedan to leave the talking to me? "Ah, regardless of all this, our leaders want answers. If we do not return with satisfactory ones, they will send more troops to investigate. Scandar Green himself will lead them," I said, making up a draconic name on the spot.

The officer snorted. "As I said, neither of you are soldiers, and neither a green nor a blue army are anywhere near us." He reached forward with his own sword and ripped the white shirt out of Caedan's hands. "That means the two of you are probably nothing more than deserters."

"If we were deserters, why in The Circle would we come here?" I pointed to the shirt he tossed on the ground. "Why would we wave a white flag?"

"Maybe you sought some information to buy your way back into the good graces of your 'leaders,' as you say, to save your own miserable lives. Whatever it may be, even if your story is completely true, I don't care." He spun his finger in a circle. "Kill them and haul their bodies away so we won't be bothered with the smell."

Caedan and I dropped back-to-back in defensive stances. I triggered multiple boosts throughout my body.

"Hm. Perhaps you know a little of fighting after all. No matter. The order stands."

The blades moved in toward us. If I could duck under one of those long ones and rip it out of the soldier's hands, maybe I could defend myself better. But even so, just the two of us versus a dozen of these armored warriors? It did not look good.

At that moment, a young man without armor raced out of the Hub, yelling. The officer raised his hand, and the soldiers stopped their advance on us. The young man, wearing a green shirt with some sort of emblem on the front, black pants that only came to mid-shin, and a golden sash around his waist, hurried to the officer and whispered something in his ear. The officer nodded, with no change in his expression.

"Bring them," he ordered, turning toward the Hub and walking away.

I relaxed my stance. Caedan did not. One of the soldiers gestured with his sword. "Move it." I put my hand on Caedan's shoulder. He relaxed at last and we followed the officer down the sloped ground and into the Hub.

We entered beside the set of railroad tracks leading to Viridia, if I had my directions right. As we passed into the enormous building, I took a quick look around. Tracks criss-crossed in every direction. Some led off into massive side rooms that lay between each entrance. Soldiers moved here and there throughout the space. I saw only one train, sitting on tracks I assumed led toward Auric. It consisted of an engine and four flatbed cars, two of them empty, and two holding piles of crates that might be in the middle of loading or unloading. I couldn't tell which.

Large metallic structures I didn't recognize stood over three of the rail lines leading out. We passed by a fourth one under construction on this set of tracks. I couldn't fathom what their use might be. Some kind of cylinder sat within each one. At first, I thought it to be a common tank car, for hauling fuel, but the shape was all wrong.

"This looks like who we need to talk to," Caedan whispered. I followed his eyes in looking ahead, where the soldiers were taking us.

A draconic lounged on an enormous stuffed chair, which looked completely out of place in the center of the Hub. They must have brought it in here by train. The draconic was gold, like the soldiers' armor, but a little less polished. Its left hand and forearm were cybernetic, and I think part of its left leg, though I couldn't be sure. It wore a pair of loose-fitting gray-green pants, but its feet and ankles were bare. The scales on the left looked more silvery to me. Also replaced?

As we approached, it looked us over with that freaky reptilian gaze. The sickly-sweet smell and heat radiating from it were stronger than any of the other draconics I had met, even Troilus Green.

"Here are the intruders, sir!" the officer reported with a deep bow. Then he turned to us. "Pay homage, fools. You stand before Taizong—"

"Gold," I said.

"What?"

"Taizong Gold. Isn't that the way draconics are named?" I looked from the officer to the beast. "Ending their name with the… color?"

The draconic spoke. Its voice, with a slight rasp, came through with the deepest intonation I'd heard yet. "The chosen ones of the other cities do follow this tradition, yet we children of Auric see no need to constantly call attention to the obvious." It looked from Caedan to me, then back. "Now. Which one of you is the cyborg?"

"Excuse me?" Caedan said.

"Which of you two is using cybernetic enhancements? It's not a difficult question."

Caedan and I both raised our hands. I shot him a look.

The draconic sighed. "I do not wish to cut you both open to find out, but if that is the process required…" It gestured to a soldier, who offered it one of the tall bladed weapons. Taizong Gold (I couldn't help thinking of it that way in my head) got to its feet and leveled the blade at us. The six-foot weapon looked almost tiny in the hands of the monster.

"It's me," I said. "How did you know?"

Taizong Gold turned its left wrist toward us. A small red light blinked on a tiny display embedded in its forearm. "You used some form of artificially generated kinetic energy. I immediately detected it, and sent a servant to bring you."

"That's all very interesting," I said (and it was!), "but we came from the opposing armies to find out what you were doing here. What are those structures?" I gestured back toward the entrance.

"Your reason for being here matters not," the draconic answered. "You possess cybernetic technology. Such tech must always be returned to Auric for evaluation, disassembly, and duplication."

"Dis… assembly?"

"Secure him," Taizong told the officer. "Load him on the train. Kill the other."

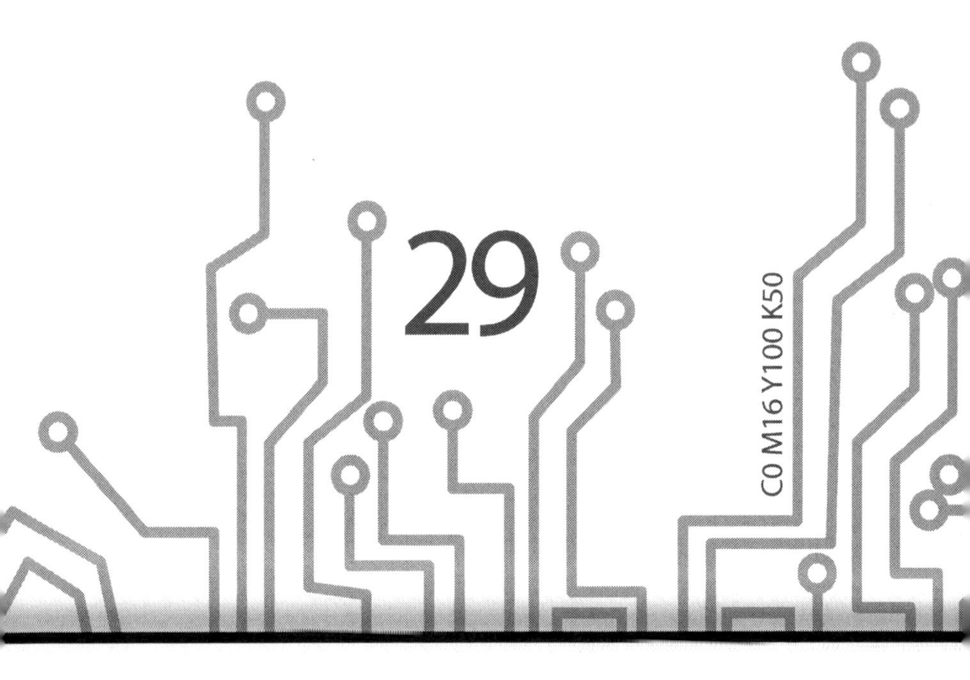

Soldiers converged on us again. I triggered boosts to my arms and legs and charged. Before the nearest soldier understood what I was doing, I seized his long weapon and yanked it from his grasp. The weapon felt unwieldy to me, but I threw it to Caedan. He caught it, snapped the staff over his knee, and spun in a circle as the soldiers closed in.

I repeated my moves, this time stealing the sword from the officer himself. I battered two soldiers aside and rushed to Caedan's side.

"We don't want to hurt anyone!" I shouted. "Let us go and it can stay that way!"

Taizong Gold rose to its feet. "Fascinating. Truly impressive. How much of you is cybernetic?"

"None of your business." I glanced around. The soldiers had stopped advancing, but over a dozen surrounded us now, weapons ready. I was no expert, of course, but I strongly suspected their armor would be stronger than the uniforms Caedan and I wore. Even with my abilities, we did not stand much of a chance.

"I will let you go on two conditions," the draconic announced.

I eyed him warily, but didn't answer. My mouth got me in enough trouble lately. I shifted the sword around, testing its weight and balance. It was longer than what I was used to, with a slight curve. I didn't know how that affected anything, but it felt remarkably balanced.

"First, you must answer a question honestly, with no guile."

"What's the question?"

"What is your name?"

"My name?"

The draconic sighed. "If you can't even do that much…"

"Beryl. My name is Beryl."

"Beryl." Once again, a draconic repeated my name as if tasting it. So weird. "Very well, Beryl. Your final condition is this:" It slammed the base of the bladed staff onto the concrete. "You must defeat me."

I looked around. Was it serious? "You mean alone? Or…"

It waved dismissively. "Your friend is of no consequence. I care not."

"No consequence, am I?" Caedan growled, stepping up beside me. Around us, the soldiers backed away.

"Careful," I warned.

With a bellow, the draconic leaped forward, weapon lifted over its head like an axe. Caedan and I dodged to either side as it came down between us. Even as it landed, it swung its left fist in a backhand that would have taken off my head if I hadn't been moving faster than normal. I sent a quick boost to my eyes, determined to use every advantage I could.

Taizong Gold lifted its weapon and swung in an enormous arc. The six-foot length of the weapon combined with the draconic's arm length would have taken out all of the surrounding soldiers if they hadn't retreated. As it stood, Caedan and I both had to duck to escape the sweep.

That reach gave it a big advantage, but it needed room to swing. As it brought the weapon back around, I rushed in close, stabbing up and under the beast's arm. I thought I had it, but at the last minute, it shifted and my blade only sliced off a few scales.

Caedan charged in, trying to distract the monster. He swung his own weapon, but the bladed piece was too awkward for him to wield effectively. The broken staff in his other hand, however, made a perfect shield for his fighting style. He deflected a blow from the draconic, but the impact made him stagger back a few steps.

I took advantage of this to spin and try to slice the creature across the back. To my shock, a tall ridge of vertical scales erupted from the draconic's backbone as I swung. My sword cracked against them, never getting near the actual skin. I didn't know draconics could do that.

Taizong Gold stabbed back at me with the butt of its staff. It caught me in the stomach, knocking the air out and punching me back several feet. I staggered, trying to catch my breath. The monster turned its full attention toward me.

Caedan yelled and launched himself at its back. I wanted to scream at him to stay back, but I couldn't even breathe.

The draconic turned its head at Caedan's yell, and swung its weapon in a backhanded sweep. To my horror, the blade sliced across Caedan's chest in a mist of blood. My friend fell.

Pure instinct and rage kicked in. I channeled all the boost energy I could into my arms and legs. I took in several deep breaths, recovering my balance. And then I charged. I battered aside the draconic's weapon and slammed into its chest with my right shoulder. It staggered, but didn't fall. I re-focused my boosts into both arms and shoved. Taizong Gold toppled.

I leaped onto its chest as it went down. I may have yelled something by this point. As we hit the ground, I stabbed down through the draconic's right forearm. With the force I gave it, the sword pierced all the way into the concrete floor. I kicked the pole weapon from its hand and caught it myself. I spun around in time to see the cybernetic left hand coming at me. I smashed the blade into it. Shattered parts went everywhere. I pulled back and hit it again. The arm fell back, a mangled piece of metal and wires where its hand had been.

"Now." I leveled the blade at its neck. "Honor your word."

"You are free to go," it said without emotion. "But we will meet again."

"Not if I kill you now." I lifted the blade.

"Kill me, and there's no one to stop all these soldiers from tearing you apart and returning you to my master in pieces."

I snorted and jumped off its chest.

"We will meet again, Beryl," it called to my back. "Auric will demand it."

I spun back around and bent down near its head. "You tell Auric that his name was the last word spoken by Caesious." I couldn't be sure, but I think the draconic's eyes widened at that. I'm not sure why I told it that. Just got too angry, I guess.

I ran to Caedan's side and dropped the weapon. That was a lot of blood. Bright red, all over the place. And still coming. I needed to bind the wound, at the very least. I fumbled with the straps on my Viridian Guard uniform. "Somebody help me!" I shouted.

"That was not part of the agreement." Taizong Gold's voice came from behind me. "Only that you're free to go. No one is under obligation to help you."

I shot a glare over my shoulder. I managed to get the top of the uniform off, then tore off my t-shirt. I ripped it in half and tried tying it around Caedan's chest.

"Besides," the draconic went on, "why are you so determined to save the life of your enemy?"

"He's human!" I screamed. "So much more than you'll ever be!"

"Good to know... you care," Caedan managed to say.

"Keep still," I told him. "I'm going to get you out of this."

"It's... been fun, Beryl."

"Shut up. Stay with me."

Caedan grasped at me with his hands. I looked around and grabbed the broken bladed weapon. I put it into his hands and he held it tight. His eyes closed. My bandaging job wasn't doing much good, but if I could get him back to the four-wheeler, maybe we had a chance. Channeling more boost energy, I stooped and picked him up.

Watched by dozens of gold-clad warriors, I carried my friend, step by step, out of the Hub. They moved out of my way, but did nothing to help me. Ignoring them, I pushed more boosts into my legs and picked up my pace.

The four-wheeler waited almost a mile away. I kept boosting my muscles, over and over, to get myself there. I glanced back every few seconds, watching for followers. Surely the golden soldiers would at least see where I was going. But I never saw anyone.

Rain began to fall, a light, misting rain that turned everything gray. In a few minutes, we were soaked. Without my shirt and the sun, a chill settled in. I shivered.

About halfway back, I suddenly realized that I shouldn't be able to do this. I was carrying a grown man while walking and running. And my shoulder didn't hurt at all.

Did the boost energy heal me? How did that even make sense? Maybe it explained how I survived the green dragon's lair. I did remember triggering a boost as I stumbled through the caves, poisoned and dying. But the boosts only strengthened my muscles. How could they possibly do anything else, let alone heal?

Caedan moaned. His condition was the only thing that mattered right now. I boosted my legs again and kept going.

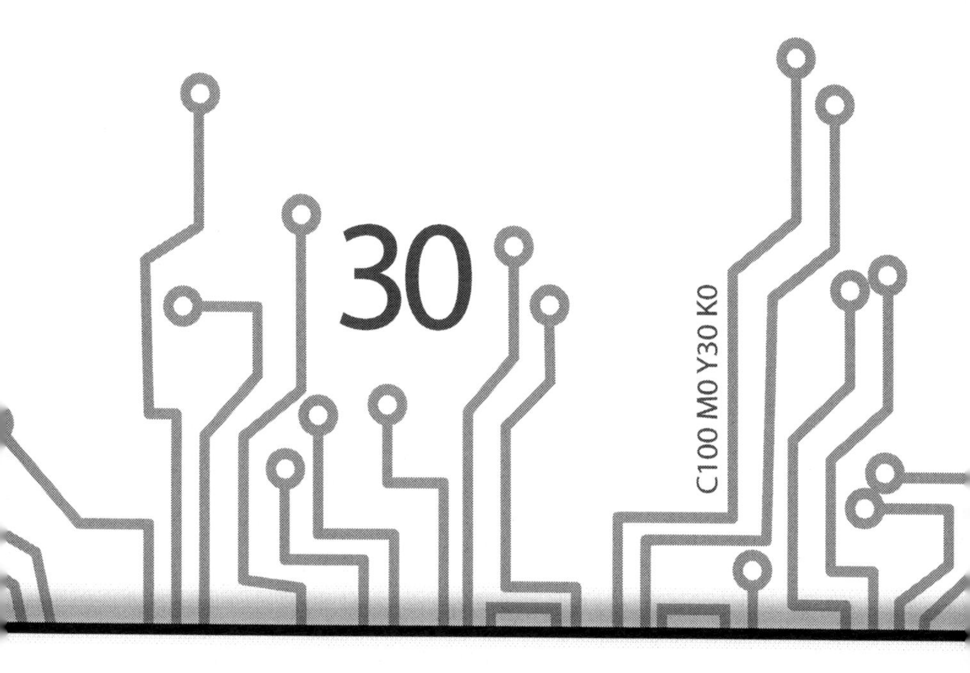

30

The trip back to the four-wheeler seemed to take twice as long, even though I ran at least half of the time. The misting rain kept falling, drenching everything. I nearly slipped at least a dozen times.

I laid Caedan on the ground beside the four-wheeler, then tried to catch my breath. I teetered on the edge of exhaustion. Only repeated boosts of energy kept me moving. I found the clothes we had left behind, and pulled on another shirt. Then I tore up the rest of them to make new bandages. I carefully removed the blood-soaked shirt from Caedan's chest and wrapped him more securely with the new material, wet though it was. Somehow, he held on to the weapon through the entire ordeal. I took it from his hands to work with the bandages. He didn't protest.

The four-wheeler had a storage rack on the back end, but it wasn't even close to large enough to hold a human being. I looked around. We had parked in a low ravine, carved out by a tiny creek that ran along the bottom. A small clump of young birch trees hung over the water not far away. I took the weapon and cut them down. After trimming the branches and cutting them to size, I laid them across the storage rack. Caedan always brought rope, wherever we went, and today was no exception. I bound the birch saplings to the four-wheeler and laid Caedan on top of them. I tied him to it around his waist and ankles, then tied one of his hands to the frame of the vehicle. It wouldn't be comfortable for him, but it would have to do.

I climbed on and started the machine. The mist kept coming as I drove out of the ravine and set my face toward the Asylum. At top speed, it would take at least three hours to get there, but I had no choice. Only Bice could save Caedan now.

Every bump made me wince for how it would feel to my passenger. Sometimes Caedan cried out. While I hated that it hurt him, at least it told me he still lived. The times he didn't make a sound terrified me. My mind filled with images of pulling up at the Asylum and finding him dead behind me.

The mist made visibility difficult. Was I going the right way? Caedan could navigate the open land so much better than I could. When I found the rail tracks again, I breathed a sigh of relief. I could follow them almost all the way now.

And there was my own exhaustion to deal with. Boosts kept me awake, but that ability grew less and less efficient the longer I drove. A single boost at the beginning kept me going for half an hour. Toward the end, I needed another boost every three or four minutes. My head nodded constantly. You'd think the constant water in my face would keep me going, but it didn't seem to matter. Between the battle and carrying Caedan for a mile, I had used every bit of strength I could muster. It wouldn't be long before the boosts no longer worked.

At last I spotted the turn-off point. The four-wheeler slid as I spun it away from the tracks. Though the rain wasn't enough to muddy the dirt, the slickness of the grass made it difficult enough. One more hill, and there it was: the Asylum.

I raced up under the covering and brought the four-wheeler to a stop near the cave entrance. I started to get off, but couldn't control my legs. I tumbled onto the ground with a short cry. I heard the footprints of the others rushing toward me, but my vision blurred. I tried to wipe my eyes, but my arm didn't have the strength to reach them.

Someone else's arms reached under my shoulders and lifted me. "No," I struggled to say. "Help Caedan."

"We'll get him, Beryl," I heard Bice's voice. "Come on, let's get them both inside."

"What has happened?" Mazarine's voice demanded.

"It doesn't matter," Don said. "Help us, priest."

Right about then, I lost consciousness.

When I woke, I heard Bice's voice griping. "...would learn eventually. His body ends up getting its rest, but only when he can't force it to go any further."

"It is the tendency of young people to imagine themselves invincible," Mazarine's voice answered.

"Yes, but Beryl is... a special case. He's driven. Sometimes, I worry that he'll try to take on a dragon by himself one of these days."

"Only if I had a sword," I managed to say. My mouth was dry, and my voice didn't sound right. I opened my eyes and saw rock above. Inside the cave, but not the workshop.

"Here." I felt movement beside me. Bice appeared, holding a glass of water. I lifted my head and drank.

"Caedan?" I asked, when I could move my lips again. I ached all over, but it wasn't as bad as it could have been.

"He'll live," Bice answered. "Mazarine, could you give me a moment alone with Beryl, please?"

The priest snorted and got to his feet. I watched him leave, then looked around. I didn't see Caedan or anyone else.

"He's in the workshop," Bice said. "He's lucky to be alive. And from the looks of things, so are you. Before I jump to obvious conclusions, how about you tell me what happened?"

Telling Bice what we had done was not pleasant. He interrupted me frequently with questions that all boiled down to: "Are you out of your mind?"

"I know, I know," I said when I finished. "It was a stupid idea, and I should have talked with you before we left."

"But you didn't... because you knew I'd talk you out of it." Bice sighed and sat back against the opposite cave wall. "What did you accomplish, Beryl? What good did this do?"

I couldn't answer. We hadn't learned much of anything, aside from first-hand experience with the weapons used by Auric's soldiers.

"Protogonus Blue has determined when the draconics will likely meet. It's eight days from now."

I perked up. That was news.

"If you want to steal the books while that's happening, guess what? You'll have to do it without Caedan. He's not going to recover by then."

Ouch.

"So you've taken your best warrior out."

"Yes, I get it. I was stupid. I know."

"Do you? It's not the first time, Beryl. You have got to stop this. You can't keep running off the second you get an idea."

"Sometimes it works," I muttered.

"Yes. Because you generally have good ideas." Bice leaned forward again. "But you need to bounce those ideas off others."

"Caedan liked it." I don't know why I was arguing, when I had already admitted I had been stupid.

"Of course he did. Caedan will agree to anything that might lead to action. You knew that when you recruited him. But if you talked to me about it, or even Don, we might have come up with a better plan, one that had a specific goal and a good chance of success."

"I get it. I do."

"I hope so." He got to his feet. "This job with the books is huge. If we can pull it off, it might be the key to everything. The plan, whatever it is, has to be perfect. You had a great idea about using the wings. That makes sense. But if Peri hadn't pointed out the problem with the size of the books, you might have run off and tried it without thinking. And then what would have happened?"

Bice turned to go, then paused. "We have eight days, Beryl. Based on what Protogonus has shared, I don't know if that can be changed. But let's make sure the plan is solid before you go flying into the dragon's lair. You're not invincible, Beryl, even with all your power. And the people around you don't have your capabilities. You have to think of them." He nodded. "I'll get you something to eat."

I drank some more water, then tested my muscles. Sore, but I could move. I wondered how long I had slept. Bice was right. My body would make me rest if I took things too far. And I kept doing that. Such an idiot.

I got up, wobbled on my feet for a moment, then walked gingerly to the back of the cave. The workshop was open. I found Caedan lying on a mattress on the ground by the wall. He slept, but his skin looked pale. His chest had been bandaged expertly. In fact, it looked like the bandage had just been changed.

"I'm sorry," I told him, not knowing whether he heard me. "It's my fault."

I sat down next to his mattress. If I had to rest, I would do it next to him.

I felt miserable.

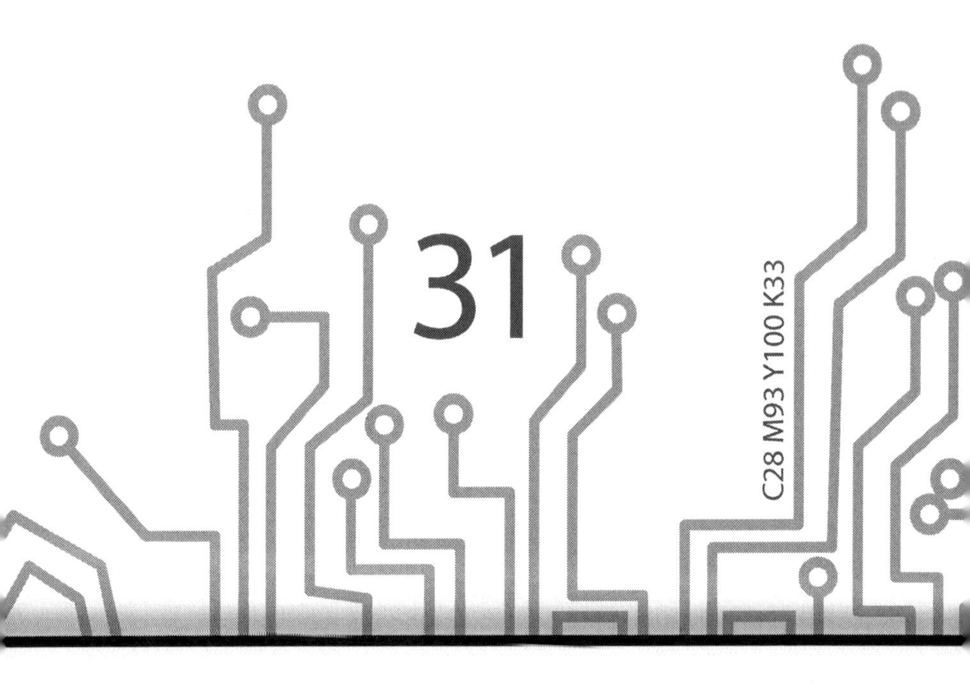

31

Caedan didn't wake up for another six hours. I helped him get a drink and tried to feed him, but he would have none of it. "My hands aren't sliced open," he told me.

"Well, yeah… I just… I feel bad. It's all my fault."

He snorted. "Shut up." He grimaced in pain. "Can you get me some more pain meds, though?"

I found Bice and got what Caedan needed. The meds took effect pretty quick, making him drowsy.

"You want to make it up to me?" he murmured.

"Of course I do." I patted his shoulder.

"You gotta let me take another flight on the wings after I heal up."

"You got it."

"Flying… it's pretty streak…"

"Yeah. Ever since that balloon thing, right?"

"Not as cool as… the wings…"

I picked up one of the backpacks that held the balloon things. "I don't know. I might want to use one of these someday, just to see what it felt like."

"You should… you could…" His eyes closed.

"I could what?"

Caedan didn't open his eyes, and I figured he was done. Then he mumbled a few more words.

"What was that?"

"Use the balloon… to get the books." His head rolled to the side. He was out.

Nice thought, though. I looked over the backpack. It had the advantage over the wings in that it would go almost straight up, very fast. But it couldn't really be maneuvered or…

"Not for me," I said. "For the books!"

I hurried outside and found Bice. I showed him the pack. "Can you modify this to hold a large bag of some kind?"

He scratched his chin. "Sure. I mean, we can attach a bag to it, but what for?"

"This is how I can get the books down from the Flame. It was Caedan's idea."

Bice turned the pack over in his hands. "You could float them away on it, sure. But… don't you have to pull one of these cords to make it come down?"

"We'll work on that. Maybe Don has an idea. In the meantime, how about you check with Peri and make sure we get the bag size right?"

Bice's smile grew. "Are you actually trying to involve everyone in this idea?"

I glanced toward the draconic's resting place. "Well, almost everyone."

Bice followed my gaze. "He has a lot of knowledge, you know."

"I'm not saying it doesn't. We wouldn't know about the superstitions if not for… it." I staggered a little and caught one of the water barrels to stabilize myself.

"You're not done resting, Beryl. Go lie down. Let your body tell you when it's rested, not your brain."

"Yeah, okay." I took a deep breath and gathered myself. "And then I need to head back to Incarnadine." When Bice's eyes narrowed, I hastened to add, "Not to go for the books, not yet. I need to talk with the others and get their input, right? I can't just show up and tell them what to do."

He smiled and nodded. "Now you're talking."

I made my way back to the workshop, put a pillow on the floor next to Caedan, and fell asleep.

I slept until I got hungry, found something to eat, and then went back to sleep again. All told, I must have slept another fifteen hours or more. When I finally got up, feeling certain that my body was saying, "I'm ready now," it was sometime in the mid-morning. Only seven days to go now.

I spent a few minutes with Caedan, who insisted he felt great as well. I told him to listen to Bice on issues of recovery. Then I headed out to begin loading up the four-wheeler.

With Peri's help, I set the mechanical wings on the back where I had carried Caedan. We secured it with more rope and straps than it probably needed, but I wasn't taking any chances.

"If I can help you, please let me know," Peri said when we were done.

"Sure, sure."

"I mean it, Beryl." The priest looked at me with a solemn expression. "I want to help. If there's a way I can be a part of retrieving the books, you'll let me know, won't you?"

"Yes." I clapped him on the back. "Yes, I will. In the meantime, check with Bice on the bag I gave him. Make sure it's big enough to hold those books."

Lovat ran up and jumped on the four-wheeler. "Can I come too?"

I caught him and lifted him off. "Not this time, buddy. But if I find a job for you, I will let you know."

"I never get to do anything fun any more," he griped.

"Hey now, you get to sneak back into Viridia once a week!"

"Not the same."

I crouched down to look at him. "Once this job in Incarnadine is done, we'll learn a lot more about the dragons," I explained. "And then we can start making some real plans." I squeezed his shoulder. "I'll be counting on you then."

"You will?"

"Absolutely. You're my right-hand man."

Lovat jumped forward and embraced me. Unprepared, I almost fell over. His little arms squeezed my neck. I hugged him back, patiently waiting until he pulled free again.

Bice approached. "Heading out?"

"Yep. But only to talk things over with the others, like I said. Once we have a solid plan, I'll come back for the supplies."

"If there's any way we can help…"

"I know, I know." I watched Lovat run to meet Don as he came out of the cave. "We have a good team here. Lots of different skills. Maybe one or two many priests throwing off the balance, though."

Bice laughed. "Give it time. The team will grow. As will your responsibilities."

I wasn't sure I liked the sound of that.

"If you're going to continue to lead, Beryl, you have to be prepared for what that will mean," he went on. "So far, our missions have been limited by a lot of factors. But what happens when you have several people available with the same skills? The longer this goes, and the larger we grow, the more decisions you'll have to make."

"Well, if a mission calls for a priest, I still don't think you have any competition."

He nodded with a grin. "But I'm a heretic, remember? Anyway, have a good trip. Tell Rick and Kelly they're missed back here."

"Sure thing." I climbed on the four-wheeler and set out.

A full day of travel to get there. One day to plan. Another day of travel back to the Asylum. And then one more back. That only left three days until the day of the peace summit. I hoped Rick and Kelly had some ideas, because I couldn't think of anything else.

As I drove, my mind wandered. If the balloon trick worked, Marcus would have to drive his truck to intercept it, wherever it landed. Cerise would be at her job. That meant Rick and Kelly would have to create the diversion, unless we brought someone else in to help. I didn't want to bring Bice, because he might be recognized. Don might be useful, but I was reluctant to put Lovat in danger. That left… Peri, I guess. He wanted to help, but I wasn't sure what use he might be. Of course, I had no idea what our plan might be, either.

I thought about the Hub, and the gold soldiers. What were those things they were setting up on the tracks? My first thought was some kind of weapon to be launched at each of the other cities. But what good would that do? Why would the gold dragon want to attack the other cities? I couldn't think of any logical reason.

Like the tower over the Blasted Lands. I could think of no logical reason for its existence either. A few illogical reasons could exist, of course, like the story of the last draconic. Or maybe the gold dragon's people built that too. Maybe there was a connection between the activity at the Hub and the mysterious tower. I don't know. Nothing made sense any more.

Making the long drive alone wasn't much fun. The monotony of the travel made me wish I had brought someone else along, just to talk. Even Peri would have been more interesting than this. At least I would get to talk with Rick and Kelly again in the evening.

At long last, as the sun was setting, I found the valley where we hid the other four-wheeler. Though I didn't see any reason for soldiers to come out that way, I was relieved to see it still there. After a stretch and a drink, I got out the talker and dialed in the frequency. "Rick, come in. I'm back. Rick?"

There was no answer.

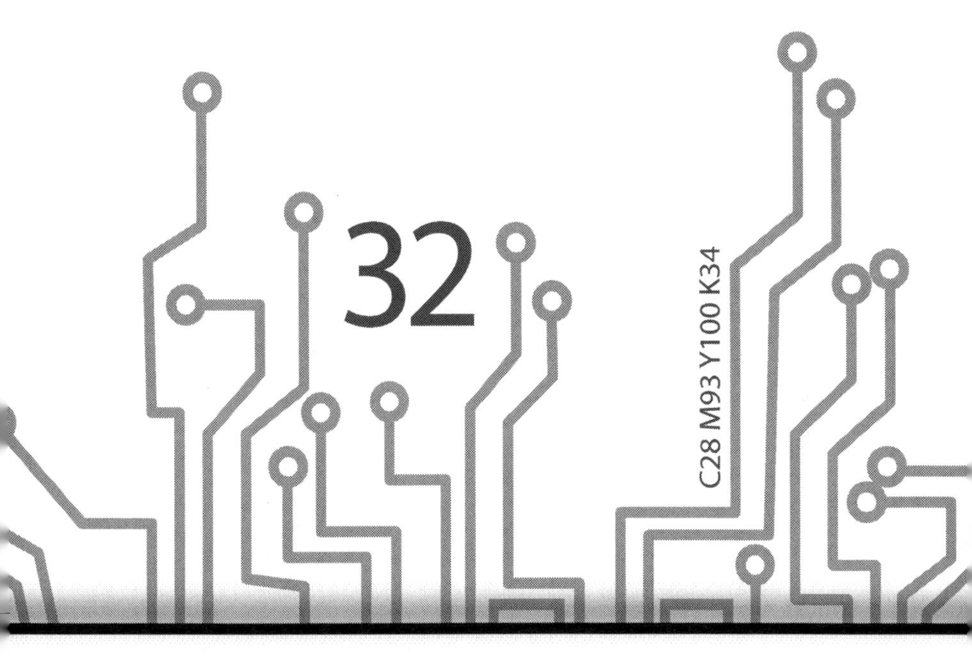

32

I tried again and again. No one answered.

Maybe something went wrong with Rick's talker. Maybe they weren't at home right now. Maybe… something bad had happened. Those were the only possibilities I could imagine.

I needed to get to the apartment, but I didn't have anyone to alter my chromark. If anyone got even a casual look at my face, I'd be denounced as an enemy spy or something. If I waited until dark, I would have a chance. Maybe.

I paced back and forth, waiting for the sun to finish setting. I needed full darkness. I tried the talker again every few minutes. With no response, I tried finding the frequency used by the Crimson Elite. No luck. Of course, I didn't know whether they even used talkers like the Viridian Guard. Maybe they had another method of communication, or none at all. It was the most forbidden of techs, after all, except weapons. Can't have those puny humans communicating. They might organize or something.

I went through my gear. Was there anything I could use, in case the situation was the worst I could imagine? I hadn't brought much with me. This trip was supposed to be for talking, not taking action. I had my sword, but I couldn't very well carry that through the streets of Incarnadine, unless I concealed it somehow. I wrapped it up in some spare clothes and considered. The bulky package might make me more noticeable, but… I would feel a lot safer bringing it along. I decided it was worth the risk.

Darkness finally descended enough that I felt safe in entering the city. As I had done while leaving, I made my way along alleys, choosing the darkest areas. As much as I could, I avoided walking near street lights. The closer I got to the apartment building, the harder it became to avoid the light. For the last bit, I waited until I saw no one else, then walked brazenly into the building. I avoided the elevator and took the stairs. After making sure the hallway was empty, I knocked at room 326.

The door flew open. Marcus stared at me. He took a quick look down both directions in the hall, grabbed my shirt, and yanked me inside.

"What's going on?" I asked. "I tried calling Rick, and—"

"Beryl?"

Kelly plowed into me all in a rush. I hugged her back, enjoying the moment. She pulled away, far too soon for my liking, and looked up at me.

"You don't look so good." It was the first thing that popped into my head, but probably not the best thing to say. She looked pale, and I think her hands were shaking.

"I've been sick," she said. "Stomach."

"Me too," Marcus chimed in. "Must have been something we ate."

"Well, I—"

"Rick's gone," Kelly interrupted. "They took him."

"What? Who? When?"

"Let's move into the living area," Marcus suggested, motioning with his hands. "We shouldn't be talking about all this right next to the door. Someone might hear."

I followed Kelly back into the living room. She sat on the couch and hugged herself. Marcus took a chair. I stood, feeling awkward, then sat on the floor near Kelly. "I tried to call with the talker," I said. "When I didn't get an answer, I came here."

"Oh. I forgot about that thing," she said. "It's in Rick's things somewhere. Must be turned off."

"Okay, well… tell me about Rick. What happened?"

"We were scouting around the other side of the Flame," Kelly began, staring at the floor. "Cerise said there must be a service entrance of some kind, so we went looking for it."

"When was this?"

"The day before yesterday." She looked at me reproachfully. "You've been gone almost a week, Beryl."

"I know. Things happened. I'll tell you later. Go on...?"

"It's not complicated." She looked back down. "I think we found the entrance, but just as we started to get a look, the Crimson Elite found us. There were five of them. Rick told me to run, while he held them off. I got away. He didn't."

I threw back my head and groaned. The story was too familiar. Rick got caught back in Viridia when the rest of us escaped. Loden and I rescued him that time, but now? We didn't know anything about the security forces in this city. I looked to Marcus. "What do you think they'll do with him?"

"I guess... I mean, I assume they'll think he's a spy from Atramentous. Since we've never been at war before, and had spies and such... I don't know what they'll do." He pulled his knee up near his face. "I guess they'll try to question him, find out what he knows... and then? I don't know."

The lab with the organ transplants flashed into my head. I swallowed. "We have to find out where they're holding him."

"How?" Marcus held out his hands. "I don't know how you got information in Viridia, but we have nothing here. I mean, Cerise has her co-workers, and I have the acting community. But no one knows anyone in the Crimson Elite or anything."

Kelly picked up a glass of water from the stand beside the couch and took a sip. Marcus offered me a drink, but I turned him down.

"Where's Cerise?" I asked.

"Working late. They extended her hours a few days ago. Not sure why."

I got up and walked around the room. "If we have no contacts in the Crimson Elite, then I'll just have to find one."

"What do you mean?"

I formed a fist and smacked it into my open hand. "I will find one of the guards and make him talk."

Marcus stared at me. "Are you insane? They're trained warriors. And have you seen those swords they carry?"

I picked up my bundle and unwrapped it. "Have you seen the sword I carry?"

"I don't know, Beryl." He shook his head. "There are a lot of ways that could go wrong."

I paused. He might be right. This... was exactly one of those situations Bice had been warning me about. I came up with a quick plan and rushed out to try it. Maybe I should wait, think things through here…

"Do it," Kelly said.

We both looked at her with some surprise. She held her water glass so tight, her knuckles were white. "I need Rick back. Do whatever it takes, Beryl. I know you can do it."

"Well, yeah. But… I don't want to rush off without thinking it through here. Marcus has a point."

"I don't care."

"What are you going to do with the guard after you get the information from him?" Marcus asked. "Are you going to kill him?"

"No! I don't do that."

"No? So you'll let him go?" Marcus got to his feet.

"I don't know. Maybe."

"And then he'll run back to his boss and tell everyone that you're on the way to rescue Rick. How's that going to work out for you?"

"Okay. So I'll tie him up and keep him stashed away until we have Rick back. Then I'll let him go."

"Where are you going to stash him?" Marcus took Kelly's glass and went to refill it. He paused at the entrance to the kitchen. "It's not going to be here. You have to keep Cerise and me out of this."

"You're right." I nodded. "We can't let anyone know about you. I'll find an empty building and hide him there."

Marcus returned with the water. "See? Talking things out makes a difference."

"I have a friend who would love to meet you," I told him.

Marcus laughed and handed the water to Kelly. "So what will you do if he doesn't have the information you want?"

I didn't know how to answer that one. The longer we talked, the less convinced I was that any of this would work. But what alternatives did I have?

"You're sure neither you nor Cerise could get this information any other way?"

"We've been trying for two days." He spread out his arms. "We just don't know the right people for something like this."

"Then it looks like I'll have to go find the right person." I slung the sword on my back.

Kelly jumped up and came toward me. "Beryl, once you find him, I'll do anything to get him back. Anything."

I nodded. "He's my best friend, Kelly. I'm not abandoning him. No matter what it takes."

For one very brief moment, the thought of leaving Rick in custody teased my brain. It would leave Kelly to me. I dismissed it as soon as it came, but the idea tried a couple more times. "What kind of a man do you think I am?" I muttered.

Kelly looked up at me. "You're a good man. I've always known that."

I tried to smile. "With an endorsement like that, what do I have to lose?"

I slipped out into the night.

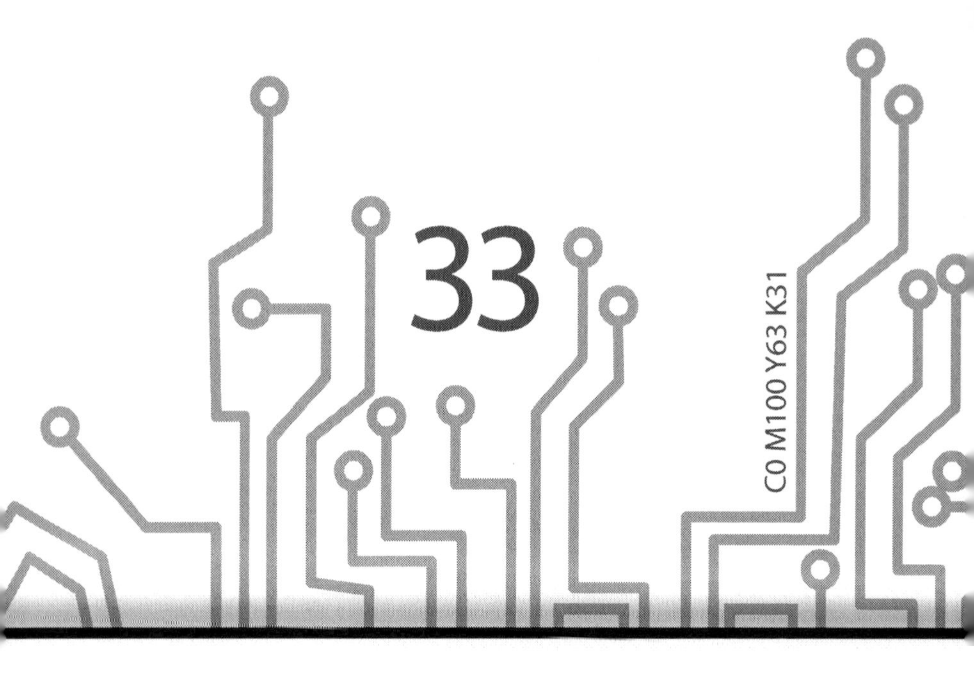

33

Prowling the dark alleys of an unfamiliar city with a sword, searching for my prey… not exactly something I ever saw myself doing. And it still didn't feel entirely right. Even if it worked, what would I do once I knew where they were keeping Rick? Storm the place all by myself? I—we—would have to come up with another plan. And that might throw off our plan to get the books.

Well, if it did, so be it. I would trade these mysterious books for Rick every day of the week. Mazarine would lose his mind, of course, but I didn't care.

Finding the Crimson Elite turned out to be harder than I expected. I assumed I would run across a patrol or something in a few minutes. I mean, it happened twice when I tried to leave this city the last time. But maybe they had been on extra duty because of the incident at the Flame, because I couldn't find them now. When you don't want them, they're everywhere; when you do, they're nowhere.

After about an hour, I found a pair of guards wandering the streets. It would have been better to find only one, but I doubted I would be so lucky. Two would have to do.

I circled ahead of where they were walking, and found a strip of shops that appeared closed down. I couldn't tell if they were permanently closed, or just for the night. None of them had any lights on. The only illumination came from a single street light. As the guards drew nearer, I took the light out with a well-placed rock. Okay, maybe the first two rocks weren't so well-placed, but the third one did the job.

"Hey, did you see that?" I heard one of them ask. I crouched in one of the store openings, waiting for them to pass on the opposite side of the road.

"What?"

"The light went out." That voice sounded young, maybe my age.

"Happens all the time." That one was older.

"Fewmets. It sure made things dark here."

I gathered myself. Any moment now.

"You aren't scared of the dark, are you, Russ?"

"I just like to see where I'm going, you know?"

I triggered a major boost to my legs and shot across the street. Before they even knew I was coming, I arrived. Using my momentum, I snagged one guard's head and slammed it against the brick wall. He went down like a sack of potatoes. I whipped my sword out and aimed it at the other guard's neck. "Don't move," I warned.

"Holy Incarnadine!" he gasped. It was the young one, Russ.

I knew the darkness kept him from getting a good look at me, but I pivoted just to be sure, keeping the distant lights behind my back. Russ held both his hands out away from his sides and kept still.

"All right, Russ. That is your name, right? You don't need to know mine," I growled, trying to sound impressive. "All I want is some information, and you won't get hurt."

"What do you want?"

"You arrested a young man a couple days ago, a spy from Atramentous. Know about him?"

"Yeah, yeah, I heard about that." He squinted, trying to get a look at me. I ducked my head a little more.

"I want to know where he's being held."

"You… you're my age, aren't you? Who are you?"

I let the cold edge of my sword rest against his neck. "You don't want to disappoint me, Russ. That's all you need to know. Where is the spy?"

His hands drifted down a little. "I can't see your chromark. Are you from Atramentous too?" The nervousness was leaving his voice. Not good.

"No," I answered. "I'm… from nowhere. I'm achromatic."

"Achromatic? What's that?"

"It means no color. Now answer my question!"

"I don't think I will. I don't think you mean your threats." He snatched at his own sword hilt. Fewmets. The last thing I wanted was a sword duel in the dark.

I boosted my arm and lunged. I smacked the hilt of my sword into his forehead. He staggered back, but managed to draw his own sword. He reeled, trying to recover from my blow.

"I warned you!" I boosted everything and charged him. I stabbed along his left side, trying to only catch his uniform. But his gasp told me I scratched along his rib cage. My sword penetrated the store wall behind him, pinning him for a second or two.

I released my sword and grabbed his right wrist with both hands. I twisted, and his sword dropped to the ground. I put my left hand on his throat, then yanked my own sword back out with the other.

"How are you so fast?" The nervousness returned to his voice. I had him now.

"Listen, I could tear you apart right now," I said. "But I don't want to. Just tell me where the spy is being held."

"I… I'm one of the Crimson Elite. Our blood is sacred to the holy Incarnadine. He will take vengeance on any who spill it!"

"Do you seriously believe that?"

"What?"

I sighed. "Do you seriously believe that the stupid dragon can tell whether or not one of his guards has lost some blood?"

"He-he promises."

"So if you cut yourself shaving, does he descend from the heavens and incinerate your razor?" It was the first thing that popped into my head.

"No, I mean… I don't—"

"The dragons are dying, Russ. One of them is already dead. The others will follow. You have to decide whether they're worth your loyalty. Do you want to go down with them?"

"You can't be serious. You think—"

"I don't have time to debate this with you," I interrupted. "The spy. Where is he?" I triggered a small boost to my hand and squeezed his neck a little.

"All right, all right!" he gasped. I released the pressure.

"He's at the fourth precinct office," he said. "But they're moving him tomorrow. Incarnadine himself wants to see him."

"Where is this office?"

He gave me directions, which I made him repeat twice. Assuming he told the truth, I calculated it would take me at least half an hour to get there. And I would have to do it now. If they took Rick to see the dragon tomorrow, I doubted we would ever see him again.

"All right, Russ, listen to me." I had to give him a final chance. "I want you to think long and hard about tonight. The dragons are not gods. You don't need to serve them. We're going to be free of them one day. You can join that effort instead."

"You're crazy."

"Maybe." I knocked his head against the wall, then dropped him next to his partner. It would have been fun to add a red-wearing warrior to our company, but I guess this wasn't the time. I considered tying both of them up, but that would take longer, and I didn't know how many hours of darkness I had left. At any rate, by the time they woke up, I should already be at this office. Just for fun, I did take his short sword. Now I had two blades.

I set off down the street, rehearsing the directions. This wasn't right. I should go back to the others, work out a solid plan, like Bice would say… but I didn't have time. Only a few hours to rescue Rick.

What would I do when I got there? If this precinct office was anything like the Viridian Guard stations, I might run into anywhere from four to a dozen more Crimson Elite. And I'm sure Rick would be locked up in some kind of cell. I never saw those myself, but they couldn't be easy to open.

I raced down the streets of Incarnadine, swords in both hands. Part of me thought I must look amazingly hue… but the rest of me knew the truth: I looked ridiculous. No one over the age of ten would run down city streets, especially not at night. And with swords?

I thought it would take me thirty minutes to reach my destination. It took thirty-five. I slowed to a walk and stopped in a dark spot, watching the building.

It stood apart from other buildings, with an alley down either side. Brick walls. Glass doors lined by two enormous windows, under a long overhang. I moved closer to see into the windows. The interior was brightly lit. I could see two of the Crimson Elite… talking to a draconic.

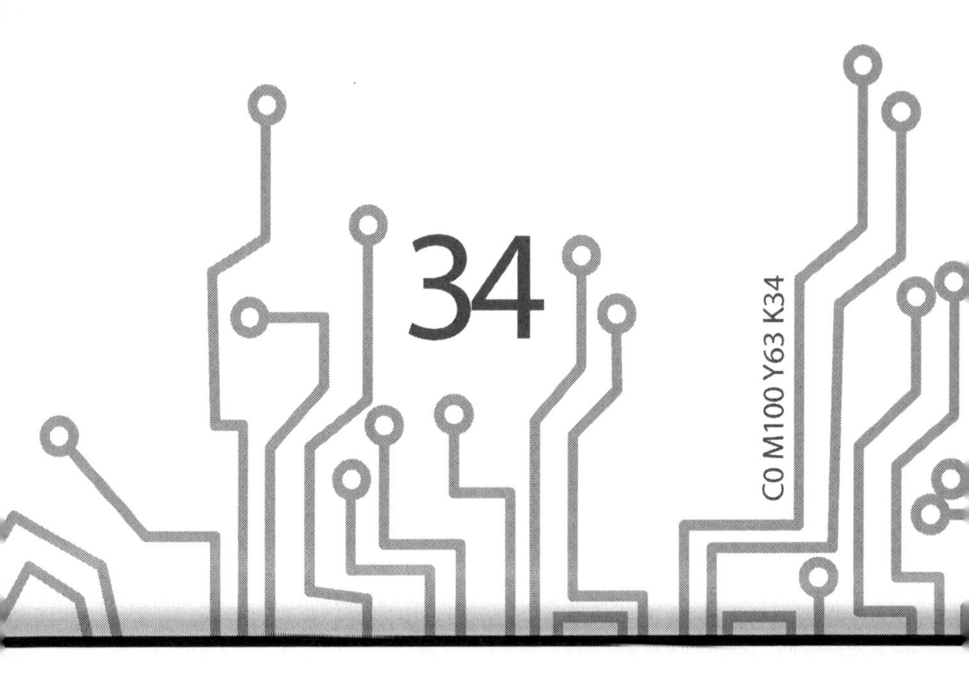

34

The draconic did not look familiar. It was shorter than Zidanta Red, maybe not even six feet tall. I guess it might be a younger one, except… according to Protogonus Blue, it still held memories from previous lives. What would that be like, suddenly gaining memories of an entire lifetime or two? I dismissed the thought. All it really meant was draconics had hundreds of years of hating humans. And yet… Protogonus Blue at least appeared to be changing. If it were possible to raise a draconic from an early age, to teach it to care about humans, to work against its old memories… No, nonsense. Focus on the present.

How could I, alone, take down a draconic and any number of the Crimson Elite? I would have the element of surprise at first, but not for long. And I had my implant. They had… a lot more. So far, I only saw them carrying short swords. I knew they had those flame-launchers on the battlefield, but that didn't seem like a weapon they would use indoors. Still, I couldn't completely rule out projectile weapons. Hadn't Rick mentioned crossbows or something?

"A projectile weapon sure would come in handy for me," I muttered. If I charged in fast enough, found and released Rick, then he could help me fight our way back out. A desperate plan, but maybe all I had.

Wait… I needed something to throw… I looked across the street and couldn't believe it. Kelly would roll her eyes at my luck this time. A hardware store.

I made my way to the door and made sure no one from the Elite office was watching. A quick boost helped me break the lock. I slipped inside and found what I wanted. I came back out, pushing a wheelbarrow, with a number of tools stuck into my belt.

I walked out into the middle of the street. If anyone inside the other building saw me, they weren't alarmed yet. I took a breath and boosted my arms. I slung the wheelbarrow in a circle and let it fly. It smashed through the huge front windows of the precinct office in an explosion of glass. At the same time, I boosted my legs and charged in right behind it. I pulled two hammers from my belt.

As expected, those inside turned away to avoid flying glass. That gave me a second or two. I threw each of the hammers at the two visible guards. Without waiting to see what happened to them, I drew both swords and charged the draconic.

I did not take it by surprise. Exploding glass did not intimidate a draconic. And whether I forgot or just neglected to do it, I didn't give myself extra speed. The draconic reached out past my swords as they approached, grabbed the front of my shirt, and redirected my momentum. It threw me behind it. I rolled and scrambled to my feet. I don't know how I didn't slice myself up while still holding on to both swords.

"Green!" the draconic roared. I'm not sure if it was an alarm or an accusation.

Either way, I didn't wait. I charged it again, this time, boosting everything. Out of the corner of my eye, I saw one of the Elite rushing at me. But he wouldn't reach me before I reached my target.

With my extra speed, I slashed up with my own sword. I caught the underside of the draconic's arm and knocked it upward. My left hand stabbed with the short sword, catching it right in the stomach. A satisfying roar of pain erupted from its throat.

My eyes locked on the Elite rushing me, his own sword raised. I spun and kicked his legs out from under him. As long as I kept the boosts flowing, I could move so much faster than the guards. I knew better than to underestimate the draconic, though.

Instead, I found the next door. I vaulted over a desk and hit the door with my shoulder at full speed. Not only did it fly open, it came loose from the hinges. I stumbled into a long hallway.

Two more Crimson Elite emerged from another door a few feet away. I ran into them with the broken door, knocking them down. I even ran over them and the door for good measure.

"Rick!" I yelled. "Rick!"

Something flew past, scratching my left bicep. I spun and saw one of the first Elite from the lobby, already reloading what looked like a very small crossbow. I knew they had ranged weapons!

I couldn't go back and deal with him. No time. I charged down the hallway, making myself as unpredictable a target as possible. I dodged, spun, ducked, kicked off the wall into the air, and then dove, sliding along the floor. Another crossbow bolt flew over me.

I rolled to my feet just as another guard stepped out of a door in front of me. I turned my arm and smashed him in the face with my elbow.

By now, multiple voices were yelling. "Get him!" "We've been invaded!" "He's after the spy!" "Where did he go?" And above it all, the roar of the draconic: "I want his head!"

I tried yelling Rick's name again, but I doubt I could be heard over the cacophony.

The hallway made an abrupt right turn. Right as I turned, another bolt struck the wall behind me. How did that guy reload so fast?

This is what I had been looking for. Five doors lined the left side of the hall, all of them with barred windows. Cells.

The fourth door down flew open and Rick stepped into the hallway, holding the remains of a lock in his cybernetic hand. "About time," he called. He could have broken the lock at any time, of course. But he couldn't fight his way out of here. That's where I came in.

I tossed him the short sword. "How many?" he asked as he caught it.

"At least four, plus the draconic behind me," I said. "One or more of them have crossbows. Is there another way out?"

"How should I know?"

We could race through the halls aimlessly, without knowing whether we could get out, or go back. But there was no way we could make it down that long hallway without getting shot. Unless…

I grabbed the door of Rick's cell. "Break the hinges!" Between his cyb hand and my strength, we ripped the door loose. Using the barred window as a handhold, I held the door as a shield. "Get behind me."

With Rick at my back, I turned the corner and started back down the hall. Two crossbow bolts slammed into the door immediately. A third struck it a few seconds later, and a fourth came through the window, narrowly missing my head.

From what I could tell from my brief looks through the window, our opponents had chosen to regroup in the lobby area. They knew we had to come back that way. Three of the Elite waited in the doorway, firing their crossbows at us. At the very least, the draconic waited behind them, and maybe more guards.

"Be ready for anything," I told Rick just before we reached the lobby. At the last moment, I gave myself an extra huge boost of speed and slammed my door into at least two of the guards. Two bolts passed harmlessly behind me from either side, the ambush I anticipated.

I took hold of the door and spun it around like I had the wheelbarrow. I caught one guard as he backpedaled, knocking him down. Then I threw the door straight at the red draconic charging at me from across the room. I didn't have time to see what Rick did, but I heard a gasp of pain that didn't sound like him.

The draconic batted down the door with ease, leveled its hand at me and shouted something I didn't hear.

A force like an invisible brick wall brought me to an abrupt and painful halt. My legs kept moving and I fell backward. Fewmets. I guess all the red draconics had the power. I was hoping Zidanta Red was the only one.

"Whatever powers you may possess, you are still nothing against one of Incarnadine's chosen!" The draconic took an ominous step forward and leveled both hands. It didn't seem to mind the bleeding puncture wound in its stomach.

"Say hello to the Chromatic Hells for me!" Rick snarled. I looked back and saw him aiming two crossbows simultaneously. He pulled both triggers.

I don't know how he made that shot, but both bolts struck the draconic's eyes. It screamed and unleashed another wave of power. Since I was still on the ground, it passed over me. I scrambled up in time to see Rick hit the ground too.

I grabbed his shirt and yanked him to his feet. Ignoring the flailing draconic and the other two guards who were getting to their feet, we ran out into the darkness.

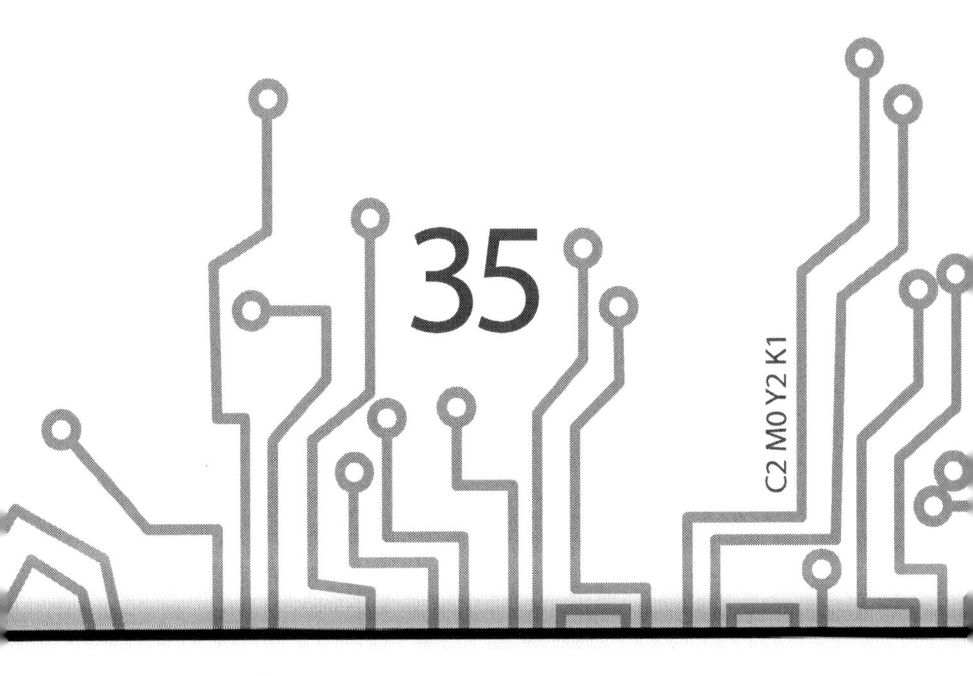

35

The roars followed us as we raced down the street.

"How is that thing still alive after you shot it in both eyes?" I yelled. "Wait, better question: how did you shoot that thing in both eyes?"

Rick waved the mini crossbow. "I used to use one of these all the time. Haven't had one since I left Atramentous."

"This way!" I led him down a dark alley, turned a corner, then another. We zigged and zagged through the unfamiliar streets, putting as much distance between us and the precinct office as we could.

Unfortunately, this also meant we got lost. I had to find the edge of town and orient myself toward the Flame and the mountains before I could even begin to find my way back to the apartments. By the time we slipped into Marcus and Cerise's home building, the eastern sky was beginning to brighten.

I don't know whether Kelly slept at all. She met us at the door, looking pale, exhausted, and disheveled. But she was thrilled to see Rick, and even gave me a fierce hug of gratitude. I tried to ignore the rest of their reunion and stretched out on the couch. I felt pretty exhausted myself.

Cerise emerged from the bedroom wearing a maroon robe. "So, how much of a disaster did you create this time?"

"Rescued Rick." I yawned. "Beat up some Crimson Elite and a draconic. Smashed some windows and doors. Other than that, it was a quiet night."

"Hm. I guess I'll have to wait until I go to work to find out how upset they are."

"Oh, and Rick..." I waved in his direction. "Rick shot out the draconic's eyes."

Cerise raised her eyebrows, but I closed my eyes. So tired. "Does anyone want breakfast?" she asked. "I have to make my own and get ready for work."

I turned her down. In fact, I barely had enough energy to do that much. While the others talked quietly, I fell asleep. I dreamed about breaking windows for some reason.

When I woke, I found Kelly and Rick asleep on the floor next to the couch, wrapped in blankets. Cerise and Marcus were gone. I found myself a glass of grape juice, and settled back to wait for the others. From the light outside, it looked to be early afternoon. Then I noticed a clock reading 2:38. I had been living in the country too long.

Kelly woke first. She patted Rick, smiled at me, then left us for the bathroom. When she returned, she had brushed her hair back, and gotten her own glass of water. She took her place on Marcus' favorite chair.

"Thank you, Beryl," she said in a soft voice.

"He's my best friend," I answered in an equally low voice. "I couldn't leave him there."

"I knew you wouldn't."

Silence stretched out for a few minutes.

"You, uh, feeling better?" I asked.

Kelly nodded. "I'm not completely okay, but better." She looked down at Rick. "It helps having him here. He... keeps me warm. He's so warm."

I didn't need to hear that.

"So, um... everyone all right back at the Asylum?" Kelly looked back at me.

"Yeah, yeah. Well, except Caedan. I got him hurt. But he'll be okay."

"Caedan's hurt? How?"

I didn't want to tell the story twice, so I pointed at Rick. "We'll talk when he's up."

She nodded. We waited. My thoughts wandered. I tried not to think about the "warm" comment. The adventure of the previous night didn't change anything as far as planning went. How many days did we have now? Five, right?

After another twenty minutes, I decided I was hungry after all. I found a box of wheat crackers and brought it back to the couch. I offered some to Kelly, but she shook her head.

"I'll take some," Rick said. His voice startled both of us.

"How long have you been awake?" I demanded.

"A minute or two." He sat up and stretched.

I tossed him the box of crackers. "Feeling okay?"

"Yeah, I'm good. So… you know what we've been up to." He glanced at Kelly. "How about you?"

I gave a quick recap of the past few days: going home, experimenting with the wings, Stacy's news, and the ill-fated trip to the Hub. Rick was especially interested in that part.

"They had one of those things set up on all the tracks?"

"All except their own," I said. "They were still building one. Wait… no. There were only four, not five." I thought back and tried to map it out in my head. "They didn't have one on the track to… Caesious."

"So the other four dragons."

I nodded, wondering what that could mean.

"They may have just not built that one yet," Kelly put in. "You said they were still building one. Maybe they're going to build the fifth."

"Maybe. We don't even know what they are."

Rick looked off toward the front door. He was thinking about something; I knew his looks by now. "What is it?"

He shook his head and looked back. "Nothing. Just weird. Auric isn't taking part in this war. Maybe he's going to do something to the other cities to make them stop fighting and go back to the way things were."

"If so," I pondered, "then he'll probably wait to see what happens with this peace gathering."

"And that's when you want to steal the books?" Kelly asked,

"Right. Incarnadine will be sending at least one draconic there. And now Rick has taken another one out. The fewer draconics around, the better."

"I'm guessing you want to use the wings to get into the Flame at the top," Rick said.

I grinned. "They're waiting outside the city with our four-wheelers." I snatched the cracker box back from him and set it on the end table. "If this is the Flame, I would fly in this way…" I maneuvered a cracker in near the top of the box. "I could get in at the top balcony, find the books and get back out. But Peri says they're too bulky to carry with me. So I'll use one of Loden's balloons to float them down. I figured Marcus could be ready with the truck to pick them up."

"Makes sense." Rick nodded. "It's the start of a plan, anyway."

"No one is used to the sight of someone flying," Kelly protested. "If even one person sees you, it won't be long before everyone is watching, including the bad guys."

"Yeah," I agreed. "Which is why I'm here to talk it over with you. What we need is a distraction, something to keep everyone's eyes focused at the ground level."

"Something so interesting they won't think to look up." Rick got up and walked around the room.

"It would have to be big," Kelly said. "We're not talking about turning the heads of a couple of guards."

"No, we want everyone inside the Flame, and anyone in the surrounding blocks paying attention." I scattered a number of crackers around the box. "What would that take? A fire?"

"A fire?" Rick repeated. "In Incarnadine. Next to the Flame."

I chuckled. "A little cliche?"

"A little." He resumed walking. He passed behind the couch and grabbed the cracker box for himself again. "No, it has to be more than a fire. That would only draw the emergency services and some onlookers. It's not enough."

"Two fires?"

Rick tossed a cracker at me. I caught it and ate it.

"It has to involve a lot of people," Kelly repeated.

"Maybe we get Bice to knock down a couple of buildings with that power of his," Rick mumbled. "Remember how the draconic took down the old church?"

"We don't know if he could do that here," I said. "He says the power only works in certain places."

"That red draconic used it last night."

"True. But I'd rather not put Bice in that much danger. And I still don't think it's enough."

"There's a war on," Rick said. "Whatever we do, it might be taken as sabotage from Viridia or Atramentous. Especially if one of us is seen."

"You need a lot of people involved," Kelly said. "None of what you're suggesting does that yet."

"Do you have an idea?"

"Of course I do. A lot of people. Drawing attention. A big commotion. You know what you call that, right?"

I shook my head.

Kelly grinned. "A riot."

36

"What's a riot?"

Kelly rolled her eyes. "Honestly, Beryl. Did you pay any attention at all during your Learning Years?"

"Sometimes. I passed, didn't I?"

Rick leaned over the couch. "A riot is a crowd of angry people causing chaos."

Kelly nodded. "Basically. But it may start as a simple protest: where a lot of people are complaining about something."

"And that leads to chaos?" I didn't quite follow.

"We haven't had anything like this in many years," Kelly explained. "The last riots in The Circle were probably the Grain Riots from, um, around 60 years ago, I think."

"Sixty-four," Rick said. Kelly raised her eyebrows at him.

"People created chaos over grain?"

Kelly threw a pillow at me. "Beryl, just listen. From what I remember, there was some kind of disease or drought or something that destroyed a lot of the grain that year. And that meant the cities were short on bread."

"But some people did get bread," Rick chimed in. "They rationed it, and started with the dragon's most loyal citizens."

"No surprise there," I said.

"Of course. Everyone expects them to get the best of anything. But this wasn't the best bread. It was the only bread."

"And people got really angry," Kelly took over. "The history books blame it on a handful of agitators, but I think it went further than that."

"But aren't we talking about becoming a handful of agitators?" Rick asked.

"Well, yeah. But I think people were already upset. The agitators, whoever they might have been, only sparked things. People left their homes and jobs and marched in the streets. Some of it was just complaining, a protest, like I said. They carried signs and stuff. Mostly, they just wanted their leaders to know they were upset."

"But it didn't stop there," Rick said. "The angriest people started getting violent. They broke windows, smashed things, and got into fights with the police groups."

"Huh." I considered the concept. "That could work. Lots of angry people in the street. No one would be looking up."

"That's the idea."

Kelly shifted on the chair. "But like we just said, people were already angry, before they got stirred up."

"People are angry," I said. "Or at least, they're afraid and stressed. Because of the war. Right?"

Rick came around from behind the couch. "That's right. They may not be angry, maybe, but they're upset. Food supplies are starting to dwindle. Some items aren't on the shelf any more. We could start rumors about rationing."

"I don't know," Kelly said. "I don't know if we should try to duplicate the Grain Riots exactly. This isn't the same thing."

"We should wait on Cerise and Marcus," I said. "They know the people of Incarnadine much better than we do."

The others agreed. Our conversation turned to other topics for a while. Eventually, we made ourselves a meal, though I couldn't say whether it was a late lunch or early dinner. Marcus returned in the early evening. He listened to our ideas, then agreed we should wait for Cerise. She arrived much later. As she ate, she listened to Kelly summarize our discussion.

"You want to start a riot near the Flame?" Cerise stared at us, forgetting her food.

"That's the general idea," Rick said. "But you know the people around here. Do you think they could be pushed over the edge?"

Cerise hesitated. "People are scared," she admitted. "But maybe not for the reasons you think. Your actions have contributed to it, in fact."

Cool. We were working on the plan before we even came up with a plan. "How so?"

"Think about it. What have the citizens of Incarnadine heard about in the past week?"

"A Viridian terrorist invaded the Flame and tried to kill the holy Incarnadine," Marcus said.

"I didn't—"

"And then a spy from Atramentous was arrested trying to finish the job," Cerise interrupted. "And then he escaped custody with a Viridian spy, possibly the same one from before, or maybe another one!"

"They're scared of us!" Kelly exclaimed.

"There's a war on," Cerise added. "They were already worried about the greens and blacks. After all, they killed Caesious, the blue dragon! They might try to do the same here. Two spies in the past week! They could be anywhere now! Who knows what they're planning?" She grinned.

"Would people march in the street over that, though?" I wondered. "Why protest against an enemy? If there really were Viridian spies, would they be discouraged by people in the streets?"

"No, no, no," Rick said. He leaned forward from his perch on the arm of the couch. "It starts that way."

"What does?"

"The march. It starts as a show of solidarity for the Crimson Elite and the great Incarnadine." He stood and raised his fist. "Glory to the holy dragon god and his servants!"

"Okay, so… we've gone from protesting to celebrating? I don't get it."

Rick took Kelly's hand and pulled her to her feet. "Picture it. The people are marching, shouting their support for their god."

"Holy Incarnadine!" Kelly cried, getting into it.

"They're using the event to mask their fears. Those haven't changed. They're scared. They're nervous. And now they're in a huge crowd of other scared and nervous people." He pulled Kelly along with him in a mock march across the room. They turned around at the wall and faced us. "And then…"

We waited.

"Yes?" Marcus asked.

Rick shrugged. "I don't know. And then we do something to set them off."

"How do you take fear and turn it into anger?" Cerise asked.

"By showing them their fears are justified," Marcus said slowly. "And that the ones they depend on to keep them safe are failing."

"They are failing," I said. "They don't have any of us."

"We can work with that," Rick said, stepping back into the center of the room. "We need to make them believe the Crimson Elite is not doing its job."

"So the crowd gathers in front of the Flame, scared of spies and terrorists, angry that they're not being caught, and then…" I shrugged. "I still don't get the last part."

"The Crimson Elite has to be seen to fail," Marcus said. "And that our enemies have gotten away with something. Something… horrible."

"Blinding a draconic wasn't enough?" I muttered.

"No, it wasn't," Kelly said. "Come on, Beryl. The draconics aren't loved, even by the most ardent servants of the dragons. You know how people see them."

She was right. "What then?"

No one said anything. Had we hit the limits of our planning ability? There had to be something…

"The grain," I said.

"We're back to that?" Rick chuckled.

"No, seriously. It makes sense." I pointed at him. "You said that food supplies are dwindling. They aren't gathering in new crops. In fact, we saw some that had been burned, right?"

"Sure."

I stood. "So what if we did something to some of the stored grain? I mean, food? Set a warehouse on fire or something?"

"That's something that would hurt the common people," Marcus said. "Like us."

I got the implication in his words, but didn't have time to deal with it. "But if it happened during the march or rally or whatever, and word spread that Viridian terrorists did it… would people panic?"

"I don't know," Cerise said. "Would they panic, or just be in shock?"

Rick grinned. "What if one of these sinister spies was uncovered right there at the rally? In their very midst?"

"That would push them over the edge, I think," Marcus said. "But they'd also probably kill that spy on the spot. Who'd volunteer for something like that?"

"I would do it, if I weren't already doing the other job," I said. "I can't be in two places at once."

"Cerise will be at work, and Marcus will be driving the truck," Kelly said. "Rick and I can't do everything else."

"We're going to need some more help," I finished her thought. "But still, I don't like the idea of leaving someone to die in a violent crowd."

"Maybe we won't have to," Kelly said, a gleam in her eye. "I have another idea."

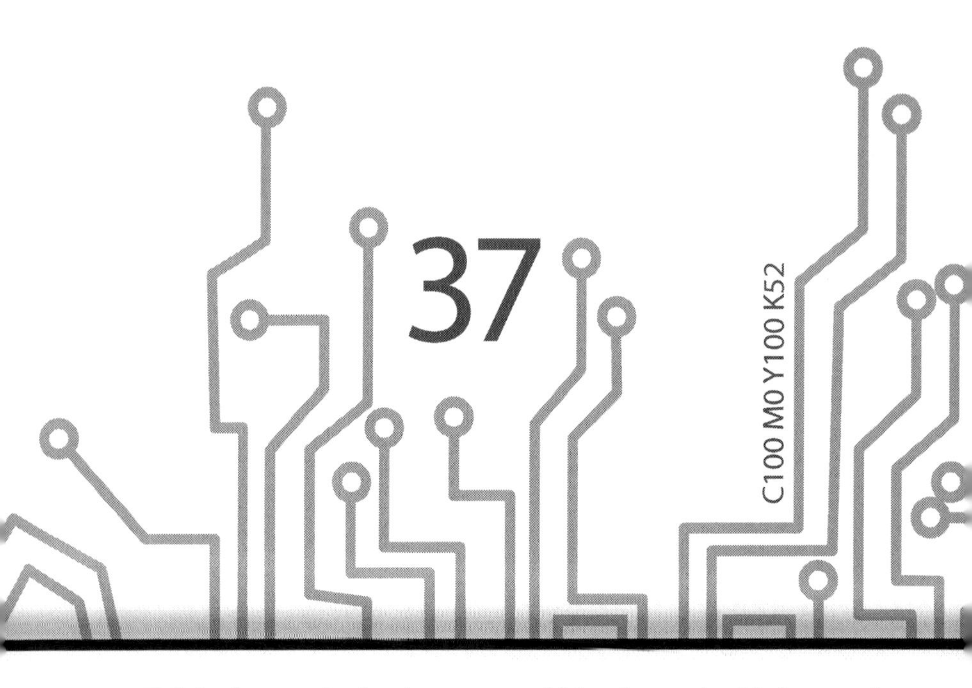

37

Kelly's plan involved judicious use of false chromarks. Unfortunately, Marcus reported that the Crimson Elite had confiscated all of his theater's supplies of the colored makeup. I would need to visit Stacy again to get what we needed. I added that to the list.

"How many people do I need to bring back?" I wondered.

"I can handle the fire alone," Rick said. "That puts Kelly in charge of the riot. How many helpers do you need, babe?"

She frowned at him for some reason. "Who can we get?" she asked. "You said Caedan is unavailable. Don would be helpful for the one bit, but we need more agitators, and I can't see him doing that."

"I don't know if any of our people would be good at that," I said. "Lovat could work his way through a crowd, but I don't know if adults would pay attention to anything he said."

"Priests wouldn't be much good," Rick said. "And Bice is still too well known, anyway. We're running out of names."

"Peri wants to help," I told him. "I just don't know if I can see him in that job. He's not very loud."

"We need Stacy," Kelly said. "You've got to visit her, anyway. Maybe it's time she got into things."

"I'll try." I looked at her dubiously. "I don't think she'll agree."

"I can help in the lead-up," Marcus said, "but…"

"But we can't risk you too much because we need you on the truck," I finished. "I know. I guess I'll have to talk Stacy into it."

"Tell her I begged," Kelly said. "We need her."

I nodded, and glanced at the window. "Well, it's already dark. I'll sneak out and see what I can do."

"We both will," Rick said. "We'll need both four-wheelers to carry that many people. And I can't show my face here any more."

"In the meantime, we'll start the arrangements," Cerise declared. "Schedule this rally, start spreading the news. I'll talk to the Crimson Elite at work and make sure some of them will come and be cheered on."

"I'll print up flyers," Marcus said. "We'll make sure everyone in the city knows."

We discussed a few more details before Rick and I prepared to leave. While he said goodbye to Kelly, I explained the use of the talker to Cerise and Marcus. "When this goes down, I want you to have one with you in the truck," I told Marcus. "I don't know who'll have the other one at that point. Probably Kelly. That way, you can let everyone know the books are safe, and we can all get out."

After a few more minutes, Rick gathered up his gear and we left the apartment again. By now, we were used to working our way through the darkened streets and alleys. More patrols were out this night, though, making our progress slower than ever. By the time we reached our hiding spot outside the city, midnight was approaching.

We concealed the wings, readied the four-wheelers, and then discussed the best plan for travel. "Should we both go straight to the Asylum?" I asked.

Rick frowned. "Can you find your way to Viridia from here?"

"It's almost due southwest, isn't it? I can pretty much follow the railroad."

"But that takes you straight through the Hub."

"I'll have to circle it on the south side, I guess. I think it'll still save us some time, rather than going to the Asylum, down to Viridia, and then back." I climbed onto my four-wheeler. "I'll just meet you back here."

"Right. You get Stacy. I get Don and Lovat. Not sure that's fair."

"You know it's the only way. Stacy… hasn't been too thrilled with you since…"

"Since I started being with Kelly. I know. She's told me." Rick got onto the other four-wheeler. "Watch out for any armies. Just because they have a peace conference coming up doesn't mean there isn't any fighting happening now."

"Same to you. And watch out for Auric's soldiers around the Hub."

We started the vehicles and took off. A few moments later, we exchanged waves and moved in different directions.

Here I was again. I wondered how many times I would end up criss-crossing The Circle before all this was over. Pretty amazing stuff for a guy who never traveled more than four or five miles from his birthplace for his first seventeen years of life. A year ago, I could barely imagine traveling to another city. Now here I was driving—driving!—back and forth between them on a regular basis.

I drove until I grew sleepy, then found a place to hide and sleep in an orchard. The next day, I circled far out from the Hub before turning toward Viridia. Rick's concerns were valid, as I did lose my way a couple of times. I don't think I lost too much time before getting back on track. I arrived on the outskirts of Viridia in early evening.

It had only been a little over a week since I came here with Kelly and Lovat. But this felt different, somehow. I was alone, in Viridia again. I walked down the street of the city I knew so well, yet hated so much. That wasn't fair. It wasn't that I hated the city, or at least its people. But I hated the green dragon and his servants and the society they created and controlled here. I would never rest until it was torn down, all of it.

And after seeing the other cities, I hated Viridia even more. At least Caesious and Incarnadine had identities and architecture. Viridia had… concrete. Why? Did the green dragon despise human creativity that much? I shook my head at the cruelty and pointlessness of it all.

I arrived at the back door of the theater once again. Stacy wouldn't be expecting me. Don and Lovat had been here a couple of days ago. Wait, more than a couple. Ugh. Keeping track of the days with all this travel back and forth was getting complicated.

Only a single light illuminated the back alley. I didn't see any light coming from inside. I knocked on the door and waited. Nothing happened. When more knocks didn't produce anything else, I tried the door. This time, it was locked. I considered breaking it, but… I couldn't be sure Stacy would be the first one to arrive the next day.

I sighed and looked around. It wouldn't be the first time I had spent the night in an alley. And at least Viridia wasn't cold, like Incarnadine. I found a place out of sight and curled up to wait.

Sunrise came and went. No one showed up. My stomach grumbled more and more as time ticked by. What little food I'd brought was still with the four-wheeler hidden outside the city.

At mid-morning, a lone male showed up, unlocked the door, and entered. I could ask him, but I'd probably come across as a crazy fan looking for an autograph. I waited. If Stacy didn't show up before too long, I would go find something to eat and come back.

It was almost noon when she arrived, escorted by four or five other people, Olive among them. I waited until they were inside, then approached the door. I brushed myself off and knocked.

Someone I didn't know answered. "I'm here to see Stacy Moss," I told him. "My name's Beryl. She knows me." He looked me over and rolled his eyes. The door shut.

I waited. Should I knock again? Just when I began to suspect I'd been ignored, the door flew open again. Stacy looked out at me, a scowl on her face.

"Really?" she demanded, folding her arms. "You use your real name? Intelligence is not your forte, is it?"

"It's a common enough name," I said.

"That's not the point." She sighed and looked around. "Come in, you idiot."

She led the way back to her dressing room. We passed the guy who opened the door for me. He gave me another curious look. Inside, Stacy flopped into her chair. "What is it this time, Beryl?"

"We've got a plan to get the books from Incarnadine," I explained. I fingered the green jumpsuit costume hanging on the back of the door. "I, uh, need a few things. Some more of that makeup to create chromarks."

"I didn't give you enough?"

"We need some green and black too. It's complicated."

"Okay, I should have that. Anything else?"

"Yeah, you're not going to like this…" I turned to face her. "We need you."

"For what?"

"To come to Incarnadine."

"That is not going to happen, Beryl." She shook her head. "It's impossible."

"We need you," I repeated. "The plan won't work otherwise."

"Even if I wanted to come, which I don't," she answered, "I can't. I have a performance in a few days."

"This would be a performance." I waved my arms. "An important one."

"Not as important as the one I have." She smiled. "I'm performing for the peace summit."

38

I stared at Stacy with what must have been a very stupid look. "You're what?"

"I'm performing at the peace summit." She tilted her head. "You know, the one in Caesious?"

"I didn't know draconics had any interest in, um, theater." I couldn't even imagine Troilus Green or Zidanta Red watching a stage play. Maybe Protogonus Blue. Maybe.

"It's all for a show of unity," Stacy explained. "There will be a singer or two, and then I'm doing a brief performance with an actor from Amaranth. We'll be showing them how humans are united, in spite of the war, and then they'll go upstairs for the real summit."

"Upstairs?"

"Yes, that's the latest news I have for you: the peace summit is taking place at Caesious Tower. They'll be meeting in the exact place the dragon lived."

Under other circumstances, this would be vital information. But right now, all I could think about was… "We really need you, Stacy."

"There's no way I can miss this, Beryl. My absence would create too many questions. Besides… what better place could I be to gain more information?"

I sat down on a large trunk. "I don't know what to do. Kelly can't handle that part of the plan by herself."

Stacy leaned over her chair. "Tell me about it. What's this plan now?"

I recounted all the ideas we conceived and how they all fit together. "Rick's gone to get Don and Lovat," I concluded, "and maybe Peri, I guess. But they're not enough. We needed you. We need someone who can act, and really stir up the crowd."

"Can you switch Marcus for someone else in the plan? He's got the ability to do that."

"He has to drive the truck." I put my elbows on my knees and hung my head. "He's the only one who can do that… or at least the only one he'll allow to drive the truck, I guess. And that's kind of the most important job, since he'll end up with the actual books."

Stacy thought for a minute. "I wish I knew someone else available," she said. "I know a girl in Atramentous that could do it, but it would take too long to go there, explain everything to her, and convince her to join the cause."

"No one here, then?"

She shook her head.

The thought popped into my head, and I couldn't ignore it. I looked up. "What about… Olive?"

Stacy snorted. "She really got to you, didn't she? Beryl, Olive is… she's an actress. Or I should say, she's trying hard to be an actress. She's not quite good enough yet, and she knows it. So she latches on to everyone she thinks can help her advance her career. She's also quite a bit, um, boy-crazy, to put it in your good-guy terms."

I wrinkled my brow at her. "I'm not a priest, Stacy. You don't have to watch your language."

She laughed. "That may be so, but I still see you as one of the most innocent guys I know, Beryl. I like you that way."

Innocent? Did she miss the part where I killed a draconic? And fought others? I didn't… okay, maybe I knew what she meant. I didn't have to like it, though.

"All of what you say may be true," I said with a sigh. "But… does that mean Olive couldn't do it? It sounds to me like she might be eager to help if we frame it right."

"She's not ready to join your little band, Beryl my sweet. She's not going to want to leave the city. I can say that much for sure." Stacy picked up a bottle of makeup or something and toyed with it. "She wants to prove herself to the dragon's servants, not fight them. She's a loyal Viridian."

I slumped back down. I couldn't go back to the others without something. My brain cycled through various possibilities, but everything came down to needing an agitator for the crowd. An agitator to stir up the people of Incarnadine because of Viridian spies…

"What if we didn't recruit her for the band?" I said aloud.

"What do you mean?"

I looked up and smiled. "She's a loyal Viridian, you say. What if I told her we needed her for an important mission against Incarnadine?"

Stacy blinked. "You mean… convince her the whole thing is a Viridian operation? That you're what? Working for the Viridian Guard?"

"Exactly!" I jumped to my feet. "You don't need her for your performance, and you said she's not a big star, so she won't miss anything if I take her away for a week or so. And we'll tell her this is an undercover Guard operation, trying to steal, um, military secrets or something from the red dragon!"

"And I thought Loden had crazy ideas." Stacy shook her head. "How can you keep your true goals a secret from her that whole time?"

"It won't be hard," I said. "It's not like we walk around every day saying, 'how can we kill a dragon today?'"

"Let me think…" Stacy put the makeup down and considered. She looked at me through the mirror. "It's… well, it's crazy. But it might work, if I vouch for you." She shook her head. "But it's dangerous, Beryl. What about after this job? What if she wants to help more? And pesters me for more information about you and your team?"

"Maybe she will. Are you saying you can't handle her?" I grinned.

"Shut up, you. The day I can't handle a wannabe actress is the day I come sleep under the stars with you people." Stacy got to her feet.

"We don't usually sleep under the stars," I pointed out.

"Didn't I just tell you to shut up?"

"Shutting."

Stacy sat back down. "Okay, before we try this, if you really want to, we need to get all of our information straight."

We sat and discussed it for a few minutes before Stacy left to get Olive. I got up and walked around the room. This was a crazy idea. Stupid, even. What would Bice think? Well, that didn't matter, because he wouldn't even find out about it until it was over. Kelly would not approve, though. That would be awkward. But she would understand. Wouldn't she?

The door opened. "...but I'd be perfect for that role," Olive said as they entered. Then she saw me. "Oh. Hellooo."

"Olive." I smiled. "Good to see you again."

She moved toward me with that walk, that sashay or whatever it was. This time, she wore the same kind of tight pants as the last time I saw her, but her loose-fitting blouse had vertical green stripes this time. "Beryl. Did Stacy finally give you that job? Are we going to be working together now?"

"In a way," I said, keeping myself from reacting to her. "I'm here to offer you a job."

She glanced back at Stacy. "I'm confused. I thought you were looking for a job."

"That... was a deception." I reached out and took her hand. She smiled, but I could see confusion in her eyes. "We didn't know if we could trust you. We had to learn more about you."

Again, she glanced at Stacy. "Who is 'we'? What are you talking about?"

"There's a war on, Olive. The dragon has need of people like you."

Her eyes widened. "V-Viridia?"

I nodded. "I represent a secret organization within the Guard. We undertake the missions that the regular troops can't do." I leaned in closer. "We're spies."

Olive pulled her hand away and put it on her hip. "Okay, you almost had me. You're good. You're very good." She turned to Stacy. "Is this the concept for the new play? The Viridian Spy League?"

"It's not a joke, Olive," Stacy said. She crossed her arms. "You know I've traveled to the other cities a lot. It's why they came to me. I've fed them all kinds of information. Why do you think they got me in to the peace summit?"

Olive lost her pose. "It's not a play?"

Stacy shook her head. "It's real. Beryl and his team are about to take on a secret mission to Incarnadine. They wanted my help, but I'm too well known. They need another actress." She walked up and put her hands on Olive's shoulders. "I wouldn't ask this if I didn't think you could do it. This is the real thing, Olive."

I stepped next to Stacy and looked into Olive's eyes again. "It will be the performance of a lifetime."

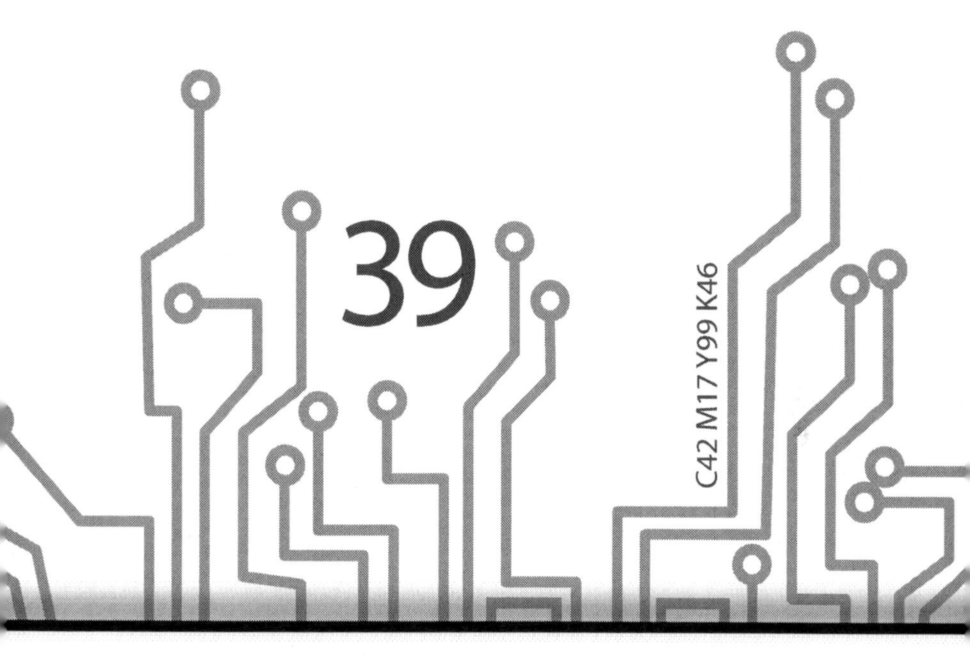

"Do you think she bought it?" I asked Stacy.

She chuckled. "The fact that she's gone to pack her things would seem to imply that she did."

"Well, yeah. But do you think she really bought it?" I shifted my weight nervously. "I mean, is she coming along because she thinks we're having fun, or because she actually believes it?"

Stacy shrugged. "Does it matter? Once you get to Incarnadine, she'll realize you're serious."

"Yeah, and then I have to explain it to everyone else, so they don't give anything away." I groaned. "This is going to be harder than I thought. I'm an idiot."

"Of course you are." Stacy put her hands on my shoulders, like she did with Olive a few minutes ago. "But you're a lovable idiot, who also happens to have super cybernetic powers. You'll be all right."

"Thanks, I think." I grinned. "I'm not sure which is more frightening right now: Olive finding out the truth, or me explaining this to Kelly."

Stacy gave me a quick hug. "Neither should scare you as much as the other thing." She turned away.

"What's that?"

"Traveling all the way to Incarnadine with Olive." She looked back at me and winked.

Oh. I hadn't even thought that far ahead. We would be traveling for a day and a half. Alone. Together.

"I do have one other bit of news for you, Beryl." Stacy looked down, folded her hands together, then pulled them back apart. "It's about that train you saw, with the Cerulean Corps soldier."

"What is it?" With everything else going on, I almost forgot about that.

"The Corps guy was returning something to the Viridian Guard, in exchange for something else. I don't know what he asked for. But I know what the Guard received."

"And?"

She grimaced. "It was the body of a green draconic."

"Troilus Green." I felt a chill run down my back. "Why would they want the body?" My mind went straight to Protogonus Blue's explanation about draconic reincarnation, but they didn't need the old bodies for that, did they?

"I have no idea." Stacy shook her head. Then she looked up. "Here she comes," she warned, just before the door opened. Olive entered, carrying a duffel bag. To my relief, it wasn't as huge as I anticipated.

"I packed light, like you said," she announced. "Just a few outfits."

"Great. I hope you packed something warm. Incarnadine is cold, for some reason. Stacy, the makeup?"

"Oh, right." She went to another trunk in the corner and returned with two bottles. "You said green and black, right?"

"Why do we need green when we're already green?" Olive wondered.

"It's part of the plan," I told her. "I'll explain on the way."

"Good luck, you two," Stacy said. "And to all the rest of the team."

"Thanks, Stacy, as always." I gave her a nod. "The dragon thanks you for your service." I wanted to ask her more about the body of Troilus Green, but what else could there be? Just one more strange thing to add to my list. At worst, it meant someone here in Viridia might be trying to unravel the truth of the dragon's death.

Behind Olive, Stacy rolled her eyes. "I live to serve," she replied.

We left the theater and started walking. I explained to Olive that we needed to keep off the main roads, as anyone carrying a duffel bag would look suspicious.

"But don't you work for the Guard?"

"Yes, but most of the common police troopers don't know about us," I said. "I'd rather not have to explain everything just to get out of the city. Better to move quietly through the back ways."

"All right." Her eyes narrowed. "We aren't walking all the way to Incarnadine, are we? I don't think the trains are running."

"They're not. I have… another means of transportation. But we have to get outside the city first." I hoped the whole trip wouldn't be like this. Olive was… nice to look at, but I didn't think I could handle hours of questioning.

"How long have you been, um, working this job? Just since the war started?"

"Oh, no. We actually started up some time before that. There are always things happening behind the scenes, right?"

"Ha. I get it." We walked in silence for a while. Then she drew closer. "Listen, I'm, um, sorry about how I treated you at first. I didn't know who you were."

I blinked. "Oh. You, uh, don't have anything to apologize for. I wasn't offended or anything."

"My flirting didn't upset you?"

"No! Um, no." I smiled at her. "It was fun."

"Good." She took my arm. "I just wanted to know where I stood for this trip. You know. Whether I had to be all business or whatever."

"Just be yourself for now," I said. "Until we need you to be someone else, of course."

She winked at me. "I can be whoever you want."

Oh boy.

We made it outside the city without incident. I led the way to where I had hidden the four-wheeler among some bushes and small trees. I pulled the pile of loose branches away, exposing the vehicle.

"What is that?" Olive's mouth fell open.

"This, my dear, is how we're getting to Incarnadine," I said with a sweep of my hand. "It's a little bit like the dragon's trucks. Here, let me take your bag." I stowed the duffel on the back of the four-wheeler.

Olive circled it. "It's nothing like the trucks," she argued. "You get inside a truck. This is… more like a bicycle."

"Is that a problem?"

"I've never ridden a bicycle in my life."

I guess now wouldn't be the best time to tell her about my former job. I climbed on to the four-wheeler and patted the seat behind me. "You won't have to do anything, except hold on. I'll do all the driving."

"Hold on to what?"

"Um, me, I suppose. Or you can lean back and hold on to the storage area there, if you can balance it right." I held out my hand.

Olive still looked skeptical, but she took my hand and climbed up behind me. She wrapped her arms around me, her hands on my stomach. "Like this?"

"Uh… yeah. Like that." Could this be any more awkward? The feel of her body pressed against my back with her hands around me… I swallowed. Then I started the engine.

Olive shrieked a little as I revved it and started moving. She clutched me tighter.

"Don't worry. It's completely safe," I said over my shoulder. I accelerated.

For the next few minutes, Olive shrieked with every change in our speed, direction, or elevation. She squeezed me with every exclamation, not that I minded.

In time, she settled down. As she got used to the movement of the four-wheeler, she relaxed her hold on me, but never completely let go. She even began to laugh when we sped up descending a hill, or jumped a small creek.

"How far is it to Incarnadine this way?" she asked.

We were now at least a couple of hours past noon. "We should arrive before tomorrow night," I said.

"Where do we sleep tonight?"

I gestured. "You're looking at it."

She leaned in closer and let her hands slide over my chest. "Hmmm. Sleeping under the stars. Sounds… exciting." I felt the warmth of her breath on my ear as she spoke.

I swallowed again. "So, like I said, your job is going to be as an agitator in a crowd," I said, trying to change the subject. "The goal is to make a big scene that will keep everyone's attention while I break into the Flame and steal some… military secrets."

"That sounds thrilling. But won't you be in danger? The Flame is where the dragon lives, isn't it?"

"Sure, but I'm used to danger by now. And I can take care of myself pretty well."

"Mm. I imagine so."

Great. Was there any topic which wouldn't take us in a flirtatious direction?

"Hey, it's not easy to talk while driving," I said a moment later, "so let's save the serious conversations until we're stopped to eat or sleep."

"Sure." Olive rested her head against my back and relaxed. I tried not to think about her, focusing instead on our direction. My stomach reminded me that I still hadn't eaten. We would need to stop for food soon.

We talked a little bit, from time to time, but avoided the main subjects. After a short supper break, we kept going until twilight. I considered going on into the night; if I were alone, it's what I would do. But I should not press too hard with Olive. She wasn't used to this.

I found an apple orchard and drove inside. The overloaded branches showed no one had been here in a while. The apples were casualties to the war.

"Are we going to build a fire?" Olive asked. "I've always heard about camping out and building fires."

"No, a fire can be seen for miles," I said. "We don't want to attract any attention. We're in enemy territory now."

Olive stretched. I tried not to watch. "Oof, that seat gets hard after a while. And we have a whole day of this tomorrow?"

"Almost. We made good time today." I took the supplies off the four-wheeler. "We might get there in the late afternoon."

"Neat." She looked around, taking everything in: the apple trees, the four-wheeler, the darkening sky, me... She took a step closer. "You know, if you wanted a romantic getaway with me, you didn't have to go this far."

"Olive, I..." I'd better say it before things got out of hand. "I need to tell you: I find you very attractive—"

"You're not so bad yourself." She moved in closer and reached for my face.

I caught her hand. "I just... I'm not sure I'm ready for a relationship just now. I, ah, lost someone recently..."

Olive nodded sympathetically. "No expectations, Beryl. I understand."

She took a seat on the ground and tossed one of the apples around while I finished unloading. "I do have one question, though."

"What's that?" I found my own sleeping bag and rolled it out.

Olive dropped the apple and looked at me. "When are you going to tell me what this is really about?"

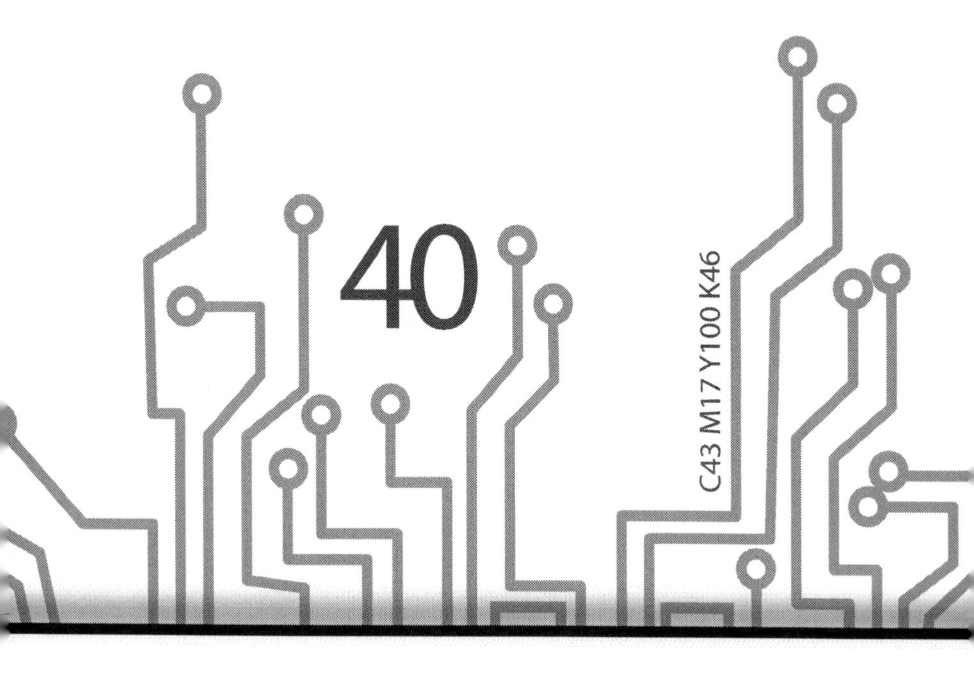

40

I looked over the sleeping bag at her. "What do you mean? I already told you."

Olive made a sweeping gesture. "Come on. You didn't expect me to believe all that stuff about the secret Viridian spy team, did you? I figured this was all some elaborate set-up to get alone with me in private—and I was going to give you lots of credit for it. Very cool. But…" She raised her eyebrows. "Now you say you're not interested in me. So I have to wonder. What is all this, really?"

I turned back to the four-wheeler and found the second sleeping bag, while I tried to think of the best way to respond. "Okay, first of all, I didn't say I wasn't interested in you," I said, turning back. I set the bag down and began to unroll it. "I'm just not ready for a relationship. I need to take things… slow."

"I can do slow," she answered. "But sleeping under the stars together, miles from the city? Doesn't feel slow."

"Everything else is real." I stood back up. "We do have a plan to steal from the Flame. And we need your help."

She cocked her head, still looking skeptical. "Come on. You're around my age, right? Why in The Circle would the Viridian Guard give something that important to you? They have to have more experienced people."

"They do, but… I'm special."

"Aren't we all?" I couldn't tell if she was being sarcastic or something else.

I crouched beside the sleeping bags. "I… four years ago, I was in an accident. It almost killed me." She leaned forward, trying to see me better in the gathering twilight. "I should have died. But a Viridian scientist gave me a cybernetic implant, back here." I patted the base of my spine. May as well stick with my original belief for now. "Not only did it save my life, it made me something special. Seeing what I could do, they recruited me into the service."

"What do you mean?" She still had a note of suspicion in her voice, but she was intrigued.

"Remember our first meeting in the theater? I kind of got carried away, showing off. Stacy covered for me, claiming I used the wires. Except I didn't."

"Aww, you were showing off for me? How sweet." She shook her head. "And that takes us back to the original idea for why we're out here."

I sighed. "You still don't believe me?"

"How can I? You—"

I boosted my legs and leaped high into the tree. I snagged an apple from a top branch and dropped back down, landing with a flourish beside Olive. I offered her the apple.

"You, you—"

I grinned. "Me."

She ignored the apple and grabbed my leg. She squeezed my calf. "You feel human, not metal. How?"

"He didn't replace my legs." I laughed a little. "It's hard to explain. It's an implant that lets me control it with my thoughts." I tapped my head. "I can send what I call 'boosts' into my legs. It lets me run faster and jump higher."

"The rest of you is… normal?"

"As far as I know."

In the semi-darkness, I could barely see her face any more, but I think she smiled. She patted my thigh, then leaned back. "I'll have to check that myself someday."

I'm sure I blushed at that. It would be so easy to push things further right now. Olive wanted more, obviously. And we were alone under the apple trees and slowly-appearing stars. But part of me still wouldn't let

Kelly go, and I knew that would ruin anything I did with Olive right now. I was thrilled she found me attractive, and I liked her, but… I just needed time.

Olive got to her feet and looked at the sleeping bags. "I've never done this before," she said. "Is it hard to sleep out here?"

I shrugged, but then realized she probably couldn't see that by now. "It depends. Some people have no trouble. For me, it depends on whether anything is underneath the sleeping bag, like a rock or root. Gotta watch out for those." I glanced at the sky. "And whether it rains."

"What? It might rain?"

"Nah, I don't think so. The sky is clear. We should be fine."

"We'd better be. Where did you put my clothes?"

I handed her the duffel bag. "I'll change on the other side of the four-wheeler," I offered.

"Whatever you like. I can't see much of anything now, anyway." As I moved around to the other side of the vehicle, she added, "And neither can you."

Why did she have to say that? As if my mind wasn't already imagining things. But I couldn't see in the dark. Or could I? I pondered the concept as I changed into lighter clothes for sleeping. If I could 'boost' my eyes to see further, could there be a way to boost them to see in the dark? I needed to find someone who could teach me about the muscles around the eyes. Maybe then I could figure it out.

"Are you ready?" I called.

"I'm already in bed," she answered.

I came back around and found my sleeping bag. I slipped into it, conscious of Olive lying beside me. Once I got settled, she scooted her bag right up next to me. "Sorry," she said. "Had to move because of a root."

With the warmth of her body right beside me, I knew one thing: I wasn't going to get much sleep.

In the morning, I woke up first. I opened my eyes and saw Olive's face not far from mine. She breathed quietly, her hair a disheveled mess. I watched her for a moment. Was it fair to deceive her this way? What if she got caught? Arrested by the Crimson Elite, and she wouldn't even know why. But wasn't it better that way? If she got caught and told them only what I had told her, it would prolong the war. For our ultimate goal, we needed that to happen. Logically.

But logic didn't account for individual people. Olive was a human being, like me, oppressed by the dragon, even if she didn't fully understand it all. Couldn't I tell her the truth if I was going to risk her life? But Stacy called her a loyal Viridian, said she wasn't ready for our cause. Did that make it right?

Olive's eyes opened. She focused on me watching. A soft smile crept onto her lips. "Hi, handsome."

"Hi." I smiled back, then crawled out of the sleeping bag. I needed to pee. "Be right back."

When I returned, I found Olive sitting on top of her sleeping bag. She wore a green tank top, and a pair of very small shorts. She looked up. "I'm really hoping there will be somewhere I can at least shower before this epic performance you want from me?"

"Huh? Oh, yeah. Sure. We have an apartment in Incarnadine. There's a couple there on our side. They, uh, sympathize with our cause. They want the war over as much as we do."

"Good." She got up and stretched. "As much as I enjoyed sleeping with you, I hope tonight is more comfortable."

"Uh, yeah. No problem."

"Where does a girl go to relieve herself around here?" She cocked her head at me.

I waved. "Um, just find a spot off by yourself."

She walked away, picking her steps with care. I watched her go for a moment, then shook my head and got busy loading the four-wheeler.

We got dressed, ate a quick breakfast of some cereal bars and juice, then set out on the rest of our journey. Olive seemed content with the information I had given her now, and didn't ask any more questions about the mission. Instead, she made observations from time to time on the landscape as we drove. Like me—well, like almost everyone—she grew up in the city and knew little of the country, aside from what she read in textbooks during the Learning Years. Little things amazed and delighted her, from the sight of some cattle to the enormous fields of wheat. When we drove past the blackened remains of the burned fields, she grew quiet. I didn't have to explain what that meant.

When we crossed a creek, she insisted we stop to freshen up. Watching her splash water on her face made me regret some of what I told her the night before. Why couldn't I move on to a new relationship? Kelly was with Rick now, and I cared about both of them. I wouldn't want them hurt. I needed to move on. I should move on. Maybe after this mission, and I took Olive home again, things could be… different.

It all depended on what happened in Incarnadine.

41

“When we get there, give me a minute to talk to the others first,” I told Olive as we drew near Incarnadine. “They’re expecting Stacy. Some of them are going to be a little… uneasy that I brought you in on this.”

“I can prove myself,” she answered behind me. She gave me an extra hug.

“I’m sure you can, but let me talk to them first.”

We drew near the hiding spot outside the city. By now, this place was becoming almost as familiar to me as the Asylum. I only hoped it stayed secret just as well. We only needed it for two more days.

Lovat poked his head up when he heard our engine. He ran to meet us, a grin on his little face.

“I know him,” Olive said in my ear. “You use a little boy in your spying?”

“He’s the perfect scout,” I replied. “He’s an orphan. No chromark of his own, so he can move about in any city. No one pays attention to him.” I pulled to a stop. “Ho, Lovat!”

“Ho, Beryl.” He grinned at us. “Hi, Olive.”

She climbed down. “Hello, Lovat.” She shivered. “You weren’t kidding about the cold. We’re not even in the city yet and I feel chilled.”

“Lovat, stay here with Olive while I talk to the others,” I ordered. I made my way down into the gully where the wings and the other four-wheeler remained hidden. Rick, Don, and Peri met me.

Rick looked past me. "I see there's been a change in plans."

"Yeah, you could say that. Have you been waiting for me long?"

"Not too long. We got here a couple of hours ago. I've talked with Kelly and Marcus over the talkers. Everything is moving along."

"Why is Miss Olive here?" Don asked.

I filled them in on the plan. Rick frowned. "That's pretty risky, Beryl." He pointed at Olive. "I mean, Lovat might have already let something slip."

Ouch. I hadn't thought of that. I guess I underestimated him too.

"We'll all have to watch our steps," Rick went on. "As if this job wasn't crazy enough, now we have an enemy among us."

"She's not an enemy."

"She's not an ally, either, if we can't tell her the real reason we're doing this."

"Then she's a tool," I snapped. "A tool to get the job done. Come on, I'll introduce you all."

The four of us joined Olive and Lovat by the four-wheeler. "Olive, this is Rick and Peri. You already know Don, I believe."

Her eyes widened as she looked at all of us. "You're a… diverse group. Green and black I understand. But blue?" She looked at Peri in confusion. That could be a problem. I didn't have an answer for why he was here.

Peri stepped forward and took Olive's hand. "That's perfectly understandable, my lady," he said. "Logically, we should be at war, no? Yet there are those of us in all the cities that want an end to all of this. That's why I've come to join these others. My only desire is for all of us to live in peace again, without fear."

My eyebrows went up. I didn't know Peri had it in him. And he really hadn't actually lied at all, come to think of it.

"All right," I said. "Where's the talker? I'll contact Kelly and update her. Then we'll decide who goes into town and so on."

"What do you need me to do, Beryl?" Olive asked.

"Ah, I do have a job for you, actually." I tapped my face. "We all need red chromarks. Can you help these guys get started on that?"

"Not a problem." She grinned. "All right, gentlemen. Bring me your faces."

Rick gave me a dubious look before retrieving the talker from the other four-wheeler. I activated it; a few moments later, I was speaking with Kelly.

"Slight change of plans," I said. "Actress One wasn't available, so I had to bring along Actress Two." I didn't know whether the Crimson Elite used similar talkers, but the possibility that someone else might pick up our conversation kept us from using names.

"Actress Two? Who...?" Kelly puzzled over it a moment. I could almost sense her realization over the air. "Her? Are you sure about this?"

"It was the only choice. Actress One has a, uh, towering performance of her own to give." I'd explain it fully in person. "For now, we need to decide how to arrange people here. We can't all crowd into where you're staying, at least for tonight."

"Right. I guess bring my guy, yourself, and... the actress, if you must. The others can camp tonight, can't they?"

"They'll be fine," I assured her. "See you soon."

I found Olive working on Rick's chromark. I told her we only needed the three of us disguised for tonight. After that job was done, we once again made our twilit way along the now-familiar route to the apartment. Olive, it turns out, had been to Incarnadine once before with a stage performance, so she wasn't as goggle-eyed as we had been at our first visit.

I expected a chilly welcome from Kelly, but she seemed gracious, at least at first. I took her, Marcus, and Cerise aside and explained the situation. Like Rick, Kelly thought it was needlessly complicated and dangerous. But when I explained the lack of alternatives, she accepted it. Marcus thought it was hilarious to be labeled Viridian sympathizers, but I think Cerise might have been a little insulted. All in all, we worked things out.

Olive finally got to take the shower I promised her, and we slept on the Vermeils' living room floor again. Rick dropped hints about my spending the night with Olive in the country, but my scowls made him roll his eyes and let it go. If I hadn't been exhausted, I think I would have felt far too awkward to sleep. So many conflicting emotions and relationships going on here.

We woke up on the day before the rally. Before leaving for work, Cerise informed us that she had arranged for a squad of the Crimson Elite to be present at the rally to be recognized. As far as they knew, they were being honored by the citizens.

Marcus showed us the flyers already spread about the entire city. "This afternoon, we're building a temporary stage next door to the Flame," he explained. He looked at Olive. "Are you willing to address the crowd?"

To her credit, Olive took a sip of water and regarded him without reaction. "How big a crowd are we talking about?"

He shrugged. "We really have no idea how many will show up. I'm hearing lots of chatter. Could be a few dozen, could be a couple hundred or more."

"I told you it would be the performance of a lifetime," I reminded her.

She shrugged. "It could be a bigger crowd than I'm used to, but as long as I think of it as another show, I'll be fine."

Kelly eyed her. "We've spread the story that a woman is going to speak who witnessed the shameless attack on our beloved Crimson Elite."

"What happened there?"

"That would be me," I said. "I kind of had to bust up one of their stations to rescue Rick."

Olive settled herself into Cerise's chair. "Give me all the details, so I don't contradict anything when I tell my story," she instructed. I described what took place. I don't think I deliberately exaggerated my actions, but I didn't downplay any of them either.

"So that's it?" she asked when I was done. "I talk about seeing an evil Viridian terrorist attack?"

"Oh, no," Kelly said. "The goal is to get them hyped up over the possibility that more of these evil spies are hidden among them."

"Which is funny," Marcus said, "because you actually are."

"And that's when I blow stuff up," Rick chimed in.

"Right. Rick sets the grain storage on fire. And then we actually do reveal some Viridian spies among them," I finished. "That's where the others come in. Peri will be in the crowd, helping agitate things. Kelly and Don are going to pull off the spy reveal, which is why I had Stacy send along green makeup too."

"So we, the real Viridian spies, will be revealing fake Viridian spies? I love it!" Olive giggled.

"Yeah, it's pretty funny. And yet deadly dangerous." I looked around the room. "Are we all in on this?"

"There's no turning back now," Kelly said. "Tomorrow, we start a riot."

And steal the Cerulean Books of Lore.

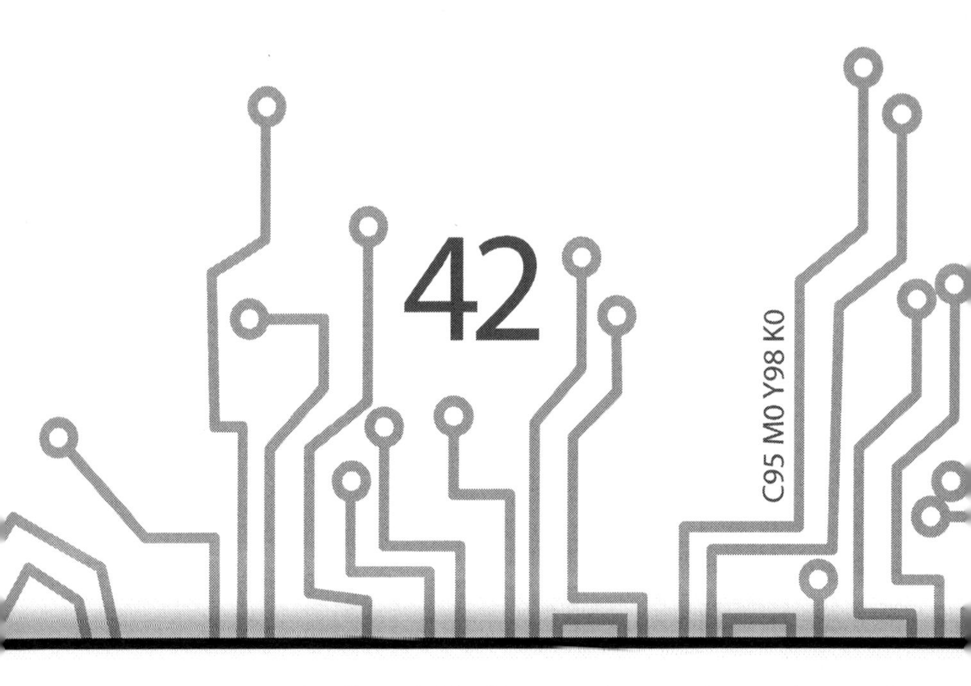

In retrospect, I really wish I had known what was about to happen. I would have spent a lot more time saying goodbye to… to certain people. But I'm an idiot. Blindly plunging into situations, just like Bice said. I mean, yes, this plan came together with a ton of input from other people, but still… I mean, we were counting on a performance from an actress none of us knew very well, and to whom we couldn't tell the truth, while I planned to fly into a dragon's fortress and steal stuff all by myself. I'm an idiot.

We spent the rest of the day going over our assigned tasks, making sure everyone knew every detail. Don, Peri, and Lovat were smuggled into the apartment, making it quite crowded. Olive and Kelly perfected the makeup process of changing chromarks. Don went with Marcus to help build the stage and get a feel for the setup. Rick took Lovat with him to look less conspicuous as he scouted the grain storage again. Kelly, Peri, and Olive worked on their plans for the rally, Olive's speech, and the other "additions."

Rick brought more talkers from Loden's workshop when he picked up the others, and we put together a system. I would have one, of course, as would Marcus. Rick and Kelly each took one as well. We would be connected for all four parts of the plan: rally, grain, truck, and the wings. My job. The whole point of all this.

Everyone seemed ready the next morning. Rick left first, to make his final preparations. If it had been anyone else, I would have worried whether he could pull it off alone. But Rick seemed to specialize on shocking displays, like when he took out the electricity in all of the Emerald Ascendancy. He never did tell me how he pulled that one off.

Next, Marcus left to get the theater's truck and wait for his part. Finally, I slipped out, heading to our camp outside the city. The others would all be joining the rally as it grew.

"Are you worried?" I asked Kelly before I left.

"About what?"

"Any of this." I spread my arms.

"I know Rick will be all right." She looked at nothing in particular, her lips pursed. "I'm not worried about you so much, though you do have a habit of unexpected trouble."

"Hey, Rick's the one always getting arrested!" I protested.

"Yes, but he has you to get him out. Who do you have, when your luck runs out?"

"I have Rick." And in that moment, I believed it. He didn't have the same capabilities as I did, but I knew he wouldn't let me down.

Kelly nodded. "The rest of us will be all right." She glanced off to the side. "I can't be sure about Olive, of course. I still don't know her."

"She'll do her part," I said confidently.

I believed that too. She had taken to all of our plotting and scheming like a professional. She seemed as ready as any of us. I told her so after saying goodbye to Kelly.

"Thanks." She grinned and leaned in close to me. "Once this is over, you are going to be the one to take me back home, right?"

"Of course."

"Good. We should stop at that orchard again."

"Um, sure. Why not?"

She laughed at me. "You can be so dense, Beryl. Do I have to spell everything out for you?"

Oh.

I kissed her. What else could I do? "Everything will change after today," I breathed in her ear after I pulled back.

"I'm counting on it."

I took the gleam in her eyes with me as I trudged out of the city. Why not? Why shouldn't I enjoy her company? Maybe it could lead somewhere. Over time, I could convert her to our way of thinking. With the aid of these books, we would overthrow the dragons once and for all. We could make our own world.

I shook my head. Grandiose dreams. I rarely thought that far ahead. At first, I had been solely obsessed with killing the green dragon. Then Rick and I decided we should kill them all. And Loden started the process. Kelly tried to get me to think about the future after it was all done, but I hadn't wanted to. Now I did. Maybe that said something about me. Maybe I was finally getting over myself.

Along the way toward the edge of the city, I passed people heading toward the rally. Some of them carried handmade signs. That had to be good.

Noon drew near when I reached the hiding place. I dug the wings out of their concealment and checked them over. Wings. I still hadn't come up with a better name for these things. Why didn't Loden name his inventions? It would make things simpler.

Only dragons could fly. That was the problem. I couldn't name the wings after the dragons. "The skies belong to the dragons," went the old saying. I hated it. I didn't want the dragons to own anything. And when I flew, they no longer did. I claimed part of the sky each time I flew this thing. "Sky Claimer," I said aloud. It wasn't elegant, or even humorous like the Achromatic Asylum. But it worked for me.

I readied Sky Claimer and then settled in to wait. I munched on a cereal bar, but I wasn't really hungry. Too much to think about.

The rally officially started an hour after noon. There would be a couple of songs, a speech by some city official Cerise recruited, and then Olive would speak. I wouldn't take flight until the climax of her speech and Rick's fire started. Only then could I be sure everyone's attention would be on the ground.

My mind wandered over all the other strange things going on, things that no longer mattered for today at least. Auric's forces at the Hub. The strange tower over the Blasted Lands. Even the peace summit. Stacy would probably be putting on her show there even now. It was a shame we couldn't do more to disrupt that event directly. With any luck, our actions here today would derail any talk of peace. I chuckled. Especially if we succeeded in making it look like Viridian agents did this.

Which reminded me. I found a cloth and some water and washed the red make up from my face. Time to stick with the green again. If I were seen, it would only help.

I examined the modified "balloon bag." As I requested, Bice attached a large duffel bag to the balloon. According to Peri, it would be large enough for the books. Bice also rigged it to lose air at a steady rate once it fully inflated. Peri calculated it would drift somewhere near the edge of the city. Marcus would be driving to that area soon.

I attached the bag to the Sky Claimer. It wouldn't be too long now.

The talker crackled. "The guards are in full regalia," Kelly reported, "just as we hoped."

I smiled. She meant the Crimson Elite at the rally would be wearing their helmets. Even now, Don would be approaching one of them and offering him a drink. He and Kelly would lure the guard away for just a few minutes. That's all it would take.

Lovat and Peri would be moving among the crowd now, tossing comments into conversations, complimenting people with signs, expressing worry about enemy spies.

"Hail Incarnadine," Rick's voice chimed in. I rolled my eyes.

I didn't respond yet. No need for it. I attached my shockspear to the side of my leg. I considered bringing my sword, but in the close quarters of the Flame's hallways, I liked the ability to incapacitate with electricity.

"Just drove past the rally," Marcus reported. "I don't know how many people are there, but it's huge. I've never seen a crowd that large. Anywhere."

More good news. Already, the eyes of the Crimson Elite and their draconic masters would be watching. Even though this rally's purpose was to celebrate them, it had to make them nervous. Humans weren't supposed to do things like this. They were supposed to be good little servants and only do what their masters told them.

"It begins," Kelly said.

I imagined the crowd cheering in front of the little stage. They would be filling the street in front of the Flame. Cerise and her co-workers would be watching, along with the guards and everyone else. That was the whole point.

I forced myself to drink some water while I waited. My nervousness pushed even the idea of hunger and thirst aside. Not long. Not long.

I strapped myself into the Sky Claimer, making sure every clip was secure. I fastened the talker onto my belt and pulled goggles down over my eyes.

"She's on stage," Kelly's voice reported.

Olive. Time for the performance of a lifetime. I put my hands on the controls. Almost time to fly.

If only I could see the stage right now. The downside to this plan, for me, was being stuck out here waiting, and not being a part of the rest of the process.

The talker crackled again, but Kelly didn't say anything. Instead, I heard another voice speaking, but faintly. I turned the volume up. It was Olive, speaking to the crowd. Kelly was keeping the talker on so Rick and I could hear events as they happened. I hadn't asked her to do that, but it definitely helped. I couldn't make out everything Olive said, but I could hear most of it. Shouts from the crowd drowned her out multiple times.

She gave a blow-by-blow retelling of my assault on the Crimson Elite. From what I could hear, she did an amazing job, including parts where she moved along the street to get a better view into the building. If I didn't know better, I'd believe she had been there. Then again, she certainly played up the more sensational aspects of the fight. I sounded like an absolute maniac in this version of the story.

I tried to listen closer. "And, and then, I heard louder noises, people yelling, but I couldn't see … the draconic screamed! I've never heard anything like it! He sounded … incredible pain." Her voice grew more rushed with each sentence. I could imagine her breathing harder, putting on a real show. "And the two men ran out. I, I hid against the wall. I was terrified! They … past me! But I saw them! I saw their marks!" She paused, no doubt pointing to her own chromark. "Green and black!" she yelled. The crowd booed and shouted for a long time.

"Watch the faces!" Olive yelled. "Don't let anyone hide their face from you! We have to find these spies!"

"We don't know how many there are!" Kelly shouted. Her voice came through extra-loud since she held the talker. "They could be anywhere!"

In the background, I could hear lots of other shouts. This was perfect.

"No hats! No headbands!" Olive continued to yell. "Don't let them hide!"

Someone in the crowd yelled something about helmets. "Yeah, no helmets!" Kelly agreed.

It didn't take long before the crowd, spurred on by our team and their own suspicions, began chanting, "Hel-mets! Hel-mets! Hel-mets!"

Here it came. I flipped the switch to start the Sky Claimer's engine.

On the stage, I could see it in my imagination. Trying to pacify the crowd, the Crimson Elite on stage would take off their helmets and…

"Viridian!" A voice screamed over the talker. "Green!" Did that screech come from Kelly? I wouldn't have believed it if I hadn't heard it.

The crowd erupted. Because on the stage, one of the Elite pulled off his helmet to reveal a green chromark. Don pulled the guard aside before the rally started, Kelly distracted him, and Don put him to sleep with a well-placed club. As soon as Kelly finished painting a green chromark on him, Don woke him back up, convinced him he had tripped over Kelly and smacked his head. Since both of them stayed to help him and even give him back his helmet, he believed it.

Even now, people were yelling, "get him!" "Find the spies!" and similar outcries. The talker stopped. Kelly couldn't keep it active now that the crowd would be getting rambunctious.

I felt a tremble in the ground before I heard the explosion in the distance. It had to be Rick. Right on time.

I twisted the throttle as hard as I could and shot into the air. I kept going straight up, up, up. I needed height and a lot of it. The higher I flew, the less likely I would be seen by chance.

I leveled off after climbing much higher than previous flights. The city of Incarnadine lay spread out below me, with Amaranth off to my right. The Flame was easy to spot. I aimed myself in that direction, keeping the throttle high. Speed mattered.

On the far side of the city, I saw a column of smoke climbing into the air. It was enormous. What did Rick do? People would be looking up at the smoke, but in the opposite direction of where I flew. That was helpful.

I descended toward the Flame. I cut the throttle from time to time, letting myself glide a little bit. Too much and I would start to fall. I kept moving much faster than any vehicle on the ground.

As I neared my destination, I caught a glimpse of the rally. Marcus wasn't kidding. I couldn't possibly guess the numbers from this height, but the crowd filled all of the street in front of the Flame for at least a block in either direction. I could see a lot of movement happening, but couldn't tell whether it had become an actual riot yet.

And I had no more time to think about it. The Flame grew closer and closer at a fantastic rate. I started to pull up, angling my descent toward the top of the structure. I wanted to get the topmost balcony, level nineteen. If I overshot, I might descend into the dragon's lair: the absolute last thing I should do.

I continued to adjust the angle until I was falling almost feet-first. Not far enough. I would miss the balcony entirely. I rotated as fast as I could, engaged the throttle for a single second, then rotated back. Now I was in position, but falling too fast. I activated the throttle again, at a very low thrust, slowing my descent. It felt very much like a mechanical version of boosting my legs when I landed after a long fall.

A boost would not be a bad idea right now. I had almost no room for error in my landing. If I stumbled, I might smash one of the wings against the Flame's wall. That would be a devastating error.

I triggered the boost and flexed my knees just before my feet touched the balcony. At the same time, I flipped the switch to turn off the engine. It worked. Only a few feet away stood the door through which I ran from the Crimson Elite.

I unfastened the straps and carefully positioned the Sky Claimer where I could easily get back in. I hung my goggles on the controls, then removed the balloon bag and put the strap over my shoulder. I would need it to carry the books back out here. I took the shockspear in my right hand, and toggled the switch on the talker with my left. "The Sky Claimer has landed," I announced.

"So we're naming things now?" Rick's voice replied.

"What's happening below?" I asked.

A moment of silence answered me.

"I've seen people running away," Marcus reported, "but I haven't driven anywhere close to the actual rally."

Not hearing Kelly's voice worried me. But if she and the others truly were in the middle of a riot, she wouldn't have time to talk to us.

"I'm heading that way now," Rick said. "I'll make sure everyone's all right."

I peered over the edge of the balcony. I wasn't at the right angle to see all of the front of the building, but I could see the fringes of the crowd. I triggered a boost to my eyes and focused. When I zoomed in, I saw angry people. Most of them were yelling, some shook their fists, some waved signs or other things. I think I saw someone throw a chair. Looked like Kelly's explanation of a riot to me. Were they directing their anger toward the Flame itself? It was hard to tell from this angle. I blinked and reset my eyes back to normal.

Somewhere in that mess were Kelly, Don, Peri, Lovat and Olive. I had no worries about Don, and Lovat could slip out much easier than anyone else. The other three might have a harder time of it. I hoped they didn't stick around too long. The Crimson Elite could not let this go on for very long. The human leaders and draconics would already be making the decision about how soon to crack down on it.

That created my time limit. I couldn't depend on the riot lasting too long. I needed to get in, find the books, and get out.

I spared one last look at the Sky Claimer. I hated leaving it just sitting out here, but even if the Elite found it, they couldn't take it anywhere. It would be here when I got back. I might have to fight someone for it, but I could handle that. After a moment's consideration, I left the talker as well. It would only get in my way if I needed to move fast.

I gripped the shockspear, took a deep breath, and opened the door to the Flame. Time to visit the library.

44

The hallway inside looked exactly as it had the last time. I jogged past the curved walls until I reached the elevator. I paused. It would be faster to just ride the elevator the remaining three floors. Except, of course, I'd be stepping out blind when the doors opened on the library. Probably not the wisest course.

I hurried on around until I reached the stairs. I made the mistake of taking a quick look over the edge. The stairs leading down nineteen floors formed a dizzying pattern. I shook my head and turned upward.

The directory listed floors twenty and twenty-one as "restricted." I paused at level twenty. The door had no knob, no lock, no visible means of opening it at all. I pushed on it out of curiosity. Nothing moved. It might not be a door at all, just a door shape completely sealed off from the stairway. I left it and kept climbing.

The twenty-second level sported an ordinary door. I confidently grasped the handle and pulled it open. And stared right into the face of an unvisored Crimson Elite guard.

He opened his mouth to yell, but never got the words out. In one fluid motion, I activated the shockspear and tapped him on the side of his face. His body contorted as the electricity attacked his nervous system. He collapsed, twitching, on a surprisingly thick maroon carpet.

I knew it might not take him long to recover, but I couldn't think of anything else to do with him, short of tossing him down the stairs. I stepped over his body and looked ahead at the library.

Unlike the other floors, when I came through the door, I did not enter a hallway. Instead, I stood in the corner of a room that appeared to stretch across the entire floor. To my left, the wall continued its usual curve around the dragon's exit shaft. The rest of the room contained row after row of shelves, each of them reaching almost to the ceiling, and covered with innumerable books.

I took several slow steps forward. How could there even be that many books in the world? Throughout my life, my family had only owned a couple of books: a collection of recipes my mother loved to reference, and a copy of the "Holy Scriptures of the Almighty Viridia" (I burned that one after my parents died). I read plenty of books during my Learning Years, but always borrowed, never owned. Nobody owned many books.

How was I supposed to find the "Cerulean Books of Lore" in all of this? Mazarine only told me that I'd know them when I saw them. Peri described seven large books with dark blue covers. I examined the nearest shelf. I spied a handful of books with blue covers mixed in among every other color. What constituted "dark" blue? I tilted my head to read the title on one of the darker ones: Structural Fractal Engineering. That couldn't be it. I looked over the shelf and saw similar titles. The books must be divided based on topics. Great. I just needed to find the "lore" topic, whatever that meant.

I stepped out on the opposite side of the shelf and noticed that parts of the enormous room were arranged differently than this section. Some had shorter bookshelves. Here and there, I saw tables with chairs. Unlike the other levels, the outer walls of this floor consisted of enormous windows looking out over Incarnadine.

Think, Beryl. These lore books were important enough to steal them from Caesious as soon as the blue dragon died. They wouldn't just slap them on a shelf in here, would they? They would be somewhere… special.

I moved into the more open areas. No sign of any people, aside from the one guard. They were probably all downstairs watching the rally/riot. Who would be reading books when all of that was happening right outside?

There had to be something… some hint of where to look…

I spotted a wall. It didn't reach all the way to the ceiling, but any kind of wall stood out here. I made my way past the short shelves and tables and followed the wall until it turned a corner. The next side of what seemed to be a square room turned out to be glass. I could see a door on the third side, and a shorter ceiling built inside.

The walled room contained a single table covered with a crimson cloth. A single book rested open on a kind of reading platform atop the table. Beside it sat a pile of six large tomes, all of them with definitely dark blue covers. The Cerulean Books of Lore. It had to be.

I hurried around and checked the door. Locked. No time to waste now. I picked up one of the chairs, boosted my arms and slammed it into the glass wall. My shoulder exploded in pain again, and the glass did not break. Not ordinary glass then.

Changing tactics, I smashed the chair against the locked doorknob, breaking it off. I boosted my leg and kicked. The door bent, but didn't open. Another boost and another kick. Progress, but still not open. A third boosted kick finally knocked it in. Immediately, an alarm began to sound, a throbbing tone that irritated my ears.

I slung the bag onto the table and opened it. The books looked even larger than Peri had described, and very, very old. Regardless, I had no time. I stuffed all seven into the bag; they barely fit. I sealed the bag and rushed back out.

The guard I electrocuted stood between two of the tall shelves, looking right at me. I would not be able to run past him to get to the stairs. I readied my shockspear and approached at a rapid pace. His eyes narrowed. Sword drawn, he stepped out into the more open area to face me.

"I don't want to hurt you," I called. "Well, any more than I already have. Just stand aside."

His eyes looked at the heavy bag over my shoulder. "You… broke in here for books?"

"Crazy, isn't it?" I shook my head. The alarm kept going. "That's war for you. Look, you can't beat me. Just get out of my way."

He tightened his grip on his sword. "I am the Crimson Elite! I am chosen by Incarnadine!"

"And I'm nobody in particular, chosen by no one. Last chance, Red."

He wrinkled his brow at my proclamation. In his mind, I'm sure I made no sense whatsoever. I sighed, boosted my left arm, and shoved the nearest bookshelf. It toppled with a tremendous crash, scattering books in every direction. "You can't win," I repeated.

"You're the one who attacked the precinct office," he realized. He took a step closer, still holding his sword in front. "I don't have to win. I just have to slow you down."

Ugh. He was right. I didn't have time to waste with him. I boosted my legs and charged.

His sword came down in an angled slash at my approach. I deflected it with my shockspear. I couldn't let him hit the spear directly with that sword; I think the sword would win. I only needed to do the same thing I did when I entered. I boosted my arm for extra speed, swept in under his returning sword, and tagged him with the tip of the shockspear.

Again, his muscles contracted and he froze. I stepped back, but to my surprise, he didn't fall. He staggered and nearly dropped his sword, but recovered somehow and kept his eyes on me. "You'll… have to do… better than that." His voice slurred, but I understood it.

"I gotta say: that's impressive. I've been on the receiving end of these things, and the fact that you're still standing?" I nodded and spread my arms. "Respect to the Elite."

He leapt forward at my apparent casual stance. I boosted everything, ducked under his wild swing, and shoved him in the chest. He flew back several feet and smashed into one of the large shelves. This time, he slumped to the floor. Surprisingly, the shelf didn't fall.

I should have left him with another quip, but he was unconscious. What was the point? I charged to the staircase door, ripped it open, and rushed into the stairway. Three levels. Just three levels down. I scrambled down one flight before I heard footsteps coming up. I couldn't tell how far they were, so I kept going. I rounded the final flight leading to level nineteen and came to a stop.

Two Crimson Elite paused at the bottom of the flight, watching me. Then they each moved to the side to allow the large figure behind them to step into view.

Zidanta Red.

"You're supposed to be at the peace summit," I said. And immediately felt like an idiot.

The draconic tilted its head—a sign of amusement or curiosity?—and took a step up toward me. "You again. You're surprisingly well informed to even know about the summit." It took another step. "But also ignorant. I'm not the only draconic in this city."

"We have a habit of running into each other," I replied. "I figured that made you important."

"And each time, you have run away. Will you be attempting that again today?" It took another step.

I backed up a couple of stairs and took a quick look around. Limited choices here. I could run back up the stairs, but that would only take me to the library or the last floor above it. Neither would help me get to the balcony where the Sky Claimer waited. I could even jump down between the stairs and fall, maybe catching hold of a railing somewhere down below, or splattering myself on the ground floor or basement. Not a good option. The only other way out was through the draconic. I tightened my grip on the shockspear. Would it even work against one of them?

"Fascinating. Are you involved in the disturbance down below?" it went on. "Or are you merely taking advantage of it?"

I stood on the landing mid-way between floors nineteen and twenty.

I held the high ground, so you'd think I had a clear advantage. Right. A clear advantage against a monster that probably outweighed me by about a thousand pounds, while I held only this shocking stick. And a big bag of books. I should have brought the sword.

I could only think of one advantage the height gave me. This could be tricky. I crouched, aiming the spear forward, as if waiting for the draconic's assault.

It took the bait. With a guttural roar, Zidanta Red charged up the stairs at me. I waited until its outstretched claws almost reached me, then leaped with a strong boost to my legs. I landed on its back and kicked off again, knocking it flat on the landing.

I came down on the two Crimson Elite. I dropped the bag of books on one to occupy him. The other moved faster, swinging his sword up as I came down. I had no choice but to block it with my shockspear. As I feared, the spear wasn't tough enough to withstand the hardened steel sword. It shattered. But at least the sword missed me.

I landed in a low crouch. With a boost to my arm, I punched the sword-wielder in the stomach. He flew back and slammed against the wall.

I turned to the second guard, who tossed the bag of books aside. Just in time for me to kick him in the chest and send him tumbling down the stairs.

I snatched up the first guard's sword and whacked him in the head with the hilt to be sure he was out. Then I spun to face Zidanta Red once more. This time, it held the high ground, but I was only one door away from the nineteenth floor. Unfortunately, I couldn't pick up the book bag and make it through the door before the draconic could reach me.

Zidanta Red nodded as it looked over my work. "Well done. I underestimate you too often. That will not happen again." It descended the stairs, no longer poised for fighting. The casual steps somehow unnerved me more. I took a step back, holding the sword at ready.

"I have many more questions," the draconic said. "But they can wait. We will have plenty of time for conversation."

"I'm in a bit of a rush," I countered. "Maybe you should ask me now."

The draconic snorted, then lifted its hand, palm up. Fewmets. That meant...

Zidanta Red roared something I couldn't understand. I boosted my legs and dove toward the door, but I was too late. A wall of air lifted me off my feet and smashed me against the wall of concrete. I was out before I hit the floor.

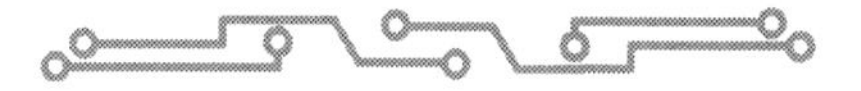

A smack across my cheek awakened me. I blinked several times and moaned. Again with the magic power or whatever. I would have bruises all over for days. Bizarrely, I wondered what Olive would think of that.

"Come, come, Viridian. With all your ability, you should be awake by now." Zidanta Red's voice. Pleasant.

I looked up at the draconic. Only then did I realize two of the Crimson Elite held my arms upward while my knees rested on the floor. Two more stood to either side with crossbows aimed at my chest.

I tried to understand the surroundings. We were gathered in what looked like one of the usual hallways, except the curved wall in front of me was made entirely of glass. Instead of looking out over the city, though, it looked into an opening within the building. I could see the same glass on the other side. It must be the shaft that led down to the red dragon's lair.

I blinked again and rolled my neck around. Aches everywhere. That's what happens when an invisible wall picks you up and smashes you against a regular wall. Ow ow ow.

Zidanta Red knelt to look at me. It reached down to the bag and took out one of the blue books. "I am fascinated by the contents of this bag," it declared. "This is hardly what I would expect a Viridian spy to steal. Was this truly your objective, or did it just look like it might be important?"

"I like to read." I was getting better at smart-mouth answers. Rick must have been rubbing off on me.

"Clever." The draconic lifted the book and examined it as it stood. "The Cerulean Books of Lore. If this was not just a theft of opportunity, what would lead you to want these? How did you even know they were here?"

"Why are they here?" I asked in return. "I mean, they're blue. You're red. What's up with that?"

Zidanta Red nodded to one of the guards holding me. He backhanded me across the face. I tasted salt and iron. Blood. Ouch.

"Your friend, the one from Atramentous, talked a lot more." The draconic turned away from me, looking out through the glass. "He tried to convince us that you two were part of a vast network of green and black spies, working to undermine both red cities. His problem was that he tried too hard. He was obviously lying." The reptilian snout turned just enough for one eye to look back at me. "Perhaps you'll be more forthcoming. Eventually."

I didn't answer.

"You're not escaping from this one. You had help on the battlefield, and you caught us by surprise the last time you were here. But now?" It turned back to face me. "You're alone. Whatever allies you possessed have abandoned you. You're surrounded by my guards. I could tear your head off without a thought." It leaned down. "And things are about to get even worse."

I was inclined to agree with him, though I determined not to show it. I could not see a way out of this one.

Another of the Crimson Elite approached and saluted. "Your excellency. We found a strange device on the balcony one floor down. It looks like… wings, sir."

One floor down. That put us on the twentieth floor, one of the "restricted" levels. But they found the Sky Claimer. At least they couldn't bring it inside yet. They'd have to disassemble it. Unfortunately for me, it looked like they'd have plenty of time to do that.

"Wings? Fascinating. That's how you got in this time, is it? I will have our techs examine this technology." It cocked its head. "Although, then I might have to kill them. Human flight is absolutely forbidden. The skies belong to the dragons."

"And me." I grinned. "It's so hue."

The draconic seemed not to have heard me. It lifted its head as if sensing something. "Ah. He's coming."

"Who?" The question popped out without thinking.

Zidanta Red looked down at me. "You're a Viridian invading the most sacred place in our city. You're clearly cybernetically enhanced in some way. You arrived here using forbidden technology." It hefted the book. "And you came to steal something very odd. You've aroused a lot of curiosity, and not just mine."

The draconic looked out the window and knelt. "Incarnadine comes."

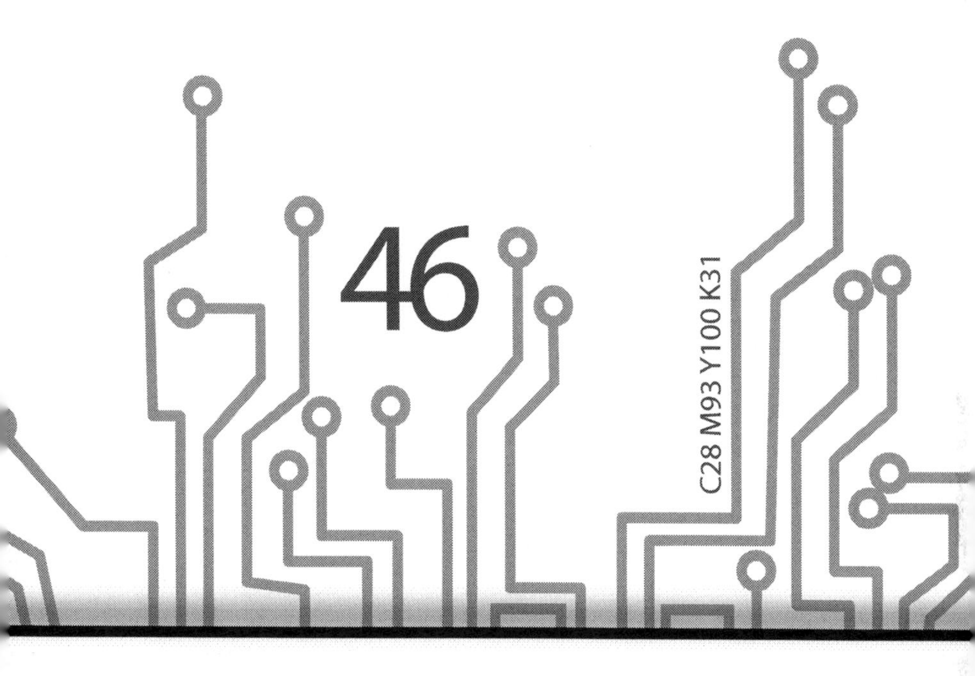

46

The dragon? The dragon was coming? As if things weren't bad enough already.

The guards twisted my arms back and up, forcing me into a lower bow. My left shoulder felt horrible, like it might pop back out. All four of the guards also knelt, though the crossbows remained pointed at me.

A low rumble shook the floor. I raised my eyes as best as I could from the awkward position. With slow deliberation, the enormous head of Incarnadine, the red dragon, rose into view through the glass. Though I'd seen him from a distance at the battlefield, it was nothing like being this close. The actual size of the dragons never ceased to amaze me, that creatures so vast could even exist. We were nothing to it. Pebbles. Toys. Snacks.

Like the green dragon, two horns rose from the red-scaled head, although these looked more like a ram's. The snout looked longer, narrower, and perhaps more terrifying. The head turned so that one gigantic eye looked in upon us. Then it turned to look with the other eye.

How was he doing this? My brain fixated on that question. He couldn't be standing at the bottom on two feet, could he? The dragon wasn't that big. But he wasn't beating its wings to float, either. Did he climb up the side and cling to the wall like a lizard? Maybe they built a massive elevator for him? I obsessed over it, maybe to hide my fear.

And that obsession almost made me miss the obvious: the second eye was cybernetic. A metal plate surrounded it, but the eye itself, glowing red, zoomed in and out at me with obvious mechanical movements. Enormous cables ran down his neck from the eye-plate to the top of his chest. My mind went back to the box of eyes Caedan and I found in Loden's workshop. This one didn't look anywhere near as realistic as those. More proof of Loden's genius.

"My lord," Zidanta Red intoned, still bowing, "here is the Viridian spy. Shall we gaze upon your glory?"

"You may." The dragon's voice sent a tremor through everything. Like the draconics, his voice came from deeper in his throat. His lips didn't move exactly with his words like a human. "Let the once-in-a-life vision of my majesty be one of the last things this human ever sees."

"Actually, you're the third dragon I've seen up close," I said. "And I have to ask—"

"Do not speak to me of Viridia and Atramentous!" The dragon's voice rose, shaking us a little harder. "They have betrayed us all, tarnished our glory, and endangered everything within The Circle!"

Regardless of anything else that happened to me, I could smile. We really did start a war between the dragons. Maybe the peace summit wouldn't get anywhere, after all.

Zidanta Red grasped my chin and lifted my head to look at the dragon. The guards loosened the angle of my arms just enough to keep from ripping them out. "Gaze upon the only god that matters!" the draconic ordered.

I almost said something snarky, but with those claws right there, it might tear off my lower jaw.

"Why did you come?" the dragon boomed. "What did you hope to accomplish here?"

"I'm… a big reader," I answered. "Wanted some new books."

The massive eye shifted from me to the books. "Are all seven accounted for and intact, Zidanta Red?"

"They are, my lord. Though why this human would want them is perplexing."

"To you, perhaps." The cybernetic eye focused on me again, with a visible movement of the iris. "I know their value. The only troubling aspect is that this one knows as well."

"Shall we torture him for information, my lord?" The draconic released my chin with a flick of its wrist, snapping my head back.

"There is something strange about all this," the dragon rumbled. "These actions… do not seem like the actions of a Viridian spy in time of war. Viridia would not send someone to steal these books."

This was bad. Very bad. If the dragon kept going down this pathway of thinking, it might figure everything out. Then the war would be over, and all of the dragons would come for my friends. Rick, Kelly, Bice… I couldn't let them down.

I started to laugh. I began with a chuckle, then grew louder. As nervous as I was, it wasn't very hard to fake. I could cry or laugh, and in this case, laughing would help me more.

"You find this amusing?" Zidanta Red moved as if to strike me again, but stopped.

"'Beware the red dragon,' they told me," I said with another laugh. "They told me how smart he was, how sinister and devious." I laughed and took in a deep breath. "Wow, what did they know?"

"Who are you talking about?"

"The green draconics. They warned me, told me to be careful." I snorted. "And yet here you are, jumping to completely wrong conclusions."

"Enlighten me, then," the dragon growled.

I looked up and glared at him. "Of course I'm from Viridia! Where else would I be from? You think I got this green mark on my face by accident?"

"Watch your tone, human, or I'll—" The draconic seized the front of my shirt.

"Let him speak," the dragon interrupted. "I want to hear this."

"Hatred, you fire-breathing lizard!" I snarled. "It's all about hatred. A thousand years of hatred! Why would Viridia want the books? For one simple reason: because you wanted them! You took them from Caesious! They're important to you. And whatever is important to you, Viridia wants!"

The dragon's eye studied me, as if judging my honesty. The head turned and reared back. He snorted. Smoke poured from his nostrils and flowed in either direction along the curved glass.

"You're right about one thing, though," I went on. "I'm not a spy. I'm not even Viridian Guard. I'm a nobody! They took me and surgically altered me. You already know I've got cybernetic enhancements. That was part of the whole thing! They took a nobody and made him into a warrior that twice defeated your best!"

"And yet here you are," Zidanta Red growled. "You're the defeated one now."

"Maybe," I replied. "Or maybe the real spy has already escaped with our true target. Maybe I'm just the distraction. Maybe these aren't the real books, but fakes."

The draconic picked up one of the books again and looked it over. "It looks genuine to me," it told the dragon.

"Like you've read them," I sneered.

The guard on my left twisted my arm again. The pain caused me to cry out this time.

"You're not so cybernetically enhanced that you do not feel pain," the draconic observed. "Let me tell you what that means, human." It knelt down to look at my face again. "We will take you apart, piece by piece, until you tell us everything we want to know. You will beg for death, but I will not give it. I will continue removing whatever real body parts you have, one at a time. Your organs will be carefully cut out and preserved, given to those more deserving of them. Whatever cybernetic secrets your body possesses will be stripped out of you and studied, so that we may reproduce it. And then, when you have almost nothing left to give…" It tapped my chest with a single claw. "Only then will I reach into your chest and take the last piece. The last sight you see will be my jaws consuming your heart."

I would like to say I stared back at the draconic in defiance. Or I spit in his face. But to be honest, that speech terrified me. I knew this quest of mine would probably get me killed one day. I always knew that. What chance did we really have, going up against all these immortal dragons? But even so, I hoped it would be quick. A sword through the heart. Even getting eaten, as horrifying as that sounded, would be over in a moment. But the torture the draconic described… I wouldn't be able to handle it. Who would? I would tell them everything. Everything. And they knew it. All of my posturing was pointless.

No one spoke for a while. Zidanta Red's words sunk deeper into my thoughts. Bice told me I wasn't invincible. How true that seemed in this moment.

"It is well that you reminded me of your previous actions," the dragon declared at last. "You did cause great pain to one of my children, and that cannot be allowed. Zidanta, before you take him away to do just as you have said, I need to see the beginnings of justice." He turned his head, moving his real eye close to the window again. It glared at me with a malice that stretched back centuries.

"Take one of his eyes."

I didn't even have time to scream as the draconic's claws hit my face.

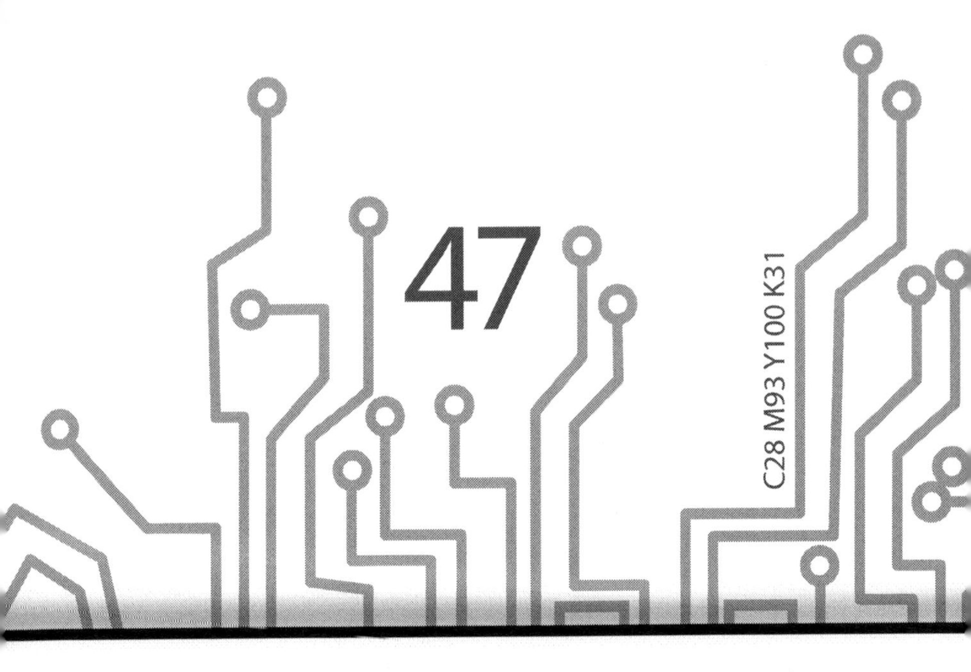

47

I thought it would feel much more horrifying and painful than it did. In fact, all I felt was something like a tearing scratch and a pop. Blood trickled down my face, but nowhere near what I expected. I looked up with my left eye and…

Zidanta Red stood there, holding my eye, with a strange look on its reptilian face. I would have to call it "baffled" or "shocked." I would call it that because I felt the same way.

The draconic held a cybernetic eye.

It looked exactly like the ones in the case I found in Loden's workshop. My eye hadn't been gouged out; it had been unplugged.

"What is the problem?" the red dragon rumbled.

Zidanta Red turned and held up the eye. "How is this possible? Our techs have nowhere near this skill."

I wondered the same thing, but for different reasons. How? How could Loden have replaced my eye with a cybernetic one that duplicated reality so closely even I didn't know it was there? And then I had a sickening feeling. The zooming I had been doing with my eyes. Sending boosts to them. Did that mean…?

I sent a boost to my remaining eye. My vision zoomed in on the dragon's head in front of me. I saw tiny detail about each of it scales. I saw metallic replacement scales painted red to match, and some from which the paint had worn off. My vision snapped back to normal.

Were both my eyes cybernetic? I couldn't zoom in if they weren't, could I? That's why the others had been so disturbed. It didn't make sense for an ordinary human. Of course it didn't. I was a freak. I had something implanted in my brain and two fake eyes. How much did Loden do to me to keep me alive? How much more of me wasn't real? I lowered my head. My remaining eye's vision blurred.

"He holds more secrets than we thought," the dragon said. "Take him and find them all."

"Secrets," said another voice. The crossbow guard on my left collapsed. I heard a "thwip" and the second one grabbed at his neck and also fell. "We all have them."

I looked up and my vision cleared. Rick stood in the hallway, reloading his crossbow. "A little help, Beryl? I can't do everything myself."

I boosted both arms and heaved. Caught off guard, both of the guards holding me lost their balance. I hurled them against the window in front of the dragon's face. I snatched a sword from one as he fell and whirled to face the draconic.

Zidanta Red looked from one of us to the other. It dropped the cybernetic eye. A massive roar shook all of us as the red dragon expressed its outrage.

The draconic yelled in response, thrusting a hand toward Rick. He fired a bolt, but it shattered in mid-air, followed by his crossbow itself. He flew back down the hall as the invisible force struck him.

But that gave me the only opening I needed. I boosted everything, stepped on one of the fallen guards and launched myself at the draconic. As it spun back toward me, I thrust the sword with all my strength… straight through the side of its throat.

It claws raked at me, but I fell and landed on my feet in a crouch. "Can't use your power if you can't talk!" I cried.

Rick scrambled to his feet and ran back toward us.

An impact threw all of us off our feet. Incarnadine slammed his head against the windows. To my surprise, they didn't break. I guess they had to be strong to resist the dragon's coming-and-going. Even so, I wasn't going to bet my life on them.

"We have to get out of here!" I yelled at Rick. I snatched up the bag of books, then reached for the fallen one.

Zidanta Red slammed into me. I hit the window, then tumbled back the other way. The beast had a sword sticking through its throat, but it wasn't dead. Not by a long shot.

"I'm open to suggestions," Rick answered. He grabbed up one of the fallen guards' crossbows. "Where are the wings?"

"One floor down!"

I boosted my arm and elbowed the draconic to shove it back. It staggered, but didn't move much.

"Can't find the right bolts," Rick grumbled. He abandoned the search and ran toward us.

A gigantic claw slammed against the glass. Cracks spread from the impact point in every direction. One more hit like that and the dragon would come through.

Rick dove. He reached out with his cybernetic hand and grabbed the draconic's ankle. He squeezed, and the monster roared in pain.

"Go, go, go!" Rick yelled.

The claw slammed into the glass again and punctured it. Incarnadine yanked it back, tearing glass and steel away. A sudden rush of wind pulled at me. I took an involuntary step toward the dragon and the abyss below him.

I regained control and ran down the hall. Rick scrambled to his feet, ducked under Zidanta Red's wild swing and chased after me. The draconic, its ankle shattered by Rick's grip, could only limp.

"We have seconds!" Rick shouted. "Go!"

The book. I didn't get the fallen book. I paused and almost turned back.

"Move!" Rick screamed, running into me. I glanced back and saw the dragon's head approaching the broken windows.

At the end of the hall, I saw a door, but from the other side, I hadn't seen anything. No time to wonder. I boosted everything and turned at the last minute, slamming into the door. It burst open.

At the exact same moment, flames poured into the hallway. Heedless of his own people, Incarnadine breathed incendiary death into the enclosed space.

I grabbed Rick, boosted everything, and dove down the stairway, pulling him with me.

Fire erupted through the doorway above us, licking the railings, the opposite wall, everything.

We tumbled down the stairs to the next landing. We both scrambled to our feet and kept going. Fire exploded out from the door again, this time even more.

Rick beat me to the nineteenth level door and yanked it open. The empty hallway looked like a peaceful refuge compared to the inferno above us. "Follow the curve," I gasped. "The Sky Claimer's on the balcony just outside. Might be guards."

"Let's go." Rick led the way. Another roar from the dragon shook the floor.

"How are you here?" I demanded. "I mean, I'm thrilled to see you, but… how?"

"You weren't answering on the talkers," he answered as we ran. "And too much time went by." He shot me a grin. "I wasn't about to let them have you, so I came to the rescue."

"Again: how?"

As we passed by the elevator doors, he thumbed at them. "I rode the elevator. I opened it before, remember? This time, I got lucky and one was waiting. I wasn't going to lose another friend and leader to the dragons!" Rick glanced at me, but didn't say anything else. I'm sure I looked horrible. The draconic's claw cut a gash right above my now empty eye socket. I still felt a trickle of blood on the side of my face.

The door stood open at the end of the hallway. Before I could say anything else, another massive impact threw both of us off our feet. Right behind us, the wall bent inward and began to crumble. The dragon was tearing this floor apart too!

We got to our feet again and ran again. We burst out onto the balcony to see two Crimson Elite staring at us with open mouths. Without waiting, Rick and I both charged them. With a well-timed boost, I put my opponent on the ground. I had meant to hit him dead on, but misjudged and only struck him in the side. It still worked well enough. Rick caught hold of the other and was about to throw him off the side when I grabbed his arm.

"Don't! A body falling from above? It'll make everyone look up!"

He nodded and smacked the guard's head against the stone wall.

"Now what?" he asked.

"The Sky Claimer can only carry one person," I said in a rush, taking the bag off my shoulder. "You take it. I'll try to fight my way down, like I did before."

"That kind of thing only works once, if you're lucky." Rick picked up the bag. He pulled the strap over his own shoulder and tightened it. "I'll ride with the books."

Another roar. The building shook. I could only imagine what the crowd below might be thinking now.

"I don't—" I began.

"Tell Marcus I'm coming!" Rick leaped off the edge and yanked the cord. The balloon expanded in an instant, jerking him higher into the air.

I strapped myself into the Sky Claimer as fast as I could, pulled on my goggles, and grabbed the talker. "Bag is en route with passenger!" I reported. "Getting out of here!" I didn't wait for a reply and shoved the thing back into its place on my belt.

I crouched, took a breath, and engaged the throttle. Once again, I shot into the sky, straight up above the Flame.

And below me, a dragon emerged.

48

While running through the halls, I noticed the change in my vision. At first, I thought everything looked exactly the same with only one eye. But I was making slight errors in judging distances and moving objects. That's why I almost missed the guard. I remembered enough from the Learning Years to know that two eyes gave humans depth perception, among other things. I would have to be much more careful flying. If I hit something with the Sky Claimer, I might not walk away from it.

All of this flashed through my brain in the few seconds it took to shoot high up above the Flame, aiming almost directly at the sun. When I looked down, a surge of pure terror gripped me, and I nearly released the controls.

Incarnadine, the red dragon, erupted out of the Flame. His wings unfolded to their full, enormous span. With one massive beat, he launched into the air after me.

Because of the dragon's sheer size, and the power of its wings, that one movement carried it an alarming distance, fully halfway to me. I could not hope to get away by sheer speed. He would overtake me in seconds.

In the distance, I saw Rick descending over the edge of the city. I couldn't let the dragon turn and see him.

I poured on the throttle, continuing my ascent straight up. Below me, the dragon flapped his wings again, eating up more of the space between us. I continued going up, higher than ever. The air grew cold, even colder than within the city of Incarnadine. I passed through a cloud, I think, or at least a damp mist.

I looked back to see how close the dragon might be. Closer than I anticipated. It loomed only scant yards below. Its massive jaws began to open, displaying rows of terrifying teeth. I once carried a discarded tooth of Viridia, but it seemed tiny compared to these blades of horror. Some were easily as big as me. A rush of warmer air, together with a smell of putrid decay, washed over me.

I twisted the left handle sharply. The Sky Claimer responded, rotating in a sudden turn. I zoomed perpendicular to my ascent. Incarnadine shot past, right behind me. I felt the heat of his passing, and the rush of wind shook my wings.

I heard the crackle of the talker on my belt. "I see him!" Marcus exclaimed. Though distorted by the rush of the wind, I could understand his words. "Almost there."

I kept holding the throttle at maximum speed. I glanced back and saw Incarnadine come to a stop in mid-air before twisting to chase after me. He might have a significant speed advantage, but I had him beat in maneuverability, even with my limited piloting skills. I only hoped it would be enough.

The wind tore at my clothes. I kept going in a straight line, letting him settle into pursuit again. I had no idea which direction I might be going. The mountains, much closer than I anticipated, loomed on my right. I guess that meant I was heading south.

For one insane moment, I considered trying to cross the mountains. There they stood, the border of The Circle, the boundary of everything I knew. What lay beyond them? Troilus Green claimed to have seen it. I might be able to cross them with the Sky Claimer. The peaks weren't that much higher than my current flight… were they?

A roar resounded behind me. "Viridian!" the dragon boomed. "You cannot escape me!"

"Yeah, I'm still going to try," I muttered. I banked to my right, heading lower and closer to the mountains before leveling off again, following the ridges. With each turn, a rush of cold air hit another area of my open eye socket. It didn't hurt, exactly, but I kept gritting my teeth against the strangeness of it.

As long as the dragon kept trying to get at me with his teeth, I thought

I had a chance to survive this. I could keep the maneuvering going, just out of his reach, at least until the Sky Claimer ran out of fuel. Maybe by then, I'd come up with some other plan. Of course, if he ever breathed fire after me, I probably wouldn't make it that far.

"Beryl!" Rick's voice came across the talker. I guess he'd given up speaking in guarded language now. "We've got them. Are you all right?"

I didn't answer. I couldn't. If I took my hand off the throttle, I'd lose too much space. And I needed the other hand to change direction right… about… now!

I twisted the handle and flipped nose-down. Incarnadine swooped right above me. One claw nicked one of the wings and knocked me off course. I lost hold of the throttle. The engine stalled. The Sky Claimer plummeted toward the ground, twisting and turning.

"Beryl?" This time it was Kelly's voice on the talker. "Beryl, speak to us!"

I flipped the engine switch off, then back on. It sputtered, but did nothing else. Above, Incarnadine turned and circled back toward me. I flipped the switch again. The engine sputtered, but caught. I engaged the throttle and stabilized my descent. Incarnadine rushed down toward me. I hovered for a moment. Couldn't move too soon, or he'd have an opportunity to pivot toward me.

"Come on, man." Rick's voice. "Tell me you're okay."

Hovering in mid-air as a monster the size of a large building hurtled toward me may have been one of the most nerve-wracking moments of my life. At the last moment, as I judged it, I engaged the throttle fully and shot back up. The heat and wind of Incarnadine's passage felt even closer this time. My singular vision might be underestimating his nearness.

I banked again and went back to following the mountains. Since my movement was in a straight line for the moment, I released the left handle and groped for the talker. I found the button. "I'm alive!" I yelled. "Trying not to get eaten right now!"

"Where are you?" Kelly demanded, her voice crackling and hissing.

"Little busy here. Is everyone else all right?"

"We're getting everybody out of the city," Marcus said. "We'll take care of them. Take care of—" His voice disappeared in a burst of static. I must have hit the range limit of the talkers.

The dragon came at me with unbelievable force this time. When I managed to dodge out of the way yet again, he almost smashed into the side of the mountains. He pivoted at the last moment, and I think his tail knocked a few boulders loose. I'm not entirely sure, because I had to focus my attention on my own direction. One of my shoes came off and disappeared behind me.

I glanced at the sun. The rally had started at one o'clock. Despite all that had happened to me since then, it couldn't be much more than a couple of hours past that. If it were later, I could hope for sunset to help me escape. But maybe dragons could see in the dark. How would I know?

Below, I saw orchards and fields flashing by. Here, between Incarnadine and Caesious, they would be untouched by the war, most likely. There might even be workers in the fields, looking up as I shot by, followed by a god on wings.

An angry god. Incarnadine's jaws snapped shut just behind me. How had he gotten that close? I should have at least smelled that breath! I swooped back toward the right, hugging the mountains again.

In the distance, I saw the landscape change. I glanced back. Incarnadine was still course-correcting. I had a few moments. I boosted my eye and zoomed my vision. Caesious. The blue city lay directly ahead. I released the zoom to regain my normal vision and shook my head.

The inklings of an idea began to tickle at my brain.

I needed more space, though. More time. I banked to the left and aimed myself at a sharp angle toward the ground. The dragon duplicated my moves, a little bit slower, but still gaining. I might be getting too predictable. I hoped I could use that to my advantage.

I needed one more turn to avoid him in my descent. It gave me just a sliver more of a gap between us. I zoomed toward an orchard. The trees rushed up to meet me. I could see individual branches… and Incarnadine was almost upon me. A wave of heat struck my lower body. A glance back showed more than I wanted to see: the dragon's open maw, teeth apart, a darkness between them.

I twisted the handle. My feet brushed leaves. I made a ninety-degree turn away from the orchard, hoping the engine didn't stall.

Incarnadine couldn't stop in time. He slammed into the orchard, smashing dozens of trees, sending an eruption of dirt and debris into the air. I coughed, trying to clear my lungs. My one good eye blinked over and over to get rid of the dust.

I rotated and sped toward the blue city. I had a destination in sight now: the tower of Caesious, former home of the blue dragon. And current host to the draconic peace summit.

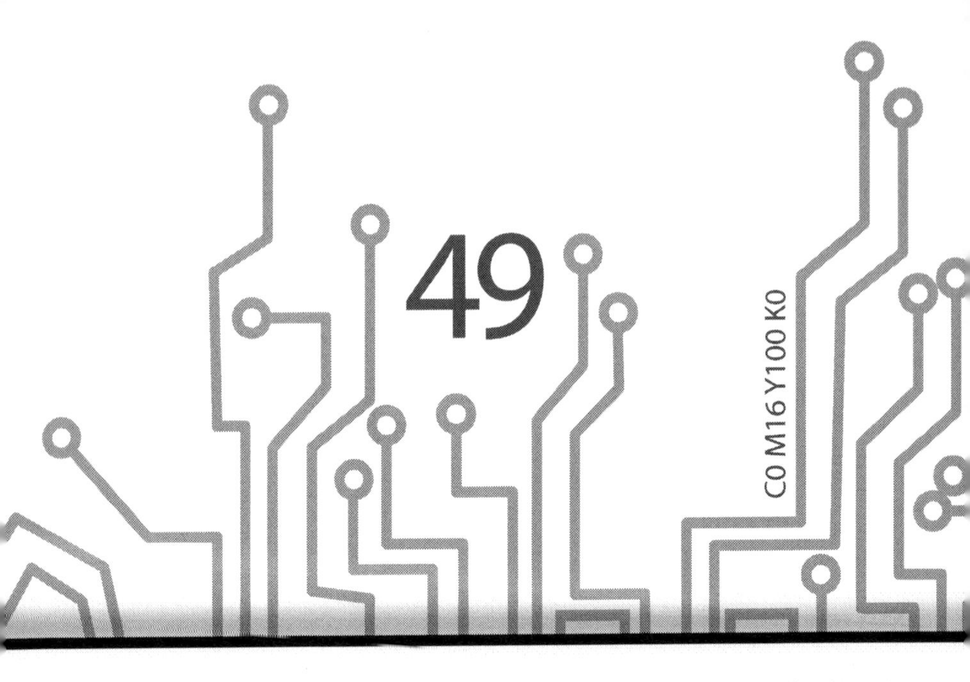

The tower. Where was the tower? It should dominate… oh, there it was. I blinked again, letting tears wash grime out of my eye. For a moment, my mind wandered on the ability of a cybernetic eye to generate tears. Funny how little details like that will distract you.

The tower of Caesious loomed over the city. While most of the buildings in Caesious consisted of metal and blue-tinted glass, the tower possessed an entirely different appearance. The steel-and-concrete structure soared above all the others in a narrow monolith, but at the top it widened into an enormous platform at least three times the circumference of the main tower. A couple dozen pillars rose from the platform to support a gigantic roof reaching high into the air above it all. The blue dragon lived on that platform. Or rather, he used to live on that platform, before we killed him.

According to Stacy, the draconics were meeting on the platform for their peace gathering. Seemed kind of morbid, if you asked me. But maybe it made sense from their superstitious point of view.

I looked behind me. The red dragon rose up from the ruins of the orchard and launched himself back into the air. I had gained a minute's respite, maybe. I hoped it would be enough.

I aimed directly for the tower's platform. No dodging and weaving now. I held the throttle at maximum. I mentally pleaded with it to go faster. Too bad I couldn't boost something other than my own body.

The gap between the platform and the roof grew larger and larger. Of course, it would have to be, if a dragon regularly came and went. What amazed me was the barrenness of the platform. Did the dragon really live up there with nothing else around him? Of course, his followers might have stripped everything from the top after he died, I suppose. Fewmets… what about the fewmets? My brain wandered to some weird places sometimes.

As I neared the edge of the platform, I spotted something near the center: an enormous table. Gathered around it were the draconics, representatives from all the cities. I even spotted a gold one. Perfect.

I entered the open space. The floor of the platform looked like lapis lazuli beneath some kind of hardened translucent covering. I couldn't imagine what could be tough enough to withstand the claws of a dragon on a regular basis.

I flew directly over the table and the draconics. I wanted to shout something appropriate and antagonizing, but nothing came to mind. The sight of a human being flying through their secret gathering had to be annoying enough, I would think.

Before I reached the opposite side of the platform, I throttled down and rotated myself vertical again. Still hovering, I turned in a circle to face the draconics. Most of them ran toward me. I released the throttle slowly and settled onto my feet for the first time in what seemed like hours. Awkwardly, I kicked off my one remaining shoe.

"Hello, everyone!" I called.

Ouch. The Sky Claimer seemed much heavier than when I strapped it on, but that might be my own fatigue. I sent a light boost into both legs.

The draconics slowed as they approached. Two red, one green, one blue, one black, and one gold: that's everyone. I could see a few more waiting back near the table. Some cities got more than one representative? That didn't seem fair.

"Who are you?" demanded the blue draconic.

"Viridian! He's green!" shouted one of the reds.

"You got me there," I answered. "Can't hide my chromark, can I?" My arms trembled from grasping the handles so long, but I couldn't let go just yet. I sent a boost to them as well.

I took a step backward. I knew I was near the edge, but not how near. Depth perception again.

The gold draconic stepped closer. "We have met before," it said in an ominous tone. "…Beryl."

Taizong Gold. From the Hub. What were the odds? At least it wouldn't matter in a few seconds.

"This human does not work for us!" the green draconic bellowed. "He is not of the Viridian Guard!"

"He wears green and uses forbidden technology!" the blue one responded. "More treachery from Viridia!"

I needed to stall just a bit longer. The gold and green draconics were coming too close.

"I bring a message from the wandering draconic!" I shouted.

That stopped them in their tracks. They looked at each other in what I hoped was consternation. "What do you mean?" one of the reds asked.

"The survivor from Onyx! He sent me here, as his representative."

The draconics erupted in their responses.

"Preposterous!"

"That's a myth!"

"But what if he speaks the truth?"

"My brother once saw the survivor. He exists!"

Wow. Protogonus Blue was right. They were superstitious. Most of them. And that's all I needed.

Three. Two. One.

Incarnadine the mighty, immortal dragon ruler of his own city, one of only five remaining dragons in The Circle, exploded into the platform area. He took out two of the supporting pillars in his rage, collapsing a portion of the roof. Flames erupted from his mouth, consuming the table and those around it. By all appearances, these draconics were in league with me, the human who raided his home. Fitting, wasn't it?

The other draconics turned at his terrifying arrival. The red ones cried out to their lord and master, while the others scattered. I took another step backward and fell off the platform.

"So worth it," I said aloud. I turned the left handle and rotated face down. Time to get out of here while I could. With any luck, the confusion and destruction would occupy Incarnadine long enough for me to find a place to set down and hide. Then I could work my way back to the Achromatic Asylum. It might take days, but I would be alive. And I might have ruined the peace summit for good measure.

At the exact moment I engaged the throttle again, an enormous weight struck the back of the Sky Claimer. Even with the throttle at full, I continued to angle down.

"You are… full of surprises," said a voice above me. The gold draconic. It chased after me and dove off the side when I fell. I have to admit, I was impressed by its single-mindedness in the midst of chaos.

"We're going down!" I shouted.

"I can survive this," it replied. "Can you?"

"Probably as well as you can." But I doubted it. The buildings of Caesious rushed toward us much faster than I'd like.

"You fought to protect a blue," the draconic said. "You incited the red dragon against the peace summit. There is much more to you than meets the eye, Beryl."

The eye. Was that a joke? I rotated the Sky Claimer, hoping to shake it off. But it hung on. Right. Cybernetic hand. It would take more than that.

I threw the Sky Claimer into a spin. I didn't know if I'd be able to pull out of it, but if I didn't get Taizong Gold off, we would crash. And I would not survive.

The wind shrieked around us. I barely heard the draconic's next words. "Should you survive this, Auric would like to speak with you."

What? I couldn't tell if that was a threat or some kind of twisted request. The Sky Claimer spun faster and faster. I closed my eye. The weight on the back shifted.

"We will meet again!" The draconic's bellow somehow rose above the shrieking wind of our plummeting descent.

The weight shifted one last time, and something snapped behind me. Taizong Gold fell. I opened my eye and fought to regain control. I twisted both handles back and forth. My spinning slowed, but didn't stop. One large building, somewhat triangular in shape, sped toward me at an alarming rate.

Screaming. Everything was screaming. The wind. The Sky Claimer's engines. Me.

At the last moment imaginable, I stopped spinning while sideways. I skimmed the side of one of the triangle building's top floors and shot back into the air.

I risked a quick look up toward the tower. Smoke poured from all sides. I think I caught a glimpse of Incarnadine's tail.

I continued to climb, but managed to rotate almost into the usual position. Something wasn't working right. I wasn't going in the right direction. The mountains waited in front of me, much closer than I would have guessed. I would much rather come down on a different side of the city.

I twisted the left handle to bank. I heard a creak, and then another loud snap. I twisted the handle again. Nothing happened. I glanced down and saw something falling: a piece of the Sky Claimer broken by the draconic.

Now what? I couldn't turn. I moved through the air, tilted toward the left, but flying up and toward the mountains. I could control my speed, but nothing else. And the fuel had to be running low by now.

After all that I had been through, all of the narrow escapes and surprises, I could do nothing else now.

I was going to crash.

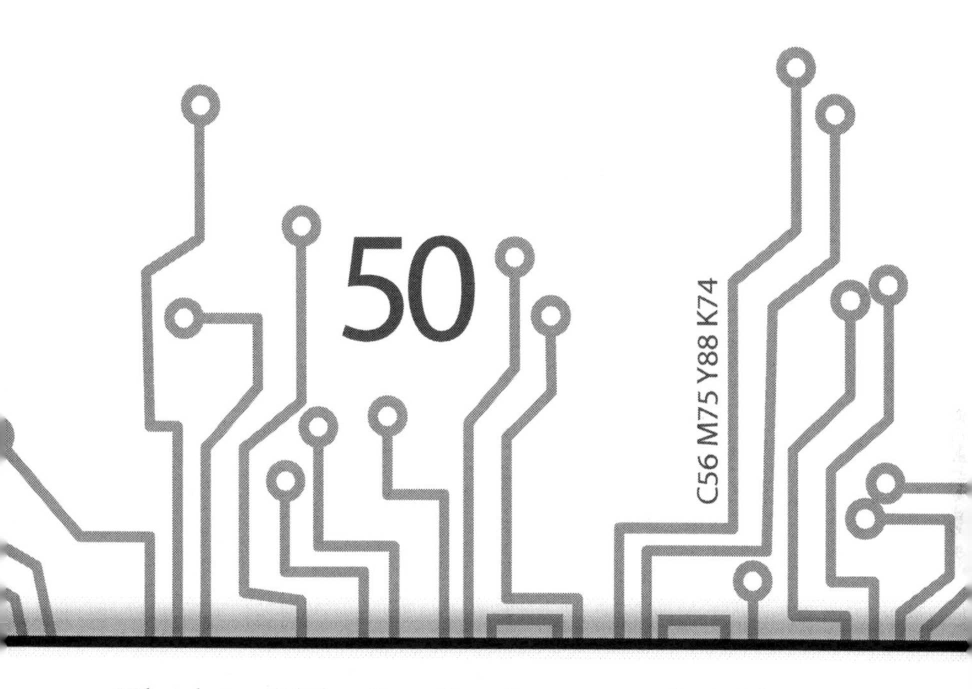

What choices did I have? I could cut the power completely. Momentum would keep the Sky Claimer moving forward for a little while, but the weight would soon transform it into a straight plummet to my certain death. Or I could keep pushing the engine, hoping against hope that I would somehow regain control. More likely, I would smash into a mountain at great speed, also guaranteeing certain death. I suppose there was a slight chance I would make it over the mountains. At least then I would get to see what was on the other side… as my last sight before plummeting to—still no question—certain death.

One last option remained. I lowered the throttle. My speed decreased, but I kept going higher. I let it drop to the bare minimum. After a few seconds of momentum, the Sky Claimer turned downward and began to fall. I re-engaged the throttle and pulled out of it, returning to climbing.

If I kept doing this, over and over, I could keep myself from falling, and hopefully keep my speed low as I approached the mountains. Maybe I wouldn't crash too hard. Maybe if I were going slow enough, I could unstrap and jump free. I don't know. But for the moment, my actions kept me alive.

As I cycled the process, the mountains drew closer. I could see steep cliffs broken up by rocky slopes. Here and there, a few trees found a way to grow. I couldn't make out much else just yet.

What would the others be thinking? The last thing they heard from me was about trying not to get eaten. As last words went, those were… pathetic. Rick would come looking for me, as he always did. He fought his way into the Flame to find me today! But how would he even know where to look this time?

The news of the dragon's attack on the peace summit would spread, and the gang would put two and two together. They would know I had been there, at least. After that, I would disappear from The Circle. No one would know. And I had no way to tell them.

Rick would be upset. Bice would be devastated. Would Kelly mourn for me? She said we were still friends, so I guess so. And Olive. I hoped Rick could get her back home to Viridia. She would be sad to hear of my fate, but she would move on. It wasn't like we had any kind of real relationship yet.

Lovat. Lovat would be sad. Poor kid. That bothered me more than any of them. I knew what it was like to lose someone you looked up to.

Wow, my thoughts were morbid. I suppose that was only natural when facing the high probability of death.

I cut the throttle again, coasted a little until I started to fall, then kicked it back in. It sputtered before catching. That couldn't be good. Fuel must be running low.

I was near enough now I could hazard a guess as to where I would impact the mountain looming in front of me. I didn't want to hit a sheer cliff, obviously. I needed to aim for one of the slopes, even a flat space if I could find one. I spotted a lengthy slope that might serve, but it was lower than my current progress. I would have to drop for a while. But I had no guarantee the engine would come back once I turned it off. I might keep falling, much further. A semi-controlled slide into a rocky slope, as dangerous as it would be, was still preferable to plummeting into rocks.

I cut the throttle. Since my speed had lessened, it didn't take very long before I started to fall again. As I did, letting it go longer this time, the Sky Claimer started to tip forward. If I let it go too long, I would be heading straight down, head first.

I twisted the throttle. It sputtered again, but didn't start. "Come on, come on." I twisted again. A couple more sputters. Again. Sputter. And then it caught. I pulled out of the dive and straightened out. I immediately lowered the speed again. I wanted to come in as slow as possible, while still maintaining my level.

I could make out the details of the slope now. It was not as level as it had looked from further away. In fact, an alarming number of rock formations protruded from the ground. The Sky Claimer would never survive this landing. I only hoped that I could.

I nursed the throttle in spurts, trying to slow myself without losing the engine again. It seemed to be working, but I was still coming in disturbingly fast.

Staying with the Sky Claimer would not be wise. I would be unable to control anything about the impact, and it would drag me along with it, face-down against the rocks. With my left hand, I reached for the central clip for the straps.

The engine quit. Now or never. I let go of both handles and fumbled with the straps. The rocky ground rushed up to meet me, faster than I anticipated. I must have overestimated my height.

The straps came loose. I fell. I tried to tuck myself into a ball to roll as I struck. I closed my eye. Rocks.

Darkness.

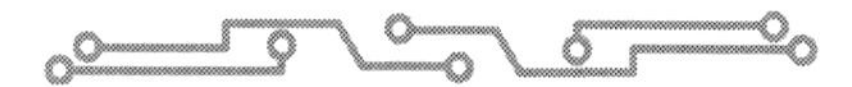

Pain. So much pain. Every inch of my body hurt, some of them far more than others. That meant I was alive, didn't it? Could there be this much pain after death?

My head swam. I couldn't even open my eye. Darkness again.

A sensation of movement caused my consciousness to half-awaken at some point. Then an explosion of pain in my head sent me into darkness again.

At some point, I dreamed. Open dragon mouths and teeth dominated the nightmares. Relief only came when they faded away into the darkness.

I dreamed of Loden. And Bice. They alternated between praising and reproving me. My parents appeared briefly, but I couldn't tell what they were thinking.

"Is he going to live?" asked a gruff, male voice. My eyelids fluttered. The voice sounded real, not the ethereal vagueness of dream speech. I didn't recognize it, though.

Cold. The air was cold. Did I have any clothes left after the wind and rocks tore them apart? What an odd thing to think about.

"I… I think so." A female voice that time. Not Kelly or Olive. She had a bit more huskiness to her voice. I wondered what she looked like. And whether I had any clothes left.

"Good," the male voice answered. "Then maybe he'll be able to tell us what's going on down there in those cities."

Down… there?

The darkness came back and I embraced it. Thinking was too hard.

Beryl's story continues in

Auric

For more information on the Dragontek Lore series,
and other upcoming books,
visit timfrankovich.com

Joining the mailing list is the best way to stay informed,
plus you get free stories!
(including Rick's story before he arrived in Viridia!)

If you enjoyed this book, please post a review
on Amazon, B&N, Goodreads, etc.
There's no better way to spread the word.

Acknowledgements

Many years ago, a young teen would ride his bike to the library once or twice a week. He would go straight to the science fiction and fantasy section and search for anything he hadn't read yet. After a while, it became difficult to find new titles that interested him, especially ones for his age level. That teen was me, and this series is written especially for him. Or, I suppose, for kids like I used to be.

I am having an absolute blast writing this series, because I can do almost anything in it. The combination of fantasy elements and technological advancement allows for all kinds of fun mash-ups. The biggest challenge is in topping myself with each new book.

I am greatly indebted to my beta readers Stephen Tallman, and Allen Perkins, who give me different perspectives and encourage me in excellence. Special thanks also to the Apex Science Fiction & Fantasy Writing Group. Our weekly meetings are inspiring and motivational.

If you want to keep track of my progress on all my writing, you can connect on timfrankovich.com, my Facebook author page, Twitter, etc. But the best way, which keeps you informed and gives you exclusive previews, is to join the mailing list. Sign up on the website. (You'll get free stories too!)

Tim Frankovich has been exploring fantastic worlds since third grade, when he cut up a grocery sack and drew a Godzilla-meets-superheroes story. Since then, he's gotten a little bit better at the writing part (not so much with the drawing).

His goal as a writer is to transport readers to another world, make them care deeply about characters in dire situations, and guide them deeply into life itself.

At the moment, he is probably suitably conscious somewhere in Texas with his beloved wife, awesome four kids, and a fool of a pup named Pippin.